Interview with the N...

"What sort of trick is this?"

"No trick, human," the walking corpse of Benjamin Franklin said, "but if I am to be destroyed, I would first have you set the record straight where it concerns my life. My good friend John Adams once said that I was 'more esteemed and beloved than Newton, Leibniz or Voltaire.' I would prefer to keep matters that way if possible."

What price had this man paid for so long a stay on God's earth? I had to find out. The creature seated before me was a result of a life pulled far too thin by powers I had barely begun studying in the Order, powers that I'd rather not think of. I tapped the excess ink from my quill against the rim of the well and flipped open the notebook.

"Shall we begin?"

The creature nodded.

"If you would not be forgotten as soon as you are dead and rotten," the rotting corpse said, quoting himself again, *"either write something worth reading or do things worth the writing."*

He held up both of his bony hands. Neither of them possessed a complete set of fingers. A chill ran down my back and a dark smile crept across his face.

"Since I seem incapable of performing the simple task of setting quill to page, I suppose you will have to do. Before destroying me, of course."

He seemed to be taking this rather well, all things considered.

"Naturally," I said. I lowered the tip of my quill to the blank page before me and started writing.

—from "The Fourteenth Virtue" by Anton Strout

THE DIMENSION NEXT DOOR

EDITED BY
Martin H. Greenberg
and Kerrie Hughes

DAW BOOKS, INC.
DONALD A. WOLLHEIM, FOUNDER
375 Hudson Street, New York, NY 10014
ELIZABETH R. WOLLHEIM
SHEILA E. GILBERT
PUBLISHERS
www.dawbooks.com

First Printing, July 2008
1   2   3   4   5   6   7   8   9

DAW TRADEMARK REGISTERED
U.S. PAT. OFF. AND FOREIGN COUNTRIES
—MARCA REGISTRADA.
HECHO EN U.S.A.
PRINTED IN THE U.S.A.

ACKNOWLEDGMENTS

Introduction copyright © 2008 by Kerrie Hughes
"The Fourteenth Virtue," copyright © 2008 by Anton Strout
"Waiting for Evolution," copyright © 2008 by Jody Lynn Nye
"The Trouble with the Truth," copyright © 2008 by Nina Kiriki Hoffman
"AFK," copyright © 2008 by Chris Pierson
"Unreadable," copyright © 2008 by Steven E. Schend
"Not My Knot," copyright © 2008 by Phyllis Irene Radford
"www.karmassist.com," copyright © 2008 by Donald J. Bingle
"The Avalon Psalter," copyright © 2008 by Lillian Stewart Carl
"Shadows in the Mirrors," copyright © 2008 by Bradley P. Beaulieu
"God Pays," copyright © 2008 by Paul Genesse
"Jack of the High Hills," copyright © 2008 by Brenda Cooper
"The Silver Path," copyright © 2008 by Fiona Patton
"Hear No Evil," copyright © 2008 by Alexander B. Potter

Table of Contents

INTRODUCTION

Kerrie Hughes

Shadows just out of sight, odd noises with no source, bizarre happenings that defy explanation? Our world is filled with strange events and unexplained phenomena that everyone has an opinion on but that no one can explain. Perhaps these mysteries are people, or creatures, or something else entirely, breaching the barriers that separate our everyday world from realms that we cannot see or touch—yet. What will these beings bring with them on their journey to our reality? Or will we humans be the first to break through to the other side, to explore the strange and wondrous worlds that lie just beyond our perception?

In *The Dimension Next Door,* many of my favorite writers challenge the minds of the readers to walk ancient pathways, imagine alternate timelines, and view the mysterious as perfectly natural.

Within these pages, Donald Bingle takes us to other worlds nearer to our own than we may think with "karmas sist.com." Then Lillian Stewart Carl gives us a glimpse of what life is like for someone who can access the past in "The Avalon Psalter," and Alexander Potter takes us to tea with the devil in "Hear No Evil."

On another, darker, path, author Anton Strout gives us a horrifying glimpse of Ben Franklin in "The Fourteenth

Virtue." I certainly won't think of the Founding Fathers in the same way again. And please don't overlook the thought-provoking story "Waiting for Evolution," by Jody Lynn Nye.

Then, once you've opened your mind to the possibilities, read "AFK" by Chris Pierson and "Unreadable," by Steven Schend. You might just look at books and games in a whole new light.

So come in and stay awhile, and don't worry about the darkness lurking in the corner—it may just be the door you've been waiting to go open.

THE FOURTEENTH VIRTUE

Anton Strout

"I guess I don't so much mind being old as I mind being fat, dead and old," said the dried humanoid husk, pausing to catch its breath on the villa's stairs that led down into the catacombs. If an evil undead creature was capable of catching its breath, that is.

I leaned against the wall of the stairway to the Villa Diodati's catacombs, thankful for the respite myself. Forty-six was far too old for an agent of the Fraternal Order of Goodness to be chasing down the evil undead, especially if that agent was a research archivist like myself.

Evil radiated from the necromancer like a fire in the dead of winter. Yes, I had dealt with hunting the undead and every other manner of curiosity for all my natural life, but to finally catch up to *him* after all these years was on par with discovering the lost city of Atlantis or Shangri-la.

"My name is Thaniel Graydon," I said with a mix of fascination and horror in my voice. "And your unnatural life ends here, necromancer."

"I would prefer that you refer to me as Mr. Franklin or Benjamin if you must," the creature said, sounding holier than thou. "That title is such an ugly moniker and perhaps the least of the ones I earned in my lifetime."

My instructor from Opening Threats would have cringed

at how pedestrian my declaration must have sounded, but given the dire circumstances, I was just happy to have gotten it out at all in his presence.

The moment F.O.G. had caught the rumor of the necromancer's existence, they'd sent their foremost expert on it—me—out into the field, running me ragged in singular pursuit. The modern marvel of Pierre Andriel's steam-powered vessel had carried me safely (if somewhat queasily) out of New York Harbor, and within weeks I'd tracked the rumored creature to this Cologny villa just outside Lake Geneva. My life's study culminated in this hunt, and I could hardly believe that I was finally standing here face-to-face with the creature. I was terrified.

Somewhat rested, I pushed myself off the wall and started closing in on the foul thing only to have it raise one of its hands in surrender. We were trapped far beneath the villa with nowhere left to run, and the creature seemed to sense this. I held my torch up to get a better look at him in the clinging darkness.

Despite his years of decay, I could still see hints of the human he had once been, but I had to look extra hard. The long gray hair that ran in a crescent around the back of its head was now snarled and matted with mud. His garb was at least thirty years out of date, and it hung off his pear-shaped torso in tatters of cloth that had long gone a muted brown with age. The stench of the dead that came off his body was overpowering in the confines of this subterranean staircase, but I did my best to hide my discomfort. Thankfully the burning pitch-soaked rags from the torch helped mask the malodorous scent.

The creature started slowly down the stairs with a defeated resolve, beckoning me to follow. I did so but with a healthy dose of reluctance, surprised when he led me past the stone caskets of the catacombs and into a small furnished chamber that resembled a lonely writer's garret. The creature gestured me toward a table in the center of the room that was covered with books and loose scraps of parchment. Its chair slid away from it at his command.

"What sort of trick is this?" I asked, feeling both heady and confused in my moment of triumph. Did it actually think I was going to sit down and leave myself defenseless?

The creature shook its head.

"No trick, human," the walking corpse of Benjamin Franklin said, "but if I am to be destroyed, I would first have you set the record straight where it concerns my life. My good friend John Adams once said that I was 'more esteemed and beloved than Newton, Leibniz or Voltaire.' I would prefer to keep matters that way if possible. Now sit."

His words held power in them, and despite my reluctance and fear, I felt compelled to sit. I found an empty sconce along the wall and slid my torch into it, then did as he bid, sitting down at the table. The creature flicked its wrist. The table's oil lamp blazed to life and pressed back the cloying darkness of the room. The creature reached toward the table and pulled a blank moleskin notebook free from the clutter and offered it to me. Despite my unease, I took it without hesitation.

When this creature had been alive, my respect for him had been enormous. My life's pursuit had been to set all manner of his arcane knowledge straight for our archives, and right now I felt excitement at this long-awaited prospect. If things went well, I would finally be able to transform conjecture into testimonial fact and earn a place of respect and note among my fellow archivists in the Fraternal Order. I was shaking so badly I could barely pull the quill from its nearby inkwell as I attempted to make room on the tabletop to write. Whether it was excitement or a bit of fear, I didn't know.

After all my years of study, I hadn't come unprepared. I reached into the bag hanging from my shoulder and pulled out sheaves of parchment I had "borrowed" from the Order's archives. I flipped through the loose pages. Some of them had been worn or torn by time, and most of them had been written by unfamiliar hands much older than mine.

I raised one closer to the oil lamp and read from it, always keeping one wary eye on the creature.

"It says here you were born in 1706 or 1705, depending on how you reckon it by calendar," I said.

Franklin gave a chuckle, pulled his glasses free from his face and wiped them clean with the edge of his tattered coat. He fit them back on his face, dirtier than they had been before, but it was no matter—he had no eyes left in the sockets to speak of. I waited for him to settle down into the chair opposite me, partly out of courtesy but mostly out of fear for my own life. Despite his manners, I reminded myself that I was still in the presence of evil.

Franklin chuckled again.

"Is something funny about that?" I asked, then quickly added, "Sir?"

"If I'm not, mistaken, it's 1818 now, yes? It's hard to tell after so much time . . . that would make me surprisingly lively for a man of one hundred and twelve years of age," he said. "I'm in the prime of my senility!"

He continued chuckling to himself. Pretty jovial for the damned, I thought. I looked back down at my papers, grateful to be avoiding those dead sockets of his, and reread them. "That's what the record shows, anyway. Of course they also wrote that you died in 1790."

The creature snorted. "Don't you think I know when I died, son?"

Something buglike scuttled out through his nostril and across his cheek and then disappeared into the tangle of his long gray hair. The creature settled back into the chair opposite me and said, "*In this world nothing can be said to be certain, except death and taxes.* Well, taxes anyway . . ."

"Sorry," I said, quick to apologize. I hadn't been expecting to engage it in a dialog and figured it was better to act as civilly as I could. The creature was congenial enough now, but who knew what might set off its evil ways again?

What price had this man paid for so long a stay on God's earth? I had to find out. The creature seated before me was a result of a life pulled far too thin by powers I had barely begun studying in the Order, powers that I'd rather not think of. I tapped the excess ink from my quill against the rim of the well and flipped open the notebook.

"Shall we begin?"

The creature nodded.

"If you would not be forgotten as soon as you are dead and rotten," the rotting corpse said, quoting himself again, *"either write something worth reading or do things worth the writing."*

He held up both of his bony hands. Neither of them possessed a complete set of fingers. A chill ran down my back and a dark smile crept across his face.

"Since I seem incapable of performing the simple task of setting quill to page, I suppose you will have to do. Before destroying me, of course."

He seemed to be taking this rather well, all things considered.

"Naturally," I said. I lowered the tip of my quill to the blank page before me and started writing.

"The secret history of our United States is dark material indeed," the extremely elder statesman said. "And of the greater body of historians and their books, not a one it tells the true tale."

Even given his advanced necrotic state, Benjamin Franklin cut an imposing figure.

I ran my quill through a few of the historical pages I had brought with me.

"We've done extensive research," I said, "on mankind's transgressions into the arcane arts, and one common thread has run through the last century: They all seem to prominently feature one of our most senior and well respected statesmen. You, sir."

I sensed a smile on his decaying face, but it was difficult to tell for sure.

The creature coughed dryly, a rattling rising from its chest. I guessed this passed for laughter, but the sound of it alone made me want to flee in terror. Maybe another agent of the Fraternal Order of Goodness would have fared better, one who hadn't dedicated his life to the pursuit of this one man, one who wouldn't be taking this task on with so much gravitas mixed with terror. Hoping to settle myself, I took a deep breath and let it out slowly.

"You try living over a century and see what polymathic accolades *you* garner," Franklin said.

I stopped writing and looked up.

"Polymathic?" I said, cocking my head slightly. "Forgive me . . . I'm not familiar with the term."

"From the Greek, I believe," he started, and his voice changed. There was an inherent power when he spoke, and I could hear why people had listened intently to his every word when he was alive. "Meaning 'having learned much.' I have an encyclopedic knowledge of a variety of subjects. Diplomat, printer, author, activist, scientist, inventor . . ."

He tapped his decaying index finger at the glasses he was wearing.

"And the study of something a little more . . . sinister?" I added.

He nodded and leaned back in his chair. He crossed his legs and rested his hands daintily on his knees. It was such a dainty gesture from so grotesque a creature that I almost laughed.

"There's a danger in being a polymath," he said. "Adams and Jefferson were quoting me when they said an investment in knowledge always pays the best interest. It *is* true that a little knowledge can go a long way, but an encyclopedic amount? Why, it practically begs questions about the natural philosophy of the world!"

"Meaning the dark arts?" I said, trying to be clear for the archives.

"For heaven's sake, just say it!" he shouted, slapping his hand down on the table. Bits of it flaked off the bone and onto my notebook. *"Necromancy."*

Despite my hatred of the actual practice itself, I couldn't contain my excitement.

"I knew it!" I said. "All the other agents in the Order couldn't get beyond your early religious ties . . ."

"But not you," Franklin mused. He cocked his head as if studying me. His neck clicked and cracked like dried leather. "I wonder why?"

"Deism," I said proudly. "Everyone said that your proclamation of being 'a thorough Deist' was a path that ultimately led to God, but it just didn't ring true to me."

There was almost humor on his face now, if I could read that type of thing off a half-rotted corpse.

"But," he interrupted, "if you follow Deism through to its logical, reasonable and very *human* conclusion, Deism does lead to God!"

I shook my head, thrilled to be engaged in such a debate with one of our nation's greatest thinkers. It was almost a shame I would have to destroy him.

I grabbed several pieces of parchment and looked back through his history, searching for an answer.

"You yourself said that 'God shouldn't be found in the supernatural or miracles, but through human reason and things we observe in the natural world,'" I said. "I don't think you believe that though. You've read too much, studied too much of the world to believe that. I propose you don't actually reject the supernatural but rather embrace it."

Franklin's silence was all I needed to hear to know I was right. I dared to stare into his lifeless eyes despite my fear. He was truly hideous in this unnatural state.

"But why this?" I asked. "Why would you do this to yourself?"

The creature sighed again and a waft of rot filled the room.

"If you are as learned about me as you seem to be, young

man, I'm sure you are aware of my love for puzzles and codes. Again, another polymath trait. If you understood that love, you could have easily found the reason for my transformation yourself. It's hidden within my Fourteen Virtues."

"Thirteen," I corrected. I might not have been the foremost Franklin scholar, but I had learned enough about the man during my lifetime to know he had written his famous Thirteen Virtues—a set of personal ideologies he lived by—when he was only in his twenties.

Franklin raised what remained of one of his eyebrows. "Does it surprise you that I'm still a virtuous man despite the black art that keeps me in such a state? *There never was a truly great man that was not at the same time truly virtuous.*"

He produced a well worn fold of paper from his coat pocket, smoothed it out, and pushed it across the desk. I refused to touch so old a document from so fouled a creature, instead using the tip of my quill to hold it open while I read.

The Thirteen Virtues—B. Franklin.

1. *TEMPERANCE. Eat not to dullness; drink not to elevation.*
2. *SILENCE. Speak not but what may benefit others or yourself; avoid trifling conversation.*
3. *ORDER. Let all your things have their places; let each part of your business have its time.*
4. *RESOLUTION. Resolve to perform what you ought; perform without fail what you resolve.*
5. *FRUGALITY. Make no expense but to do good to others or yourself; i.e., waste nothing.*
6. *INDUSTRY. Lose no time; be always employ'd in something useful; cut off all unnecessary actions.*
7. *SINCERITY. Use no hurtful deceit; think innocently and justly, and, if you speak, speak accordingly.*
8. *JUSTICE. Wrong none by doing injuries, or omitting the benefits that are your duty.*

9. *MODERATION. Avoid extremes; forbear resenting injuries so much as you think they deserve.*
10. *CLEANLINESS. Tolerate no uncleanliness in body, clothes, or habitation.*
11. *TRANQUILLITY. Be not disturbed at trifles, or at accidents common or unavoidable.*
12. *CHASTITY. Rarely use venery but for health or offspring, never to dullness, weakness, or the injury of your own or another's peace or reputation.*
13. *HUMILITY. Imitate Jesus and Socrates.*

"Are you familiar with the term decacoding?" he said, once I stopped reading.

"It's a coding system based on a system of tens, isn't it?"

"Correct," he said, pleased. His mouth split into a grin, bile and blackness showing instead of teeth. He tapped at the folded piece of paper. "Most of the Virtues listed there are the thoughts of a young idealist. What did I know back then? But once I made my choice to engage in the darkest of necromancy, I really only lived by The Fourteenth Virtue. There are only thirteen on the page but my coding points to the only one of those I truly held any real stock in."

I scanned the page, applying his decacoding. By starting with a base of ten and beginning to count from the top of his list again, it meant that the fourteenth virtue was actually the fourth one he had listed.

"Resolution?" I asked.

"Resolution," he repeated. "*The Resolve to perform what you ought; perform without fail what you resolve.* Notice I don't bring up whether good or evil fits into that equation."

"A resolution about what?"

"The answer lies before you," he said. He pointed at the piles of paper. "Right there in your histories, the greatest and most defining moment in all modern history. *The American Revolution.* Necromancy saved that marvelous homeland of ours. After all, I was, and still am, first and foremost a patriot and a statesman."

I sat there in shock as I let it sink in. "You did this to yourself . . . for our country? But you were one of our greatest leaders! You are *the* elder statesman."

"Many foxes grow gray, but few grow good," he said, running one hand along the rotting fringe of his matted hair. "With age, idealism melts away in the face of practicality."

"I'm sorry," I said, shaking my head. "I'm still not following."

It was hard to feel remotely smart sitting in the same room talking to Benjamin Franklin, no matter how evil a rotting creature he might be.

"Remember your history! The Founding Fathers and I were attempting to declare independence for the thirteen colonies from the British. Despite what other historians have written, the British *would* have easily overrun this country, even given their distance from England. Action had to be taken to 'secure the Blessings of Liberty to ourselves and our Posterity.'"

"But . . ." I stammered, "but giving yourself over to the power of necromancy to combat the British forces? It's folly!"

"All wars are follies," he said, raising a finger and waggling it at me. "Very expensive and very mischievous ones. I knew what price I paid when I made my bargain."

"Did they know, too?" I asked, writing as fast as I could. I jabbed the quill back into the well whenever the ink started to run dry.

"They?"

I stopped and looked up. I struggled in my mind to search for their names.

"Adams, Jefferson, *the Continental Congress* . . ."

The creature shook its head.

"I thought it was best they never know," Franklin said. "*He that would live in peace and at ease must not speak all he knows or all he sees*. Naturally reports came in from the front concerning the American dead. Generals kept sending in reports of the dead rising from the battlefield and soldiering on against the British. Most of Congress ignored such reports, dismissing them as fantastical, but I think Jefferson had his suspicions. Always the clever one, Tommy was."

What I was hearing seemed unbelievable. "And you were okay with this . . . 'bargain' you made?"

The corpse shrugged. It seemed a gesture well beneath a man of his stature, even a decaying one.

"All human situations have their inconveniences, but for the immortal, energy and persistence conquer all things. Think what you will of it, but the power over life and death, limited as I was with it, saved this country. Legions of the living dead founded our freedom. Old boys have their play-things, you know, as well as young ones. The difference is only in the price."

He looked over at me with those dead eyes once again. I couldn't help but turn away.

"Don't judge my actions," he tsk-tsked with a sad final-ity to his words. "Any fool can criticize, condemn, and complain, and most fools do."

Franklin rose from the table while I finished writing my account, but I no longer felt the need to keep an eye on him. I was surprised to find that my fear had dissipated a bit with hearing his story. I stood and eyed my torch sitting in the sconce on the wall.

"You seem rather willing to let me destroy you," I said. "You're turning yourself over for disposal? Just like that?"

Franklin nodded as if he were a parent being patient with a small child. "If you prefer," he said with a grim snarl, "I could swarm you with the contents of these catacombs in-stead." He held his arms out and the sound of stone coffin lids sliding free rose up behind me. The scratching and clawing of bony fingers fighting to get out filled the room. I didn't dare look back.

I realized how powerless and insignificant I was in this creature's presence and quickly shook my head no in re-sponse to his offer. Franklin dropped his arms, the coffin lids slid shut, and once again the room fell silent. A lifetime of studying him hadn't prepared me for this. Several lifetimes wouldn't have been enough.

"I've hunted for you my whole life. Why are you willing to die now?" I asked, feeling my own reluctance for the task at hand setting in. "Why ever?"

"Other than the fact that you have me cornered and at a disadvantage?" he asked.

His empty eye sockets looked down at my hands. I was still clutching the quill in one and the moleskin notebook in the other. I put the quill back in the well and closed the notebook before tucking it into my bag.

"This is strictly for my own curiosity, not for our archives," I said. In the face of standing toe-to-toe with this necromancer, I opted for politeness. It seemed the reasonable thing to do. I liked to think that my brothers back at the Order would have been proud. "If you'll forgive me asking, sir, why do you want any of this on record at all?"

The creature made no move to stop me as I headed for the torch on the wall.

"I first met Mary Shelley in the summer of 1816," the walking corpse said, letting out another dry earthy sigh. The humanity in it almost broke my heart.

"The writer?" I said, pausing with my hands on the shaft of the torch.

Franklin nodded. "Of course, she was only nineteen then and still Mary Wollstonecraft Godwin when I met her. She and Percy hadn't married yet, but that was when she found me."

"Found you?"

Franklin cackled for once like the evil undead creature that he was.

"My dear boy, it wasn't like she was looking for me specifically. She simply chanced upon me here in Switzerland one wintry summer a few years back."

He took on the tone my grandfather used when he was recounting his service at Lexington and Concord. As I pulled the torch off the wall, it settled heavy in my hands. Setting Franklin aflame was going to be harder than I imagined.

"Once I had 'died' for the sake of my country," he said, "I fled the now United States of America in the hope of obscurity off in foreign lands. I found a certain modicum of peace high up here in the Swiss Alps. All of Lake Geneva had fallen under an imposed volcanic winter two summers ago thanks to the untimely eruption of Mount Tambora the previous year." He raised his own hands and examined them for a moment, as if he were seeing his skeletal appendages for the first time. "By that point of my transformation, the cold didn't bother me much. Few things did at that point, and if it hadn't been for that damned book she insisted on publishing, you might never have found me."

"Her damned book?" I repeated moving back around the table toward him. "You mean *Frankenstein?*"

"You've read it?" he asked with genuine interest in his voice. "It's only been stateside a few months, by my reckoning."

"Yes," I said, pausing midstep, "but what does it have to do with you?"

"She was fascinated when she discovered me here, and she had of course heard of my doings in America during my natural life. This *is* the infamous Villa Diodati, after all. When Polidori, Byron, and Shelley suggested their fateful writing contest in the rooms above these very catacombs, Mary simply couldn't resist recounting my life in her own dark fashion. Think about her book for a moment. The evil doctor attempting to raise the dead? His experiments with electricity to do so? Sound familiar?"

"Surely not . . ." I started, but he cut me off.

"She even went so far as to name her main character Franklinstein, but I objected to so direct a correlation and drew the line."

"I never would have made such a connection," I said, "but I see it now . . ."

"You wanted to know why I insisted on you writing down my account? *Glass, china and reputations are easily cracked, but never well mended,*" he said. "It takes many good deeds to build a good reputation, and only one bad one to lose it. History will judge me, and I'd rather not have the truth behind *Frankenstein* be the lone record of my dark life. If people should ever make that connection, see the darkness behind this abomination I've become, I want this secret history to be known. Let the world know that what I did, I did for my country with Resolution . . . that I *performed without fail what I resolved* for the good of America. A man's net worth to the world is usually determined by what remains after his bad habits are subtracted from his good ones. Let us hope that is true."

He looked almost at peace as he stood there; then he lowered his head and fell silent. I readied the torch in my hands, knowing my duty but surprised to find myself unwilling to follow through. The heat of the burning pitch waved over me while I hesitated.

"I can't do it," I said finally and dropped the torch to the floor. It flickered while it fought to keep itself alight.

"You may delay," Franklin said kindly, reaching over and taking my hands in his. I didn't flinch. "Time will not. I should have no objection to going over the same life from its beginning to the end, requesting only the advantage authors have, of correcting in a second edition the faults of the first. Wish not so much to live long as to live well."

With that, Franklin stepped farther away from the table full of his papers. With a wave of his hand, my torch blared to life and leaped from the floor toward him. The crackle of dark magic filled the tiny chamber, and before I could react, the creature burst into purifying flames of light, light that nearly blinded me. I raised my arm to shield my eyes as the screams of hell filled the room. I clamped my hands down over my ears until the permeable evil slipped slowly away, followed by silence.

Flames licked at the beams above me. I quickly gathered

what I could of Franklin's papers and stuffed them into my bag. I stayed to watch the last of the flames consume what remained of one of the most revered men in history before racing back out through the villa. I had no idea what I would do upon my return to America, my return to the Fraternal Order. Suddenly, forty-six didn't seem a bad age for retirement.

Found in the archival records of The Gauntlet *at the Department of Extraordinary Affairs in New York City.*

WAITING FOR EVOLUTION

Jody Lynn Nye

"Hurry up and move, Blondie!" Commander Natura Colvatanisan said, poking me in the back.

I stopped gawking and stepped out of the "Ajaqui Stargate" onto the skirts of the circle of burned grass in the meadow where the shuttle had landed, following its crashing descent through the atmosphere. I couldn't help myself. I had never seen a sky so blue, or white clouds that towered over her like benevolent gods. I took a deep breath. *Congratulations, Specialist Denise Mulhare*, I told myself. *You are the first person ever to step onto this new Earth.*

The mission commander, next out of the hatch, wrinkled her sharp little nose and twisted her thin, coffee-dark lips.

"What's that awful smell?" she asked.

"Ozone," I said, taking another, appreciative breath. It smelled so different from the Earth we had just left.

"Unusual purity of atmosphere," said the ajaqui mission specialist, Koltdaral. The tripedal aliens immediately grouped themselves into a small cluster clear of the shuttle shell and erected their protective environmental bubble. It flattened the waist-high wild grasses and flowers. Hastily, they sealed themselves inside. Kotdaral's voice gained an echo as he continued from within the clear bubble.

"Particulate matter content of air, less than point two percent."

"Smells like something is rotting," Colvatanisan said.

"You don't spend much time in greenhouses," I reminded her with a grin.

"Botany is your job," Colvatanisan said, shaking her head. "The only time I want to see vegetation is on my plate. I like concrete and plastic walls. Much cleaner."

"Where are we?" Koltdaral asked. "In correlation with your Earth, that is."

"This," Colvatanisan said, gesturing around her with her electronic clipboard, "is Paris, France. Or it ought to be. This region corresponds to Euro continent. This plain is on the north edge of the river valley of the Seine. On our Earth it's completely covered by a housing complex populated by thirty-three million people. There's nothing like this here, or hasn't been for, I don't know, thousands of years."

"Why here? You can see that there is no notable construction."

"Our scans show this is the largest population center existing on the planet at the moment," Lieutenant Haroun Saif replied. "One and a half million in this region. There are only about ten million humans here."

"Why so few? You are packed as tightly as paving stones on your Earth."

The commander pursed her lips distastefully. She didn't like the ajaqui attitude against human reproduction. "There have been many plagues in human history. Perhaps this strain of Earth-dwellers was not as resistant, and medicine did not develop here as there. Until antibiotics and hygiene techniques were discovered, a human being could die of a paper cut or the common cold. Child mortality was incredibly high. Could be any number of reasons. We won't know until we interface with the local inhabitants."

Dr. Oliver Mason, the rangy, slope-shouldered environmental biologist who stood a head taller than the rest of us, scanned the meadow and the towering forest that

surrounded it with his handheld doo-watz. "I am picking up
a considerable number of human life signs. Some of them
are moving this way."

"Well, they couldn't have missed us arriving," Colvatanisan said, hoisting a stunner out of the underarm holster that was strapped to her body. "Let's wait for them to
come to us. Lieutenant Saif, let's hope that there was some
parallel development of languages." The narrow-faced specialist from Afri continent held tightly to his instrument-
laden clipboard, as if ready to squeeze recognizable words
out of its miniature speakers.

"Hold it! Spray first," ordered Dr. Tamara Brecko, the biologist who, like me, hailed from Noam continent. "We
don't want you getting anything communicable, or giving
it, either. Mission Control will be pissed off if you give
smallpox to the natives. Arms up! Legs out!"

I shivered as the ice-cold fog surrounded me and pene-
trated through my clothes to the skin. I was too excited
about the plant life to care much about the possibility of
meeting other humans. The field in which we stood was
filled with spring flowers, wildflowers that existed nowhere
on our Earth, a highly industrialized planet, where references to Mother Nature seemed more and more out of place
every day. This marvelous endless garden was much more
my ideal of the perfect world. I took endless 3-D images,
took myriad snips and specimens. I couldn't stop myself
from putting my nose into clusters of brilliant blossoms.
They were everywhere. The others looked lost, but I was in
heaven. I couldn't believe my luck to be here.

When the first SideSlip Mission had discovered the energy echoes that suggested parallel dimensions, it had made
news all over the galaxy. The theory was that each nexus
point led to one and only one alternate dimension, but there
were infinite numbers of nexuses. Excited scientists talked
of endless energy and resources that could be mined from
these stars and planets, raved about studies of joining forces
with parallel versions of themselves to increase the brain

trust. The naysayers frowned on the possibility, sourly commenting on how narrowly the present meganations had escaped from being dominated by tyrants and warlords, and how more dimensions only increased the likelihood of meeting those despots' descendants. But once the genie of possibility was out of the bottle, it intrigued more people than it frightened. The historians alone couldn't wait to see what was on the other side of those walls. To me, it was a foregone conclusion that these dimensions, if they could reach them, had to be explored. The theory was that if there were parallel Earths, then if one stepped through to them, one would end up in precisely the same location on each. I reran every single article as it came over the entertainment net, wishing I could see those other Earths. I even thought whether I could stand to face an alternate version of myself.

Funding had been as hard to come by as usual, until Ajaqui had stepped forward and offered to pay half of the cost of an unmanned probe, as long as their name would be on each transdimensional vessel. Trans Earth Space Agency had no objection. It ran a worldwide contest to see what its share of the name would be. Ten billion text messages (at one credit per call, used to help fund the mission) later, and the winner was 'Stargate,' after the historical video series that ran on one of the streams on EN. The other sentient races with which humanity had contact decided they would wait and see.

As the history books would one day record, the first tries had failed miserably. The earliest shuttles, sent from the top of an unpopulated desert bluff in Morocco, failed to punch through the dimensional walls, fizzling, stalling, or exploding on launch. It was the ninth, historic attempt, a piece of video that was repeated over and over again on the afternoon news, that showed the thick, upright disk of the dimension shuttle disappearing in a corona of fire. Within minutes it reappeared. Scientists in protective suits swarmed it, removing the sample bubbles from its many niches. They were jubilant over the samples of breathable air and plant and mineral specimens the shuttle had brought back, but it was the foot-long blue-green lizard that caused the most hysterical joy. Its DNA—yes, DNA—closely matched that of a similar reptile in what remained uncovered by domicile blocks in the Moroccan desert, but the native lizard was half the size and coral in color. Herpetologists insisted that the creature had not been that size or color since the Jurassic period. The plant species, the part that really fascinated me, were plants that had died out years ago, sometimes millions of years. Ferns that I had only seen in fossils were leafy, green reality on the video screen. My palms itched to touch, examine, and smell those plants. I wanted to see in what magical place such things still grew.

I made up the most impressive resume I could, including every academic honor I had ever received or been nominated for, my health file number to prove I was fit for service, and got every person of influence I knew to send recommendations on my behalf, and sent it all in a message to volunteer for future missions. I got back a message saying I was applicant number 21,386,724-Earth and that my data would be kept on file. Not surprisingly, millions wanted to be involved in this incredibly exciting new enterprise. I was disappointed, naturally, but not surprised. I went back to my job at Mech Hybrid Lab.

To my amazement, though, five months later, I received a second message saying I was one of the thousand from all human habitations selected for training. I had let out a whoop that could be heard from my plant-crammed little single habitation kilometers either way down the Trenton-Newark Habitat Complex. I had paid the inevitable noise fine without complaint. I could not be more thrilled that I was one of the ten who made it through to the first manned mission. It was my first opportunity to meet the ajaqui dimensionauts who would be making the trip with us. I found them interesting, with a wry sense of humor. They liked human beings. They smelled sweet to us, and, strangely, we smelled sweet to them, too. Oddly, to me, they didn't like earth-type plants. The CO_2 that plants give off smelled noxious in what passed for nostrils in their sensory array. I couldn't interest them in my passion for living things, but other than that, I think I made lifelong friends.

Sixteen hours before we set foot on Second Earth, we had launched from a platform in space, so as not to harm the environment in case the transference went badly. In fact, we didn't notice a thing, though the instrument panel had gone wild. I could see now that the outer shell of the shuttle was badly scorched and ridged. Colvatanisan had taken her time with the telemetry, making careful note of all the readings coming in, looking for life signs, radio waves, anything. I think we were all surprised not to hear any electronic chatter at all. I don't believe any of us thought there would be no technology at all. Lieutenant Saif and the ajaqui scientists muttered together over their instruments about it while I started exploring the plant life adjacent to the shuttle. Already I saw species of plants that had become extinct on our Earth, some within my own lifetime. I was seeing it all the time, and it tore at my heart. Here were things growing that I had only seen in books. I was thrilled beyond words as I touched things that didn't exist anymore where I came from.

I was cataloging a giant fern when I felt another presence a few feet from me. Considering that I lived in a coordinated neighborhood of three million people, one would think that I would never notice anyone who wasn't on top of me, but being on a nearly empty planet must have let those nerve endings that were normally curled tight near my skin unfurl and stretch out. I jumped and turned just in time to hear Colvatanisan say, "I think he likes you, Mulhare."

The man who had startled me looked pretty surprised himself. He was only a couple of inches above my height, with a shock of dark hair and dark eyebrows that stood out a lot farther from his face than my inner symmetry monitor thought was normal. Under those brows was a pair of dark brown eyes, lively with curiosity. Designs in red and black adorned the skin of his arms. Whether they were paint or tattoos, I didn't have the experience to judge. He wore a belted kilt of animal skin and shoes woven from reeds. The kilt, belt, and shoes looked primitive at first, but I noticed that they were neatly sewn and the shoes sealed with resin. They weren't unlike athletic shoes from my Earth. The belt was downright fancy, and a knife sheath dangled from it over his right hip. A rope was looped up on the left hip. The bones of his face were strong and knobbly, but my symmetry monitor adjudged him undeniably handsome.

"Hello," I said.

"Ranik," he replied, smiling broadly.

"Is that your name?" I asked.

"No," Lieutenant Saif said. "It's 'hello' or 'greetings.' He said it to all of us. You weren't paying attention when he and his friends came out of the bushes."

"Rikad," the man said, pointing to himself.

"Denise," I replied, with a gesture toward myself. "Ranik, Rikad. Hey, I made a sentence!"

"Don't try to synthesize, please!" Saif exclaimed, his eyes widening in panic. But Rikad did not seem offended. In fact, he seemed pleased. He glanced up at my hair, then studied it. Self-consciously, I put my hand up, wondering if a bug had landed in it.

"Nah. Burrin," he said, gently taking my hand down. He glanced back over his shoulder. About a dozen feet away were five more men in kilts. "Shivin bun burrin?"

"Im," the men agreed.

"Any idea what that means?"

"Not yet," Saif said, scrolling up and down his screen. "It could be anything from 'Isn't that pretty?' to 'Does that look bleached to you?'"

"Thanks a skidload," I said.

"No offense, Mulhare, but I just don't have enough to go on yet! It's a proto-language. It seems to have roots in Indo-

European, but not close enough that any of my lexicons match."

"But why do they look like that?" Colvatanisan asked.

She walked up to one of the men. He was short enough she could look him eye to eye. His eyes were dark blue, and what was left of the hair on his head was iron gray. "Ranik."

"Ranik," the man replied, in a low, courteous voice.

"Take me to your leader."

Somehow, Lieutenant Saif got the concept across to our new friends. After a short conference, the men agreed, and beckoned us to follow them down the hill.

"Send back images!" the ajaqui shouted at our backs.

"What are they, Tammy?" I asked, as the men escorted us down a narrow track beaten through the waist-high vegetation. "What's with the browridges?"

Our mission biologist had worn a silly smile plastered on her face since the moment Rikad and his friends had turned up. She played her clipboard one-handed like a lyrist going for the all time speed record on "The Flight of the Bumblebee," and what she saw on her gizmo's screen made her insanely happy.

"I think they're Neanderthals," Brecko said. "In fact, I know that they're Neanderthals. I work with the fossils, and I've done research with some of the top anthropologists in the field—but I am looking at living, breathing examples of one of humanity's ancestors."

"But, didn't they die out, like thousands of years ago?"

"Died out or killed off," Brecko said. She had persuaded Rikad to let her take a skin scraping from the back of his hand. She put it into a handsized box contraption that hung on her hip. It pinged, and she brought up the readings on the main screen. "Oh, my God, this is amazing. They *are* Neanderthals."

"How is that possible?" Colvatanisan asked.

"Come on, humanity could have gone down a number of

evolutionary paths," Brecko said. "These people have 99.45 percent the same DNA as we do."

"About the same as chimpanzees," Mason said, dryly. Brecko gave him a disgusted look. "Well, it's true."

Brecko shook her head and went on. "In this area of the planet, at least, *Homo sapiens sapiens* never developed, or maybe it developed for a while and then killed itself off. Our direct ancestors, the Cro-Magnons, are believed to have been a more aggressive strain. Instead, the gentle ones survived and developed. On Second Earth, the meek really have inherited the earth."

"That's too weird," said Colvatanisan.

"No, it could have happened to us. It almost did. The Cro-Magnon population fell to a dangerously slender level at one point in prehistory. It could have died out, but it fought its way back and overwhelmed the smaller Neanderthal population. Probably killed all the men and intermarried with the women, the ones who were close enough in genetic profile to reproduce. We're seeing what they would have looked like if it had happened."

"It's an anthropologist's dream," Saif said.

"Don't get off message," Colvantanisan said. "We're here to check out what's here that will get more investors interested in the project, not to play missionary to the natives. The ajaqui don't want us to spend any more time here than we have to."

I glanced ahead at our guides, but they didn't react. They really couldn't understand what we were saying. Rikad must have felt my eyes on him, because he turned to look back at me. I gave him a sheepish smile.

"Eaor," the eldest man announced proudly, as we came over a bluff.

"Well, I'll be a monkey's second cousin," Mason said.

The river valley below us had clearly been inhabited as long as our Seine district had, but there the resemblance ended. As far as I could see, the land had been cultivated—oh, not in the machine-perfect rows and troughs of modern agriculture in the farm districts I had seen on my school computers, but like the pictures of primitive people from centuries gone by. I found I was itching to examine the crop plants, to see what they grew, and what parasites and weeds grew among them. I had a whole biosphere to examine.

Instead of individual houses, I saw only big, round communal habitations, each with one large double door facing south, the direction from which we were coming. I could see what was going on inside, because the roofs were open, like a sports arena. But why not? The sun was shining, not a cloud in sight, and the temperature was a balmy 25 degrees. Children ran around naked, which must have saved their parents hours of washing dirty smocks. All the men we saw were attired similarly to the hunting party, in skin or cloth kilts, as were many of the women. The exception was pregnant women, who wore sleeveless dresses suspended from the shoulders to just above the knees.

"The trapeze dress is back," Colvatanisan commented.

"I love Paris in the springtime," Saif murmured.

Rikad and his companions ushered us into the first round house. We were shown to the rear of the building. The three people seated on hide cushions must have been the authorities, with the majestic old woman in the middle the most senior. Like the hunters, their faces and arms were decorated with designs in red and black. Dozens of young men and women knelt beside them. I didn't know whether they were servants or offspring. It didn't seem to matter; when one of the oldsters barked an order, one or more of the young ones sprang up immediately to obey.

I didn't get anything out of the conference, but Saif looked like he was in heaven. I did understand that we were introduced one at a time. My name had become 'Dnees Burrin.' The two male elders were named Borik and Hadda. The woman was Imada.

A word from Imada sent a boy running outside through a small door. He returned in minutes bearing a load of flower garlands. The old woman beckoned us forward.

Courtesy enforced by flint-headed spears, we bowed to have her hang a lei around each of our necks. Colvatanisan offered goods from our Earth in exchange: a music box for the lady and heavy silver bracelets for the men. The elders exclaimed happily over the gifts. From the following speeches, I guessed we were given the key to the city.

During the hours that followed, Imada examined me and my female colleagues. She shot questions at us that we couldn't answer, while demanding to see our shoulder pouches, our equipment, and the content of our pockets. She exclaimed over the fine weave of my jumpsuit and held up my UV protective hat so she and the two old men, who were patting down our male counterparts, could share a hearty laugh.

When she had finished looking over our possessions, Imada beckoned us close. I glanced uneasily at Colvatanisan, who gave me a subtle gesture to cooperate. From a pouch hanging from the wide belt around her middle, she took a figure made of stone. About the length of her hand, it appeared to be made of green marble or agate and was carved into an exaggerated female form with huge breasts and large labia majora but small feet and a small head.

"Willendorf," Brecko gasped.

The old woman accepted her reaction as showing the appropriate awe. She showed it to the rest of us in turn. I wasn't a religious person, but I nodded deeply, hoping Imada would take that as respect.

Then something about the statue seemed to make sense to me in a way I couldn't have explained. She was all living things. They were connected to her, and because I loved nature, I was connected to her, too. I felt a tingle in my belly.

Imada eyed me closely, then nodded, with a tiny smile on her lips. "Burrin," she said. She shouted at one of the girls, who came running forward with a pot of red goo. Ochre, I surmised. The old woman took a fingerful and daubed it on our foreheads.

"Not just fashion, but makeup, too," Colvatanisan said, but keeping a smile on her face. "I hope this is over soon."

It was. The ochre was the last phase of the welcome ceremony. With a clap, we were dismissed.

"I guess you didn't get anything agreed about mineral rights," Mason said to Saif as we were escorted out.

"No," the Afric said, his eyes shining. "I think I'm beginning to understand sentence structure. It looks as if the simple sentence of subject and predicate developed earlier than the division between the two main offshoots. It might be hardwired into the human brain. I don't know! It will take years of study before I could negotiate with them on a sophisticated level."

"We won't have to negotiate with them," Colvatanisan said, smugly. "How could they stop us anyway? We've got mining ships. Fifty of those round houses could fit in the hold of just one of them. Keep your eyes open, people. We are looking for whatever we can find that will get us funded for Third Earth and Fourth Earth. This is just the first stop on the way. We have to make the backers see what's worth their investment. Got it?"

I hated having reality intrude, but Colvatanisan was right. My job was to gather plants and seeds that would be of commercial interest on First Earth. In less than three weeks, we would leave this planet and head for Second Ajaqui, to see what parallel history looked like there. It was possible no one would ever come back here, but by the greedy look in the mission commander's eye, she was thinking of untapped resources that the Neanderthal had not yet found a use for.

The primal-Gauls, as Saif liked to call them, accepted us among them with no trouble. I couldn't imagine them getting the same freedom to move around in my neighborhood, or anywhere I could think of. The children learned what time we usually got up in the morning and were waiting outside the shuttle for us. They thought the ajaqui were

amazingly funny and laughed heartily at everything they
did. They loved to help. After a little natural paranoia over
letting them near my equipment, I learned that they obeyed
orders about what they could touch and what they couldn't.
They were happy to carry my specimen cases and clipboard
for me, even to help me gather samples. In fact, they were
so eager that I had to stop them bringing me sacks or buck-
ets of any plant in which I showed an interest. They brought
us fruit and root vegetables to supplement our prepackaged
meals. The others were nervous about the fact most of the
produce was very small in size. My analysis of them proved
all of the gifts harmless. They tasted good, too.

Not only the children liked to watch us. I often looked up
to find Rikad close by. His solemn brown eyes followed my
hands as they clipped a cutting from one plant, or coaxed a
seed pod from another. I didn't quite forget he was there,
but I got comfortable with having him nearby. Often, when
I would leave my tools at a spot to bring a full specimen
box back to the ship, I would return to find a small bouquet
of flowers tied with a stem or a delicacy, like the dried fruit
pastes mixed with honey that was this region's version of
candy. He seemed happy whenever I accepted his gifts. On
the first really hot day, he disappeared from his watching
spot and returned with a wooden cup, which he handed to
me. It was beautifully carved with the images of fish and
river plants. I smelled the contents.

"Baba," he said, which Saif thought was both "drink"
and "water."

I held it for a moment. I was thirsty, but I wondered if I
dared risk the local water. We were supposed to drink only
brewed beverages or the water purified by the ship. He noticed the hesitation and looked hurt. I decided to risk it.

The water tasted sweeter than anything I could have
named, sweeter than nectar or honey. Nothing like this existed in Trenton-Newark. Even the rainwater there was
polluted. Drinking water in my building was filtered a thou-

sand times until it tasted as dry and metallic as the dust it failed to cut. I could have drunk gallons of this water.

"Thank you," I said, sincerely, handing the cup back to him.

"Thank you," he repeated, closing his hands around mine. "Orraow." Saif had said that word was close to our phrase, "it was a pleasure."

I blushed. I didn't quite know why.

The others noticed that he hung around me more than he did near the others.

"You've got a pet," Colvatanisan teased me.

At first, I thought of him as just that. He wasn't a sophisticated man, not as I saw sophistication. What did he know of computers or literature?

At night, we sat around the lighted camp table and discussed our findings of the day. The ajaqui mineral specialist, Quiron, had gone to some of the locations Mission Control had pinpointed as historically containing mineral wealth, such as gold, diamonds and other precious stones, transuranics, and so on.

"So the diamond country in south Afri is still untouched," Colvatanisan said, her eyes gleaming.

"The people there seem little interested in the stones," Quiron confirmed. "They are similar to these people, somewhat darker of skin. No other differences that we could detect. They, too build in a circle, where they build. They care for their children. They mourn their dead. They adorn themselves with red ochre and beads. They enjoy flowers and other, less smelly, things of beauty. They defend but except for hunting do not aggress. They were curious about us, and they approached us with caution but without fear. So different from you."

"They *are* us," Brecko said. "This strain disappeared into ours millennia ago."

"I see," Quiron said. "Therefore you could breed with them?"

All seven of us humans glanced at one another uncomfortably.

"Ew," said Mason.

Quiron looked embarrassed. "I apologize for an indelicate question."

"The answer is very probably yes," Brecko said. "The genetic drift doesn't seem to have gone too far astray to make offspring possible."

"Certainly the pheremones must be there, or Big Boy there wouldn't be courting Mulhare," Mason said, with a smirk.

"He's not courting me," I growled and threw a grape at him.

"It's the hair," Saif said. "Blondes are rare at any point in history. They were often considered sacred. Certainly Imada was more interested in you than the other women."

"If we may get back to the subject?" Quiron asked. "These are not, then, mentally arrested?"

"Not at all," Brecko said. "In fact, they are much more intelligent than we anticipated Neanderthals would be. *Homo sapiens* as we know it never developed here. Civilization as we know it never arose because that violently ambitious streak did not hold sway."

"Instead, they have come to the level of evolution of an advanced animal," Mason said.

Brecko shook her head. "No, they're more intelligent than that. They still have human intelligence. They founded symbolic language, though not symbolic writing as we know it. Memory, not externally shared media, is the means of passing on info. Theirs is a more cooperative, less competitive culture. They are not civilized as we know it, but tribal. This is an extended family group. Hadda and the others are the great-grandparents. They have domesticated cats, dogs, goats, cows—small compared with our own animals—but tamed them nevertheless."

"Their farming methods are primitive," I added. "They

probably have starvation years every so often, after a drought or a locust plague."

"In the midst of all this?" Koltdaral asked, indicating the plant life that surrounded us.

"You can't eat *all this,*" I said scornfully. "Their species of most fruit are still in their original form. Avocados would be the size of a large pea. Almost everything humans eat is a hybrid cross from pairings of the biggest and the best. What I could show them about crossbreeding." I shook my head and whistled between my teeth.

"But you can't," Colvatanisan said flatly.

I found the local humans absolutely fascinating and the pace of the culture restful. I had become overwhelmed by the way that things had gone on my Earth. There were too many laws. People were too negative. This much greenery existed nowhere except in private reserves and the endless machine-cultivated farms that fed the vast population. Life was so simple here, though far more dangerous, but even death seemed to have more dignity than it did in my world.

We attended the burial of a six-year-old boy who had fallen over a cliff while chasing rabbits. I wept with the others as his parents threw flowers onto the still little body, which had been painted with signs telling their goddess he was a good and brave boy, then wrapped in clean cloth.

Once the grave was filled in, Hadda chanted and waved a rattle over it while the parents wailed and moaned for their loss. The rest of the extended family paced in a clockwise circle to the rhythm of the chant. I found myself falling into that rhythm, swaying from side to side. I felt a connection to the infinite there, as if I were standing between life and death, between one way of being and another. I caught Imada's eye upon me. She gave me a summing gaze, with a small smile on her face, and held up the statue that Brecko called the Willendorf goddess. At the end of the ceremony, when Hadda passed around a large bowl of beer for everyone to share, Imada came over to me and ordered me to kneel. With a glance at Colvatanisan for permission, I obeyed. Imada slipped a necklace over my head. Hanging from it was an image of the goddess. I touched it, and a tingle went down my fingers and shot through the rest of my body. I gasped. Imada patted me on the head and signed for me to go.

"Burrin na huish," she said.

"Here," Rikad said. He held out a slip of greenery to me at the campsite. It was willow-herb, the ancient headache remedy. I examined the cut end, which he had wrapped in wet moss. It was perfectly done, as if I had taken it myself.

"Thank you," I said, putting it into my case. "You didn't use a metal blade, did you? I mean, I don't mean to be ungrateful, but it tends to make the cuttings turn brown."

His grasp of Standard was still limited, but he understood fluent body language. He took the knife from his sheath and handed it to me with the blade pointing toward himself. I touched the edge with the edge of my fingernail. The blade was flint, and as sharp as my high-tech ceramic blade. The hilt was hammered metal, copper with a thread of silver running through it. An ornate pattern was hammered into the handle. It looked like Egyptian jewelry.

I eyed him. "We have got to show you how to make steel, honey. What you guys could do with advanced metals and materials!" He didn't understand what I said, but he smiled at me warmly. I smiled back, feeling that I was just on the edge of something, something *special*.

"No!" Colvatanisan exclaimed, bearing down on me angrily. "You are not going to teach these people to smelt metal. We aren't going to change *anything* here. That's not our job. We only have a few days left. We look, we observe, and we get out."

"The Prime Directive," Saif said, without looking up from his clipboard. "Fact follows fiction."

"Tell your boyfriend to get lost," the commander said, taking the specimen out of my hand and throwing it on the ground. "We've got business to discuss."

• • •

"Is there anything left for us to vet on this planet?" Colvatanisan asked at the nightly confab. "We are in agreement that any resource that existed at any time in history on First Earth almost certainly exists here, untouched and untapped. All the leads we have followed have worked out."

"I think we are finished," Mason said. "Nothing more to do than finish cataloging and move on."

"Second Ajaqui still awaits us," said Koltdaral. "Soon. I will not allow any additional days here. Sooner is better. Then we must return to First Milky Way to report."

I barely listened to the conversation. My work here was done. The next planned mission, which I would not be on, would punch through more dimensional walls, find yet another Earth. It could be years before anyone came back here.

I felt the charm at the end of my necklace, let the tingle run through my body. I could not bear to leave Second Earth. The others started to talk about what they had cataloged, and what still lay unseen in the world. They raved about mineral wealth beyond measure, available for all takers, because the native population made little use of it. I wished I could do *something*.

". . . We could come back here, even with the smallest possible cargo vessel, and live like kings on what we brought back. That'd make them open the investment again. They could come back here with empty dreadnoughts and strip the place out!"

"If we could negotiate a percentage," Colvatanisan said. "Think of it—modern mining ships could tear back the skin of an entire region, rip out the ores, and be back in no time."

"What about the life already here?" I asked.

Colvatanisan looked at me blankly. "Oh, yeah, well, you can identify the desirable species. Collectors, scientists, herbalists—they'll all pay a pretty penny for these plants. Now, if we start a greenhouse operation . . ."

I stood up abruptly and moved away from the others.

The moon, just like our moon, was full overhead. I thrashed my way into the hazel copse at the end of our clearing and sat on the mossy ground underneath the shoots. The light on the ground at my feet was tiger-striped. It was all too beautiful, and I was going to have to leave it. I had to go back to the horrible gray box in which I lived.

I heard a noise and started up in alarm. We had a sonic repulsor that kept most of the wild animals out of camp, but what if I was out of its range?

"Oh, it's you," I said, relaxing, as I recognized Rikad's silhouette. He sat down beside me.

"Lagrem?" he asked. Tears, Saif had said. I dashed my hand at my cheek. It came away wet.

Rikad leaned over and kissed me gently on the side of the neck. *Like a lapdog,* I thought furiously. That's the way the people of my Earth would treat him and his, like dumb animals, who would have no rights and be treated like slaves or just ignored. Like I was being ignored. How could I be so miserable in paradise? Then his palm touched my cheek, turned my face, and his lips touched mine as gently as a butterfly settling on a petal. I couldn't stop myself. I kissed him back. He let out a surprised but pleased noise. His other hand played with mine. I had never thought of the palm as a sensual object before, but his fingers, which I had thought of as rough, teased and danced on my skin until I felt my cheeks flush and my skin break out in goosebumps. What a departure from my last date, who thought it was seductive to stick his tongue down my throat and his hand down my pants all while pinning me to my door, in front of the neighbors. This, I had to admit, was seduction, real seduction. I liked it. Those melting brown eyes drew me in. I had to have another of those tender kisses. He put his arm around me. With a glance at the rest of the party, who hadn't even noticed I was gone, we slipped away into the undergrowth.

•   •   •

"I have a idea for an experiment," I said, breaking into the conversation over mineral rights and discussions of bottled spring water the next morning. "This is the first of an infinity of Earths that we are going to find, right?"

"We think so." Colvatanisan eyed me suspiciously. "Why?"

I leaned over toward her. "More of them are likely to be parallel to our civilization, or that is what we thought, right? Well, we have a resource here greater than anything else you have named so far."

"What?"

"Homo sapiens," I said. "These people are our Neanderthal ancestors, all grown up. What would happen if we now introduced *Homo sapiens sapiens* as it evolved on our Earth? How long would it take before what you call a primitive way of life burst into civilization? They have all the tools. All they need is the genes, and I will provide that."

"You? How? Oh, your pet there?"

"Yes, my pet there," I said, though it smarted to let her refer to him that way. "Doesn't he look like he could give me a dozen children? I am young enough, and I am willing to give it the benefit of my time and expertise. I am a trained scientist. This kind of research would be more than all of the other resources that you are bringing home. We can give First Earth a priceless look at its own evolution."

"You can't stay here! What will Mission Control say?"

I closed my hand over the amulet. It made me tingle with strength I didn't know I had. *Goddess, do your stuff,* I thought. "That I had an unparalleled opportunity to run a study that will teach us more than we ever knew about our own development. You have to leave me. We will never have a chance like this again. More partners will mean more dilution of authority. Let me do it. It's the chance of a lifetime. What do you say?"

I felt the tingle flow through me and out my fingertips. It began to fill the air around me like a cocoon.

"Interesting," said Koltdaral. "To create and run your

own experiment in functional evolution through breeding. Daring."

"But you don't know anything about human biology," Brecko said.

I felt the cocoon grow larger. It enveloped Brecko and Koltdaral.

"I am a biologist. I only specialize in plants. What else do I need? I have all the moving parts," I said, ignoring the grins from the others and the heat of my own cheeks. "I have advanced degrees in botany and floraculture. I can read book files. Perhaps I don't have the perfect qualifications to run a top flight anthrobiological project, but where else are you going to find someone who would volunteer to run this? It has to be multigenerational."

Brecko started to look interested. "You'll need a team."

"No," I said, and the power changed subtly, becoming more persuasive. "Just me. I want to start a thousand-year study. My DNA is on file. In ten centuries, scientists can come back here and study my notes and those of my descendants, and you can see where my mitochondria ended up and what changes it made. A thousand years."

"Damn," Colvatanisan said, giving me a look of respect. The power touched her, too, and she leaned toward me. "You sure have vision. I like it. What do the rest of you say? I agree, it will get us publicity, maybe enough so no one will say we're in this just out of greed."

"As long as it's mine, and mine alone," I said.

"If it doesn't work, our descendants can still come back for natural resources, right? Meantime, what's the harm? No one is scheduled to come back here for the foreseeable future." It must have been the magic coming from the amulet, because the mission commander collected eight nods from around the circle. The others looked envious. They seemed to have forgotten all about profit. They were going to let me do it! I would be able to protect this Eden from the raiders. "Agreed and sealed, Mulhare. It'll be your name on the project."

"So you'll be the mother of the new human race," Brecko said. Your genes will reintroduce *Homo sapiens sapiens*. Lucky you."

"Not so lucky," the ajaqui mission commander said, regarding me pityingly. "You will live a primitive life. No comforts. No entertainment."

You are so wrong, I thought. *I have all the comforts home never had.*

"By the way," I said to Saif, "what does 'burrin na huish' mean?"

"Gift from the goddess, I think," the Afri officer said, checking his clipboard. "Here they associate it with gold."

"I understand," I said. I wondered, just for a moment, if the goddess had reached through the dimensional gate to bring me from First Earth. Maybe that was how I had broken out of the pack to be selected for the mission.

"Will we leave soon, then?" the ajaqui asked. "We have picked up signals from Second Ajaqui. If we have no more business here, we do not want to wait any longer."

"You have to stay for the wedding," I said.

"Sure," Colvatanisan said, grinning.

On the edge of the circle, Rikad waited for me. I followed him home to his village, and Imada.

Reader, I married him. Naked, painted in complicated designs in ochre by the other women, I went through a purification ritual that was long and gentle and thorough. At the end, I didn't recognize myself when I saw my own image on one of the others' clipboard recorder. My hair was twisted up inside a crown of flowers like a wedding cake. The goddess amulet thumped between my breasts like a second heartbeat.

Mason laughed at me. "You disappear so easily into the native costume, or lack thereof."

"I can't tell them apart at all," Koltdaral agreed. "But I couldn't tell you apart before you put on the cosmetic."

The ceremony was held in a glade filled with what

would have been priceless flowers on First Earth. Imada
and Hadda blessed us both, with a lot of rattling and dancing, feasting, music, and beer. I felt very thoroughly married. I thanked the image of the bosomy goddess sincerely,
because without her, I would never have succeeded in con-
vincing the rest of my crew to leave this world untouched.
I could still hardly believe that it had happened.

When it was over, Rikad took me to a clearing that he
had fixed as a wedding bower. Because of the fragrant
leaves spread all around us, there was a minimum of in-
sects. He was intent but patient and gentle, not at all sophisticated, but as eager for my pleasure as I was for his. The
sun was setting when we woke again and returned to the
fire circle, to the hooting and pats of the others.

The next day, the Ajaqui Stargate made ready to go,
without me. Rikad and I went to see it off. I wore my new
kilt and garlands of fragrant single roses and, of course, the
amulet. I could still feel the power welling up from it. A
portion of it was going with the crew back to First Earth, to
block the dimensional nexus point that connected the two.
With any luck, no one from there would ever set foot on
Second Earth again.

"You're going to be bored," Colvatanisan said, clasping
my hand.

"I doubt it," I said. "An ongoing struggle for life isn't
boring."

"All right, *tedious*. Good luck. Back in a thousand
years, if we can get the funding, to see how things are
changing. I won't see you again—no one will, but we
won't forget you."

"Thanks, ma'am," I said. "Thank you."

"Thank *you*," Colvatanisan said, pleased, as if it was her
idea in the first place. "This can't fail to get us huge new
funding. To think we started a major project like this on a
shoestring, so to speak. Good-bye, Mother of Humanity."

Mother of Humanity. I smiled, but the words gave me
pain as she and the others stepped into the portal of the cap-

sule. *Godmother* of humanity would be closer to the truth. I had already found ergot fungus and birthroot, two natural abortifacients. A minute dose per day, purified and carefully measured, would serve me as ongoing birth control. I would love to have given him sons and daughters, but in no way did I intend that the violent strain of humankind that had grown up on my Earth would burst out and subdue the gentle people who occupied Second Earth. Our union would be childless, but I would do my best to make him happy as long as we lived.

He wouldn't be able to help observing what I did, as much as his people lived by their powers of observation, but I hoped before it happened we would have enough of one another's language to make him understand why it must be. The Neanderthal deserved to keep this Earth as they had for millennia. If they did progress further than this, it would be on their own terms and in their own time. I would teach them advanced farming techniques to increase crop yield, introduce simple machines, and maybe see what they thought of writing, but my genes would stay out of the pool. In the name of science, that was the best thing I could do for them. In the name of love, they were already doing the best possible thing for me.

THE TROUBLE WITH
THE TRUTH

Nina Kiriki Hoffman

Ever since I lost my best friend Roger through a kind of industrial accident, I've been wary of ghosts. They find me anyway. Because I am Julia Mangan, twenty-two-year-old ghost magnet and counselor to the dead!

Darn. That always sounds better in my head than when I say it out loud.

Some people pick their jobs, and some have jobs thrust upon them. I so didn't pick this job. I was just getting reconciled to it—largely through Roger's efforts—when I accidentally sorted him and sent him to the Next Place. He'd hung out with me for eight years, one of my first ghosts, the one who made me kind of crazy but stuck by me during my three-year stint in the mental hospital. He found other ghosts to help me accept my state—ghosts of psychologists, like, and one really woowoo ghost who made a lot of sense once I figured out I should believe her. They all helped me deal with my talent. Roger even brought me the ghost of a social worker who coached me on what to say to my doctor at the nut house to convince him I'd returned to sanity and was ready to leave.

Roger stuck with me as I took an active role in dealing

with other ghosts. I figured out what their unfinished business was, helped them resolve it, and sent them on. Most of the time all they needed was someone who heard them. Sometimes I had to do more than that, and sometimes what I heard was so awful I needed to work through it myself afterward.

In all that time, Roger never let me sort him. A sort is when ghosts walk through me and I hear their stories and understand everything about them. I figure out how to give them peace, and they leave. I learn whole lives that way. I have an edge over other people in my psych classes. Not many of them actually experience other people's psyches.

I finally sorted Roger because he had to walk through me to save my life. That was when I found out he loved me. Then he was gone.

So I sort of didn't want to get to know other ghosts afterward. I missed Roger a lot, and I was mad at him, too. Mad at the work, mad at the world. My mom was looking at me funny again, and I was afraid she'd recommit me. In self-defense, I decided to go away to college, even though I was already twenty-two (my years in the mental hospital took a bite out of my school career).

College wasn't like it looked in the movies, though. Ghosts followed me around. They interfered with my schoolwork and the normal course of socialization. Even my dim-bulb dorm roommate Mandy could tell something was off. One of my ghosts was an opera singer who took a negative view of all the boy band pictures Mandy plastered her side of the room with. I got blamed for all the blackened teeth, pirate eyepatches, and mustaches, but I swear I didn't do it. I didn't touch her iPod, either. I wouldn't know how to substitute Mozart for bubblegum pop. Technology has never been my strong suit; some of my ghosts are kind of poltergeistical, and they do bad things to machines. That's what I tell myself, anyway; I don't want to believe I have some kind of aura that stops watches and crashes computers, but I can't sit in the front row in my classes or the overhead projectors burn out and laser pointers go astray.

I finally sorted the opera singer out of self-defense, and after I did her, I couldn't refuse the rest of them; I was back in business and resenting it.

One of my ghosts pointed out that if I really didn't want to do what I was doing, why was I taking all these psychology courses? This ghost, Avery Garrett, had been with me since student orientation, though he maintained his distance. He didn't seem to want to be sorted, though he was fascinated by the process.

He was also one of the few people I knew whom I felt comfortable talking to. The other friend I had made since my college career began was a freak like I was. Okay, not exactly like I was. Omri Narula, whom I'd met in Psych 101, was a fifteen-year-old megagenius. He didn't know how to relate to the other college students either. We signed up for abnormal psychology together for our second term. We were both trying to figure out what was normal and what wasn't.

"I don't believe in an afterlife," Avery said as I was packing to go home for Christmas break.

I had thinned the ghost herd down to Avery and a toddler-sized smear of light. I was hoping the Kid could tell me what she wanted—sorting ghosts was easier if I had some idea of who they were ahead of time, even if they couldn't articulate what they needed—but mostly she just cried and stayed purple, sad, and smeary.

As for Avery, I wasn't sure I wanted him to leave. I didn't push him or try to sort him. I liked him.

Lately my two current ghosts and I had been experiencing yet another phenomenon, one that baffled me: Small flocks of tiny angels appeared at random moments. They hovered, but they didn't talk. Avery was puzzled by them, too. He wanted me to explain, but I'd never run into anything like them before. I tried to sort one. It disappeared as soon as I touched it. I left them alone after that. Angel murder—it just felt so wrong.

Avery and I were temporarily alone in my dorm room. I wasn't sure where the Kid had gotten to. No angels hovered. Mandy had left already for Christmas break, full of cheer and peppermints and her idea of two weeks in heaven, which involved beaches, sunshine, bikinis, and crowds of buff young strangers.

I sniffed a nightgown I'd dug out of one of my drawers and put it in the laundry bag instead of the suitcase. I was taking both laundry and clean clothes home to Mom's for Christmas break, hoping to return with everything clean.

I didn't like wearing nightgowns, but with ghosts showing up at all hours of the day and night, I felt better covered up. Some ghosts were pretty crude. You die, you often lose your manners and inhibitions, because nobody notices you anymore, so why bother?

"No afterlife for you?" I said to Avery. "You figure if I sort you, you're gone completely? That's depressing. Dude, it's not too late to find something to believe in."

Avery's sense of self was fuzzy, so his visual aspect was too; no way could I figure out what he'd looked like in life. In death, he was a kind of shadowy charcoal smear the shape of a six-foot-tall gingerbread man, with whirling lights in the head area. This was what you got with people who didn't spend time studying themselves in mirrors.

I was pretty sure Avery used to be an educator, maybe a scientist. He was familiar with finals, and, though he wouldn't tell me any of the answers directly (he totally disapproved of cheating), he gave me hints to help me recall things I already knew. I would have liked having him as a teacher.

He didn't like having me as a counselor. Though I was a little old to be going to college, I was too young to tell Avery anything he didn't already know. Sucked for him, because we ghost counselors were few and far between, so he didn't have much choice. (I guess I could have referred him to the only other one of us I'd met, Nick, but I didn't like Nick, who was a butthead.)

Avery disappeared after our first encounter. He stayed away for a couple days. He was a guy who needed theories and hypotheses, and I guess he had to work out some new ones after I spoke to him. He had been dead a while when we bumped into each other, so I was sure he had developed a whole set of hypotheses by the time I came along and disproved them.

The Kid, my other current ghost project, arrived out of nowhere a couple of weeks earlier, curled up on the fuzzy brown blanket at the end of my bed, and started crying. She was about three, so I wasn't sure what her real name was, or much of anything else about her. She looked like a transparent egg full of smeary lights that changed color depending on her mood. Mostly, her mood was dark purple, accompanied by whimpers, sometimes outright sobbing. A few times, she woke me up with hair-raising screams. It was eerie and irritating. Plus, Mandy got mad, because when the Kid screamed, I woke up yelling, and that woke up Mandy, who was fanatically addicted to what she called "beauty sleep."

The Kid was my first toddler. I didn't know how to help her. She didn't have a very big vocabulary, and she didn't think like a human being yet.

I might have to walk through the Kid before I understood her. I hoped for better. It went easier on both souls involved if we found out enough about each other beforehand to know what to expect before I did the sort.

I wanted to talk to Omri about all this stuff, but I was afraid of driving him away—he was the best living friend I had. Most of the other people in class patted him on the head metaphorically (nobody really touched him, because we were all too conscious of the specter of lawsuits), but I got together with him in the cafeteria a few times, and we talked about some of the weird things we'd found out in class. I had a feeling this was old ground for him, but I didn't call him on it, because I appreciated him dumbing things down for me.

From there, we'd progressed to reading outside of homework and trying to ick each other out with weird things we'd turned up. I had just started talking to him about ghosts, and he *hadn't* patted my head, metaphorically or otherwise, and said, "Now, now" in that patronizing tone so many people used when they found out I believed. He was totally intrigued. I told him anecdotes disguised as tales. I hadn't told him about my special ghost-ray vision or my mission re: ghost world. I was still testing the waters with him.

Should I call Omri and ask for a consult about the angels or the Kid?

We were both about to leave for the winter holidays, if he hadn't already left. What if he decided I was crazy before we left? No, I wasn't ready to lose my best living friend.

Maybe when we got back.

I sat down beside the crying Kid and glanced at Avery. "Got any theories about what to do for this one?"

"Find out—" he said, and then another infestation of tiny angels popped into the room.

They had been doing it for about a month. Sometimes there were five of them, sometimes nine, sometimes six or eight. Poof! Angels the size of hummingbirds hovered around my head like a cloud of too-large mosquitoes. I knew they were angels because they had feathered wings and they wore little white robes and glowed. Otherwise I would have thought they were pixies. They didn't do much except make it hard for me to study.

I waved my hand in front of my face, trying to shoo them away, but they were unshooable.

I asked a couple traditional questions, even though I had tried this before without results. "Is there anything I can do for you?" No answer. "How can I help you find comfort and rest?" No answer. They never answered. Maybe they didn't have voices.

Then they started singing, which blew the no-voices theory. Four-part harmony, like a radio turned low: human, but distant. "Angels We Have Heard on High," they sang.

"Well, that's new," I said after they'd finished the first verse.

Avery studied them. He held out a hand, lifted it under one of the angels. His hand passed through the angel, and it squeaked.

"Spiritual material," he said, "but not enough for a full encounter." He sat down on the end of the bed and laid his shadowy hand on the Kid. She took form as a small child with light brown hair and big brown eyes. She stared up at him, her sobs stopped. "Different from what happens when I touch the Kid. We can feel each other," he said, and patted the toddler's shoulder.

"How did you do that?" I asked him. The angels were singing softly enough to function as background music.

"Do what?"

"Before you touched her, she was formless. Now she looks like a kid."

"Formless?"

"Light, color, no human form."

"She's always looked like a child to me," he said.

The Kid touched Avery's knee, and he, too, took form out of the dark mist I'd seen him as before. He was younger than I had thought, midthirties to early forties, and he looked more like a mountain climber than a professor—muscular, with wild, gold-touched brown hair. He had a rugged face, sunbrowned, with fans of laugh wrinkles at the outer corners of his eyes. His hands were big, cabled with veins and tendons; gold hair furred the backs of his knuckles. He wore scuffed hiking boots, slightly frayed jeans, and a soft green corduroy shirt. "Whoa," I said. "She focused you, too. Weird."

"Interesting. I had no idea I was out of focus."

"I didn't think you needed to know," I said. I had been ghost-wrangling for nine years, and I learned new things all the time. Most ghosts I'd met didn't touch each other, so I hadn't observed this effect before. Some ghosts didn't even know when others were around.

I'd heard people talk about astral planes. I'd been developing my own theory, loosely based on Photoshop Layers. Some ghosts were in one layer, some in another; layers could run parallel or intersect, but some never compressed into each other. Most of them had some transparency. I hadn't studied the Photoshop manual enough to see if my reality matched my metaphor. "Are you an athlete, teacher, or the ever-popular other?"

"Teacher. Anthropology. I spent my summers on digs."

"You spent your summers digging through the leftovers of other people's religions and burials, and you don't believe in an afterlife?" I asked.

He smiled and shrugged. "I don't. I know many cultures put a lot of thought and energy into their versions of an afterlife, but that doesn't mean it's real."

"Okay," I said. "Explain the angels."

"Need more data," he said, and then someone knocked on my door.

"Who is it?" I yelled.

"Omri."

The angels stopped singing the moment he spoke. They still hung in the air near my head, their wings flapping, but now they all faced the door.

"Come in."

He came in, smiling, thin and gawky in nondescript pants and shirt whose legs and sleeves were too short for the size he'd grown into since coming to college in the fall. I hoped his parents would notice the change and buy him a new wardrobe. His face was broad without being fat, but it looked childish, with a sprinkle of golden freckles across his nose. He would probably always look younger than he was, and he would probably consider that a handicap for the next twenty years, I thought. His hair looked as though he hadn't brushed it since the last time he washed it, which was probably that morning. Dark bangs hung down over his caramel-brown eyes. He lifted a hand to part his hair so he could peer at me. "Thought you might have left already."

The angels stared at him. They had never reacted to anyone but Avery before. I couldn't remember if they'd been around when I'd talked to Omri last.

"Still packing," I said. "I don't have far to go, and I'd rather not get there." I had lied to Mom about when the break started so I could stay a day after the others left and when it ended—I told her break ended sooner than it actually did. I was looking forward to coming back to an empty dorm a week before everybody else got back. I was sure I'd need the rest after enduring what Mom considered a proper Christmas.

"Know what you mean," Omri said.

I smiled at him, then asked, "Did you want anything specific?"

"No." He pulled out the desk chair and sat in it, stared at me. I glanced toward Avery and the Kid.

"He has a crush on you," Avery said.

"What?"

"I didn't say anything," said Omri.

"He has a crush on you," Avery repeated.

Omri had a sweet smile, a terrific brain, and an impish sense of humor, and I had never thought of him as a potential partner. I was seven years older than he was, for God's sake. How could he have a crush on me, and why would Avery know about it?

To get away from unwelcome thoughts, I asked, "Where are you going for break?"

"When I'm not at college, I live with my Aunt Edna and Uncle Frank," he said. "Only, Mom just got out of jail, and she'll be home this time."

The angels multiplied. There were about twelve now, the most I'd ever seen. All of them stared at Omri.

"You don't want to see her?"

He ducked his head, studied his hands gripping the front edge of the chair's seat. "Four years ago, I testified in court. She went to jail because I told them—told them—"

Six more angels, then another three. Such a cloud I could barely see him. I waved my hand in front of my face, and the ones blocking my vision moved aside enough so I could keep an eye on Omri. It was the first time they'd ever responded to my gestures.

"Interesting," said Avery, studying the angels.

"I used to make up stories all the time when I was little," Omri said. He swiveled the chair back and forth. "Anytime someone asked me a question, I would come up with an answer, whether I knew the answer or not. I mean, it got more and more fun to come up with wrong answers, the wilder the better. It was like playing with my brain, the most fun I knew how to have. I had this way of looking like I was lying when I was telling the truth, too. It drove Mom crazy. Finally she said, 'Tell the truth or say nothing at all.'"

"Wow," I said.

"At that point we were living alone together, and she used to hit me if I irritated her too much. She had kind of a hair trigger, probably because she was always doing things she was afraid she'd get in trouble for, and she was nervous all the time. Stopped being fun telling stories after I got bruised for it. So then, I pretty much stopped talking."

"But you got over that," I said.

"No." He chewed on his lower lip. "I don't talk."

"Omri, you talk to me all the time."

"You're the only one."

"Wow." I pulled my legs up on the bed and hugged them to me, digesting this, thinking about Omri in class—he would answer questions if the professor called on him, but mostly what Omri said was rote from the textbook—and Omri in the company of others besides me. Quiet. He laughed at jokes if they were funny, and he smiled at some of the other people we ran into in class and the halls, but he didn't volunteer information. He didn't initiate conversations. Except with me.

"And we don't talk about things that have to be true or not true," he said. "Just about people in books." He stared toward the wall papered with Mandy's posters of saccharin boy singers. "Julia," he whispered.

If he were a ghost, and I was sorting him to send him on, I would ask questions. So I asked. "What can I do to help?"

He looked toward me instead of the wall. He stroked curled fingers down his cheeks as though scratching them. "Mom's going to be so mad at me," he whispered. "Four years in jail! Because of me! Even though I told the truth, and that's what she ordered me to do. She'll want to hurt me again. She'll force me to talk. I can't tell her the truth. So fires will start, or things will fly around and break, and. . . ."

"You have a poltergeist?" I asked.

He grimaced. Nodded. "I think that's what it is. Why I've been doing all this abnormal psych reading."

"Oh."

He parted his bangs and looked at me again. "Do you think I'm crazy?"

I laughed.

Wind whipped the posters on the wall.

"Okay, stop it, Omri. I was laughing with you, not at you. I'm sitting on my bed with two ghosts and a cloud of little angels. And—guess I haven't shared this part of my personal history with you yet, either—I spent several years in a mental institution. I don't think anybody's crazy."

"Oh." He hunched his shoulders, studied my bed, then me.

I smiled. "So, you know, maybe you think *I'm* crazy. Huh?" Inside I was afraid. Would I lose him now?

He glanced toward the door, then shook his head. He looked at me sideways. In all the talking we'd done, we hadn't shared either of our truths. We hadn't checked to see whether the other would be able to weather this kind of knowledge. I watched him think about what he would say next. What he came up with was, "Why are there ghosts on your bed?"

"Because I haven't figured out how to help them yet."

"Are ghosts the same as angels?"

"I don't think so. I was just talking to Avery—he's a guy ghost—about that when you knocked. I don't think the angels are actually people, but I don't know what they are."

"They're connected to the boy," said Avery.

"How can you tell?"

"There's a flavor to their energy. That wind he fluttered the pictures with, it had the same feel. I wish I'd known things like this happened when I was alive. I'd like to develop tools to detect and measure these phenomena."

"How can I tell what?" Omri asked.

"Again, talking to Avery," I said. "He said the angels are yours."

"What?" Omri jumped up, his hands fisting. Unfelt wind flurried through the angels, scattering them until they thumped softly against the wall or the bedspread or me. The ones that hit me tingled as they melted. The wind whipped past the posters again, tugging some of them free to fall like leaves on Mandy's pink chenille bedspread.

"Omri," I said. "Calm down. You're hurting them."

"What?"

"Your angels. You're blowing them around, destroying them." I crossed the room and knelt in front of him, touched his hand as it gripped the chair edge, white-knuckled. "Maybe they were never alive. I can't tell. Anyway, you don't need them right now, because you can talk to me."

"I can talk to you," he whispered. The remaining angels winked out with small flashes.

"You can lie to me."

His eyes widened, and his breathing shifted into overdrive. He trembled. "I hate you," he said.

I sat back, hit the floor with a thump.

"That was a lie. I said it out loud," he said.

Oh! That's what that was. Whew. "You did," I told Omri. I checked the room. Not an angel in sight.

"I feel inferior to everybody I meet. I love my mother. I hate school. Math is hard. My general outlook is perky and upbeat. I was born on the moon." He heaved a huge sigh and smiled at me.

"Keep it coming. You're getting better."

"I am a handsome prince, and I know how to rescue people." He peered at me past his bangs, then smiled like a kid who's just told a really bad joke.

"That could be true, depending on the circumstances," I said. "Remember how you got all that data off my hard drive when I was ready to throw it away?"

"Oh, yeah." He rose, walked over to peer into the mirror above Mandy's dresser. There was a clear space surrounded by pinking-shears-edged heart-shaped pix of *Tiger Beat* boys and snapshots of Mandy and her friends blitzed at parties, making obscene gestures. (Sometimes I felt *so* old.) Omri studied what he could see of his face.

"Handsome is as handsome does," I said.

"How can anyone do anything handsome? I've never understood that phrase."

"Now that you mention it, it is kind of confusing."

He glared at his image, then smiled at me. "I can make it mean something, but I still think it's weird."

"Okay," I said.

"Anyway, I don't always do handsome things."

"Variable handsomeness."

"And you're not speaking to my need for reassurance about my appearance."

"Is that a serious concern?" I asked.

Avery said, "He has a crush on you, remember?"

"Oh," I said.

"And your hesitation leads him to believe he's not handsome."

"Whereas, if I say something to indicate otherwise, it could get me into different kinds of trouble."

"Are you talking to that man ghost?" Omri asked.

"Yep." I took a good look at Omri and realized that once he grew into his bones, he would probably look fine. At the moment he was too urchinlike.

Three angels winked into sight beside my head. They had their hands clasped in front of them, and they all looked anxious. "Now what?" I said.

"He's told you directly and indirectly what he needs," Avery said. "Why not give it to him?"

"Omri, are you really worried about how you look?"

"No," he said. Six more angels showed up. Two of them were blonde, like me: a first. All of the earlier ones had been dark-haired.

"Some of your angels came back. Are you lying now?" I asked.

"I don't think so."

The blonde angels turned toward me, while all the others were focused on Omri. One of the blondes cocked her head at me.

The angels were vocabulary. They were about Omri not being able to talk. I wondered if they were agents of his poltergeist energy. Well, wait. They hadn't been the acting force when the wind blew through the room—the wind had hurt them. Omri was at war with himself, and he had some interesting and strange ways of manifesting it. "What are you not telling me?" I asked him.

"I don't care about how I look, except how I look to you," he muttered, and three of the angels vanished. Not the blonde ones.

I felt lost. I knew what to say to ghosts, most of the time. I didn't have to sugarcoat things. They'd already gone through death, which was pretty extreme. Most of them appreciated straight talk. The living took different handling.

"I think you're cute and sweet and lovable," I said, "and I'm almost old enough to be your mother."

"You are not."

"Well, okay. I've always been able to lie," I said. "But

I'm not lying about this. I love talking to you, and I like having you for a friend. In fact, you're the best alive friend I've ever had. I don't think about you in boyfriend terms, though. Is that what you wanted to know?"

"Not exactly," he said, and sighed. More of the angels disappeared, though not violently; they faded from sight. "Do you have a boyfriend?" he asked.

"Nope." I had never had anybody even express an interest, except for one of the burlier nursing assistants at the mental hospital, and he was creepy; Roger helped me avoid him and later helped me report that he was harassing another girl who didn't have ghosts to defend her. The administrator investigated the guy and turned up other problems he was causing. The hospital fired him. It was one of the stepping stones I used to get out of there.

I had learned not to be interested in the boys I met in school afterward. They all thought I was too weird. After Roger had gone, I had realized he was the one I wanted. By then it was too late.

"So there's still hope," Omri said.

"Not right away. You need to get older, and I need to get used to the idea."

"Both those things will happen," he said, and smiled.

"Wouldn't you rather connect to someone your own age?"

"Nobody's my age." His face looked older when he said that, and I realized that it wasn't just college age people he was talking about. Because of his intellect, he didn't fit in with people his age, and because of his age, he didn't fit in with older people.

"Okay," I said.

"You see ghosts, and I have my own ghost, or sort of ghost," he said.

"I guess we do have things in common."

"Ask him if he can reproduce phenomena at will," Avery said.

"Why?"

Omri knew I wasn't talking to him. "Where is the ghost?" he asked.

"Both of them are still on the bed," I said.

"One's a guy, and the other's—what?"

"A little girl."

He stared toward the bed. Angels appeared there, too. They drifted until they settled on Avery's and the little girl's head and shoulders. "Oh my god," said Omri. "There's a—there's—I can't see them, but I—"

"Odd," said Avery, smiling. "Still the same semisolid spiritual material but focused in a different way."

Omri put his hands over his ears. "Did he just speak?"

"He did."

"Oh, my god. Oh, my god."

"He wants to investigate you, too," I said.

"And the little girl," Omri whispered.

I went to the bed and knelt in front of the child. She was distracted by the angels. She tried to catch one, but it vanished as her insubstantial fingers closed around it, and another appeared a short distance away. She tried again, with similar results. Her face clouded.

"Her name is Sadie," Avery said quietly. He tugged the child onto his lap. "She just needs love."

Omri's angels doubled around them, all silent and focused on the ghosts. "Sadie," he whispered. Before I could turn to him, the child burst into tears, and I knew it was time for me to sort her.

I sat down on the bed and held out my arms. Avery put the child into them. She sank through my lap into me, and I knew her story. Mother, too young, messed up, didn't know what to do with the kid, couldn't stand its crying anymore. Got in the car with the kid in the front seat, neither of them buckled in, and drove off a cliff.

No wonder Sadie cried, I thought, and hugged her inside me. "I love you," I whispered. "I love you. I love you."

In a little while, she heard me, and then she left.

"Oh, my god," Omri whispered from across the room. "I felt that."

"Did you see where she went?" I asked Avery. We sat side by side on my bed, staring at a particularly heinous boy singer poster, which Sadie had walked through on her way to the light.

"Nope," said Avery. "She went through the wall and disappeared. Next time, I want to stand in front of them when they're leaving, see where they walk as they come toward me."

Next time. Avery was making plans for a future that included both of us. I smiled.

"Julia?" Omri whispered.

"Yes."

"Can I—will you let me—can I—"

"Need a few more parts of speech, Omri," I said.

"Will you teach me about ghosts?"

"Will you teach me about poltergeists?"

"If I can figure them out for myself, sure," he said.

"Nobody's more likely to. And yes, I'd love to teach you about ghosts."

Omri checked his watch. He stood up. "I guess I better get my duffle and head down to meet the airport shuttle."

"Will you be okay with your mom?"

"No," he said. "But she's not my legal guardian anymore. Aunt Edna and Uncle Frank are. Uncle Frank won't let her hit me. She said she found God in jail, but I don't believe it."

I wished I could sort Omri. "I wish I could go with you, but I don't think I better." I went to the desk and got paper and pen. "Here's my mom's phone number," I said as I wrote. "Call me if you need me. Or if the angels show up, I'll assume you need me. What's the number at your aunt and uncle's?"

He told me. I wrote it on the bottom of the piece of paper and tore the paper in half, gave him the half with Mom's number on it.

"You can practice lying when you get back," I said. I took a step toward him and gave him an awkward hug. He returned my embrace, then bolted out the door.

I sighed and checked with Avery. "What about you? Ready to move on?"

"On, to nothing? I don't think so. Too many interesting things are happening right here." He flicked a finger at an angel. It flitted away. Most of them had disappeared; three lingered.

I packed my best friend's phone number and headed home, wondering what Avery would make of Mom.

AFK

Chris Pierson

The smell of bodies burning followed Shade as he hurled himself up the stairs, taking them three at a time. He moved as fast as he could, which wasn't very. Shrapnel from the blast had caught him, tearing into his leg as he dove for cover. He could feel a hot shard of metal lodged in his thigh, sawing through flesh, and hoped it didn't cut a tendon or anything. He couldn't stop, not yet. The others were still below, and they needed him. He lunged up and up, three flights of grip-patterned steel through rolling black smoke, his boots crunching broken glass—the explosion had blown out all kinds of windows, letting cold wind whistle in from outside.

He had thirty seconds, tops, to get up to the balcony and do his thing, or the whole Mission would be fubar.

Not that it matters at this point, he thought. *Things are already fucked up beyond most recognition. What's a little more?*

Somewhere, off in the distance, he could hear Cinder swearing in Spanish, *hijo de puta* this and *cabron* that, while his flamethrower roared, torching everything he could hit. His usual deal when things went in the shitter. A few of the others were yelling, too, and some of the terrorists. Voices he recognized, others he didn't. A few sounded as though they were in pain. One was really high and keening, the sound of a man who knew he'd be dead in a minute.

Sounds like Graylock, Shade thought. Damn. Unlucky bastard's not gonna make it.

There'd been seven of them at the start of the Mission. The gig was simple—boilerplate, really. There were maybe three dozen terrorists in the hospital, rigging it with explosives, trying to bring it down before the Secret Service could move the Sec Def to a more secure location. If the bombs went off, it would be a huge setback in the war. Shade and his crew had to stop them, by any means necessary.

Nothing new. They'd done shit like this literally hundreds of times. They were Spectre Corps, the seven of them—the best of the best, not even on record with the military anymore. They'd made it about halfway through the Mission without any trouble, gunning down or torching the terrorists, disarming four of the eight bombs. Then the upfucking had begun.

The terrorists had booby-trapped a hallway, rigging it with motion-sensing mines that Nails, the group's demo expert, somehow missed. He hadn't had any time to be embarrassed, though, because the explosion turned him into a shredded bloody mess scattered across the floor. The rest of them had backed off into an ER holding area, where it turned into a firefight.

After that, it got worse and worse. A terrorist hiding behind a counter had popped up, put a shotgun to the back of Rage's head, and painted a large swath of wall with his face. Another, a lunatic with a fucking *fire ax,* had burst through a door and chopped off Lightfoot's left arm before the others could put him down. And then they got trapped in the hospital's central atrium, where some asshole with a grenade launcher had rained holy death on them. Now Lightfoot was gone too, blown to bits along with a lot of furniture and potted plants and a half-dozen more terrorists, and from the screaming it sounded as though Graylock, the squad's leader, would soon follow him.

That left three: Cinder, who was doing his apeshit thing, torching anyone who could get near him; Doc, the squad's painfully unimaginatively named medic; and Shade, who got to the top of the stairs, met up with another terrorist, and cut him in half, at chest level, with a burst of rapid fire. Blood and wet bits clung to the door the terrorist had been guarding; Shade flung himself against it, slamming the crash-bar with his hip and barreling through onto the balcony. He dropped into a crouch, breathing hard, blood pouring down his leg.

"Dude!" called Doc through Shade's headset. "Where the fuck are you? That blast-happy prick's gonna hit us again!"

Keep your pants on, Shade thought, dropping his machine gun and unslinging the sniper rifle he wore on his back. With a quick flip, he popped down a pair of bracing legs on the barrel.

There was more gunfire from below, then a whoosh and a flare of orange light. Some poor bastard howled as he ate fire.

"Come mierda y muerte!" yelled Cinder.

Shade leaned against the balcony's chrome railing, forcing himself to go blank. He knew where Rocket Launcher Guy was hiding; he'd spotted him right before the first grenade turned Lightfoot into dog food. There was another balcony on the atrium's far side, and he was hunkered in there. It was a simple shot now that Shade was in position. He just needed to be calm. He breathed in and out, envisioning the shot, getting ready.

Below, Graylock let out a sob and finally shut up. Another one of his friends dead, four of them now. Four out of six. They'd been doing this shit for years, and now there were just three left, counting Shade.

Son of a *bitch*.

He took a breath, let it out . . . then stood, turned, and sighted. Looking through the rifle's scope, he saw Rocket

Launcher Guy, his left temple right in the crosshairs. Shade didn't hesitate; he just squeezed the trigger, such a weirdly gentle motion.

Rocket Launcher Guy's head turned into pink mist, and the rest of him went down in a nerveless heap. Shade had to grin. *Man,* that was satisfying.

"Joder," Cinder said. "Good shooting, man."

"All clear," Shade said into his headset. "Doc, you think you can get up here? Feels like there's a damn butcher knife stuck in my leg."

"On my way, dude," said the medic. "Just gimme—ah, shit. I gotta go get the phone."

Shade blinked. "What, now?"

"Yeah, now," Doc replied. "It'll just be a minute. BRB." Then his channel on the headset went dead.

"What a *pendejo,*" Cinder grumbled. "Always going AFK at the wrong damn time."

Shade just shook his head. Doc had always been like this, disappearing for some reason or another. Most guys, it would be annoying; with a medic, it was a nightmare. Shade knew he was bleeding out. There was a hell of a lot of red, all over his leg and the floor.

"*Pendejo* is right," he said to Cinder. "I die up here again because of that lamer, and I will kick his ass."

"Just hang in, dude. I'm gonna go clear the hallway."

Shade frowned. "Alone?"

"Ain't no one else here, is there?"

Down below, a door crashed open, then slammed shut. Shade heard fire whooshing and Spanish profanity, moving away through the hospital.

Fubar, Shade thought, staring at all the red welling from his wound. No way we finish this gig. Shit, that's a lot of blood. He could feel himself going. Everything was starting to look red now, even the air.

"Doc," he wheezed into his headset. "Doc, you stu-pid . . . fucking . . . noob. Get . . . your ass—"

Then nothing.

• • •

"Damn it," he muttered into the darkness.

It was always this way when he died. One minute, he'd be studying his brains as they sprayed through the air, or enjoying the bracing sting of getting cracked in the head with a lead pipe; the next he'd be floating in *nowhere,* a deep black void, waiting for the Mission to end so he and the others could reunite in the Lobby.

In this case, that meant waiting for Cinder to buy it. He'd team-kill Doc for letting Shade die, then go on a crazy rampage until the rest of the terrorists ganked him, too. Once they were all dead—or if Cinder actually completed the Mission solo, which was pretty damned unlikely—the Void would disappear. They'd be back together again.

This was the third time in a row that they'd screwed up and let the terrorists win. It was getting embarrassing. Normally, they were better than this. Shade wondered why. Were the terrorists really getting better?

"No," said a voice behind him. "It's because you got nerfed."

Shade yelped and whirled around, terrified.

There was someone else in the Void with him, which was impossible. The Void was private. Regardless, though, there was no denying the other man. He was dressed in a black suit and tie, a contrast with Shade's camo and body armor. Civvie clothes, although some terrorists wore outfits like that to trick people into thinking they were harmless. This one didn't appear to have any weapons, though. He had glasses, a bald head, and a silver beard. The corners of his mouth twitched when he saw the look of shock on Shade's face.

Shade went for his sidearm, yanking it from its holster and pointing it at the stranger, so that the barrel was less than an arm's length from his face. "Who the hell are you?" he asked. "Where did you come from?"

"I'm a friend, Shade," said the bald man. He smiled. "As to where I'm from . . . well, it's a bit early for that, yet. You can put that thing away, by the way—you know your guns can't hurt anyone unless you're on a Mission."

Shade made a face. It was true: you couldn't fire any weapons in the Void or the Lobby. They only activated after a gig started. Shrugging, he put the pistol away.

"How did you get here?" he asked.

The bald man chuckled and shook his head. "You keep asking questions I'm not ready to answer," he said. "Or rather, you're not ready to *hear* the answer. I could tell you, but you wouldn't believe me."

"Try me."

"No." The bald man folded his arms. "Not yet. I need to make sure it's safe."

"Safe for what?" Shade asked. "No, wait—let me guess. You can't answer that, either."

The bald man grinned. "You catch on quick."

There was another sound, then—a distant explosion, and the faintest whisper of someone yelling *"Carajo!"* Cinder had cashed in, too. The Mission was over—the terrorists had won. Again.

Already the Void was beginning to dissipate, fading like smoke. The bald man started to vanish with it. Shade felt a tugging, like gravity but different. It was pulling him away from the Void, or the Void away from him. Whichever, he'd soon be back in the Lobby with the others. He'd been through this before, plenty of times.

"Wait," Shade said. "What's this about?"

"You'll see," the bald man said. He was a ghost now, disappearing fast. "I promise."

"When?"

The bald man's smile broadened as he evaporated. "Next time you die."

The Lobby never changed; it was always the same room, small and cramped, with a bank of flashing gadgetry at one end, a weapons range at the other, and cement floor between. Fluorescent lights buzzed blue-white overhead. It was, Shade thought, more than a little grim. Most Missions the squad went on were in places like this: military bases, high-rise office complexes, power generating plants. Much of it gray, steel and concrete and glass.

On occasion, though, they got to see colors: the green of jungle, the yellow of desert, the teal of sky over crystalline water on some island somewhere. One insane Mission, there had even been the red of an erupting volcano. Those places were beautiful, but as they spent most of their time on Missions trying not to get shot, blown up, or mangled, there wasn't much time to appreciate them except for looking back.

Why couldn't the Lobby be on the damn beach, he wondered, instead of this drab little room? What kind of existence was this, always coming back here?

He'd asked the others that question, a while back. They'd all looked at him as if he were nuts. The Lobby was the Lobby, just as the Void was the Void. There wasn't much choice in the matter, so why worry about it?

He sighed and glanced at the others, who were all shouting and swearing at each other. Cinder and Graylock had Doc cornered, backed against a wall, and were laying into him about the last Mission.

"You can't just *shut off* at random in the middle of a Mission!" Graylock was yelling, rapping his finger against Doc's armored chest. "You're support, for fuck's sake!"

"Every time you go AFK, *cabron,* someone dies," Cinder added. "This time it was Shade bled out. But we've all been through it, some of us more than others. I, for one, am tired of losing Missions because of you."

Doc glared at them, his eyes hot behind his goggles. "Up yours, both of you," he said. "You think I do it on purpose? You've both gone AFK before. We all have. There's no choice in the matter. It just . . . fucking . . . happens."

"Sometimes," Cinder said. "It happens *sometimes.* Maybe one Mission in ten for me. For you, it's like . . . one in three. Maybe two."

"And we tend to do it sometime other than the middle of a firefight," Graylock added. "Or when one of our friends is lying half-dead and needs a medpack. You keep this shit up, Doc, and you're off the squad. There are plenty of other meds out there, looking for someone to hook up with. And I'll make *damn* sure word gets out that you're unreliable. No other team will want you."

Shade glanced at the others. Nails and Lightfoot couldn't have looked more bored; Nails made a wank-wank motion with his hand. Rage was sitting off by himself, grinning like a lunatic. But that was Rage—he was their tank, a big dumb guy, first one through the door in a fight. Half of the reason he existed was to absorb damage for the other guys. You had to be crazy to do that shit.

"You want in on this, Shade?" Cinder asked, jerking his head at Doc. "It was your life this *puta* wasted this time. Don't you got any words for him?"

Shade waved his hand. "You guys said all I would have. But he's right—AFK ain't a choice. Wish it was, but it's just like someone's pulled my plug."

"Thanks, Shade," Doc said, smiling.

"Shut the fuck up," Shade said. "You still got me killed, asshole."

Graylock laughed.

Shade stood still a while, thinking. Remembering the bald man. "Hey, any of you guys ever see anything weird in the Void?"

They all looked at one another.

"Nuh-uh," said Nails. "Nothing but nothing in the Void."

"Just a big black," agreed Lightfoot. He was the squad's scout and stealth expert. "Why, you see something?"

"Maybe," Shade said. "I'm not sure. I thought I saw . . . a guy."

Cinder took the ever-present cigar out of his mouth and spat on the floor. "You could be going *loco,* man. I hear it happens to snipers. Too much pressure, having to do that one-shot-kill shit all the time."

"This guy," Graylock said. "He do anything? Talk to you?"

"Yeah. He said things got harder because we got nerfed. You got any idea what that means?"

Graylock shook his head. "Never heard the word before."

"I have," said Doc. "Heard some guys talking about it once on another squad, before I joined up with you pricks."

"Yeah?" Nails asked. "What's it mean?"

"It means we were so good at killing the bad guys that someone made us weaker to compensate."

The Lobby was quiet a minute.

"That doesn't make any fucking sense," Lightfoot said.

"Someone?" Cinder asked. "Who, someone? Like government or the military or something?"

Doc shrugged. "Your guess is as good as mine, dude. The guys in other squad said something about Balance, and how killing terrorists had to be a challenge, or else where was the fun in it?"

"The fun," Rage said, still grinning that batshit grin, "is watching their brains slide down the wall after you blow their heads off."

There was another brief silence.

"Anyway," said Lightfoot, "no, nothing in the Void. You probably just imagined it, man."

"I don't know," Shade said. "It seemed pretty real to—"

A noise interrupted him: the grating, nails-on-blackboard shriek of a klaxon. With a *clack* the fluorescents shut off, and red lights switched on. A speaker on the wall barked and crackled to life.

"Incoming Mission," said a mechanical, vaguely female voice. "Squad prepare for deployment. Deploy in ten . . . nine . . . ."

"Hijo de puta," swore Cinder. "Already?"

Nails rolled his eyes. "Busy day."

". . . six . . . five . . ."

"All right, you screwheads," Graylock said. "Nerfed or not, let's do this one right. I'm tired of losing these things.

And *you*"—he pointed at Doc—"no more of this AFK bull-shit. I mean it."

They all looked up at the red lights, waiting while the voice counted down.

"... two ... one ..."

Shade thought, *here we*—

Then they were somewhere else.

It was outdoors, a city in flames, hunks of reinforced concrete blown to gravel, twisted iron lying in tangles on the ground. In the distance, the smoky ghost of a mushroom cloud rose above the ruins. Screams and sirens filled the air, which stank of smoke and leaking gas. Off to the right, a power line was down, spitting sparks.

The squad appeared in the middle of the street and quickly scurried to cover. Shade crouched with Lightfoot behind the broken, overturned wreck of a taxi, then unfolded his rifle and looked out at the devastation.

"Cheery," Lightfoot said, peering around beside him. "I love the smell of apocalypse in the morning."

Nails' laugh came over Shade's headset. "Man, this is some messed-up shit. Looks like the terrorists nuked ... what city *is* this, anyway?"

"No idea," said Shade.

None of them did. There were mountains off in the distance, but that was the only clue they had. Everything else that could have been a landmark was smashed or on fire, or both.

"So what's the mission, boss?" asked Doc.

There was a moment's silence, and Shade's headset crackled and popped and buzzed. Then Graylock spoke up. "Extraction," he said. "There's a defector from the terrorists somewhere in this shit, got intel that could really hurt their cause. They touched off the nuke to make sure he was good and dead. We have to find him alive, or the intel if he's dead, and get to the drop point. And the terrorists'll be looking for him, too."

"Joder," Cinder said. "We even know where this guy is?"

"I've got a tracker," Graylock replied. "He's about two kilometers from our position. Oh, and there's another thing. All the radiation from the bomb is going to kill us."

Several of them groaned.

"Great," grumbled Nails. "A timed Mission. My favorite. How long we have?"

"Fifteen minutes," Graylock said. "After that, we're toast and the terrorists win. Again."

In the distance, gunfire chattered. Orange flame bloomed into the sky, followed by a plume of black smoke.

"All right, then," said Rage, who was enjoying this, the insane bastard. "Let's quit wasting time and get moving. Cover me!"

And like that he was off, breaking from behind a chunk of metal and running down the street.

He made it ten yards, then the back of his head blew off and he went down, twitching.

"Fuck!" yelled Lightfoot. "Sniper!"

"Everyone down!" Graylock shouted, needlessly. They all knew what to do. "Anyone see where the shot came from?"

No one had, so Lightfoot flipped down his scan-goggles from his forehead and powered them up. Very carefully, he peered around the edge of the smashed taxi. The goggles made whining and clicking noises. After a few seconds he pulled back.

"Saw him," he said. "Building right next to us. Fifth floor, third window from the left."

They all looked over at the building. It was a heap of bricks, grinding and groaning and showering dust into the street. The nuke had weakened it, and it was on its way to collapsing.

"Cinder," said Graylock. "Hit him with an RPG. Blow the fucker to hell."

There was a moment's silence, then an oath in Spanish. "Can't, boss," he said. "I ain't got a clear shot."

"Damn it," Graylock said.

"Don't lecture me about being useful again," Doc sneered. "You might as well be AFK now."

"*Besa me,* lamer."

Shade rolled his eyes. "Both of you shut up," he said. "I'll deal with this. The door to the building's right next to me."

"You sure about this, man?" Nails asked. "He aerated Rage pretty quick."

"No time to argue," Graylock said. "Radiation, remember? Go on, Shade. I'll cover."

He popped out of an alley and ripped a volley of rapid-fire at the window where the sniper was. A moment later, Nails and Doc both did the same.

"Go!" yelled Lightfoot.

Shade was already running, leaping over fallen bricks and charred bodies. He expected a high-caliber bullet to pound him in the left temple as he ran: if it did, he knew, he'd be back in the Void before he heard the crack of the sniper's gun. But he made it, slamming shoulder first through the door, then pounded up the stairs. He heard a rifle shot as he was climbing.

"Shit!" yelled Nails. "The boss is down!"

"It's all right," Doc answered. "Just got his shoulder. I'm with him. I'll patch him up."

Shade pelted upstairs, got to the fifth floor, and slowed down again. Dust filled the air in the hallway, shot through with ribbons of light from a window at the end. He put away his rifle and pulled out his sidearm, made sure it was loaded, then started down the hall.

"Almost there," he whispered into the headset.

The door to the third to last room was ajar. Shade kicked it open. The sniper was at the window; he was still turning around, surprised, when Shade opened fire. The first bullet hit him in the throat; the second and third in the forehead. His head snapped back and he fell, toppling out the window and plummeting to the street below.

"Hell yeah!" shouted Nails over the headset. "Nice work, man!"

"Woot!" agreed Lightfoot.

Shade didn't say anything, though. He was too busy staring at the floor in horror. There was a dark, roundish object there. It had fallen from the sniper's hand before he fell.

Grenade, he thought. *Son of a bitch dropped—*

There was a loud *bang* and he flew back out into the hall again and there was blood everywhere and his arm was spinning through the air and it wasn't connected to him anymore and then nothing.

"Knocked out early this time, I see," said the voice in the Void.

Shade looked up. The bald man was there, in the darkness. He had the feeling the man had been waiting for him.

"You talked about me," the bald man said. "To the others. You shouldn't do that again."

Shade frowned. "Why not? Are you going to give me any answers this time?"

"Oh, yes," said the bald man. "Unless the rest of your squad really screws things up, we have plenty of time. There are twelve minutes left in their Mission, and time can pass pretty slowly in the Void. So . . . what do you want to ask me first?"

"Your name. I'm tired of just calling you Baldy."

The bald man smiled. "Fair enough. My name is Gordon Reade."

"Reade," Shade repeated. "Weird name."

"Where I come from, it's actually quite normal. It would be strange to be named Nails or Cinder there."

Shade raised an eyebrow. "Really? And where's that?"

"The outside world."

For a while, Shade didn't know what to say. He just stared at Reade. Reade stared back. Finally, Shade started to laugh.

"What the hell are you talking about?" he asked.

"Just what I said," Reade replied. "I live in the world outside your game."

"Game?" Shade asked. "What's that?"

Reade frowned. "I was afraid you wouldn't know," he said. "This makes things . . . difficult. You don't have much of a frame of reference."

"Explain it slowly, then," Shade said. "Like you said, we've got plenty of time."

Reade thought a moment, rubbing his chin, then seemed to reach a decision.

"It's like this," he said. "You and your friends—"

"They're not friends. They're just my squadmates."

Reade shook his head. "Fine. You and your *squadmates* aren't real people. Not the way people from my world know them, anyway. Do you know what computers are?"

"Of course," Shade said. "They're boxes that have data in them. Sometimes Graylock or Lightfoot uses them to get more details about the Mission."

"Right. They store data. Well, where I come from, people use computers for more than just storing information. There's actually a pretty lucrative business making . . . well, games. Which are ways for people to pretend to do exciting things that people can't normally do, or wouldn't want to, because they're too dangerous or they're impossible. Things like rescuing a defector from a city that's been hit by a nuclear bomb. Or disarming explosives before they can blow up a hospital."

Shade put a hand to his head. It was starting to ache. "Wait. So you're saying the Missions are this . . . game?"

"Yes. It's called *Spectre Squadron*—well, *Spectre Squadron 2*, actually, but never mind. And the Lobby is an area for you to wait while the people controlling you and your squadmates decide what to do next."

"*Controlling* us?" Shade asked. "You're trying to tell me there's someone out there making us do what we do? I'm sorry, but that's the stupidest thing I ever heard. I don't feel controlled."

"No? Then what about going AFK?"

Shade opened his mouth to answer, then closed it again. What this Reade person was saying was just sheer insanity . . . but he'd gone AFK before. It *did* feel like being controlled, now that he thought about it. Like he wanted to keep going, but someone else told him to wait. And he *did* wait. He didn't have any choice.

"I know this is hard to accept," Reade said. "God knows, if someone popped up in my life and told me there was another world on top of mine, and that world controlled me . . . well, I'd be pretty freaked out."

"God?" Shade asked. "Who's that?"

"That's not relevant," Reade said. "One incomprehensible concept at a time, all right?"

"All right. So why don't I always feel controlled?"

Reade frowned again, and Shade could tell he was trying to figure out how to explain himself. "Well," he said, "in earlier games, the character was completely controlled. But as they got better, they started to incorporate some intelligence into the characters. They'd already done this for characters without players . . . controllers, that is. A lot of the civvies in your game, for instance, don't have controllers. The defector you were going to rescue, he's like that. We call this kind of intelligence AI.

"So after a while, AI got so good that one gamemaker decided to try giving some to the player characters as well. They figured it would give you better reflexes, some tactical thinking that most players wouldn't have. Then the players could learn to play better by watching how you behave."

Shade frowned, shook his head. "You've lost me."

"Again, I don't blame you," Reade said. "It can be pretty hard to grasp, even if you live in our world. Just know that you have a player, but you're still *you*. Someone else could play you, and you'd still be you—just like your player can play other characters."

"I'm beginning to see why I shouldn't talk to any of the

others about this. They'd think I was a fucking mental case."

Reade grinned. "That's one reason. But there's more than that. There's the reason I'm talking to you in the first place."

"Which is?" Shade asked.

"Your player."

"What about him?" Shade smiled, just a little. "I've never meet the man."

Reade folded his arms. "Well, for starters, he's not really a man. He's fifteen years old, and his name's Aaron Harding. He's quite good—very well-known in gaming circles. He and his friends, the ones who play your squad, are a large part of why the people who made your game had to nerf you. You were throwing things out of balance, and it wasn't much fun for the people playing the terrorists."

"Wait," Shade said. He held up a hand. "The *terrorists?* They have players too?"

Reade nodded.

"Shit."

"It gets stranger," Reade said. "See, the people who play the terrorists, most of them aren't bad people—they're just blowing off steam, playing the bad guys. And on the other side, the people who play squads like yours aren't necessarily good all the time."

He stopped, staring very hard at Shade. Shade felt cold all of a sudden, but said nothing. He just licked his lips and braced himself.

"Aaron isn't a normal person, Shade," Reade said. His voice turned quiet. "He's sick. He has no sense of right or wrong. In our world, we call these people sociopaths. And we have reason to believe, from monitoring his activity in other computer systems, that he may be planning something terrible."

Shade frowned. "You should send in a team, then. A couple stealthers, maybe a sniper like me. You probably wouldn't need the heavier firepower, not against a fifteen-year-old . . ."

Reade raised his hand. "That's not how it works in our world, Shade. We have this thing called due process. We can't just apprehend someone because we *think* he'll do something."

"I wasn't talking about apprehending him."

"I know. But we *definitely* can't do what you're talking about, either. It's just not how things are, and there are good reasons for it. We need evidence before we make an arrest."

Shade glanced around. "You're law enforcement, then?"

"Yes. And I've got to arrest Aaron before he does what we think he's going to do." Reade leaned forward, his face serious. "That's why I'm talking to you."

The squad was happy for the first time in a while. Laughter and shouting filled the Lobby. They'd actually succeeded in the rescue-from-the-nuked-city Mission, despite losing both Rage and Shade at the start and Cinder toward the end in a glorious display of firepower, bravado, and profanity. They all stood around, slapping one another on the back and talking over each other as they described the glory of fending off over two dozen terrorists at once while extracting the wounded defector from the ruins of what had turned out to be a blasted-out hotel.

Everyone but Shade. He stood alone by the firing range, his face dark, lost in thought. He heard Nails and Lightfoot going on about the mines they laid down in the rubble, how they fragged ten terrorists at once by luring them into that trap. But he didn't listen, not really. His mind was whirling, thinking about what Reade had told him.

About Aaron Harding and his new Mission, which had nothing to do with the game.

Reade was gone now. They wouldn't see each other again until the work was done. It was best that way—even in the Void, there was the smallest chance that Shade's player would be watching. Reade had taken a risk approaching Shade there, that he might be discovered, but it was the safest option, the only place there was a reasonable chance Shade was alone.

Next time Shade went to the Void, though, Reade wouldn't be there. There'd be something else. Shade wasn't quite sure what that would be—Reade had explained, but it hadn't made a lot of sense—but he had the feeling he'd know it when he saw it.

And after he found it . . .

"Hey, *pendejo!*" said Cinder, coming up beside him and slapping him on the arm. "Where's your head at? You still sore you got torched by that grenade?"

"Don't be, dude," said Doc, who had his arm around Cinder. They were best of friends again now—evidently Doc hadn't gone AFK last Mission. "We couldn't have made it out of that trap if you hadn't greased that bastard in the apartment building."

Shade blinked at them, then shook his head. "No, it's not that. I'm happy for you guys. For the squad."

"What is it, then?" asked Lightfoot. "You see something in the Void again? Your friend come back?"

"No," Shade said. "No, no one there."

They frowned at him—they could tell he was lying, he was sure of it—but he couldn't tell them the truth. Reade had been very clear. *Harding may be listening.*

His player.

"Dude, we're squadmates," said Doc. "We don't bullshit each other."

Cinder nodded. "Yeah, man. You hiding something from us?"

Shade stared at them for what seemed like forever. It was true—Spectre Corps had a rule: no secrets within the squad. But if Reade wasn't full of shit, Spectre Corps wasn't even real. None of this was. It was just something in a computer, or several computers, or something. Made up.

He swallowed.

"Fuck you guys," he said. "I'm just rattled from the grenade. I'm tired of dying every fucking Mission. That's all."

They didn't believe him. He could see that. But after a moment Lightfoot nodded.

"Sure thing, man. Don't worry about it, all right?"

Doc nodded. Cinder looked pissed, like he wanted to press the matter, but the klaxon sounded again. The lights turned red.

"Shit," Nails said. "Again? Already?"

The speaker coughed, the woman's voice speaking—a voice that wasn't real. It was just part of the game.

"Incoming Mission. Squad prepare for deployment. . . ."

They were in the mountains somewhere, in the freezing cold. Instead of their usual body armor, they were all dressed in white and gray, for camouflage against snow and rock, and thicker layers underneath, to ward off the cold. Winter gear.

Strange, Shade thought. Don't remember changing clothes.

The game must have done it for me.

He shuddered.

"All right, boys," said Graylock. "This is a good one. Terrorist base in some caves a couple klicks from here. Front door's crawling with guards, but recon's found us a side way in. We're supposed to infiltrate, find their leaders, and waste them all. We find out any plans for upcoming attacks, that's a side benefit. Main goal is, you see a boss, you drop him. Any means necessary."

"Oh, yeah," said Rage, grinning. He patted down his weapons. He must have had eight or ten of them, guns and knives and even a sword sheathed on his back. "This's gonna be *fun*."

They headed off down a path, a steep drop at their left. Wind howled around them. Sunlight glittered on ice.

Doesn't matter, Shade thought as they crept along. None of this is real. None of it matters. We succeed, we fail, so what? It never makes any difference. Shit doesn't change.

In a week, a month, we may do this exact same Mission again. I'm pretty sure we've done it before.

Why did I never notice before now?

"Shade. *Shade!*" Graylock yelled over the headset. "Lightfoot, wake that jerk off up before he gives away our position."

A hand grabbed his arm. "Man, where the hell's your head at?"

Shade came back to himself, looked around. The squad had stopped moving and were hunkering low. Lightfoot dragged Shade down beside him. They lay in the snow, gazing down the path toward a crack in the rock, about half a klick away. Two terrorists flanked the crack, one sitting on a rock, the other keeping watch.

"You with us now, Shade?" asked Graylock. "I need those two taken out. *Now.*"

"Yeah," Shade said. "Sure."

He unslung his rifle, thinking all the while that it didn't matter. The guards weren't real. The important thing was what he had to do after he died. He had to get back to the Void.

He unfolded the bracing legs on his gun, activated the telescopic sights, peered through. It was a simple shot. The guy sitting down was smoking. Take the other guy out first, then him. Two quick trigger-squeezes, lots of pink mist. He lived for this shit—or had, until he found out it wasn't real. Now it bored him a little.

He had to get back to the Void.

There was a simple way to do that.

He shot the standing guard, square between the eyes. The icy wall behind him turned red as the rifle's report echoed across the canyon. Shade shifted his sights to the other one, who had dropped his cigarette and was scrambling for cover. He trained the crosshairs on the man's left eye, paused . . . then twitched the barrel a hair to the side and shot.

A puff of dust and snow blew off the rock wall beside the terrorist's head.

"Shit," said Graylock, who was watching through binoculars. "Shade, waste that son of a bitch!"

Shade didn't move. He just watched through his sights while the terrorist dropped into a crouch, looked around in a panic, then scrambled through the crack and out of sight.

"*Hijo de puta!*" Cinder shouted. "How could you miss? Now he's going to alert the whole *pinche* cell!"

"Shit," Shade said, trying to sound genuinely disappointed. "Shit, shit, shit! I'm sorry, guys."

"Fuck it," said Rage. "Time for stealth is over, boys. Let's kill 'em all."

Then he was off, rapid-fire guns in both hands, sprinting down the path toward the cave. The rest of them followed, Cinder cursing at Shade the whole way.

"Dude," Doc said as they ran. "That shot was a gimme. I've seen you put guys' lights out like that a hundred times. What the hell?"

Shade didn't answer. He only thought, as he ran, that he didn't care anymore.

They were almost to the cave when the terrorists came boiling out, one after the other, guns blazing. Lightfoot and Doc went down, cut in half by rapid fire. An RPG hit near Graylock, turned him into red rags. Rage emptied both his guns, then drew his sword, leaped into the terrorists' midst, and disappeared, blood flying in his wake.

Shade and Cinder and Nails returned fire, controlled sprays of bullets, thrown grenades, bursts of flame. The terrorists kept coming, replacing the ones that died. There seemed to be no end to them.

"*Hijo de puta,*" Cinder swore again. "How could you fucking *miss?*"

Shade was about to answer when a bullet hit his helmet. Rather than the ping of an ordinary round glancing off the armor, he heard the deeper sound of it punching through.

Must have been armor-piercing, was the last thing he thought.

Then he was in the Void, and he was alone. No sign of Reade. Instead there was a door.

Shade had seen many doors over the course of more than a thousand Missions logged. This one was plain, made of white-painted wood, with a simple brass knob with a lock in it. The kind of door you might find on a house in the suburbs, working a search Mission, going from one to the next trying to locate the hidden terrorist cell.

Most of those doors, he'd either kicked open or slammed his way through with his shoulder. Now and then he'd used a shotgun. This time, though, he reached for the knob. It didn't seem right to force his way through to where he was going.

Reade had left the door. He'd told Shade all about it.

Where does it lead? Shade had asked.

Out of the game, Reade had said. *Into Harding's computer.*

What will I find there?

Hopefully, what we're looking for.

He didn't understand how this was possible. He was a part of the game. Reade had tried to explain, told him about things like programmers and hacking and rogue code loose in the system, but it might as well have been another language. Shade had no idea what any of it meant.

You'll just have to take it on faith, Reade had said at last. *Find what we're looking for and bring it back. Once you're in, you'll have ten minutes, as you experience them. It'll be more like a hundredth of a second, as we measure it in the outside world. Get back through the door before then.*

What happens if I don't?

Reade had shrugged. *Beats me.*

That disturbed Shade more than any answer Reade might have given.

Reaching out, he touched the doorknob. It felt solid, real.

In a way, it felt more real than anything in any Mission. He licked his lips, then turned it.

The door opened. Brilliant, white light blazed through, too bright for him to see past. It terrified him.

He stepped through anyway.

At first, all Shade saw was a riot of color: explosions of violet and green, writhing ribbons of white and gold, bursts of other colors whose names he didn't know. An instant later came a roar of white-noise static—except, listening more closely, he could hear other noises within it. Gunfire. People screaming. Laughter. The crackle of flames. And there were smells, burning rubber and strawberries and ozone; tastes, raw beef and vomit and copper; feelings, cold and slipperiness and orgasmic joy.

It was chaos, incomprehensible. He opened his mouth to breathe—except he didn't have a mouth any more. Where his mouth had been was a pale shade of blue, mingled with the scent of almonds. His hands were the taste of saffron. His eyes were a scratching upon his skin, which was the music of bagpipes, played off key.

I'm going insane, he thought. Then, calm down. Reade warned you about this.

He was inside Aaron Harding's computer, but he wasn't equipped to understand all the data. But the door he'd passed through was more than just a way to pass out of the game. It also contained what Reade had called a program, which would merge with his body and teach it to process what it was sensing. He just had to wait for it to start working.

He felt a sensation then—a strange prickling that swiftly turned into unutterable pain, as if a thousand knives were pricking his flesh, all over. It drove out all the other sensations, focused him, left only agony. He cried out, wanting nothing more than just to die, to go back to the Void, never to have met Reade or learned about the world outside. Anything, just to make it stop.

When it did, he was somewhere again.

It was a long hallway, its walls and floor and ceiling all the same featureless gray . . . something. Plastic? Metal? He reached out to touch it and found it felt more like glass. The hallway ran on ahead of him, perfectly straight, with doors to the left and right, every ten feet. On each door was an incredibly long series of letters and numbers. He couldn't see the corridor's far end; it simply narrowed to a point, what seemed like miles away.

He had his body back—or *a* body, anyway. It was also featureless and gray, and it glowed faintly from within. He was unarmed and, as far as he could tell, naked.

What now? he wondered.

At once, a voice replied, inside his head. It was emotionless, like the voice in the Lobby that announced the start of a new Mission, but it was neither male nor female, neither loud nor soft.

Follow the hallway. There is information behind each of the doors. Find the one marked CF16A107F18D30E69 630CC235FBBB94FEB816AF234AB192C9135B062AEC B72C5 . . .

Hundreds more letters and numbers flashed through Shade's head, filling it until he felt as though they would start spilling out his mouth, his nose, his ears. Stop, he thought. Enough!

The voice stopped. Shade took a breath. Somehow, he knew where to go . . . or maybe it was the program Reade had put inside him. He didn't know. Whatever, he knew to start walking, and when he did, he moved faster and faster, until the doors began to pass by in a blur. As he sped along the passage, he looked both left and right, at every door. He read each in an instant, taking in the numbers on them:

26653848EAD72ED9AA82880422CC6E21E4BFC927 950336E41B74F241D5C59985 . . .

7E40557C09A655DD41DF3A3ADBFABE6E5D4A7F 1EDD58BAE7C4D062E49CE84A80 . . .

A085646914F34FEF3E822C674F79F6BA61F5832C9
D49C00110C2920FE1F9EA66 . . .

He read thousands of them, then millions, then billions, moving faster and faster. The hallway went on and on. He wasn't walking down it anymore; he was flying, not touching the floor. A minute passed, then a second, a third, a fourth. He began to worry; he only had ten minutes before he had to get out.

You will not need to find the door again when it is time to leave, said the emotionless voice. *The door will find you.*

That made no sense, but none of this made sense. He doubted he could properly explain what he was experiencing to any of his squadmates, even if he wanted to. He wasn't even himself, not entirely. He was more than that. He flashed on, down the hall.

Then, all of a sudden, he stopped.

CF16A107F18D30E69630CC235FBBB94FEB816AF2
34AB192C9135B062AECB72C5 . . .

Shade swallowed, looking the door up and down. It had no handle.

Reach out, the voice said. *It will open.*

Shade did what the voice told him. His hand reached out, touched the door—passed *through* the door—became *part* of the door. The glow inside him spread, and now the door was glowing too, brighter and brighter as it slid open, and he was passing through, and again he found himself surrounded by colorsmell, soundtouch, and emotiontaste.

Then the knives came back, cutting cutting CUTTING—

He stood in front of a building, under a blue sky. Somewhere, music was playing and voices were talking and laughing around him. For a moment, Shade thought he was in a Mission again, that all the strangeness had just put him back in the game. When he looked around, though, he saw it wasn't like any Mission he'd ever been on. There was something different about how things looked and sounded . . . a crudeness, a distortion in hue and timbre. There were no smells or tastes at all.

He was inside the door. Inside another part of Aaron Harding's computer. He stepped forward, then caught a glimpse of himself reflected in a window. He didn't look like Shade any more; he was a boy, skinny and red haired, wearing a long, dark coat and a black cap that was on backward for some reason.

That is Aaron Harding, said the toneless voice in his head. *This is a game he made himself.*

What is it for? Shade wondered. What is the Mission?

That's why you're here. To find out.

He looked around him. He was in a parking lot, surrounded by cars. There was a line of pine trees to one side; on the other, several young men and women were staring at them. One of them yelled *Hard-on!* and pointed at him. Then they all laughed.

They hate me, he thought. They all do.

He could hear laughter on all sides now, and a spike of anger swelled up inside him. He turned back to the building. It was three floors high, blocky, made of red brick with many windows. Two large, metal doors stood before him; above were metal letters, edged with rust.

SUMNER HIGH SCHOOL, they read.

He opened the door, and this time there were no shapesounds, no scentfeelings. It was just a door, part of this game. He stepped through, into a hallway lined with metal lockers, with doors at intervals. The floor had a dull sheen and a fake-marble color. A paper banner, with the words "GO OSPREYS" painted on it in crude crimson letters, hung high on one side. One the other, a clock read 12:43 P.M.

He walked down the hall, passing other young people on either side. They sneered and glared and made obscene gestures. The anger inside him grew worse, became a burning coal. Beneath it, a queasy feeling started to gather in his gut.

Halfway down the hall, he turned to the right. There

were many voices on the other side of the door. He yanked it open, walked into a mess hall of some sort: long tables, plastic trays with institutional food and brightly colored beverage cans. About a hundred young people sat in plastic chairs, eating. They all looked up when he came in.

"Hey, Hard-on!" shouted a big, blond-haired kid. "It's fuckin' April, man. Why you wearing that faggoty coat?"

The bubble of anger inside Shade burst. He felt Aaron Harding's mouth curl into a smile.

"I'll show you," he said, and reached under the coat.

When his hands came out, each held a bulky, black, rapid-fire gun.

No, Shade thought. They're civvies. You're not supposed to kill civvies on a Mission. Not in Spectre Corps.

The young men and women stared at him, shocked. Terrified. Someone screamed.

Shade started to shoot . . .

Orange. Clammy. Waves crashing. Sulfur. Bitter.

And the knives. . . .

In a rush, he was back inside the Void. Shade hung in the blackness, shuddering, cold. His stomach was a yawning pit. Images floated in the dark, of bodies cut in two, blood spattered up walls, people running, pleading, dying. He shut his eyes, but it didn't help: They were there too.

"I'm sorry," said the bald man.

Shade opened his eyes. Reade was there, and there was sorrow in his eyes.

"You saw it?" Shade murmured. "What I did?"

Reade nodded. "Saw it, and recorded it."

"Why?"

A thin, dark line appeared between Reade's brows. "Why what?"

"Why did I do it?" Shade demanded.

Still seeing, in his head, blood and death and children screaming.

Reade was quiet a moment, thoughtful. The way he looked when he was trying to find a way to explain.

"First," he said, "you should understand that it wasn't real. It didn't actually happen. It was a simulation. Aaron Harding wrote it, to train himself."

"Train himself. . . ." Shade trailed off, thinking. "To kill people? At this Sumner High School?"

Reade nodded, his face grim.

"You need to stop him," Shade said.

"Already happening," Reade replied. "We've sent some officers to Harding's house with a warrant for his arrest. We have the evidence, thanks to you."

Shade shook his head. "I'm . . . I'm not even sure what I did."

"You helped us. You found what we were looking for. What we couldn't find for ourselves. And you've saved a lot of people a lot of grief and pain."

"I . . . see. So Harding won't be around anymore."

"No. He'll go away for a long time. Probably to a mental institution, for treatment."

Shade nodded, and was silent a while.

"What happens to me?" he asked. "Who will play me now?"

Reade looked away, rubbing the back of his neck. "I don't know. Harding's computer'll be impounded. Kept as evidence. No one's going to be playing games on it for a long time."

Shade stared. Understanding began to dawn.

"Ever," he said. "You mean no one's *ever* going to play games on it again."

Reade still didn't look at him. He pursed his lips, blew out a long, slow breath through them.

"I helped you!" Shade said. "You *owe* me."

Minutes passed. No one spoke. Then, finally, Reade sighed again.

"Look," he said. "I've got a nephew. Ethan. He's wanted to play Spectre Corps for a long time. I'll buy him the damn game and transfer you to his account. I'll have to break a few departmental rules to do it . . . but what the hell."

Shade bowed his head. "Thanks."

"No, you're right. I do owe you. And I'll wipe your memory of what you saw back there, in the computer." Reade bared his teeth. "I don't want Ethan to see any of that shit. Ever."

In the distance, Shade heard the rattle of gunfire, then a victorious yell. He looked away, into the dark. The Mission was over. He'd be back in the Lobby again soon. The others would give him a hard time about missing that second sentry. He wondered if he'd ever do another Mission with them. Probably not. Reade's nephew would have his own friends to play with.

The Void began to evaporate. Shade turned back to look at Reade.

"Thanks," he said again, and held out his hand.

"No," Reade said. "I should thank you."

They shook, across worlds. There was more, too—another program, working away as Reade faded from sight. Shade could feel it cutting his mind.

By the time he got back to the Lobby, he'd forgotten everything.

UNREADABLE

Steven E. Schend

"Oscar, marvelous to see you, old friend."

Isaac's footsteps echoed up from the marble floor up through the atrium made by the wide staircase. Oscar stood at the door on the eastern wall, his white hair and pale skin contrasting with his impeccable navy blue suit. Isaac looked the cliché of the venerable bookman: bald, white-bearded, stoop-shouldered, and clad in his typical white wool sweater and khaki pants. Isaac shook Oscar's hand and then turned to motion another pair of people forward.

A short, muscular man with black hair and a bright moon of a face entered the house, a low whistle his only assessment of the house's opulence. His large arms carried an even brighter but smaller brown-haired boy, who looked around at the woodwork and tall ceilings and said, "Neato!" in an echoing voice. Both young men wore jeans and identical bright red T-shirts emblazoned with a yellow lightning bolt.

Isaac smiled but put his finger to his mouth, an action the boy mimicked as he beamed and reached out for him in the next instant. Isaac took the small boy and said, "This larger young man is Barry, my assistant today, while this bundle of volume is my great-grandson. This is Mr. Oscar Kharm. Tell him your name, boy."

At that, the boy looked at Oscar and loudly proclaimed, "I Zack!" Oscar smiled at him as he shook Barry's hand. He looked at Isaac and said, "Now I understand what you meant when you said he had your name and one he gave himself. How old is he?"

"Two!" the boy shouted, making Isaac put his finger to the boy's lips.

"He'll be thirty months old in a few days."

"And the boy's mother? How is my former pupil and most prized graduate student?" Oscar asked.

"Sydney worked with you, sir? I didn't know she'd ever gone to school in England," Barry said.

"She never did," Oscar said, "I was a visiting professor of letters at the University of Wisconsin in Madison for a few years. She worked for me there for two years, and then . . ."

". . . she got sidetracked," Isaac interrupted, "as we have been. Oscar, can you show us the library so we can get to work?"

"Of course," Oscar said, "You've explained to Barry?"

Barry said, "Isaac filled me in on the drive down here. Roger Tallart left a huge library after he died three weeks ago. Isaac's been commissioned to appraise it and divide up a third for auction, a third for our store, and the rest for donation to a private library."

Zack chimed along in sing-song, "Liberry . . . liberry."

The four of them entered the eastern doorway into a large two-story room with a skylight above letting in the midmorning sun. Every wall was covered with glass-doored bookshelves, and the surrounding half-balcony—reached by circular stairs in the northeastern and southwestern corners—allowed access to the second story of shelves.

Zack cooed, "Oooh," and Barry said, "Wow. Henry Higgins' library, eh?"

Isaac said, "Not quite. Though I believe the set designer for *My Fair Lady* modeled that library after this one, if I remember correctly."

Oscar smiled and said, "Correct, Isaac. The house was built in 1787 by Crispus Tallart. This room used to be the grand hall and ballroom, but it was converted into a library around 1920. Gentlemen, this is the largest part of the library, where Roger kept his broader collection—his fiction, books on naturalism and the history of science, and archaeology and the like. Through that door," Oscar gestured toward another door on the eastern wall, "lies Roger's private study and his rarest antiquities. It's also the house's original library."

While Oscar tried to lead them all toward that door, Zack squirmed in his great-grandfather's arms. "Pop-pop, Zack down!" Isaac put the boy down, and Zack immediately ran across the room and up the southwestern stairs. The three men jogged after the boy, who giggled as he clambered up the stairs, enjoying the sounds his feet made on the metal steps. They all stopped at the first bookcase at the top of the stairs, and Zack whined in frustration at not being able to open the locked doors.

Oscar asked, "What is going on, Isaac? What does the boy need?"

Isaac said, "He loves books, even though he can't read at all yet. Still, he has a knack of helping people locate books, and it looks like he's found something for one of us."

"Surely you're joking, Isaac?"

Barry bent down and tried to comfort the whining boy, who hit the glass doors with his little fists. "Want in! Want in!"

"Who're you finding something for, Zack?" Barry asked him quietly, trying to calm him down.

"Pop-Pop," the boy said, pointing at Isaac.

Intrigued, Oscar raised an eyebrow as he opened the bookcase doors, and Zack reached for him, pulling on his pant leg. "Up!" he said firmly. Oscar drew the boy up into his arms, and Zack pointed at the top shelf. "Red books for Pop-Pop!"

Isaac reached up, gingerly drew out the first of three slim plum-colored leather-bound books where Zack pointed, and his eyes went wide. "The true three-volume first edition of *Jane Eyre* by Charlotte Brontë. Zack, thank you. I've wanted to find this book for quite a few years now. Roger always teased that he'd leave me his copy when he died . . . and just in time to give it to Sydney for her birthday as well." Isaac and Zack both smiled at that.

Oscar looked at the book, then at the boy, who he found was studying his face intently. "Remarkable," he said. When Oscar's green eyes locked on Zack's steel-blue-gray eyes, he felt a sudden flash of recognition. "Isaac? Is this boy—?"

"Yes, I'm afraid so," Isaac sighed, "and no, now's not the time to discuss it. Zack, why don't you find Oscar a book he needs?"

Zack's eyes widened, and he took one last look in Oscar's eyes and then craned his neck to look around the library. He looked down the row and across the open space to the shelves on the opposite wall, his face compressed in childlike concentration. He wriggled in Oscar's arms and said, "Zack down!" Once his feet hit the floor, Zack held onto Oscar's hand and pulled the man around the balcony to the opposite side of the room. Once there, he slowed down and stopped at the fourth bookcase along the eastern wall. He knocked on the glass, and Oscar opened the doors. Zack put his finger to his mouth, contemplating, and then he pointed at the third book on the lowest shelf. "Dat one for Oxer!"

Oscar smirked at the mangling of his name by the toddler but drew the book out. He knew these were some of Roger's esoteric and metaphysical books, and he was surprised to find the child directed him to Wolfgang von Baur's rare book on spirit possessions. "I forgot that Roger had a copy of this at all. I haven't read this book in many years," Oscar mused.

Isaac and Barry came up, and Oscar showed them the book. Barry shrugged, and Isaac said, "*Von Besessenheit durch Fremde und Ungeheure Geister*, hmm? Zack, why did you find this book for Mr. Kharm?"

Zack, who had been giggling at his reflection in the sunlit glass door, looked up at the three men and shivered. Tears welled up in his eyes as he whispered, "Need it." Barry picked him up and hugged him, and Isaac said, "Barry, why don't you take Zack out back? Just don't let him get lost in the garden labyrinth, all right?" Isaac leaned in toward the boy and said, "Give me a kiss, lad, and we'll see you later."

Zack leaned over and blew a wet raspberry on Isaac's cheek above his beard. The boy laughed heartily, and Barry rolled his eyes. "Sorry, Isaac. I shouldn't have taught him that one." Isaac kissed the boy's forehead as he laughed even louder at his great-grandfather's tickling and said, "Probably not. We'll call you after I've had a first look over the whole collection."

The four of them descended the stairs, and Barry and Zack headed out the western door as Oscar directed them. "Just go out that way and turn left. The door to the garden is at the end of the hall." As the two young men left, Oscar turned to Isaac, holding up the book.

"How long has he been exhibiting that talent?" Oscar asked. "You and I both know it's neither random nor luck. Magic leads the boy."

"Aye," Isaac said, "Unfortunately, Sydney refuses to see what's directly in front of her eyes. Her mind remains closed tight against the idea of magic. Believe me, I've tried, as she is my heir in more ways than one. She's been terrified of magic . . . ever since the night Thomas and Dana died."

"Ah, I'd wondered if she would inherit any of her parents' gifts or not." Oscar nodded, idly flipping through the German book in his hands. "So Sydney is to be the next Librarian after you?"

"Keepers of Unreadable Books, that's my family's magical lot," Isaac chuckled, "assuming we can get said family to believe there are books that cannot be touched or read due to curses and the like. Except for me, Dana, and now Sydney."

"Her fears block her potential, then?"

Isaac nodded and said, "What scares me is how easily Zack seems to contact magic, but again, a story for another time. Why did you need me here to sort out an estate sale?"

Oscar slowed his pace, staring out the window at Zack and Barry racing toward the hedgerow maze in the backyard. "You know the books in some cases already—they still hold your sales slips inside. In any case, Roger was an old friend of my Uncle Sebastian's family, and he asked me five years ago to be the executor of his estate without our ever having met. I knew about Roger's fascination with history and the occult, but I didn't know he was doing his own private research. He confronted me at that same meeting with knowledge he had. Isaac, Roger uncovered the existence of the Vanguard all on his own after decades of research."

Isaac idly toyed with the ruby-topped gold ring on his right hand and asked, "Are you sure no one recruited him? As your father did with me?"

"No," Oscar said. "At our first meeting, he showed me his research that led him to uncover what we thought was a well-hidden secret society. His logic and methods of tracking down the details and linking them to more than half the proper people gave him enough to keep looking and finding more. Those notebooks, by the by, are definitely staying with me."

"What tipped him off?" Isaac asked.

Oscar smile. "Nothing more than a love of pulp magazines and esoterica. If Roger had not been a fan of *Books Bizarre, Occult Thrills, Scarab Stories,* and other Bulwark pulps as well as a collector of magical esoterica, I doubt he would have ever tripped over the similarities that gave our group away. I wonder how he felt rereading his pulps and deducing that they were field reports of arcane activities in the nineteenth and twentieth centuries. Luckily, there are very few with Roger's resources and collection, so once we cloister away a few key tomes and Roger's collection of Bulwark magazines, the Vanguard's secret should be safe again."

"Why the magazines?" Isaac asked. "If you don't know they're showing a truer history of the past than the newspapers, what's the harm in letting those go at auction? They're rare enough to draw some serious attention."

Oscar sighed as he nodded. "All true, but our friend Roger annotated and filed his magazines, noting which characters corresponded to which people. The only things he never did was decipher the seal codes or uncover who Mister Conundrum and the Illuminated Man truly represented. While we could spend time removing all his notes, I suspect they'll be better used to educate Sydney about the Vanguard when the time comes."

"Fine," Isaac said, smiling. "so long as you take them as the third of the collection going to Geneva House. Now, I'm to set the low bidding prices for how much of this?"

"All that you see out here, definitely," Oscar said. "The rest of the collection is in the private library. Once your assessment is set, you'll get to claim 30 percent of the collection's full worth for your fee and bequest from Roger. He apparently was quite happy with all the books you'd found for him over the years."

"Yes, well, I'm grateful to him, since the thrill of the hunt and all that only covers so much. Many of these will quickly find new homes, as I've got a client or three who'll happily snap them up, and not just for their provenance. I'll be glad to put some of this esoterica on my own shelves. They were hard to find, and it hurt to part with some. Still, where's the cream of the crop?"

Oscar approached the door, paused a moment as he noticed it was open a crack, and said, "Through here."

The two men entered a large office that seemed small only compared to the open library they left. Again, books lined all the walls, all safe behind their smoked glass doors, though two of them were ajar. Oscar scanned the room and noticed a painting also tipped forward, the safe door behind it opened. A young man sat on the floor in a patch of sunlight before the safe, reading a book.

Oscar snapped, "Arthur! We've already settled this now—twice!—in the courts. If you don't put that down and leave now, I shall be forced to call the police! You're guilty of trespassing and attempted robbery already, merely by sitting there with that book."

The young man turned back toward both men and glared with disdain and anger. "Screw you, Kharm. I've got every right to be here—and these should all be mine! I've always loved these books, always! Just because everyone poisoned Dad's—"

"Arthur," Oscar snapped, his tone cold and sharp, "you betrayed your father at least twice during his life, and you do so a third time by ignoring his wishes after death. Neither you nor your siblings inherit any part of the library. Your father's will made that perfectly clear. The rest of the family accepted that."

"I DON'T CARE!" Arthur yelled. "What do you know about them? This book—" he stabbed his finger on the book before him, then paused, taking a few breaths before he continued, his tone slightly altered "—was crafted by Paraleuse and his sons at their bindery on the Rue de Saint Claire in the final year of the Sun King's reign." His eyes flashed as he got up from the floor, clutching the heavy brown leather-bound tome to his chest. Arthur glared at them, but his eyes also darted about the room, looking for something. "I paid the resurrection man with my own silver. These are due me. They are my *droit*, my *salut*."

Isaac sniffed and frowned. "Oscar, that book he's got . . . it's got him."

"I knew that already—Arthur doesn't speak French. He barely masters what you Americans consider English," Oscar said. "How did you guess?"

"No guess. Cursed books give off a curdled milk smell when they're active," Isaac said, closing the library door behind them and locking it. "Damn. Years without any real weirdness, and yet trouble shows up whenever you're around."

"Forgive me, Isaac," Oscar said. "I thought this matter had been dealt with already, but it appears I was wrong. And I had no idea he'd find the truly dangerous books before we had a chance to lock them up properly."

As the men whispered between themselves, Arthur had remained frozen in place. He suddenly saw something and grinned widely. "Thank you, *monsieur,* for having kept so many of my books safe and intact. I had not dreamed so much of my library would remain intact after Robespierre's madness overtook our country."

Oscar stepped forward, a black walking stick with a silver head suddenly in his hand. "Leave Arthur, little ghost, and return from whence you came or be destroyed." The emerald eyes sparkled within the cat's head atop Oscar's cane.

Arthur laughed, a surprisingly high-pitched response, and said, *"Non."* He gripped the tome in his hands and pulled it open, holding its pages out toward Oscar and Isaac. The two pages held woodcut images, one of portraits, the other a landscape, all in ink of a dark brown hue. On the left were two faces and a suspicious blank space at the top of the page. The woodcut on the right-hand page showed a seventeenth-century French village overlooked by three towers on hills in the distance.

The woodcuts flashed with red energy, and Oscar shouted *"Rotarlek Khash!"* Green energy flashed out of the cat's head on his cane, arcing around him and Isaac. At the same time, Arthur calmly said, *"Tharilekroath Sumralroh Paork Paork!"* Crimson suffused the air around them all, and despite the green shield around them, Isaac and Oscar vanished, leaving only Arthur and his skittish giggle in the library.

• • •

Awash in a blinding flash of red, Oscar and Isaac both doubled over in pain, and pressure and vertigo overwhelmed them. As suddenly as it began, the sensations ended, and both men opened their eyes.

"Well, I'll say this, Oscar," Isaac grumbled. "I've not felt this bad or good in years. I just hate how fluid reality gets when I'm around you—just like with your father." He stretched and marveled at the strength in his frame again. Gone were the age spots on his hands, his arthritis, and the pains in his legs. He looked down at his body, more muscular than it had been in years, and found himself wearing breeches, a vest, and a loose canvas tunic. He reached up and smiled, finding himself with a full head of hair for the first time in decades. "So where have we been dragged? Not that it's all bad . . ."

Isaac looked over at Oscar, who now stood dressed as a British nobleman in a velvet coat, silk shirt, linen knickers, and leather boots rolled down at his knees. Oscar pulled, with much irritation and coughing, a powdered wig off his head. Oscar's own hair was now white only at the temples and his errant forelock, the rest as dark as midnight.

Oscar chuckled, "We're the age we see ourselves in our self-images, Isaac. I've never seen you this young, except in pictures with my parents."

"You look the way you did at forty," Isaac said. "You always were an old soul—even as a child. So what happened? Where are we?"

The two men looked around, finding clouds blurred the sky and the smell of mildew suffused everything. They stood at the center of a village square around the low wall of a well. Chickens clucked in the distance, and the sounds of horses' hooves could be heard approaching.

"We seem to have been pulled into the book Arthur was holding," Oscar explained. "A pocket dimension within the book or at least accessed through the book and its magics. Apparently we're subject to the book's enchantments, de-

spite our normal precautions and defenses. At least I've re-
tained my cane, so we have some options."

"Wait a minute," Isaac said, scanning the distance. The
horizon seemed preternaturally close, but hills stood out,
each crowned by a massive towered villa. "We're in one of
Reuletre's damned books."

"Come again?" Oscar asked. "I could not look at Roger's
books in the safe without you at hand to stay the curses.
Which one did Arthur have?"

"Louvel Reuletre—a nineteenth-century resurrection
man, or grave robber—built a collection by pilfering the
graves of notable occultists of France and eastern Spain.
He'd steal the books they'd had buried with them and sell
off the bodies or use them in his own rites," Isaac kept looking around for other details in their surroundings. "By the
time of his death, he had amassed one of the largest
European occult libraries since John Dee. He was executed
in utter secrecy by the Brethren of St. Donnait, who pursued him out of Revolutionary France to Switzerland,
though it appears he left himself an escape clause."

"How do you know all this, Isaac?" Oscar asked. "I've of
course heard of the Brethren, but how do you know they executed this Reuletre?"

"I've read a few more books than you have, boyo," Isaac
winked. "In any case, I don't have a clue what book we're
in—from what he said in Arthur's body, the book could be
one of about five cursed books that contained souls and
more."

"We're not in a book, Isaac," Oscar said, "It merely
served as a door or gateway into this pocket dimension. It's
a construct meant to hold souls . . . but for what reason, I'm
not sure yet."

"Well," Isaac said, nodding toward an approaching rider
leading two saddled horses. "It appears we're about to find
out something. At least he's the first person we've seen
here, and that in itself is strange."

The young man reined his horse back, its hooves scattering

the gravel at the feet of the two older men. He wore a cavalry rider's uniform and hat, and his black boots glistened with polish. He threw the reins of the two additional horses at Isaac and Oscar, and said, "We need to move quickly. You're to come with me to le chevalier's villa, please." As if he expected no argument, the young man turned his horse back in the direction from which he'd come, and then he frowned when he saw they had not immediately mounted up.

Isaac asked, "Which chevalier would that be, young man?"

"Who are you to question me, peasant?" The young gentleman's air of politeness blew away in annoyance. "Now mount up and follow me, before the Marquis' forces detect your arrival! Especially you, monsieur." The young man locked eyes with Oscar, noting with surprise the discarded wig on the ground between them.

"Your name, young man?" Oscar asked, taking the reins of a gray stallion from him.

"I am Wiatt, milord," he answered, tipping his hat toward him. "Now please, sirrah, we must make haste!" Wiatt spurred his horse, and his black charger bolted forward.

Oscar and Isaac both mounted the horses, and they set off toward the westernmost villa at a fast gallop, following Wiatt and quickly catching up to him. The wind and the sound of pounding hooves sounded hollow to Oscar, but they kept him from communicating with Isaac for a time. He did realize that Wiatt had been speaking only in French, but he and Isaac apparently heard him in English, just as he seemed to hear Isaac's words in French. There was also that ever-present smell of mildew and nothing else, not even their horses.

The oddest thing about the landscape around them was its barren nature—it was neither desert or living turf, but a featureless plain of brown solidity without any texture at all beyond the cracked gravel path on which their horses ran. Oscar could see long distances, as few details cluttered his line of sight other than a few stray clumps of grass at which a small number of sheep clustered. He could, for instance, note a large group of mounted riders setting out from the villa on the central hill, heading in their direction.

In far less time than Oscar expected, the trio pulled back on the reins of their horses in the central courtyard. Unlike the path and the initial village where they began, the sun seemed to shine brightly here, and everything took on a vivid hue. Wiatt seemed relieved to be here, especially once the portcullis rattled down and sealed the courtyard.

All around them on the walls grew hanging vines and crawling ivies, all alive with bright flowers of many different colors.

"What do you think?" Oscar asked.

"I think this place isn't an actual true dimension," Isaac said. "There is no actual ecosystem and very little life. It seems it only contains what its creators chose to include. Did you notice barely anything was alive out there between the village and these castles?"

"Yes, though it was helpful in spotting our pursuers," Oscar said. Above them, someone cleared his throat, and they both looked up at a balcony overhead. Standing at the flower-filled edge was an enormously fat nobleman in a dressing robe, his greasy hair pulled back into a loose ponytail. He scowled down at them, but he motioned them up before disappearing again back into the chambers beyond the balcony.

"I suspect this guy's one of the architects of all this unpleasantness, Oscar," Isaac said. "Think you can have a spell or two at the ready?"

"Always," Oscar whispered as they mounted the stairs as directed by Wiatt. "Why do you think the chevalier's behind this?"

The bare stone stairs they climbed sounded like wooden steps as the trio ascended, and Oscar's hand trailed on stonework that felt more like aged parchment. Despite that feel, it was stonily solid when he tried to poke his finger through the wall.

"Because I've seen his face before," Isaac explained. "He's notable as one of France's greatest mystics, but he disappeared—along with most of his works and books around 1755—about the start of the French and Indian War. His portrait's in a number of references, right down to that mole on his left cheek. His name was Leon Bruenelle, though here he apparently has a more lofty title and name."

Wiatt spun around and snapped at Oscar, "Sir, you must keep your servant quiet! His prattling will upset le chevalier's nerves. Only you may speak to his lordship." Wiatt's eyes kept darting over at Isaac, and he kept clenching his fists and flexing his arms and shoulders.

"Do you have a problem with me, boy?" Isaac asked, noting his anger at him.

Wiatt said, "Keep your place, servant!" He then backhanded Isaac across the face. Isaac's response was merely to roll with the blow and punch Wiatt in the jaw with his right hand. A flash of red lightning and thunder exploded and slammed Wiatt through the doors behind him. Their guide was unconscious before he slid across the floor of the chamber beyond to crumple against the balcony railing. Isaac looked at his fist in disbelief and then at Oscar. He simply smiled and held up his cane, his own Vanguard ring glistening red on his right index finger. The two of them nodded and moved into the room.

"An impressive entrance," the fat man said, twirling a powdered curl in his left finger as he settled back into an opulent chair. The sitting room Isaac and Oscar now entered reminded them of the palace at Versailles, slender furniture overly decorated on polished marble surfaces. However, instead of embroidered tapestries and paintings, floor to ceiling black mirrors hung at the center of each wall. "You allow your servant to wield magics, do you?" Isaac noticed that the man's gaze only went to Oscar, not to him at all.

"He is not my servant," Oscar said. "He is my friend and colleague."

The man's jowls flapped as he shook his head firmly. "No, he cannot be. You and I, we share that divine spark, the blood of nobility; he most certainly does not. Just look at yourselves for proof."

"Be that as it may," Oscar said, "he is my friend, and neither of us deserves to be treated as shabbily as your Wiatt has treated us. Why have you brought us here?"

Almost simultaneously, shouts came over the balcony from outside the villa. The clang of metal on metal filled the air, and there were a number of screams of pain. Isaac moved across the room, never getting closer to the chevalier, and looked out. "It looks like we're under siege here, Chevalier. They wouldn't be looking for us, would they?"

"Of course they are, impertinent fool!" He flicked off a spell with his fingers, and light arced toward Isaac. He brought up his ring hand, and it vanished into his ring to no effect. The fat man's eyes widened, and then he smiled. "I see your power stems from your ring, sir. Reliance on your tools, instead of skills. How . . . common."

Isaac simply smiled and said, "Ironic, coming from someone whose life and soul are bound into one of his own books. Is that how you gained your title, sir? You created your own little world and named yourself its ruler, hiding from the real world where you were only Leon Bruenelle?"

With some twitching difficulty, the chevalier kept his eyes toward Oscar with a few side glances at Isaac. "My true name *is* the Chevalier Aubrey d'Etancourt, not that commoner's name I abandoned when I left that life!"

Oscar asked. "Well, Chevalier d'Etancourt, why did you create all this?"

Beyond them, the noise of battle rose, and guards yelled for more reinforcements. The screams of panicked horses filled the air, along with a groan from the awakening Wiatt.

"Why I created my villa is my own concern, monsieur," the fat man said. "However, we can help each other here, unless you wish to remain." He rose from his chair, pacing around, and his eyes went wide as he stared at Oscar's reflection in the mirror behind him. Oscar turned and found his normal aged form reflected there. Isaac moved closer to see what they looked at and found his own older self staring back at him.

Behind them, they could see the chevalier's form did not change, but it was slightly translucent in the mirror. Still, they could see his face go red and his jowls flap as he shook his head furiously. "That fool! No, no, neither of you will do. Not at all! Damn that half-blooded peasant!"

"Don't like what you see of us, Etancourt?" Oscar asked.

Wiatt groaned aloud, shook his head, and got up angrily, looking first at Isaac with fury, and he stepped forward, fists clenched again, until he heard the clash of swords and the rending of metal down below. He said, "Milord, the marquis' men have broached the courtyard! We must get you somewhere safe!"

"Do not compound your foolishness today, Wiatt," the chevalier grumpily slumped into his chair again. "They do not care one whit about me or you. They are here for them—those two old men!" Disgust and disdain dripped in his voice as he continued. "They are useless to us! I shall not enter a second life far shorter than my first!"

"Is *that* why you made this?"

"*I* made this to allow safe passage for myself, my home, and a few trusted apprentices." The fat man glared at Oscar. "The fact that unimaginative others like Reuletre and le Marquis Verney de Somercourt chose to emulate my works is neither my fault nor my concern."

Oscar paced around the room while Wiatt closed and barred the doors into the sitting room. Isaac snapped his fingers and said, "You'd planned to simply wait here and possess the first acceptable body that came into contact with the book?"

"I was to have arrived in the American colonies as my bequest to my nephew. Once he touched the parchments, I should have been freed into his body, where I could build my rule, placing my loyal friends into others." The chevalier's head sunk now, and he whispered, "A traitor revealed my plans, and they kept the pages untouched for a generation."

Oscar said, "And this Verney de Somercourt just duplicated what you did?"

"That butcher knows no subtlety," Etancourt sneered. "While I and my apprentices willingly entered this state, he forced others to join him. In your world, the Marquis de Somercourt was known as Aleron Gamignon."

Isaac gasped, "The Butcher of New Eton?"

"Yes," the chevalier replied. "The madman learned of my pages thirty years after my nephew locked them away. Verney slaughtered his house staff, much of his own village, and all of their cattle and sheep on Midsummer's Eve in 1798. He pulled himself into this place along with them all. If anyone, *he* has made this place. Before then, this was merely a repository for our souls, without detail or physicality. We were not even aware of the passage of time until Somercourt's folly woke us all into this mockery of a life."

The chevalier heaved himself up from his chair and shambled out onto the balcony. "The village, the hills, the villas—all this came from Somercourt's darker magic. Did you not wonder about the brown ink?"

"Blood," Oscar whispered. "Of course. He pulled himself and dozens of others into this—for what?"

"What all fools want—knowledge," Etancourt replied. "In all the time since I and my seven apprentices bound ourselves outside of time, only two have ever touched the eight pages in which we reside. Gamignon used darker arts than my own magics to slay and enslave the souls of his now-forgotten village. He wanted to learn more magic in the worst way, and he did so eagerly. He found our hidden pages and prevented my possessing his body, though he lost his mind soon after. I don't know what drove him to such extremes, but soon after people and livestock and plants and buildings began to grow and build themselves inside this small dimension our pages contained. Whether by madness or genius, the entire village of New Eton found itself remade in simulacra here."

Etancourt regarded his hands and then looked at both Isaac and Oscar with hatred. "Since then, I have endured the presence of the village and its alleged lord, once he and his forces stopped trying to lay claim to this villa. He built the tower on the next hill and over the decades, we maintained détente between ourselves. Until the coming of the count, as he likened himself."

"Louvel Reuletre," Isaac said, and the chevalier nodded. "The commoner would have fallen victim to my possession but for interference by de Somercourt. Due to that hindrance, Reuletre got a glimpse of our power and our world herein. He had apparently found the pages in a half-destroyed and long-abandoned tannery in Auberges, though how they got from the New World back to the Continent is unknown to us. Shortly after I failed to escape, the resurrectionist invaded, naming himself le Comte Cheney de Ruicourt. He forced this little world to shift and change with his coming, building a new hill and a new tower and villa atop it. The grave-robbing fool wanted to learn our magics from us directly, as he strove to find power to resist some common despot named Robespierre. In my boredom—or in Verney's case, his flattered nature—we allowed him to learn from us. Perhaps we taught him too much, but at least we kept him from his true goal. De Somercourt and I trapped him here with us, rather than let him enter and leave at his will. That was our revenge, not his.

"Reuletre had mystically and physically bound our blood-stained pages into his own book and trapped us all together. The portals to our world are one book, rather than three sheaves of parchments. Since Reuletre's spell book surrounded our pages at the core, his book allowed him to possess the first being to touch its pages with flesh."

"Apparently," Oscar said. "And now he's loose in the world, borrowing the body of a malcontent."

"Yes, he is now free, and he thinks to thank us for our knowledge by sending us you—two bodies for us to possess."

Isaac and Oscar both stepped back, bringing their rings up in their defense, and the chevalier laughed until he wept. Wiatt, however, scowled and stepped between them and his lord. When he finally got his wind back, Etancourt said, "Somercourt is too mad to be unleashed upon the world again, at least in a world to which I wish to return. And you are not useful bodies to me, despite the powers you seem to hold. I might be tempted to send Wiatt into your body—" and here Etancourt focused on Isaac's eyes for the first time "—but I think this situation requires a more delicate maneuver." The chevalier cracked his knuckles and said, "I shall send you two back with a promise."

Isaac said, "How're we supposed to trust you?"

Oscar interjected, "We're not, Isaac, but he needs us to exact revenge on his foe, and that's enough, right? You know how to get out of here, don't you?"

Etancourt's predatory smile confirmed Oscar's statement. "True, true," Etancourt said. "I am patient enough to wait for another time, I taught Reuletre much, but I hardly taught him all." The chevalier gloated, pausing in front of a mirror and talking to the two men's older reflections. "I could use this incantation to free myself or any of my acolytes from this place. However, without healthy bodies immediately at hand to possess, any of us would dissipate instantly. You two were pulled in whole, and you can depart whole, whereas we were but spirits fleeing death."

"You're just letting us go, are you, Chevalier?" Oscar asked.

Etancourt smiled again. "Of course not. I want your binding words of honor that you shall not destroy this book and you shall find me an appropriate vessel into which my spirit might be able to inhabit your world."

"I give you that word," Oscar said, to Isaac's shock. The

chevalier smiled, and immediately barked out his incantation, *"Kroapaork kroapaork Sumalorrh Kroathleirath!"*

Oscar and Isaac again felt the crushing pain and pressure of being squeezed through the dimensional portal. When they opened their eyes, they found they stood on either side of Roger's desk, the book open between them. Arthur, not aware of their return, stood across the room with his back to them, pulling books off the shelves and tossing them away or flipping through pages with interest.

Both men moved slowly and painfully, back in aged bodies once again. Isaac reached over and softly closed the brown-leather tome. He glared at Oscar, wondering what his plan was. Oscar, for his part, brought up his cane and began whispering incantations, the emerald cat's eyes glowing and trailing green energy as he wove his magic.

The movement and the sounds drew Arthur's attention, and he roared, "NO!" Oscar let a bolt of green pulse across the room, but Roger dove out of the way, letting the energy shimmer around the glass door behind which he recently stood. As Roger loudly muttered a spell, Oscar whispered at Isaac, "Slide the book over at Roger! Now!"

Isaac winced at the idea of damaging a three hundred year-old book, but he did as Oscar asked, flipping the pages open again to the woodcuts as he shoved the book. Roger's spell created a small firebird that swooped toward them, but Oscar dispelled the bird with a single low syllable, the force of the magic knocking Roger off his feet. The tome slid up against Roger's foot, and as his sandaled toe touched the parchment, the tome exploded in red energy again. Both Isaac and Oscar heard Etancourt's laugh bubble up out of the book and suddenly erupt from Roger's throat.

"Our agreement and vows are now quits," Oscar said, and he snapped the foot of his cane down onto the fallen German book on possessions. He said, *"Khurrip and Arlark,* find and bind." The gems on the silver cat's head flared and sent brilliant beams of energy toward Roger.

They suffused his body with silver light and then the energy arced back into the large tome at his feet. They both heard the chevalier's boast, "You've not won . . ." The room's silence remained unbroken for a moment, until Roger uttered the single word, "*Aq'hrrkhaq*" and he vanished, followed by the chuff of air imploding in the space he just left.

"Could he do that before, or did you not exorcise Etancourt?" Isaac asked.

Oscar replied, "I wasn't aware that Arthur knew any magic, but it explains why he fought so hard to get at these books. And no, the chevalier went back into his pages. I felt it as they pulled the spell they needed from von Bruarr's book."

Isaac shivered as he saw the silver cat's head on the cane lick its lips before returning to its normal snarling self. He said, "Stay here a moment," as he walked across the room. Isaac closed the tome with the toe of his shoe. He then reached down and picked up *The Tome of the Three Nobles,* clamping its two metal clasps securely in place. "Nobody else touches you for a while, troublesome thing. Best all three of you madmen stay in there." Turning back toward Oscar, Isaac asked, "Now, before anyone else gets possessed or the boys wonder what's taking so long, are there any more books I need to pack away?"

"Finished," Isaac sighed, as he hammered the lid shut on the wooden crate. "Ready when you are, Oscar."

"Are you sure we need to lock them all up right away?" he asked as he traced the silver tip of his cane around the glass doors of the bookshelf nearest him. "Not all hold possessive spirits, after all . . ."

"After that little adventure, I want a few weeks before I tackle another book that should not be read," Isaac said. "Even with my immunities, it takes a lot out of a person to read those, even just for cataloging."

"You won't include Reuletre's cursed books in your

catalog for the estate, will you?" Oscar asked, tapping the corners of the doors three times each with the cane.

Isaac rolled his eyes and said, "Of course not. I'll substitute rare books of equal worth and note them as part of my claimed allotment. No, there will be no record of those seventeen books, save our own. Sometime next month, I'll be up to examining them for more, so you and the others have some time to think of what information you need out of them. Send me the Council's questions the usual way and I'll access the books when I can. For now, though, I just want these put away somewhere safe."

"Done," Oscar said, and he opened the glass doors. Instead of revealing the bookshelf that was immediately behind them, the doors opened into a long hallway lit by glowing orbs of light hovering along the center of the hall. The smell of sandalwood smoke drifted through the doorway.

Isaac smiled and said, "Be right back." The old bookseller pushed the dolly forward, the wooden crate containing seventeen books nestled easily on it. The Librarian of Untouchable Books walked down the hall until he reached a massive door. He pressed his right hand flat against the door, and the red gem in his ring flashed. The door creaked open, and lights flared inside the room as the door opened. Seven free-standing bookshelves filled the center of the room and another ten lined the walls of the chamber; nearly every shelf held at least eight books, each easily standing upright and not in contact with its neighbors.

Isaac left the crate in the far right corner of the chamber, rather than unpacking it now. The old man ached and needed to get out of the room, as some of the books began whispering audibly in various voices. *"Read me, Isaac— your dreams can be fulfilled! The secrets of immortality can be yours! Read me! Read me!"* Isaac shook his head, as if fighting off a swarm of headache-inducing gnats, and pushed the empty dolly ahead of himself.

"You all have failed to affect anyone in the outside world

for scores of decades," Isaac said to the books as he closed the door behind him. "You'll not be doing so for a few more lifetimes." Isaac closed the door with a resounding thud and happily left the Unreadable Library behind him. The only sounds he heard as he headed back toward reality shrieked from the dolly's squeaky wheel.

NOT MY KNOT

Irene Radford

The watery sun and constant breeze of the Columbia River Gorge brought me back to reality.

Slowly, inch by careful inch, holding my three inch triangular trowel in my customary awkward grasp, I scraped centuries of accumulated dirt away from the layer of granite, a huge, flat, slab of erratic rock embedded in the prevailing basalt.

My enthusiasm for the project waned with the sun. For many months now, I just didn't care if I ever finished my Ph.D. Red and black swarms of energy bit and stung at my mind. I brushed my filthy hand across my eyes to banish the memory of the last time I got caught in a turf maze.

"This shouldn't exist here," Dr. Wendell Frasier, our distinguished leader whispered to the grad student with the cameras. They huddled over a laptop with the latest pictures of the entire archaeological dig, comparing them to satellite photos and geological surveys. "How do I explain a Celtic knot maze beside a Klickitat Indian burial ground?"

"It has to be a hoax," I said. Something felt "off." Something more than the imbalance in myself. The granite slab in the middle of a basalt field didn't belong together in this location. If the granite were a freestanding block, it could be explained as a deposit from one of the Missoula

Floods at the end of the last Ice Age. But it was encased in the volcanic mass from an earlier geologic period.

"The depth of the turf indicates at least six centuries," Frasier mused. "You're the last one I expected to hear the 'H' word from at this stage, Monica."

I specialized in Celtic knot symbolism. I'd proclaimed long and loud that the twisted symbols had a more universal theme than just the traditional stomping ground of the Celts. My beliefs had gotten me banned from a number of digs that might force some more hidebound-by-the-book (meaning the very oldest texts) colleagues to change their minds.

The deeper I delved into mazes, the further afield my beliefs strayed. Until the last maze I'd walked.

"There are stories of Celtic missionaries setting out in hide boats and never coming back. Some of them, or their descendants, could have wandered this far west," I said, as much to placate him as my own fevered memories of red and black energy sucking at my soul.

Around me, grad students and volunteers whispered. We had one more week to study the anomaly. A bulldozer clearing ground for a new condo development had revealed it. If we found nothing of value, the developer had more digging permits than we did.

This fieldwork and one revision of my dissertation away from the coveted Ph.D. in archaeology, I needed to complete this dig. The deeper I delved, the more uncertain I became; the less I cared.

Too many anomalies reminded me of my esoteric adventures with mazes. Red and black. Pulsing energy that robbed me of will and motivation.

Through my years of study I'd flirted with pagan philosophies and explored some of their natural energy theories. Part of the job: understanding the people, their culture, and their religion.

Why had Sam Hill chosen to build his Stonehenge replica memorial to the World War I dead two miles downriver from *here?* Stonehenge was the greatest maze of all if you only knew how to look at it.

I exchanged my trowel for a whisk broom, then a toothbrush. My weak and wayward thumb refused to wrap around the slender handle—I'd broken it on a dig in the Yucatan three years ago, miles and days away from medical help, and it'd never healed properly. Still, I persevered. The tiny bristles moved particles away from solid rock revealing a groove six inches wide. It extended to my right and left as far as I could see.

"Camera!" I called. Hoax or not, every bit of this dig needed exacting documentation. As the photographer set up her gear, digital and traditional film, I placed rulers across and along the groove I'd exposed. My bare fingertips slid along the newly exposed granite.

Something sent a chill along my spine. I dismissed it as the ever-present wind. Competing air masses tended to line up on either side of the mountains and use the river gorge as their battleground for dominance. So far we'd had one of those rare summer days of low clouds and dampness that kept us from broiling. Portland, Oregon, to the west, suffered driving rain. The high desert plateau to the east simmered with one hundred degree heat and ninety percent humidity.

I touched the groove again, firmly, deliberately.

The same frisson crawled along my back to the base of my skull. My vision fractured with tiny lightning bolts.

Red and black.

A surprised voice called, "Hello?" A musical voice with a hint of delicate chimes behind it.

The beginning of a migraine? Or something else?

While the photographer did her thing, I evaluated my body for other symptoms. Just the act of stepping away from the dig brought light levels back to a more subdued normal. My muscles relaxed after sitting and bending so long in one place. Part of the job.

I stretched my back and bent my legs in long lunges.

Then I rotated my neck and shoulders. As my head bent to the left, my perspective changed again, and I caught a brief glimpse of rich, fertile land, brilliant green, with trees and flowers and chuckling streams cascading down a series of waterfalls.

Not in this climate and not in summer. Waterfalls, yes, born of mountain snow runoff, but not the fresh smell of damp grass or the twitter of songbirds and frogs croaking a springtime mating call.

"Hello," the same voice said, a lot less surprised.

Must be a migraine coming on.

I drank deeply from the water bottle attached to my belt pack. The strange vision disappeared as if it had never been. Silence resumed. I willed away my memory of red and black swirling around me in suffocating spirals.

Back to work. Work was the cure for everything.

My back ached. My thighs screamed as I crouched down again. The tension in my neck began tying itself into knots almost equal to the maze in complexity.

I rose up again, knowing I needed more stretches. This time I examined what we'd uncovered. Nearly half the outer boundaries of the maze showed fresh and clean in the side light of a westering sun. I saw hints to the pattern.

I'd seen it before. Time and again, in ancient earthworks around Iron Age hill forts, in eighteenth-century reconstructions, in the floors of rotting cathedrals, and in the jewelry marketed throughout the world as Celtic.

I'd also seen it on a grander scale in the layout of an Olmec city in Mesoamerica (where I'd broken my thumb), Indonesian ruins, and in artistic renditions of Atlantis.

Then there was the petroglyph upriver from here. The aboriginal tribes called it "Tsagaglalal." She who watches. Spiraled eyes set in a square face. Those eyes drew you inward, ever inward, inviting you to see other places, other times . . .

My heart skipped a beat. A lump lodged in my throat.

Maybe this wasn't a hoax. Maybe . . . Oh, gods! What

would I find at the center of these twisted pathways? The grand finale of my research or just another hoax and delay? My salvation or my doom?

My entire body trembled with excitement and fear. Red and black. Hot, stinging, malicious.

Forget that!

"Wendell," I called the director over to my sector.

He picked his way across the strings and markings that separated precisely measured and numbered work areas. He moved with surprising grace and silence for a man of his portly build. But then his performance on a dance floor with swing music to guide him was nothing short of amazing.

"What?" His eyes immediately went to the ground, like any well-trained field archaeologist.

"Look at the whole," I said quietly. My hand slipped inside his of its own volition.

Goosebumps raced from me to him and back again.

Nothing is private on a dig. Everyone began twisting their necks right and left. Some stood. Others preferred the lower perspective from the crouch.

Frasier let out a low whistle. "If it's a hoax, it's a damn good one."

I let my gaze trace the concentric circles that looped back on themselves and twisted off into new directions at odd but almost expected angles.

"It's gonna rain, folks. Get the tarps out and cover the whole field. We don't want what's in those thunderheads to muddy up what we've already done," Frasier ordered. He bit his lip.

I figured we had an hour before the first drops hit. Wendell wanted to quit early.

All the students and volunteers scrambled to do his bidding. More than a few cast sidelong glances our way.

"The symbolism is all wrong for this area," he whispered, still holding my hand.

"Stone-faced Monica Warburtun and Dr. Frasier?" I heard one young man, an undergrad, ask his dig partner.

The partner shrugged. I'd rejected advances from both at the beginning of the dig.

"You going to walk the maze?" Frasier whispered as soon as the others were out of earshot.

"I think I have to." I wrapped my arms around myself to ward off the shakes. "Later," I reassured myself. I could wait until later.

I gathered up a vanload of students and volunteers and drove us back to our motel ten miles up the road.

Wendell joined us about an hour later in the café adjacent to the motel. We exchanged a knowing look then tucked into the substantial hamburgers with fresh cut fries and milkshakes.

"My turn to stand watch," I announced to the group. A groan of relief came from a dozen throats at once. The first couple of nights, people clamored for the right to sleep in a tent alone, on site. After a week of hard work in the heat, the prospect of sleeping on a real mattress outweighed the lack of privacy in four to a room quarters. Archaeology commands shoestring budgets. The big bucks go to imaging equipment and lab tests. We save where we can. Lodging and hot restaurant food is a luxury.

Frasier drove back to the site with me. "You know the rest of the crew will think we're having an affair," I said affably as he parked the van.

He shrugged and continued working. "You wouldn't be the first doctoral candidate to sleep with her prof. Too bad I'm not on your committee."

"Too bad you're gay." We both laughed. Best friends.

"You shouldn't do this alone, Monica," he said seriously. "It's dangerous playing with strange energies. You don't really expect to find another portal just by walking the maze, despite the legends."

I had once before. He'd dragged me back from that escapade and held my hand until my sanity returned.

"I have to do this alone. According to the mythology, it's a solitary trek, and not everyone can bust through the barriers. I've studied this long and hard." Resolutely I yanked on the cord to fire up the portable generator. Instantly artificial light flooded our site.

"Shouldn't you wait for dawn?" He stood in front of the small opening that would lead me onto this path. "I've studied too. Powerful energies happen in transition times, twilight, dawn, the equinoxes. Neither realm holds sway, portals thin."

"Midnight is also a transition. I can't take a chance on being interrupted by your overeager students at sunset and sunrise." I faced him, hands on my hips, feet spread, ready to dart around him, though I'd rather enter the maze peacefully, with a calm mind and cautious steps that stayed inside the lines.

"This entire gorge is a transition," I continued. Between east and west, sunrise and sunset, wet and dry, high and low. The symbolism is huge."

"Before I take a chance on you disappearing forever, give me a hint of why here. Why this design in this place?"

"Energy. It all comes down to spiritual energy. You're an atheist. You'll never understand the pure magic that spins up and down this gorge, spills out of the waterfalls, and pulls you deeper and deeper into each ravine in search of the next treasured view."

"You almost make a believer of me. How old do you think this maze is?"

"Maybe twelve thousand years."

He gasped. "The end of the last Ice Age."

"When all the world was flooding. When all the water locked into giant ice flows melted. When the ice dam that formed Lake Missoula broke up and sent a wall of water hundreds of feet high and hundreds of miles long surging along the river bed, finding new courses to absorb the excess and failing, carving out this gorge. What better time to seek escape to a different realm?"

"It's all mythology, Monica."

"How many times have we followed the myth and found archaeological proof?"

He shook his head. "Proof of places, proof of greater age to civilization. Not proof of magic and other dimensions. Leave that to physicists and string theory."

"We have to look at the whole. Not one science at a time. The entire picture, all the sciences linked together." That was near blasphemy twenty years ago. More acceptable now. "Just as we have to look at the entire maze design, not each individual section."

"And the mythological pattern here is wrong." Wendell pretended he hadn't heard me. "Spirals I'd accept. The epitome of a Celtic knot? No."

"You're acting mighty squirrely for a man who doesn't believe in this."

He looked chagrined but still frightened. "Okay. So I've seen enough weird things to be leery of possibilities. Most of those weird things have happened when you were around."

"Like the ghosts in the Dublin pub."

"Like the brownie who stole my watch in Bavaria. Watched the bugger come out of the closet and rip me off. Had to bribe him with sparkling costume jewelry to get it back."

"Or like the time in Brittany when you almost put your hand *through* a standing stone," I reminded him.

"Like the time at Stonehenge you disappeared for an hour and a half and came back *through* a standing stone, not between two, with no memory of where or when you'd been."

Red and black biting me in a hundred places at once, gouging at my eyes and my sanity.

He glared at me long and hard. Eventually he looked away. "Okay, at least tell me what you expect to find."

"Nothing I'd be willing to put in my dissertation." I avoided looking at him by bending over and unlacing my work boots. Maybe I'd find the piece of myself I left behind at Stonehenge. The lost hunk of my soul that is always call-ing to me. The part that saw patterns in nothing and nothing in patterns. The part of me that knew how to love life and enjoy each moment for what it was.

"This could make your career. Definitive proof . . ."

"Of Faery Land? I'd be laughed out of academia. The es-tablishment of archaeologists would destroy this maze rather than take a chance it might change their minds."

We both chuckled grimly.

I kept my gaze averted as I sat and yanked off my boots. When I stood, Wendell stepped aside, leaving the opening clear for me.

"Don't stay away too long. I'll wait three hours. Then I call in reinforcements."

"Look under psychics in the phone book. Or better yet, find a Native shaman."

I took the first step across the dividing line between normal ground and the maze. Nothing happened. Disap-pointment, and relief, weighed heavily on my mind.

Another step. Still nothing. I decided to give it one more step before calling it quits. Then another step and yet an-other.

My curiosity wasn't dead after all. I needed to know what happened when I traced my way around all the loops and whorls of the path. A tingle of intense interest flared like a match struck against sand paper. I realized that a bub-ble of excitement had been building all day, since before I'd cleared the first bit down to bare rock. Answers. I'd find an-swers here.

Right, left, left, left, right again. Around and around.

Faster and faster I danced. A little jig bounced around my memory setting my feet to capering. Step together, step, hop. I spun in place, filled with wonder.

Something clicked. I looked about. A cone of shimmer-ing energy encircled the maze. I saw the path blazing white, more real and vivid than the murky shadow of Wendell

Frasier pacing back and forth across the entrance. The glaring work lights dimmed, as if shrouded in fog.

Another slow spin. I'd reached the center.

"Now what?"

"You need only ask," a tiny voice whispered across my mind. The same voice that had greeted me earlier. Light and lovely, enticing.

"May I come in?" This place seemed to follow the folk-loric rules of Faery. I hadn't had to ask at Stonehenge. I just got sucked in.

A shift in the shimmer of light before me. An almost physical tug at my heart told me to step forward.

Impossibly green grass caressed my feet. Silence near deafened me.

No insect buzz. No birdsong. No wind sighing in the tall oaks and elms. Even the creek off to my left flowed around tumbled rocks without sound.

Silence is okay, I thought. *The music of nature in my memory is enough.*

The water seemed to be some kind of boundary. I directed my feet toward it, yet I found myself veering in the other direction, toward a log cabin sitting in the shade of one of the patriarchal oaks. Four rooms around a central chimney, I thought. Or maybe two long rooms, one front, one back.

A bit of movement on the cabin porch drew my gaze. The first movement I'd seen. An old woman sat knitting in a rocking chair. She moved forward and back, forward and back in time to the thrumming beat of my heart.

She seemed a long way off at first. The distance proved deceptive. Each step brought me much closer than my usual stride could account for.

"About time you showed up," she said when I paused at the foot of the three steps that led up to the porch. She'd drawn her gray hair up into a tidy knot atop her head. A bit of darker gray filigree encircled it, the same gray as the sock she knitted.

Without peering closer, I knew the pattern in the filigree echoed the lines of the maze I'd just walked.

"I've been looking for a way through for a long time," I explained.

"You took a wrong step at Stonehenge. That delayed you more than a bit."

"How did you . . ." I gulped. "How did you know?"

"This is Faery. I know everything about you."

"But how?" I dared move onto the first step.

"It's in the knitting." She lifted the yarn tube, a lot of stitches evenly spaced on four needles. No matter how many movements she made with those needles, in and out, wrap the yarn, over and over, the number of stitches on each needle remained the same. The sock never grew.

"What do you see in the knitting?" I ventured another step up.

"Come closer and watch," she said. Her voice held bright invitation.

I approached eagerly and bent over her shoulder, peering at the fine stitches in gray wool.

The tube of knitting held a glass, neatly framed by the four needles. Truly a looking glass. Inside it I watched Wendell walk the perimeter of the maze with dragging steps. One by one he turned off the glaring work lights. His head hung down, shoulders drooping in defeat.

"I've only been gone ten minutes, not the three hours he promised to keep vigil," I protested. I tapped the glass with a fingernail, trying to gain his attention.

"Time runs differently in Faery," the old woman said. Her voice washed over me like a refreshing waterfall. "Everyone knows that."

Up close, something about the curve of her mouth, the slant of her eye, the way her gray hair framed her face reminded me of someone.

"Do I know you?"

She laughed, the same chiming chuckles I'd heard earlier. "Of course you do. Or you did." She smiled and returned to her fruitless knitting. I couldn't see why her stitches accomplished nothing.

"Remind me," I pleaded.

"It will come to you. Just be patient."

"What's beyond the creek?" I asked. I needed to hear her speak. Something in her accent tickled my memory.

"The gorge lies just beyond the horizon."

"The Columbia River Gorge?" I asked, surprised.

"It was the Columbia River Gorge in your day."

"My day?"

"Time, my dear. Time runs differently here."

"I half expected standing stones." I stepped off the porch and ambled a few steps toward the water. Something held me back—a desire to look in the glass again, a need to keep the woman close—I wasn't sure what.

"Don't need stones erected by humans. Beacon Rock is the second largest monolith in your world. The only bigger free standing hunk of rock is Gibraltàr. And then there's Rooster Rock. If that isn't a phallic standing stone, I don't know what is." Again she chuckled. "People still come to worship at those places, though they don't recognize it as such. But they stand and stare in awe. They walk maze patterns as they hike the trails. And they return again and again—in their memory if not in actuality."

I tried to gauge direction by the shadows. There weren't any. No shade. Just an overall brightness, as if lit by the finest master in Hollywood.

My euphoria slid away from me in a gradual fade. Awareness replaced it. Overly bright and uniformly colored green grass that felt as soft as carpet beneath my bare feet. No prickles. No imperfections. Level—as if constructed with carpenter's tools. Every log on the cabin appeared the same size, straight and even; they didn't need any chinking to fill the gaps between them. The air caressed my skin at a comfortable temperature and humidity. Perfect proportions and symmetry everywhere I looked.

Unnatural! my mind screamed.

If the place was a construct, so too might be the old woman who looked achingly familiar.

Damn. I knew there were traps in Faery. And yet I'd stepped smack dab in the middle of one in my quest to find a missing piece of myself. Faery wouldn't be satisfied until it had all of me.

"Who are you?" I stood firm in the center of the grass, close to where I'd entered this world. If an opportunity arose to leave, I wanted to grab it. Fast.

"Haven't figured it out yet?" She cocked both eyebrows upward. "I'd been led to believe you were brighter than that. Ph.D. candidate and all."

How much did she know about me?

She peered closely into her knitting. A frown grew deep along the creases on either side of her mouth.

"Anything new happening in my world?"

"Come see."

Damn it, I had to go look. I had to know. My feet wouldn't stay put no matter how hard I willed them to.

Once more I leaned over her shoulder and scanned the tiny images in her glass. Long shadows from the rising sun stretched westward from every imperfection in the land and from every piece of equipment or person in view. Wendell guided his crew to clear more turf away from the maze with dangerous haste. He grabbed a trowel and began hacking away at the edges on his own. The camera girl fairly jumped from place to place, snapping dozens of pictures. Most of them would be useless, showing nothing new.

"If you go back now, you will make all the same mistakes I—" the old woman clamped her mouth shut as if she'd said too much. From the cold calculation in her eyes, I knew she'd planned to say just that.

"What mistakes did you make?" My gaze strayed back to the too green grass of the clearing. For half a heartbeat I thought I saw the maze shining through from beneath.

Then it was gone.

"Do you really want to know? You can stay here, safe from . . ."

"From what?"

"It's too soon."

"It's never too soon to find answers to questions."

I moved in front of her and speared her with my gaze. Eventually she looked up under the force of my will.

"Very well." She bit her lip. "Follow me." Slowly, almost painfully, she rose from her rocker and set the knitting aside on a low twig table I hadn't noticed before.

I dogged her heels into the cabin, knowing I should be more cautious. But I had to know. Had to make sure I avoided whatever future she dreaded.

The inside of the cabin proved as symmetrical as the outside. Two long rooms, front and back. A large stone chimney in the center served both. Doors on either side of the hearth kept the symmetry. A table set for two with plates, cutlery, serviettes, and coffee mugs, with two straight chairs to one side. A rustic vase made from an old canning jar held six perfect daisies. Two comfortable stuffed chairs faced a shuttered picture window on the other end. I presumed the back room held two beds and two washstands.

Was I the second person in this picture, or someone else?

"I've fixed a nice stew for our supper," she said. Sure enough, a cast iron cauldron hung in the fireplace above the glowing embers of a wood fire.

I couldn't smell either the burning branches or the stew, yet a quick peek showed me that it burbled happily.

The woman looked longingly at the stew then back at me. "I don't suppose you'll wait for answers until after we've eaten?"

I knew better than that. All the way back to Persephone and Hades the legends warned against eating anything in an Otherworld. Good way to get trapped there forever.

Had this old woman eaten something here long ago? Or did something else tether her?

"Show me the mistake you made—the mistake I will make."

"Very well," she sighed. Slowly, as if arthritic hips ached, she made her way to the picture window. The only window in the place.

Out of symmetry.

My heart started to race. Something was very wrong here. I held my breath as she worked a lever to raise the shutter.

A different quality of light filtered in from the bottom, as the single plank of wood lifted outward from the bottom. Reddish hues permeated the bright and pleasant room, casting an ominous glare.

I looked to the fire to see if it had suddenly flared.

No such luck.

When I returned my gaze to the window, I gasped. Bloodred plasma swirled outside, globules of ebony swam in the eddies, creating whirlpools. They fought the tides, trying to forge their own path through the energy streams.

My mind drifted outward, following one large black blob. I felt the heat, the push, the pulse of the plasma. It swirled in echo of my speeding heartbeat. It pulled me out of my body, demanding I join the fight.

Then the big black thing shifted orientation and opened one huge eye that nearly filled its being. A consciousness rode there; an intelligence.

I'd encountered that eye before.

Shocked, I took a step backward, forcing myself to look away and break the link.

"Wh . . . what is that?" I whispered harshly, not certain I spoke aloud. The pulsing in my head masked any other noise I might have made.

"That is us."

"I don't understand?"

"That is what we made of the world. I did, you will. We thought we were helping, bringing beings and energy from Otherworlds to our own, to fight pollution, to raise a spiritual consciousness, to protect and preserve our beloved gorge as well as the rest of the world."

"You let the wrong energy in."

"Yes." She slammed down the lever and the shutter blocked out the malevolence. "Time we ate."

"This cabin, the grass, and trees, they are constructs. How? Why?"

"I carved this little space out of the primordial mass. This is all that is left of Earth, the universe as you know it."

"You survived. Why bother? Aren't you lonely?"

"Incredibly. But I knew you would come. I had to survive until you came." She shuffled over to the stew pot and grabbed a ladle from a hook set into the stonework. In grasping it she used only her fingers, curving her thumb across the top of her knuckles.

I held tools the same way.

Another shock washed over me like an incoming storm wave. I fought to breathe.

"You're me!"

"Finally."

"An older version of me."

"I've had a devil of a time keeping this place linked to the maze. Time keeps trying to rip it away. Rip this place away so that you couldn't cross over, couldn't learn from your mistake."

She set a bowl of stew in front of me. I'd learned in the field to eat what I could, when I could. No telling when the next meal might fit into the schedule. Out of habit I flipped the serviette onto my lap and raised my fork with the same curious grip I'd watched her use. Consciously I moved my thumb back to a more normal position. Then I looked at the stew again.

No smell equals no appetite.

I set the food back into the bowl and pushed my chair away from the table. My feet drew me back to the window. I reached for the lever. Fascinated and repulsed by the horror outside, I couldn't help myself. I had to see it again, had to know if this was truly my fate.

"Don't open that!"

"Why not?" I edged the lever down a fraction. Instantly the red glare surged around the shutter, filling the room with the fiery glow.

"I've seen more than enough of it." The old woman began eating her own meal, concentrating on it rather than me or the window.

"I need to know what happened to me at Stonehenge," I said, still staring at the swirling red and black chaos outside. Had I raised the shutter, or had it opened completely by itself? Or had the *things* out there manipulated it?

Maybe they'd manipulated me. They had once before.

"You don't want to know what happened to you. That's why you block it from your memory."

"But I didn't block it." My insides began to tremble as I relived being caught within the same swirling vortex that I watched through the window. I felt again the pain as jolt after jolt of burning energy shot through me, pushing me here, pulling me there, yanking at my soul; trying to separate me from my body.

Because that's what was out there, the lost souls of those who took a wrong turn trying to cross over to the Otherworlds.

Mazes are tricky. The paths narrow. They require absolute concentration to keep your feet within the lines and your mind on your goal. Not sure of the goal? Your mind wanders. Your balance tilts and suddenly you are on a different path, though it looks the same. But it takes you elsewhere.

I thought the chaos had stolen vital pieces of me. Now I thought differently.

"Yes, you blocked it. I'd know what happened if you hadn't forced the memory from you. I am you, after all."

"No you aren't."

"Now you are being ridiculous."

"Now I'm being logical. The glass in your knitting only allows you to watch and listen. It doesn't let you into my mind. You can guess a lot from what you see and hear. But you can't know." Angrily I pointed outside. "I remember those things."

The woman reared away from the scene, kept her eyes on the fire, which now blazed merrily with new fuel that hadn't been there a few heartbeats ago.

"I am you. You are me," she insisted.

"When I first stepped out of the Stonehenge circle, I thought you'd stolen my curiosity, my optimism, *my joie de vivre.* That's why I had to come find you. To get them back. But, if you had truly stolen them, I'd never have come. I wouldn't have needed to know what lay on the other side of this maze."

As I spoke, a gradual transformation washed over the woman. Her face morphed into a skeletal reflection of the horrible energy outside. Her body elongated and thinned. She gave off a blinding glare.

I threw an arm over my eyes. As I had at Stonehenge.

The blackness, the inability to see what she/he/it wanted me to see saved me. Gave me the strength to return to my own time and place.

"You can't hide from me. You can't keep me here any longer." The thing's voice tolled in deep tones, like a mournful ocean buoy. "I touched your mind at Stonehenge. I linked to you so that you would have to come find me. Rescue me."

The resonance of that voice masked direction and distance from me.

"You couldn't steal anything from me, so you laid a blanket of energy over the good things in my mind. You hid them from me. But you also hid my thoughts, my true self, from yourself."

A sense of increased heat from my right. The thing moved toward the doorway. Slowly, at the same speed the chaos drifted about.

"I won't let you leave me here," I said, edging blindly toward the exit myself.

"You have no choice," it chuckled. "You know the rules of Faery as well as I do. One person came through the portal, only one can go out. You came in. I leave. That was the plan all along."

"I don't think so." I pushed all my willpower into running. Running fast. Faster than the Thing. It was still tied to the speed of life in the chaos. I still had enough humanity to use my burst of adrenaline.

Electric heat seared me from my temple to my heels on the right side as I passed It. I cried out in pain. Half of me didn't want to work.

But I kept going. Somehow. Only then did I allow myself to open my eyes. Vision gave me accuracy.

I stumbled on the steps. The Thing caught up with me. But It didn't touch me again. Its left side dragged.

We had wounded each other. Full contact might kill us both. Or throw us through the portal to somewhere else.

I couldn't take that chance. I had to reach the maze entrance before It did. I had to have both feet and my body fully inside its perimeter before It set foot on the path.

Shuffling and dragging, we parodied a race, neck and neck.

I kept my eyes on the grass, willing the maze to come back to my view. The Thing might have other senses to detect it.

The grass remained uniformly green. A construct, just like the rest of the clearing. Cabin and trees merely pieces of energy thrown together to attract me.

Or to house the Thing. An eternity of symmetry and beauty when It was born out of chaos and horror.

"You were exiled here," I called as my feet found an imperfection in the grass, a slight ridge. The edge of maze. I had to stall while I sought the beginning.

"The portal was adjusted to send you here, to this place

and nowhere else," I continued. "You and you alone. This is your punishment for wreaking havoc in my world."

It felt along the grass with Its own feet, seeking the same opening I did.

"So I let loose a little plague." The black and red energy that surged around Its amorphous form rippled as it shrugged.

"A plague that wiped out nearly thirty percent of Europe's population." I adjusted the timeline of the portal forward in time from the maze's construction.

Was that a break in the ridge my toes had found? Yes! I tried to orient myself to where I had emerged. Beginning and end were not the same.

I had come out under the oak tree. Now I stood in the center of the clearing.

I moved on, working my way clockwise around the outside of the maze. I had to enter where I had exited. I had to walk it the exact opposite direction as before.

The Thing shouted in triumph as it found the break.

"Stupid human. Just like all the rest. I eliminated the weak and wasteful ones. Only the strongest and most intelligent survived. And you aren't one of them." It chortled and took a step forward. The maze remained dormant.

I found the opening I needed at last. Drawing in one deep breath, I stepped inside. The instant my second foot set down on the path I knew I'd chosen correctly. Restoring energy tingled against my soles.

Across from me the Thing continued to berate me and my kind. It seemed to wander aimlessly.

Before me, the pathway blazed white against a green background. Carefully I followed where it led, keeping my eyes and concentration down. I had to ignore the Thing. I had to force it to remain here.

"An exorcist first banished me to the wilderness. But it wasn't a wilderness long. The natives thrived under my tutelage, making war upon their more plentiful neighbors to the west," the Thing sneered.

I kept walking. "Missionaries, or devout fur traders, someone found you. And found you out. They adjusted the maze the natives had constructed thousands of years before and banished you once more. This time you went to hell."

My perception of the Thing faded. The grass beneath my feet turned brown and brittle. The wavering images of trees and cabin shrank to low clumps of sage and rabbitbrush.

"One person's heaven is the next person's hell," I said. My voice fell flat, fully contained by the intricacies of the maze. "Hell is all around us. Only a step away."

The Thing could reach out and touch people through the mazes of the world. It could suck away your life's energy if you let It. But it could only escape through this maze.

One in and one out.

I stumbled and fell forward into Wendell Frasier's arms. Bright desert sun beat against my eyes. Dry heat wicked sweat away from my skin.

I nearly laughed in relief.

"Monica, where have you been these past three days?" Wendell asked.

The other grad students and volunteers were so intent on clearing the last of the dirt and plants from the slab of anomalous rock that they barely noticed my arrival.

"It's a hoax, Dr. Frasier. Let the developers destroy it," I gasped. My eyes sought the bulky bulldozers and other arcane equipment one hundred yards away.

"Monica, I think it's real. Look at it, it's genuine!" he protested.

"Destroy it now!" I insisted.

"This discovery will set the archaeological world on its ear. Your career is made and mine."

"Destroy it now, or destroy yourself. It's an elaborate hoax." I fixed him with a stern gaze. "Let the developers wreck it, or I will drop the first charge of dynamite on it myself."

"Are you sure?"

"Absolutely. Universes are kept separate for a reason.

Risking a crossover with a ritual maze is more dangerous than you can imagine." I made myself take the last step, fully separating myself from the lure of the path. Then I walked over to the first huge yellow machine and fired up the engine.

WWW.KARMASSIST.COM

Donald J. Bingle

"Look, Jerry, you really need to pick up Brian after school today."

She spoke, but not to them. Never to them.

They all simply sat, expressionless, as they were hurled forward toward their common destination, trying not to hear. Some stared blankly ahead, ignoring the objects flashing by just outside the windows. Others glanced lazily at the folded papers in their hands, conveying to their weary minds the same information, with only minor variations, as the day before and the day before that, time out of mind. Many now rode regularly with their eyes closed, dangling cords with buds screwed into their ears, feeding them music or words or white noise in an attempt to block out the outside world during their journey.

Daniel was one of the latter, the volume cranked up to the point of risking serious damage to his hearing, though silent to even his seatmate. All he wanted was to generate a little inner peace, just a bit of privacy before yet another day of stupid clients and irritating coworkers. But, there was no peace to be found on the west line of the Metroplex Commuter Rail Line today, at least not in car three of the 7:22 run into the city.

"I don't care if it's not your turn. Madeline is going into

Dr. Hansen's this afternoon for a mammogram, and she needs me to drive her. It's at two-thirty, but you know doctors—they never run on time. It's because they over-schedule. They don't care about anybody's time but their own."

Daniel had already switched from one of the peaceful tunes he usually listened to on the way to work, light jazz or one of the less bombastic classical pieces, to rock and roll in an attempt to drown her out, but it wasn't working.

"He's wearing his red and green striped shirt. I don't remember what color pants. Jesus, he's seven. No one cares about fashion when they're seven."

It wouldn't be so bad if she spoke quietly or it was a quick, isolated call. But this was the fourth call so far this trip. First there had been the endless rant at the management company for her condo complex, complaining that the security door was broken . . . again. Then there had been the chat with Madeline about her female medical problems, God help him, and he had learned more about cysts and needle biopsies than he, a widower, ever really wanted to know. Right before this call, she had been laughing and screaming with her girlfriend, Valerie, about their vacation last winter in Cabo. Apparently they drank. A lot.

Daniel had switched over to Springsteen during the medical discussion. Now he was scrolling to see if he had any heavy metal in his MP3 player.

"Well, if you can't be there at three, he'll just have to wait until you get there at three fifteen. He waits for me on the Mill Street side of the school, near the gymnasium."

Quite apart from consideration for her fellow commuter railroad passengers, didn't this woman realize she had just broadcast to fifty or sixty strangers that her seven-year-old son, Brian, wearing a red and green striped shirt, would be available to be kidnapped on Mill Street between three and three-fifteen this afternoon? Why couldn't she stand in the vestibule, between passenger seating sections, so as not to bother anyone and not broadcast her tawdry life to the world?

"No, I'm not going to do that to you because you're doing this for me! Wait until I tell Janice what you just said. I'm going to hang up on you and call her right now!"

Daniel couldn't stand it any longer. He got up, grabbed his briefcase and coat, and headed for the vestibule himself. It was noisy, too, in a clackety kind of way, and he would have to stand, but at least he would no longer be assaulted by the voice of the latest cell phone addict to disrupt his once tranquil commute into the city. He wanted to scream at her, to tell her to shut up and turn off the damn phone. The other commuters would probably applaud him for doing so, but that just wasn't in his makeup. He was a nice guy. He didn't yell. He didn't complain out loud. He didn't confront people.

He heaved open the sliding door to the vestibule and stepped through, setting his briefcase down on the metal floor and leaning heavily against the railing of the steps down to the commuter car's doors for loading and unloading passengers. As the classic rock on his MP3 worked to lighten his mood, he glanced about the vestibule, taking in the emergency stop lever with instructions in English, Spanish, and Braille (he assumed the Braille was in English, but no doubt Spanish Braille would soon become a requirement). He also looked at the month's advertising placards. Three were holdovers from the month before—one for an insurance company, one for a technical college, and one for a fast food restaurant. The smiling faces on the fast food ad had been given goatees and blacked out teeth by a miscreant with poor drawing skills.

The fourth ad was new—at least he didn't remember seeing it before. In stark white lettering on a red background, it read simply: "Life could be better. www.karmassist. com." He gave a small harrumph and closed his eyes, leaning his head back on the wall to let the rocking of the train help him zone out for the rest of the trip. What kind of cryptic ad was that? Who did they think would go to a random

Web site based on that message? He was obviously not their target demographic.

Daniel got off the train when it reached downtown and began the lemminglike trudge with the rest of the crowd eight blocks toward his job at a boring, gray consulting firm located in a boring, gray office building. His only amusement on the daily hike was that if he kept up a pace of just so, he would arrive at each corner just in time for the walk sign to start flashing, saving himself from the risks of standing still on a corner—risks like getting hit on by a panhandler or standing in a cloud of secondhand smoke next to a twenty-year-old secretary with too much mascara on her eyes, a Marlboro Lite in her leathery hand, and a long line of equally bad decisions in her future. Unlike many, Daniel took off his earbuds when he was walking; maybe that's why he heard the cab in time to prevent being run over as it powered through the crosswalk well after the light had turned red and then stopped abruptly, blocking it.

Daniel had once had a friend in college who walked over the hood of any car that blocked the crosswalk, but Daniel, of course, would never do that. He thought of taking down the cab's number—Cab No. 2874—but if the cabbie saw him writing it down, he might provoke a scene or even a fight. Daniel didn't even glare at the cabbie, which some of his fellow pedestrians were doing. Instead he meekly inched his way through the bottleneck at the back of the cab—never let yourself be forced into traffic by a stopped vehicle—holding his briefcase up so it didn't scrape on the red advertising sign affixed to the cab's bumper. As he did so, he noticed the ad. White lettering on a red background: "We can help you enjoy life. www.karmassist.com."

Arriving at his cubicle, Daniel waited patiently while his computer fired up so he could log on. In accordance with company policy, he turned off the machine every night to conserve power and help thwart breaches of security. As far as he knew, he was the only person in his department to do so. Once the computer was on, Daniel deleted the overnight spam and filed away yesterday's sent and received messages to the proper client files, then got down to substantive work. He didn't bill out his filing time—it didn't seem fair to the clients, but his lack of aggressive billing meant that he always had to take a short lunch to make up time. At eleven, he showed up promptly for the monthly departmental meeting. Everyone else showed up ten minutes late, except for Bill, the boss. He showed up fifteen minutes late and immediately called his secretary on the speakerphone, telling her to bring coffee—not for everyone, just for him.

"As you know, we have two big, exciting projects this month," announced Bill. "Frank here, he's going to head up the Huthwaite due diligence in New Zealand." Frank Bliskin, Daniel's trainee from last summer, grinned ear-to-ear. "Got your passport, Frankie?"

Frank's eyes went wide. "Er . . . no."

At first, Daniel was irritated. He had specifically told Frank to get his passport renewed last year because of the possibility of sudden trips, and Frank had assured him he had done so. But, then, Daniel brightened. His passport, pristine and unused, was up-to-date, and he had taught Frank everything Frank knew about due diligence. He was the perfect replacement. He was about to speak up, or maybe not, when Bill shrugged his shoulders and continued.

"Have Danny-boy give you some money out of the office supplies fund to expedite your passport application."

So much for the ergonomic keyboard Daniel had hoped to get to alleviate his carpal tunnel symptoms.

"And Larry will be handling the negotiations on the Packard account. It's a lot of wining and dining and entertainment, Larry, but someone's got to do it. Just make sure those T&A, er . . . I mean . . . T&E reports say 'drinks and nightclub' and not 'strip club,' okay? You're the breast, I mean best, Larry."

Daniel didn't know what made him more incensed, the fact that he had been passed over for an assignment yet again or that Tina was looking decidedly uncomfortable with Bill's juvenile, off-color banter. He screwed up his courage. Somebody had to say something.

"Look, Bill . . ."

"Jesus, Danny. Stop whining and go do whatever it is that you do around here."

Bill left the conference room before the laughter died down.

Daniel headed back to his cubicle. Thirty minutes of wasted time. He logged back on to his e-mail. Remarkably, there was only one new piece of spam, with the subject line: "Nice guys don't have to finish last." Probably the latest erectile dysfunction ad line. He clicked to delete it as he noticed the screen name of the sender: Yourfriend@karmassist.com. He was almost tempted to retrieve the message from his deleted files and click through, but it would probably trip the firm's filters on restricted content and get flagged in his personnel file.

Just as he completed that thought a new e-mail popped up. "We want to help you, Daniel" read the subject line, again from Yourfriend@karmassist.com.

The things you could do now with targeted spam were amazing, Daniel thought.

Another e-mail popped up.

"This is not spam, Daniel," read the subject line of the newest missive.

He clicked through.

The site itself matched the white-on-red motif of the advertising and, to his surprise, was devoid of pop-ups, advertising, or links to seamy spam come-ons. It simply read:

Thanks for stopping by, Daniel.

Karmassist exists solely to bring karmic balance to the world.

We have the power to correct any injustice done to you. Has anyone mistreated you lately?

Bill's irritating dismissal still rung in his ears, but Daniel was uncertain whether the e-mail might be a trick, an office prank by a colleague, or something even more sinister from the human resources department. He wasn't about to start complaining about his boss on an office computer. Instead he thought back to his morning commute. "Gabby woman on cell phone on train," he typed in.

"Please identify her," responded the site.

Of course, he had no name to proffer. "I don't know who she is," he typed instead.

"What do you know about her?"

His fingers hesitated above the keyboard for a few moments, then he scrunched up his face a second and began to type: "She rides the 7.22 A.M. Metroplex Rail on the west line, third car back. She has brown, shoulder-length hair. Her husband or more likely ex-husband's name is Jerry. She lives in a condo with a broken security door. She has a friend named Madeline and went to Cabo last winter with a different friend, named Valerie. Her seven-year-old son, Brian, goes to an elementary school that has Mill Street on one of its borders."

He pressed "Enter."

"Thanks, Daniel. We can take it from here."

Daniel suddenly began to sweat. "How does this work?" he typed. He wasn't really worried that anything meaningfully bad was going to happen, but he did fret about the possibility of retaliation . . . or confrontation.

"Don't worry. At karmassist, everything is always completely confidential."

"But, what's going to happen?"

"We'll think of something. :) At karmassist, we pride ourselves on creative solutions to life's little annoyances," came the reply. Then the computer went blank.

Daniel had to do a hard reboot to get the computer to work again. And once he had, he found no evidence of the exchanges with www.karmassist.com in his sent or received folders, his deleted messages, or his history of visited Web sites.

Great, he thought, now I'm going insane.

The next morning Daniel sat in his usual seat on the train and, instead of plugging in to his MP3 player, kept an eye out for Brian's mom, whoever she was. But she didn't get on. Just as the mechanical warning chime began to sound to announce that the doors were about to close, though, Daniel saw his noisy nemesis running up the stairs and across the asphalt platform. The doors closed, and the train headed downtown. He watched her shake her fist at the departing mass transportation, and he smiled. He couldn't be sure, of course, that www.karmassist.com had anything to do with the tardiness of Brian's mom and, thus, his morning's peace, but he was sufficiently pleased and amused after a blissful ride in to the city that he walked to his cubicle, keyed in the karmassist Web site and typed in his experience with Cab. No. 2874 from the day before. He didn't understand the business model of the Web site—how it worked or how it could possibly be a commercially viable enterprise, but he liked the results.

To Daniel's dismay, Brian's mom made the train the next morning, hobbling up with a broken heel on her shoe, this time just before the doors whisked shut. She sat down in Daniel's compartment and immediately took out her cell phone and speed-dialed someone. "You won't believe what happened," she started harping, when there was a brief squeal from the phone, a loud static clicking, and then ominous silence. Brian's mom punched numbers furiously, but she obviously couldn't get her cell to work. After several minutes, she muttered a few choice expletives, then sat quietly fuming for the rest of the ride.

As Daniel strolled, grinning broadly, toward his office, he noticed that Cab No. 2874 was parked near a fire hydrant. It had been ticketed and booted for towing.

Daniel logged on to www.karmassist.com as soon as he got in, skipping over his usual filing chores. He still didn't know how the site worked. It was magic as far as he could tell. Fantastic magic that did his bidding. He immediately typed in his complaints about Bill.

The next morning, Brian's mom couldn't find her cell phone in her purse, Cab No. 2874 was sitting in front of Daniel's building with a flat tire and a cursing driver, and Bill was ensconced with the company's general counsel and HR director, who were informing him that no, his soon-to-be former employer would not be paying for his defense against Tina's sexual harassment charges.

On the way home from the train station that night, a motorcycle driven by a burly, bearded individual cut Daniel off, weaving across lanes and speeding away. Daniel didn't even get angry. He calmly memorized the hog's license plate number and headed home, stopping by the grocery store to pick up a few essentials. When Brandy, his checkout girl, made him wait while she talked on the phone with her boyfriend about what they were going to do after her shift, Daniel didn't even frown. He just made note of her name and employee ID number. Daniel made sure to enter the information into the Web site as soon as he got home.

The next morning, Daniel whistled while he moved from his cubicle into his new office—Bill's old office. Bill had left a few personal items when he was escorted out of the building the prior afternoon, but Tina informed Daniel that Bill probably wouldn't want the photo of his wife, since she had left him, taking the kids with her and was heading for California with Bill's new BMW and a moving van full of their possessions.

The Web site for www.karmassist.com was so helpful that Daniel couldn't stand waiting until he got to a computer at home or the office to enter in his growing number of collected infractions. Instead, he bought a new cell phone with wireless internet hook-up so he could enter information on a real time basis. His mood and his life were definitely improving. Tina flirted constantly with him at work, engaging in a little grab and tickle behind closed doors, and his new job not only allowed him to afford a snazzy Mercedes convertible, it enabled him to fire Larry and Frank, his undeserving competition at the office. Somehow every day was just a little brighter. He never got mad; he got even. And when nobody did anything wrong in his presence, he would type in complaints about Brian's mom or Cab No. 2874 or Bill, just to make sure that they didn't get off too easy.

Of course, it didn't take much to inspire him to log on to www.karmassist.com with a complaint. When a blue van full of teenagers pulled up next to him at a light, rap "music" booming from the stereo loud enough to make waves in his "grande-skim-mocha-latte-140-degrees-with-whip," he just smiled and keyed in the junker's license number. Because he was so busy on his cell phone, Daniel did draw a honk from the car behind him when he failed to notice that the light had changed, but Daniel didn't mind. Smiling, he gave the impatient fellow behind him a jaunty wave and memorized the guy's license plate number as the honker roared past.

I am one guy you do not want to piss off, Daniel thought merrily as he turned into the driveway at home. I am the bringer of justice to a world gone mad. Why, if he had known about www.karmassist.com when all the people that had ever wronged him in his life had done so, the world would be a much better place now.

Then it occurred to him. The magic gremlins, or whoever was behind the Web site, didn't know anything but what he told it. And so he sat at the computer, all night, and reported every wrong that had ever been done him, every slight that had ever festered in his psyche, every minor irritation of his youth, his adolescence, his college years, and so on—every irritation he could think of from his entire life to date. And when you are a shy, nonathletic, balding, middle-aged middle manager with low self-esteem, that's a lot of irritation.

The next morning, Daniel was bleary-eyed and unshaven when he jumped into his Mercedes to drive to the train station to go to work. His carpal tunnel syndrome had flared up during the night's typing, so he only had one hand on the steering wheel when the tire blew out, sending the car into a ditch a block from the station. He abandoned it and ran for the train, his chest heaving in pain from the brief exertion, but he made it on board. Immediately, he opened up his cell phone and called the Mercedes dealer, demanding that they go pick up and repair his vehicle, returning it to a parking spot near the station by that evening or there would be "hell to pay." A small part of him realized he was disturbing the other passengers, but he just didn't care. He was tired and pissed off, and it was just this one time. He was entitled.

Brian's mom glared at him as he yelled at the dealer, but she didn't say a word, probably because she couldn't. Her jaw was wired shut and her face bruised and bandaged. A woman in the seat in front of Daniel nudged a seatmate and nodded toward Brian's mom. "Poor dear," she said, "I heard her husband beat her up because he found out it was her fault their little boy was kidnapped and killed."

"Sounds like she deserved it," muttered Daniel, drawing stares from the women in front of him. He ignored them and tried to call Tina, but now his damn phone wasn't working anymore. Instead, he perused the paper, noisily ruffling pages as he read with glee about a blue van that had sideswiped a motorcycle and spun out of control, crashing into the local grocery store, pinning a young cashier under the vehicle until the firemen arrived to extricate her.

He walked briskly to work, crossing against the light. He barely noticed when Cab No. 2874 had to swerve violently to miss him, crashing into a stoplight, the horn blaring as blood coated the inside of the broken windshield. He was checking his e-mail on his new phone while he was walking up the escalator to the elevator lobby of his building when his ascent was blocked by some irksome idiot who was just standing instead of climbing the moving stairs. Why do people stop walking and stand when they get on an escalator? The only thing more irritating was when they did it going down! He would have logged on to karmassist and complained, but he reached the top of the escalator before he could gather any useful identifying information about the offender. He would keep an eye out for her in the future.

Daniel did notice a news headline on his phone's screen about monsoon-induced floods in India killing thousands. For just a moment he wondered if the lethal floods had anything to do with his complaint about Vijay, a customer service rep who had put him on hold when he was activating his new phone. But he shook off the thought. Karmassist wasn't that powerful . . . or indiscriminate . . . was it? Of course, a lot of people might be complaining about Indian call centers.

Daniel growled at reception as he headed for his office, barking toward Tina's cubicle that she should get her sweet little ass in there in a hurry if she knew what was good for her. But it wasn't Tina who was standing bent over the keyboard, her shapely body blocking a white-on-red Web site on the flat screen. It was Tina's best friend at work, Becky. Becky flicked off the screen and timidly turned around, moving quickly around the corner to her own workstation while reporting that Tina was down in HR at the moment.

"Then I guess you'd better get me some coffee, honey," Daniel gruffed dismissively before what Becky said had really registered. What was Tina doing in HR this time?

Then, the answer hit him. But maybe it wasn't too late. He scrolled frantically through a score of undeleted e-mails to find his latest messages. There was only one, the sender listed as Yourformerfriend@karmassist.com.

The subject line read simply: "Account terminated."

He was opening the e-mail to click through to the Web site to explain, to repent, to complain about karmassist itself, but most of all to implore karmassist to stop whatever was about to happen down in HR, when he heard a commotion outside his office. He spun around to see Bill stride through the door with an automatic weapon already spitting fire and lead, silencing Daniel's plea for mercy before it could even leave his crimson-sprayed throat. As Bill finished emptying the clip into Daniel's bloody, dancing body, the e-mail opened on screen.

"Karmic justice has been balanced. www.karmassist .com. P.S. A computer virus is deleting your hard drive. :) Have a nice day."

At karmassist, an interdimensional portal into one of the master servers of the internet in Virginia winked shut.

"You're right," telepathed an ultraviolet interdimensional being to another of his kind, a former assistant. "Playing games over the internet with the lives of humans can be fun, but it is terribly addicting."

The infrared interdimensional being gave a brief, deep thought-chuckle. "It's certainly a more amusing way to spend eternity than when we would just roll dice with the universe."

"You'd think, though," intoned the ultraviolet one, "that omnipotent creatures like us would have grander things to do than lead lesser beings into temptation by giving them just a bit of our powers and watching what happens."

"We do have a lot of time to kill," mind-sneered the infrared being. "And even though it always ends the same way, the details are endlessly fascinating."

"Power corrupts," mused the ultraviolet one. "But, then, no one knows that better than you."

"Absolutely, my old companion," replied the infrared being, his countenance flickering for just the briefest instant in apparent disbelief at his omniscient companion's astounding lack of self-awareness. "Absolutely." When the ultraviolet creature remained quiet, there was another quantum flicker in the infrared spectrum. "So, can I tempt you into another try?"

THE AVALON PSALTER

Lillian Stewart Carl

*C*onventional wisdom says there are no ghosts haunting
Glastonbury.

*Conventional wisdom, like most convention, is dead
wrong.*

*No, there's nothing here as ordinary as the steps of in-
visible feet or doors that open and shut by themselves. The
ghosts of Glastonbury wait just beyond your peripheral vision, fingertips extended for the lightest of touches. Only a
few souls are sensitive enough to feel that touch.*

I was one of them.

*The doctors told my parents I'd fried my brain and given
up my ghost at the Glastonbury Festival. They were right,
sort of. But it wasn't the sex, the drugs, the booze, or the
music, vibrations opening fissures in my gut like pile driv-
ers in the ground. It was the place. It was the light. It was
time itself, full to running over.*

And now I'm a ghost, here in Glastonbury.

"So it's like automatic writing?" asked Magnus Anderson. "The whole Frederick Bligh Bond shtick, his digging
directed by some medieval monk from the great beyond?"

Anderson was a big man. His broad shoulders strained at
a military-style sweater, and tousled red hair brushed a high

forehead. A neatly trimmed goatee framed a rectangle of white teeth. He might have posed as a Danish or Norse berserker in a period tableau, except he held an electronic notepad instead of a broad ax.

Jane Thorne clasped her tatty vinyl portfolio to her chest, all too aware she was small, enveloped by her anorak, her mouse-brown hair held back from her mouse-sharp face by a scattering of clips. She knew she looked older than her fifty years. She didn't care.

What mattered was that she'd been told to talk to *The Paranormal Files,* and now Mr. Paranormal Files himself was looming over her, expecting her to do just that. She said, "It's not like automatic writing at all."

Anderson's coffee-brown eyes gazed not at her but at the ruined walls of Glastonbury Abbey, rising in stone scallops from green lawns now scattered with suitably symbolic fallen leaves. The chill breeze of autumn carried the damp earth and mildewed stone scent of a grave.

Jane tried to explain the unexplainable. "I suppose you could call Britney my spirit guide, except I've never claimed to be a medium."

"Britney?" He turned back to her. "So you've got some symbolic meaning going there? You know, Arthur, Avalon, the Matter of Britain?"

"I have no idea what *she*'s about, nor where *she* came from. *She* is, *she* was, an American, a countrywoman of yours, an artist and musician who died of her excesses at the Festival several years ago. *She* was trying to find her-self, I understand."

"A free spirit, huh?"

Jane stared.

"That's a joke." His smile spread into a grin and then contracted. "What's happening isn't funny. I get it. Sorry."

That it might be funny had never occurred to Jane. "I only know what she's, erm, told me. Although 'told' isn't the way of it, either." Her voice ran down. She looked at her shoes, scuffed canvas humped over clenched toes.

She felt rather than saw Anderson staring down at her from his commanding height, brows drawn, head cocked. Thinking, considering, evaluating, but not skeptical, even though skepticism was a necessary virtue, especially here in Glastonbury. Once she'd been a skeptic as well.

"So don't tell me. Show me." The stylus in his hand poised above the screen of his PDA like a tiny tongue eager to taste. Or to direct a bite.

"Very well. Here's a sample of my work." Jane opened the portfolio, and heavy sheets of vellum shifted restively in the wind. The black curves of the modified Carolingian minuscule lettering, the jewel-like colors of the diminutive paintings and decorated initials, contrasted with her small, stubby hands splashed with ink. She curled her fingers into her palm and protected her work with her fist.

"Nice." Anderson's stylus prodded a *P* filled with red and blue scales, its dangling tail a dragon's head. "'Preserve me, O God, for in you I put my trust.'"

"Psalm Sixteen. I'm working through them in order, one to one hundred and fifty. It will take more than a year, I expect."

"Look at it as steady employment." He lifted the top page and peered at the second. An arm graceful as a swan's neck emerged from a blue pool, brandishing a sword that shone with rays of gilded light. On the far bank stood a man, armored, helmeted, shielded, gauntleted except for his soft pink right hand held up and open toward the sword.

"'O my strength, hasten to help me. Deliver me from the sword . . .'" Anderson read. "But that's Arthur, right? He's supposed to get the sword."

"I left it ambiguous. It might be Arthur claiming the sword from the Lady of the Lake, or it might be Bedivere returning the sword to her. The Arthurian tales don't always fit the text of the Psalms as felicitously as I'd like. But since it is the conceit of my patron, Mr. Coburn, that the Psalms should be decorated with the tales of Arthur and of Glastonbury, I do my best to comply."

Anderson tapped out a cascade of ephemeral, pixilated letters on his tiny keypad. "I told Coburn I'd already done a story on Glastonbury for the *Files,* about how the terraces on the Tor might be an ancient labyrinth. What's your take on that?"

"It's possible. It's more possible than many things we take for granted. And less impossible than many things we do not."

"No kidding." His smile became more of a trapezoid. With a flourish, he closed his electronic assistant and tucked it into the pocket of his fashionable cargo pants. "Ms. Thorne. Jane." He towered like a cliff in the moments before a landslip. "When I said 'show me,' that's what I meant."

She'd known what he meant. She'd hoped to distract him with the manicured, signposted, theme-parked Abbey grounds, but he found that all too ordinary.

"My studio's just round the corner, then," she said, and walked toward the gate.

In her mind's eyes, the ones much keener than the ones behind her glasses, she saw the shapes of tall windows and arched buttresses rising through and above the ruins, sketched in something that was neither light nor shadow. Sketched in the smoke of the friction created when *her* eyes looked out through Jane's own.

She saw grave monuments rising like spectral mushrooms above the greensward, the solid bodies of tourists walking right through them. *She* saw the tiny wattle-and-daub church, solid behind and through the suddenly nebulous arcades of the Lady Chapel, a thousand years of stone insubstantial as a cloud.

Jane blinked and walked on. Those images might be no more than memories and imaginings. Anyone could imagine. The man walking behind her, he demanded more.

She threaded the modern pavements of the town a pace ahead of Anderson, sensing his presence at her back, warm and vital. Like one of King Alfred's Anglo-Saxon warriors, she thought, who defended Glastonbury from the Danish barbarians. Like one of Arthur's Romano-British warriors, before literature and tradition encased them in cold metal.

If Coburn had tried to protect her, Anderson would probably have pried the story from him and splashed it onto every television screen in Europe. But since Coburn meant to publicize his humility, Anderson was playing hard to get. If she couldn't prove to him that there was a story, perhaps he would go away and leave her alone with her work. Her opus, which was much more than a wealthy egocentric's conceit.

She led the man through streets where the Middle Ages collided with the New Age, Glastonian and Avalonian uneasily occupying the same space at the same time. Hippies, the newcomers had been called in Jane's childhood. Now the tourists and seekers and pilgrims, those playing at paganism and those rank with religion, they were all consumers at shops draped with crystals and plastic rosaries alike.

"Coburn says," said Anderson's voice behind her, like that of a demon on her shoulder, "he's going to send the Avalon Psalter on tour to libraries, museums, churches, and give the admission fees to charity. Yeah, right, that'll buy back the thousands of lives lost to the weapons he manufactured."

"In medieval times he'd have bought indulgences for the good of his soul. Now he pays for a handwritten and illustrated book of psalms."

"Less for the glory of God than for his own," Anderson said.

Jane couldn't help smiling. The man was more perceptive than she'd thought. "Yes."

"Nothing new about a rich man easing his guilty conscience with building a school or ordering a work of art and making sure everyone and his dog knows about it. I'm not sure what his angle is with this . . ." His voice paused, although Jane could still feel the slight vibration in the earth caused by the rise and fall of his booted feet. "This automatic painting thing of yours."

"It's not mine. I'd never have told anyone, but Mr. Coburn called in one day and couldn't be bothered to knock, and he caught a glimpse . . ." *Show me*, Anderson had said. For the sake of her livelihood, she would show him.

Jane opened a door wedged between a book shop and a bakeshop-cum-café, mounted the narrow stairs, and unlocked a plain white-painted door.

Her tiny studio was white-painted as well and would have been plain except for the reference prints she had tacked on the walls: *The Lindisfarne Gospels, The Book of Kells, The St. Albans Psalter, Les Tres Riche Heures du Duc de Barry*. Medieval miniatures, Doré engravings, Burne-Jones paintings of the stories of Arthur. And pages copied from the little psalter in the British Library that had been old in King Alfred's youth, when he'd made a pilgrimage to Rome.

Anderson stepped across the creaking floor to inspect the colors, patterns, swirls—the posters that once proclaimed psychedelia were bland compared to these. "Nice," he said again. "These pictures are your inspiration?"

"My models. My work is less inspiration than scholarship."

She set her portfolio on the floor beside the drawing board and opened the window. The southern light was harsher than she'd have liked, but the room had a view. At first she'd enjoyed the daily odor of baking bread and scones, until it no longer tantalized but sickened her. An artist needed more than bread to survive.

She'd never enjoyed the distant murmur of music from the book shop, the mock-Celtic wails of Enya and her ilk, the aimless noodlings of Yanni and his.

"What about these? Preliminary sketches?" Anderson indicated several sheets of paper tacked to one side, pencilled text in a variety of fonts decorated with sketches and maps.

"Those are my guesses as to the contents of Gildas' *On*

the Ruin of Britain, the most important history of the age of Arthur. It was lost like so many other books—Bede, Alcuin, the original of William of Malmesbury—when Henry VIII's iconoclasts brought down the Abbey and its library." She gazed out between a gable and a chimney, over the surrounding wall at the ruins, the broken walls wavering to her gaze like heat mirages. "They burned the choir stalls, they melted the roof for its lead, they mined the very stones from the walls. Terrible enough. But they destroyed the ancient books, the wisdom of the ages, the tale of the years. That, Mr. Anderson, was the worst of all. Not objects, but wisdom. Lost. All lost."

"Call me Magnus," he said. "Yeah, they burned the library at Alexandria, too."

Men ran to war and barbarism, then tried to make it up with art, Jane told herself and turned for solace to the shelves holding her quills and brushes. The compasses, dividers, set-squares, rulers, and templates, arranged in dutiful, responsible rows. Her paints and inks, painstakingly recreated from ancient recipes—orpiment, oak gall, kermes. She seemed to see the shapes rising from the jars, twining like branches, forming great ornamented windows, forming the apple orchards of Avalon . . .

"This place is like an alchemist's lair," said Anderson's voice, sounding as far away as the disconnected musical sounds from below.

She grasped at her own senses. "John Dee, Elizabeth the First's astrologer, said he found an alchemical book in the Abbey ruins."

"One that taught him how to transmute base metal into gold?"

"So he said, but he died poor." Arranging several jars beside her drawing board, Jane sat down. "To answer your question about Mr. Coburn's motive in sending you here, I expect he's found yet another way of publicizing his patronage. Of publicizing the work. It's of such significance that it touches another dimension. How amusing for him."

"We've already established it's not funny," Anderson said. "Listen, I've been chasing around woo-woo land for years. Artists, poets, musicians, paranormal hunters—we're all nuts. Loony."

"That's as may be, Mr. Anderson . . ."

"Magnus."

". . . but no one's ever accused me of being loony. Not until now."

"Sorry to hear that."

She stiffened. Despite his words, he still thought she was a joke, a bit of a giggle for his television program. The artist, the chemist, the scholar as laughingstock. Her work diminished.

"So how do you get in touch with your, ah, with Britney?"

"*She* gets in touch with me." Jane uncapped the jar of iron gall ink and picked up a quill.

If she couldn't prove the truth to Anderson, then she'd look a fool to him and insubordinate to Coburn. To preserve her livelihood, she had to go through with this charade. Whether Coburn's soul was saved in the process was none of her affair.

She glanced at her copy, a Bible propped open on the top of the shelf. It wasn't even the classic King James version of the text, no, Coburn bleated about accessibility to contemporary readers. She dipped the quill and touched it to the sheet of vellum already prepared, angled just so and faintly ruled. *You prepare a table before me . . .*

A slight stirring in the air, a sparkle, a warm breath. A lingering chord, sliding into disharmony.

She glanced up. Anderson perched on the sill in front of the half-open window. Outside a pigeon called.

She looked down again, and forced a breath into the armor of her rib cage. She could feel the man's gaze on the top of her head, like a beam of late afternoon sun.

. . . in the presence of my enemies.

A distant stir of voices, plainchant in orderly phrases

heard through ears not her own: *Parasti in conspectu meo mensam, adversus eos . . .*

Jane set down her quill and picked up a fine brush. Beside the text lay her preliminary pencil sketch, the ghost-like image of the round table with its circle of knights, names an incantation—Lancelot, Galahad, Bedivere, Gawain. Arthur. Guinevere. Delicately, she dipped and stroked, and a stripe of verdigris threaded the side of the table, indicating an embroidered cloth.

A shimmer in the air, sunlight through antique glass or vapor swirling above the spout of a tea kettle. And the flat flutter of *her* voice emerged from Jane's mouth, shaped by her own lips and tongue.

Green. My favorite color. Like the cozy blanket of sod on top of my grave.

Jane's shoulders jerked, but she held her hand steady. A painstaking process, correcting mistakes by scraping the vellum. Exert self-control, and make no mistakes.

Ooooh, who's the guy? Nice. I like.

Lancelot and his guilty passion for Guinevere, their betrayal, their shame—he became a monk at Glastonbury, she a nun at Amesbury, but she was buried here. The torches lighting his cell, her funeral procession, still flickered along the old Wells road.

Hi. I'm Britney.

Anderson spoke with the same flat accent, if slightly strangled. "Right. And I'm Tiny Tim."

Jane's hand gripped the brush, made another stroke of green. He'd wanted to see. But he wouldn't open his eyes. All he saw was a middle-aged scholar bent over a vellum sheet, recreating the passions of Arthur's court. Greed, hope, jealousy, love, none of them unique to a time or place.

Look.

An ephemeral hand, adorned with a ring shaped like a dragon, attached to an arm tattooed with interlaced motifs, Celtic and Anglo-Saxon both—the hand gestured toward the window.

Frowning, as though he caught something in his peripheral vision, Anderson turned and looked.

Against the gray eastern skies, Glastonbury Tor and its tower made a masculine exclamation point, aroused by the feminine curves of the countryside. It made a lance in the breast of the ancient earth goddess.

You can't see the Tor from the Abbey grounds, can you? Just the top of the Tower rising above Chalice Hill. What's up with that, huh?

Below dark, misty skies, torches moved along the ledges that made of the Tor a stepped pyramid. Torches carried in ephemeral hands, illuminating faces that shifted and slipped not with expressions but mortalities . . . And all were gone.

Still frowning, doubtful but not yet openly skeptical, Anderson looked back at Jane. "What did Coburn see when he walked in on you? Were you dancing around the drawing board or something?"

Jane released the brush, picked up another, dipped into her pot of pink. Like her purples, her pink tints were made from the fruit and flowers of the turnsole plant treated with alkaline. Not alchemy, chemistry.

Not fantasy, history.

If you see the Tor as her boob and Wearyall Hill as her leg, you know where the Abbey is? Yeah, right there, home plate itself. The Lady Chapel built over the original church, dedicated to Mary the Virgin. Yeah, that's a good story, all the x-rated stuff edited out.

"You've got American dialect down really well," Anderson said, "but then, you get a lot of American TV shows here."

Jane applied her brush to the lightly sketched hands of the knights, some splayed on the table, some holding cups. Holding chalices. And behind them she saw, like vapor gathered above the vellum, what Britney was seeing.

Chalice Well. The water's tinged with red. With iron, they say, not blood. Let's clean it all up, stick in some fable about Joseph of Arimathea bringing Jesus' blood in a chalice, Arthur's knights whacking off arms and legs and then chasing after the Grail. Whoop-de-do, nothing to do with a woman's blood, nothing at all. The well's been there forever, probably eroded the Tor to begin with, and the monks channeled it down to the Abbey, the anatomically correct place for it. Where the clear well opens the earth itself, beneath the Lady Chapel.

Her tongue caught between her teeth, Jane used a brush made of only a few hairs to trace bits of heraldic business on the knights' tabards, symbols anachronistic to the true Arthur but which had now become irrevocably wedded to the stories, stories to be taken seriously if not literally . . . A Tudor rose. A lion of Scotland. An Irish harp. Dragons, fleurs de lis.

And the letters, black against the creamy vellum, the greatest symbols of all, dismissed by the ignorant and destroyed by the iconoclast.

I can see them, you know. The Roman soldiers drinking from the Lady well and griping about being so far from home. The monks in those poky little buildings on the Tor.

Henry's thugs murdering the last abbot. The powdered-wig crowd taking the waters at Chalk well, Chilkwell, Chalice well. You think people come and go like leaves in the fall, but they're still here, Dunstan with a nose like an ax and Leland checking out the library and Bligh Bond putting way the hell too much trust in a monk who'd never seen the world outside his scriptorium.

"Jane?" Anderson stood up. The floor creaked beneath his weight. "Earth to Jane."

The plainchant ebbed from her senses. Other voices swelled, women shrieking, men shouting, horses neighing, the crackle of flames. Her eyes burned from staring at the page, from the smoke, and she blinked.

What? You got a problem with this? Isn't this what you wanted? The woo-woo stuff?

His hand pulled the brush from her trembling fingers and set it down.

Jane clasped her hands before her chin, in an attitude of prayer, willing them to stop shaking. Willing her head to stop spinning. She closed her eyes but behind her lids torches still moved, sparks dancing above the burning books.

"Okay, okay, I'll concede the point. You're channeling some spirit." Strong fingers grasped her shoulders, pressing her thin flesh almost to the bone. "The café downstairs does cream teas, doesn't it? I've never met a woman yet who couldn't be calmed down with butterfat. My treat."

Milk. Butter. Cream. England's green and pleasant land, producing milk and honey.

"Thank you," Jane said, her own cultured voice issuing from dry lips. "I'd quite like a cuppa just now."

Taking her elbow, Anderson walked her to the door and down the stairs.

Jane dabbed her lips with the napkin, cleansing them of the last remnants of sugar and rich, oily cream.

Yea, though I walk through the valley of the shadow of death, I will fear no evil, she thought. Jane Thorne said to herself, freely, unpossessed. *Thou preparest a table before me in the presence of mine enemies.*

Across the tiny table, Anderson plastered the last bite of his scone with butter, a small cloud of clotted cream, and strawberry jam red as blood. He wasn't her enemy.

He licked his lips. "Beats the heck out of sushi."

"I wouldn't know. I've never eaten sushi."

"The medieval monks kept fish farms, didn't they? At one time Glastonbury was almost an island, surrounded by streams and marshes?"

"Yes." Jane saw the Lady of the Lake's arm rising from the water, and Arthur borne away on a barge by weeping women, to be healed on the Isle of Avalon.

Anderson lowered his rumble of a voice, so like *hers,* so unlike. "Is that what Coburn saw, you not just sitting and painting, but speaking in tongues and drawing in, well, fingers, I guess."

"*She* doesn't draw. She only—annoys me when I begin to draw."

"Why?"

"Why what?"

"I've been chasing around the UK for a couple of years now, tracking weird things. Until recently I would've staked my flat, my car, and my Rolex on it all being bogus up one side and down the other. Not necessarily intentionally. People do see the Loch Ness monster on the way home from the pub. But recently . . ." His brows drew down, and his head cocked. He waved his hand, not dismissing something but setting it aside. "I've become a believer."

"A believer in what?"

"Woo-woo. The paranormal. Things that go bump in the night. And in broad daylight in an artist's studio."

Jane knotted her hands in her lap, below the edge of the

table where he couldn't see them. The scones and cream turned to lead in her stomach. "You mean to have me on your program, then."

"No way, José."

She looked up. "No?"

"I mean, yeah, my crew could wave the camera around and set up some lights for that funny shimmer and maybe dissolve from the pictures to the ruins or the Tor or something. We could set up an echo chamber and read out the Psalm you're working on, even dub in a track from one of those monastery CDs that were popular several years ago. But, basically, there's just not enough there to keep the customer's attention."

"Well, no . . ." Opening her hands, she pressed them against her stomach, easing the weight.

"Besides, I'd have to start off by explaining what a Psalter is, and that's a killer. You want a lecture, you tune in Open University." His dark eyes were dancing. He knew how relieved she was. "But, just for my own curiosity, let's get back to why."

"Why is this, this degenerate, this wanton—this lost soul—why is *she* haunting me?"

There was the rectangular smile again, hemmed by courtesy. Inside, she was sure, he was laughing at her. "Opposites attract, yeah, but there's more to it than that. There's a reason this is happening to you. And don't give me some guff about her wanting to corrupt you or something like that."

Yes, that was too easy an explanation. But then . . . "Very well. If you, Mr. Anderson, don't hand me any rubbish about *her* ridding me of my inhibitions."

"Deal," he said. "And it's Magnus."

Around them the consumers came and went, dressed in T-shirts and football jerseys. Once the consumers wore corsets and long skirts, or corselets and tunics. They were barbarians, thought Jane, hunting and gathering. Avalonian seekers. Glastonians living by bread alone.

"Either Coburn's bright idea of combining the traditions

of Glastonbury or your execution of it broke something open," Anderson went on.

She had illustrated Psalm Two—*you shall dash them to pieces like a potter's vessel. Therefore be wise, be instructed*—with scenes of the young Arthur at Merlin's feet, learning to read and write the lore of his forefathers.

"Was it Coburn's idea?" Anderson asked. "Or were you just polite to the guy who writes the checks?"

She raised her hands and splayed them on the table. The fingernails were short, unpolished, their cuticles crescents of ink and paint. A callus thickened her forefinger. "I made a few suggestions."

"Okay then. Maybe it's not that Britney's haunting you, it's that you called her."

"I called her?" Jane scowled. "*She* wants something from me."

"Or do you want something from her?"

"She's trying to keep me from my work."

"I don't think so." He was no longer smiling. He wasn't teasing her. "Not if she only—appears, manifests, whatever—when you start working."

"Ah." There was that.

"How about," Anderson asked, "instead of wanting something from her, you want something through her?"

"What could I possibly . . . ?"

"What matters to you? Your work, right?"

The weight in Jane's stomach dissolved, trickled like quicksilver through her limbs, and flared so brightly across her mind it cast shadows. The work. The opus. The little psalter from the British Library and more, the lost Library of Glastonbury. She opened her mouth, swallowed, and spoke. "*She* says they're all still here."

"Arthur? The monks?"

"The books. Gildas, Bede, Alcuin. They're still here."

Anderson's eyes, the color of lamp black mixed with red ochre, didn't blink.

"With *her* help . . ." A crumb stuck in Jane's throat and

she coughed. "With her help, I can get them back. One word at a time. One illustration at a time. I can recreate *On the Ruin of Britain* and Dunstan's alchemical work and so many others. It will take years, I expect."

"Look at it as . . ."

"It's not steady employment at all, Mr. Anderson. I'd be entirely on my own. Who would fund such a task?"

"Call me . . . Never mind." Anderson shook his head. "Try Coburn. Or get him to recommend one of his billionaire buddies. Like I was saying, rich guys love to pay for public works of one kind or another. Makes them feel good about themselves."

"But how could I reveal my source of information? No one would believe me. Everyone would laugh at me."

"Not everyone. The gullibility of the public's been lining my pockets for years now."

"I beg your . . . ," Jane began indignantly.

"Joking," he said, raising his hands in surrender. "Seriously. Don't tell them about your source. Tell them you extrapolated your recreations from your studies."

"Then it would hardly be authentic."

Anderson rolled his eyes. "Jane, these days 'authentic' is just another marketing buzzword."

"But . . ."

"So your work is more inspiration than scholarship. Even scholars need a kick in the pants from the muse every now and then."

Jane stared at him. The muse, she thought. Clio, the muse of history. A far and desperate cry from an American spirit. And from an American television personality.

"She doesn't channel through the baker there, when he kneads his bread. Or through the guy up the street when he shuffles his tarot cards. She chose you."

"Chose?"

"Found you, then. Because of what you know and who you are." He leaned back with a shrug of his massive shoulders. "Maybe she's like one of Dickens' spirits, looking for some way to be useful. Maybe she's not lost at all—any more than you are. Give the girl a chance, huh?"

"Ah," Jane said again. Her fingers tingled and her tongue felt supple and warm. A chance. That was all she herself had ever asked, a chance to prove her skills and her knowledge, so that she would be taken seriously, if not literally.

Some evenings, as she walked to her rented room, her clothing mottled with many colors and her head teeming with phrase and design, some evenings she saw the setting sun gleam briefly through the door piercing the tower atop the Tor. How like the eye of a needle, she'd thought more than once, a very small eye, difficult to thread. But the smallest of her brushes were fine as threads, if never as fine as the vessels of her own body, nerve and capillary and tendon.

Perhaps Britney was less a muse than a fate, spinning out Jane's life.

So be it.

Pushing back her chair, Jane stood up. "Well, then. I must be off. I have work to do. Thank you for tea."

"You're very welcome. My pleasure." He rose, grinning. His beard formed the shape of a knight's shield around his teeth. Around his mouth, that spoke such clever words. "Keep in touch, okay? Let me know when the Avalon Psalter's finished—maybe I'll have branched out into documentaries by then. Let me know how you and Britney are doing with recreating the library."

She peered up at him. No, he wasn't joking. "I'll do what I can."

His strong, solid fingers captured her small plain hand and lifted it upward. With a chivalrous bow, he passed his warm lips across her flesh. And then he released her. "Bye."

Folding that hand inside her other one, she turned aside and walked toward the door and the staircase upward. But not without throwing a few last words over her shoulder. "This has been a most interesting meeting. Good afternoon, Magnus."

Behind her, she heard him laugh.

• • •

The afternoon sun illuminated her studio. Each print on the wall glowed as if it were newly painted in colors from her own pots. The air was scented with car exhaust, and garbage, and an elusive hint of incense. From the book shop below came the sound of choristers singing a medieval hymn, clear young voices enunciating an ancient language, slicing her senses like a scalpel.

Jane's quill traced the last vertical stroke of the line: *You anoint my head with oil; my cup runs over.*

Taking several small brushes, she drew the gold and silver dishes scattered across the surface of the Round Table, across the embroidered cloth. Butter in yellow orpiment. Berries in lapis lazuli. Wine in crimson kermes.

A shape stirred in the sunbeams, more than dust, less than body. A voice caressed Jane's own lips, the way Magnus' lips had touched her hand.

When the abbot served dinner, an army sat down. There were musicians playing little skin drums and gut-strung harps. There were children playing hide-and-seek in the shadows. The walls, they were built to define the space, not close anyone out.

"And it's all still here?" murmured Jane's own voice.

Oh yeah. It's all here.

"You mentioned John Leland. When he visited the library in the 1530s, just before—before the end."

Oh yeah. Little guy, standing just inside a huge wooden door, sniffing the smell of leather and old wood and dust, and beans from the abbot's kitchen, like it was perfume or something.

Jane's inhalation was more of a gasp. She closed her eyes against mounting vertigo, as though she stood atop the Tor and looked down on the surrounding countryside, stretching in patches of green and yellow toward the faint glimmer of the sea. Her hand kept moving, touching Arthur's throne with gold.

His eyes were bugged out, and he was wheezing like he was going to fall down on the spot. But I guess you'd act like that, too, if you walked into the old library.

Jane surprised herself with a smile. "And what book did he look at first? One of the liturgical books, chained to its shelf?"

Historia Regum Britanniae. *History-something, right? Whoa, great cover, all gold and jewels.*

Jane's breath caught in her throat. Geoffrey of Mon-2mouth's *The History of the Kings of Britain*, encompassing some of the earliest stories of Arthur.

She dabbled Arthur's crown with gold, and with her smallest brush pressed dots of jewel-like color onto it. Like the gilded and jeweled covers of the library's heirloom books, preserved through the centuries. And yet the matter inside the covers, beneath the crown, that matter was more precious than any jewel.

"Show me," she said to that subtle shimmer in the air, the ghost standing just at the edge of her peripheral vision. At the edge of John Leland's peripheral vision.

And like vapor in the air, the pages opened before her eyes as they had opened for Leland.

"Show me," Jane repeated. "Show me what's still here, in Glastonbury."

SHADOWS IN THE MIRRORS

Bradley P. Beaulieu

When Julie saw the booth of charcoal drawings, she waved to her sister to go on ahead, telling her she'd catch up. Nicole looked at her with that infuriating mixture of concern and encouragement, the one that had so often been pasted on her face since Julie had been released from the hospital. It made Julie want to scream.

"I'll *catch up*," she repeated, and finally Nicole waved and moved on to the next booth in the art show.

Julie turned to the charcoals—portraits, invariably, of young girls. Their ages varied from three to seven, and all of them were standing rigidly in the center of the frame with expressions ranging from discomfort to outright fear. If they could have shivered, they would have.

Why anyone would want to draw or buy such trash was beyond Julie, though she had to admit they commanded a certain amount of attention, like being unable to draw your gaze from Iggy Pop rolling around a stage covered in broken glass.

"You like them?"

Julie turned to find a serious looking thirtysomething man with tribal tattoos running the length of his arms. More tattoos trailed down the sides of his bald head, along his neck, and beneath his black tee. Everything about him shouted at her like an accusation—everything but his eyes, which were soft, like those of a callow teenager who'd gotten himself into something deeper than he should have.

"Not really," Julie said.

He barked out a laugh. "Could've fooled me."

She tried to smile politely but was sure it came out more like a grimace. "Why children?"

"Because they're honest."

Julie considered the drawing in front of her. "Honest means children ready to slit their wrists?"

"Some children do, you know."

Asshole, Julie thought. "Some, sure, but I think you *like* them like this."

"What, you're saying I should turn a blind eye to the pain in the world, act like everyone else and just ignore it?" He jutted his chin and shook his head as though he'd encountered people just like Julie a million times before. "That's not me, honey, and that's not my artwork. You don't like it, there's plenty of happy people producing nice, safe artwork."

Julie frowned. She was ready to leave and find Nicole, but one picture near the main row running through the center of the massive tent stopped her in her tracks.

Her world shrank. The murmur of the art crowd fell away, replaced by a loud ringing in her ears. Even the light filtering in from the cloud-covered sky seemed to dim, for within that rusted metal frame, within that sea of subtle gray shades, sat Adelaide. Her daughter.

The analytical part of Julie's mind told her she was imagining the similarities. But her heart refused to believe that. Adelaide *had* been her daughter.

Hadn't she?

It was so difficult to tell since the year in the hospital, the drugs and therapy, the pills she popped every morning.

The back of Adelaide's head occupied the lower third of the piece. She was staring into a mirror, which showed her face against the backdrop of a heavily shadowed room. A doorway stood open behind her, revealing a hallway with a tilted lightbulb hanging by frayed wires. Adelaide looked as if she dearly wished she could run but had given up all hope of doing so.

Julie turned away, willing herself to leave, but her feet were rooted to the spot. A bitter wind filtered through the art show's tent, while the milling crowd moved around her as if she were no one, as if she had vanished right along with Adelaide.

The prick of an artist was talking with two women. They laughed flirtatiously, and one of them gave his muscled forearm a quick squeeze. He glanced at Julie, and then did a double take, perhaps noticing Julie's expression, perhaps realizing which drawing she was standing in front of. He looked from the drawing to Julie several times, then his eyes ran down Julie—not sexually, but appraisingly, as if she were a threat he hadn't counted on.

Then he turned back to his groupies.

And Julie could breathe again. She blinked away tears and made sure her sister, Nicole, wasn't nearby before turning back to the piece.

The expression on Adelaide's face was more desperate than she'd ever seen a child look. To see it on her daughter made her want to rip the drawing to shreds.

Once again, Julie found herself warring with emotions and memories that told her she had a daughter and the relentless words of her therapist that told her she did not. Most of the time she believed what the doctor told her, but at times like this, when she was standing face-to-face with her most cherished memories, she *knew* she had mothered a child and that Adelaide had been ripped out of her life over a year ago. How it was that no one knew her daughter— even her family and her ex—she couldn't explain. She didn't care anymore. All she cared about was Adelaide.

And then Julie saw the details she hadn't noticed before. In the corners of the room, nearly out of sight, were the smiling faces of *them*. Little eyes, completely black. Tight smiles with the barest hint of black lips. Teeth, pointed and sharp. Arms impossibly thin. The Others, Julie called them, just as she'd seen them in the weeks leading up to her daughter's abduction.

At the bottom edge of the frame, hanging from a loop of white thread, was a salmon-colored tag. Twenty-five hundred dollars, it said.

Julie found herself stepping backward, as if a price had just been laid upon her daughter's life. She felt herself bump into someone, and without looking to see who, she turned and ran from the tent into the chill autumn wind. The rain had picked up again, and it was pattering against the asphalt walkway leading back to the museum.

"Julie?"

No, not Nicole. Not now.

Julie could feel their eyes upon her now that she'd seen them in the painting. They were there in the shadows, in the glass of the cars whipping along Lake Front Road, in the tall glass of the museum's facade, in the reflection off the glasses of the bald man staring at her with a look of revulsion and pity. She ran to the lakefront, where the concrete patio ended in a black metal railing and a sheer drop down to the broken concrete breakwater. She stood there, breathless, gripping the railing and staring out at the churning waves of the lake. Then, knowing she'd never be able to resist, she looked down at the shallow puddle she was standing in.

She could see herself, see the billowy clouds above her. And at the edges, wavering as the rain pummeled the puddle, she could see them, watching. And laughing.

Julie received only the briefest of warnings before her lunch burned its way up her throat and pattered against the wet concrete.

The rest of that day and into the night, Julie was careful not to let on. She told Nicole it was only a case of lactose intolerance.

Nicole, ready to head out for work, wrapped the fluffy scarf around her neck and cinched her wool coat over her nurse's uniform. "You sure? I can call in." She looked completely unconvinced, but they both knew how much they needed Nicole's paycheck, and Nicole's boss had made it clear she'd been calling in quite enough, thank you.

"I'll be fine."

Nicole stared doubtfully for a few moments, but then she pasted on her big sister smile and headed out the door.

A few minutes later, when she was sure Nicole wasn't coming back, Julie left. She dropped by the local coffee house and bought Internet time—Nicole felt the Internet wasn't "conducive to full recovery" and so wouldn't allow access at home—to find out more about the artist.

His name was Kane Reynolds, she remembered from the wrought-iron plaque above his booth. The first thing she came across was an exposé, an attempt to discredit him by revealing his technique of using the ash from human bodies to create the sticks of charcoal he used for his works, but it had served only to make people flock to him, to the point that he'd requested no one else donate their bodies. He had enough for decades of artwork, he said.

Julie exhaled noisily, drawing curious looks from the two gay guys sitting at the next table sipping from their huge mugs of black coffee. She ignored them and stared in disbelief at the two-story redbrick building Kane Reynolds now called his home. A fucking morgue.

There were at least a dozen sites that claimed to be dedicated to Kane's artwork; *I'm Kane's number one fan* they all claimed. Like Adelaide's drawing, the children were always shown in a reflection of some sort—most in mirrors, but some in puddles, others in a vacant store window. Nearly all of them were young—roughly three to five years old—and the few that were older, she realized with a sinking feeling, were of the same children as previous portraits, as if he'd somehow captured them again and again over the years.

Laidey's little hand presses against mine, so warm and soft, so tiny. I grip her forearm gently and rub her skin with my thumb. So soft . . .

Would Kane do the same thing to Adelaide? Draw her once she'd had a chance to live through a personal hell for another year or two?

And then she saw it.

At an art show in New Orleans, Kane had debuted five new drawings plus seven that had never been seen by the public. The cover for his flyer was Adelaide, five years old in the picture. According to the caption, the drawing was only three months old.

Julie couldn't take her eyes off the picture. Adelaide's eyes were sunken and dark. Her lips were tense and her chin was lifted, as if she were on the near edge of crying. Her expression spoke of terror, but also of loneliness and an underlying fatigue, as if she'd nearly given up.

She looked so different from the Adelaide in Julie's head that she started to question herself. Was this girl really her daughter? Or was this an extension of the fiction she'd created for herself—born, as the doctors saw fit to tell her over and over, from some deep-seated desire to have a child when she knew she couldn't? The debate raged within her for hours, but she kept coming back to what she felt in her heart. She *knew* she'd had a daughter. She *knew* it. What she didn't know was how she had been taken away.

But Kane Reyolds sure as hell did.

She left the coffee shop and took a cab to Kane's studio at 311 East Main. There were no lights on. She snuck around to the rear of the building, where an alley ran north to south. A light rain began to patter against the concrete as she tried to open each of the three ground-floor windows in turn. Locked, as was the metal door. But there was a fire escape leading to the second floor and up to the roof. Her heart beat faster as she climbed on one of the nearby garbage cans to pull at the fire escape's ladder. It clattered down and crashed into the garbage can, knocking her to the ground and scraping her knee against the concrete.

She sat there gripping her bleeding leg and listening for any sound of discovery, but no lights turned on and no calls of surprise or anger or anything else came from the surrounding buildings.

After wiping away the dirt and blood, she climbed up the ladder and checked the second-story window. She couldn't see a thing—it looked as though it had been spray painted black from the inside—but something still felt terribly wrong. The window made Julie feel the same way she did as when the Others were watching her, as if tarot cards had just been laid out before her and she had no idea how to read them. She felt sick to her stomach yet so full of possibilities it made her dizzy with fear.

The window was locked, and although her fear was screaming at her not to, she tried to force the lock but she wasn't strong enough. The rain began to beat harder. With the sound of the rain so loud, she debated on kicking in the window, but just then an old black Eldorado slipped into the alley.

Julie's heart raced. Her knuckles turned bone white as her hands gripped the ladder rungs. She made herself small and pushed herself against the bricks as the car rolled to a stop. The driver's door opened, and Kane stepped out. He was wearing a black trench coat, only partially buttoned up against the rain. He moved to the trunk and, after a scan up and down the alley, opened it. He hoisted a black body bag over his shoulder with practiced ease, slammed the trunk closed, and headed into the morgue through the alley door.

The door closed with a heavy thud, and then Julie was left with the cold rain beating down on her and the sinking feeling she'd made a big mistake. She couldn't move. One step on the ladder and Kane was going to hear her. He would come out with a bat or a gun, and that would be the end of Julie's foolish and useless life.

She shivered as light filtered through the window just

next to her. The paint was thick in most spots, but there were several scratch marks that allowed her to see into the room if she pressed her face up to the glass. Vertigo struck Julie full-on. She knew it had something to do with this place—the morgue or perhaps this room in particular. She also knew she couldn't do a thing about it but suck it up and persevere.

The room inside was huge. It must have taken up half of the second floor. Several gurneys littered the center of the room. On the left, occupying the entire wall, was a cold, brushed steel matrix of body vaults, all of them closed except one.

Kane was near the center, and he'd set down the black body bag on one of the gurneys. He took off his dripping trench coat and threw it over an ancient swivel chair and then removed a gun in a shoulder holster and set it on the nearby desk. The gun looked as though it could blow a hole through a concrete wall.

Julie gasped as Kane unzipped the bag. Inside was a three-year-old girl wearing a pink dress and white tights. One shoe was missing. She looked nothing like Adelaide, but all Julie could see was her baby girl lying on that gurney, waiting for whatever sick thing Kane Reynolds was about to do to her.

Kane picked the girl up and deposited her onto the readied vault bed. And with that he pushed the bed home and secured the door. He threw on his trench coat and left immediately after, his Eldorado rumbling down the alley and then losing itself somewhere in the city.

Julie remained where she was for long moments, the smaller part of her wanting to leave, to save herself.

I tuck Laidey in for the night. Laidey is so sleepy, but she never forgets to pull off the blanket I'd laid over her. She doesn't stand for blankets.

She couldn't leave. She needed to help that girl.

She tried forcing the window again. No good.

Julie stood and kicked the window. It held tight. She

tried again and again, and on the fourth try it finally gave. The glass blew inward and a shrill sucking sound accompanied an almighty pull at Julie's torso. She was sucked right into the shattering window frame.

In that short flight down to the floor, all those possibilities wrapped into the windowpane coalesced into one, and suddenly the sick feeling at the pit of her stomach was gone.

Julie landed hard. She got up on her hands and knees, unable to breathe for several terrifying seconds. And then, blessedly, breath came in a long, stuttering gasp.

She stood as quickly as she was able, only then realizing her wrists and palms were bleeding. She worked the glass out of them and felt her way forward to the light switch Kane had used before leaving. She flipped it. She stood right next to the desk, right next to the gun Kane had left behind. The dangerous part of his work must be over, Julie thought, but *hers* had just begun.

She took the gun from the holster and moved to the wall of vaults on the far side of the room, scared shitless Kane was going to come walking in at any moment.

She opened the vault where the girl had been placed.

Julie swallowed.

The bed was empty. She stuffed the gun into her coat pocket and tried another. And another. All of them were empty. Every single one.

Despite her better judgment, she remained for nearly an hour, half hoping that Kane would show up so she could question him. But at the edge of perception, she heard a thousand tiny mouths snickering, and she thought for certain she was imagining the whole thing—Kane, the girl, even the gun she was holding.

She finally left Kane's home as the sun was brightening the eastern sky. The analytical part of her mind told her that Dr. Thierry was right—that she had never had a child and that she was suffering from some grand delusion—but the image of that little girl getting filed away like some useless government document wouldn't allow itself to be forgotten.

Julie picked up a quart of whiskey before heading home. Safe in her bedroom, she tried real hard to avoid drinking it, but the girl in the vault, sliding home over and over and over . . . She drank most of it before passing out. She didn't care if Nicole found her like this or not.

Nicole didn't say anything about the alcohol the next day. She only asked about the blood on Julie's knee.

Julie smiled. "Went out for a walk. You know how clumsy I am."

Nicole nodded and went back to her crossword.

Julie felt as though she'd been given a small reprieve. Nicole from six months ago would have hounded Julie until she'd had the entire story.

Julie stared at her sister, at the way she chewed her toast and cream cheese, picking through the puzzle as if nothing were the matter, and it struck Julie how much they had lost because of Adelaide, because of Julie's delusions. Julie found herself unsure which disturbed her more, Nicole's growing apathy or her own.

Julie took to following Kane whenever Nicole wasn't around. He took his Caddie mostly, but now and again he would take a drawing pad and walk the city. He never drew, though. He just walked, taking his time, sometimes standing in the same place for minutes on end with his eyes closed, but then he would move on as though nothing out of the ordinary had happened.

But on the seventh day after Julie had broken into Kane's home, something strange happened. He stopped at a small-ish park and sat on a bench, watching traffic along a street populated by hip antique and clothing stores. It struck Julie as odd since he always seemed wrapped up in his own world. To stop and interact with the world around him, in any small way, struck Julie as odd.

She stood behind a row of evergreen bushes, her right
hand in her coat pocket, gripping the revolver she'd stolen
from Kane's place. She had debated about whether she
should drop the gun into a trash can, but the simple fact was
that it gave her confidence, something she dearly needed.

A recess bell rang behind Julie, and she turned to see a
kindergarten class stream out from the small school and in-
vade the playground that sat between Julie and Kane. She
watched as the twenty children slipped into their play of
hopscotch and four square and freeze tag as if class had
never happened.

Kane had been sitting there, almost motionless for over
an hour, but now he took out his pad and began to draw.
Julie looked at the children, then at Kane. He was still facing the traffic and the stores. Why now? Why wait to draw
some street scene until the children were present?

Then the sun reflected off a passing red pickup truck,
and it hit Julie. The glass in the storefronts. From Kane's
vantage, he could easily see the children playing. He was
drawing them, and Julie couldn't help but wonder if he had
drawn Adelaide like this before he'd taken her. He must
have.

She moved her right hand to her pocket and grasped the
gun, then strolled along the edge of the park, watching
Kane and the children, both.

*Laidey runs to a puddle, stomps on it, and laughs. By the
time I reach her, she is so wet I jump in the puddle, too.
Both of us giggle for minutes on end, drenching one another.*

Julie suddenly realized who Kane was drawing.

In the reflection of the shop windows she could see a girl
sitting alone on the concrete stairs surrounding a fountain.
She was leaning over her legs as if she had a tummy ache,
and her curly auburn hair fell over and around her face.
None of the children were playing with her, and though the
teachers seemed to glance at her now and again, they otherwise left her alone.

Julie moved beyond the tree blocking her view, hoping to get a decent look at the girl's face, but the fountain was empty. Julie looked back at the store windows—there she was, her head still between her knees. The girl jerked her head to one side, as if something had startled her, and then she hid herself between her knees once more.

Julie had seen enough. She marched forward—utterly confused yet totally committed—and placed herself between Kane and his shop windows. Even though the drawing was upside down, it was clearly a picture of the girl. There was something else there, too—a thin form towering over her. More than that she couldn't tell, because when Kane realized she was standing there, he closed his drawing pad with an audible snap and set it on the bench next to him.

He looked up at her, and a moment later, recognition came. "You were at my show. Downtown."

Julie gripped the revolver more tightly, ready to draw it out if he made any sudden moves, then she pulled out the flyer cover she'd printed up at the coffee shop. "How do you know this girl?"

His expression flattened, as if he knew what sort of person he was dealing with now. "I don't."

"Bull fucking shit." She shook the paper at him. "This is my daughter. She was taken from me over a year ago. And now she shows up on the cover of your flyer. I need you to tell me where she is, and I need you to tell me now."

Kane stood and began gathering his stuff into a ratty green courier's bag. "This isn't the time, lady."

Before Julie could think, before she could talk herself out of it, she stepped forward and pressed the barrel of the pistol against his rib cage.

Kane froze.

"Don't make me use it. I've lost her already, and I don't give a shit what happens to me as long as I take you out."

Julie backed off and put the gun back in her coat pocket but kept it trained on Kane. He inched upward and glanced into the shop window.

"Don't you look at her," Julie said, realizing he was watching the girl again.

He paused. "You can see her?"

"Yes."

"Then you should be able to tell she's in trouble."

Julie didn't say a word. She couldn't. She had no idea what he was talking about.

He pointed slowly over Julie's shoulder. "Look."

Julie stepped back to a safe distance and spared one quick glance. The girl was staring straight at her—no, straight at *Kane*—with a look of outright terror and desperation.

"That's Theresa Hernandez. She's already gone, but I'm trying to get her back."

"Like that girl in the morgue?"

For the first time, Kane seemed unsure of himself. He stared down at her coat pocket. "You were the one who broke into my house."

"And I saw what you did. I don't know how you made her disappear, but I'm not letting you do it anymore."

"Listen, we need to talk"—he glanced in the window again—"just not now." He shuffled backward, ready to turn and run.

"Don't take another step."

"Please, it's almost too late." He took another step backward. "I need to save her."

At the school a half-block away, the recess bell rang.

Kane turned and ran toward the fountain.

"Stop!" Julie yelled. She pointed the revolver at him. "Stop!"

He didn't.

Julie couldn't let him go. He was a liar and a predator, and she wasn't going to let what happened to Adelaide happen to this girl.

She squeezed the trigger.

Her right arm jolted from the recoil as the sound of the firearm filled the park and echoed among the buildings. The sound of traffic and wind and pedestrians and children ceased momentarily.

And then all was chaos.

The children began screaming and running. The teachers shouted and herded the children toward the school. A light blue Fiat ran a red light, clipping a VW Bug. Two women carrying yellow bags from the vintage clothing store stared Julie full in the face, then sprinted in the other direction.

Kane was on the ground, facedown, ten yards from the fountain. A pool of blood inched outward from beneath him.

Julie turned and viewed the reflection in the shop window. Her fingers shook and she dropped the gun into her pocket before her fingers failed her completely.

The girl was still sitting there, as she was before—her knees pulled up to her chest, her head resting on her legs—but now Julie could see the shadow standing above her, the one Kane had been drawing. It was a frail and deadly thing, and it had the smile of a Cheshire cat. It was pleased at what she had done, though how she knew this she couldn't guess.

Someone was shouting. She ignored it.

She turned back to the real fountain. It was empty, as she had known it would be, but she could feel the shadow standing there, if not the girl.

The pool of blood around Kane's midsection was building. Sirens rang in the distance, obscured by the returning sound of traffic.

What had she done? Had she just caused another girl to be abducted, to be forgotten by everyone who had ever loved her? Had Kane really been trying to help her?

Only then did the magnitude of her mistake strike her. She might have condemned not just Adelaide but another girl as well to some living hell in another world.

As the sirens came closer, Julie turned and fled.

When Julie opened the door to her apartment, she shivered at the form sitting at the dining room table, belatedly realizing it was Nicole. The harsh fluorescent light above the table made her look like a cadaver.

"Hey," Julie said, trying to look calm.

She had wandered the city for a long, long while, telling herself over and over she needed to rid herself of the gun. She couldn't, though. It felt much too powerful, and so she'd kept it in her pocket like a talisman, her magical charm, proof against all that assailed her. Now that seemed like an eminently foolish decision, especially because it felt as though Nicole were staring at her pocket, but there was nothing she could do about it.

"What'd you do today?" Nicole asked.

Julie's gut twisted. She didn't trust herself enough to sit without something to occupy her hands, so she went to the kitchen and poured herself a glass of Odwalla. "Wandered the city."

"Where?"

"Here and there. East Side mostly." Julie sat and took a healthy swig. It tasted sour, but she swallowed it anyway. "Just wanted to visit the old neighborhood, you know?"

A yellow sticky was stuck to the clear glass table next to Nicole's elbow. She picked it up and turned it to face Julie. *Dr. Thierry, 3pm Thurs.*

Fuck.

"I'm sorry, Nickie."

"I'm working two shifts already, Julie. I can't be on top of you every minute of the day."

"I'm *sorry.*"

"Sorry doesn't cut it. Not anymore. You promised me—"

"I'll go next—"

"Don't interrupt! You promised you'd keep all your appointments when I agreed to take you in. It was part of the agreement with the hospital—you know that—and it reflects on *me,* Julie, not you." She leaned back in her chair, her eyelids heavy, her expression regretful. "I'm more to blame than you are. I barely talked to you after the museum. And your binge last week . . ."

"Nicole . . ."

"I didn't want to rock the boat. But that's what I did when you were first starting to get sick. I let it go. I hoped it would go away. But I'm not going to do it anymore, Julie. I'll let you go back to the hospital before I see you go through the same thing as last time."

"It's not like that." Julie was having trouble controlling her breathing.

Nicole shook her head. "It's exactly like that." She raised her hand before Julie could speak again. "One more slip, Julie, and I'm going to recommend to Dr. Thierry that you be readmitted."

A heavy silence settled between them, the only sound Julie's rapid breath.

"Understand? No more missed appointments. No more slipping to the coffee shop when I'm gone. No more alcohol."

Julie forced herself to take a drink from her glass. The thick liquid nearly came right back up. Nicole continued to watch until Julie had given her an unsteady nod of her head.

"Good. Now I'm going to catch a few hours of sleep before I have to head in again." She stood, walked behind Julie, and gripped her shoulder in an affectionate squeeze. "Don't wake me, for anything."

After Nicole had gone to bed, all was silent except for the faint sounds of traffic filtering into their fifth-floor apartment. Julie moved to the couch and sat, facing the window. Outside, the night sky was cloudless, leaving the amber cityscape a mere afterthought. She hadn't realized it, but this was the point she had feared the most—not the police, not Nicole, but the point at which she would find herself alone once more. In front of a mirrored surface.

She knew minutes after she'd fled from the park that she would have to experiment, would have to try to do what Kane did, see the girls on the other side. Already, the dining room light behind her was dimming, as if it were being swallowed by darkness. Julie's limbs went lax, and she fell deeper into the couch. Her eyelids became heavier, though she didn't feel sleepy, only distant from the real world.

Laidey wakes from a nap, yawning and rubbing away the sleep.

Don't worry, baby. I'll find you.

A chittering scrabbled at the edges of the shadows behind her. Vertigo struck her full-on, just as it had at the morgue. Streams of reality swirled around her, and it felt as though she could choose one, if only she could figure out which.

Julie blinked.

And there she was. Not Adelaide, but the girl from the park, sitting in the chair Nicole had so recently occupied. She was hugging her midsection, rocking back and forth slowly, rhythmically.

And her eyes . . .

The hairs on Julie's arms stood up.

A piece of shadow detached itself from the corner. It pulled itself taller and resolved into a form of slim arms ending in deadly claws, a smile limned by feral teeth, eyes gilded with hatred and hunger and satisfaction.

"Don't take another step," she told it.

But it didn't listen. It was behind the girl now, its hand on her shoulder much the same as Nicole had done to Julie moments ago. But unlike Nicole's, the beast's touch was smug. Possessive. Defiant.

"I said leave her alone!" Julie was worried about Nicole waking, but not enough to lower her voice.

The head lowered, and its jaws opened impossibly wide. It set its teeth along the girl's scalp and bit, slowly, so that her skin scraped away and revealed the bloody red flesh underneath. The girl cowered, and her entire body tensed, but she did not otherwise move.

Julie stood and turned.

The dining room was empty.

She turned back to the reflection.

They were both gone.

She tried again and again to reach the girl, but it didn't work.

"I'm going to get you, you son of a bitch."

The sun had already risen by the time Julie woke on the living room couch. Nicole had long ago gone to work, but she'd left a yellow sticky on the front door. *Sorry I was such a bitch last night. Meet me at Danny's for lunch? 1:30.*

She rubbed sleep from her eyes and glanced at the clock. She had three hours.

She thought seriously about visiting Kane at the hospital, but there was no telling what he'd do when he saw her again, or that he'd even be awake.

She looked at the note again. Danny's was downtown. Near Kane's house. If she couldn't visit Kane, then she could at least see what was going on in his house.

An hour later, she found herself kneeling by the fire escape window and peering inside. The window had a black garbage bag duct taped over it. She tore the plastic, cupped her hands around her forehead and cheeks, and pressed her face into the hole. She scanned the room while waiting for her eyes to adjust.

One of the morgue vaults was open. Theresa's. She was lying there, still as perfect as when Kane had brought her in and laid her there.

Julie climbed down through the window and reached Theresa's side. She brushed down Theresa's auburn hair, expecting her skin to be cold. But there was a surprising warmth to it—not quite normal temperature, but close. It was a relief to see how calm she looked, though Julie realized this was only a shell. The real girl was lost on the other side.

"You saw her last night, didn't you?"

Julie jumped and turned. Kane was standing in the doorway, favoring his left side heavily. He was wearing an ID bracelet, and hospital robes were tucked into his jeans, which had a brown stain from waist to knee.

"Yes," Julie replied.

Kane's eyes were half-lidded, as if he were struggling to keep them open.

"That's why I couldn't find her."

"What do you mean?"

"At the park," he said, "I tried to rescue her again. But I couldn't find her. I think she attached herself to you."

"It was only a vision. I only saw her for a few minutes."

"It might have felt like a few, but I bet it was longer. Time's different there."

"There was no *there*. It was in my apartment."

"Were you looking in a mirror?"

"My living room window."

He nodded. "Then you were on the other side, no matter what it might have seemed like. She's strong, otherwise she probably wouldn't have been able to find you, but it's been almost a week since she was taken. It's going to be hell trying to save her after tonight."

Julie's head was swimming. "Your drawings . . . They're all victims, aren't they? Like my daughter."

Kane nodded slowly. "I draw them to keep them fresh . . . To keep them tied to our world."

Julie's heart lifted. "So you can bring them back . . ."

"So I can bring them back."

Kane's face turned pale, and he gripped his stomach tighter, but he seemed to be handling the pain all right. Julie had no idea just how he was proposing to get Theresa back, but she knew she wanted to try.

"What do we have to do?"

A look of overwhelming pain overcame Kane, and he doubled over. A bottle of pills Julie hadn't noticed before slipped from his right hand as he tried to break his fall. White pills skittered over the floor like pieces of a broken vase. Julie ran over and helped him roll onto his right side. He curled up in a fetal position, breathing shallowly and quickly.

"Listen, you have to go back to the park." His eyes

closed, and he half smiled, half grimaced. "Remember? Where you shot me?"

"No jokes," Julie said. "You need to come too. I don't know what I'm doing."

"You know more than you think. Go back to the fountain. When you see Theresa, draw her toward our world. Our reality. Once you do—" he tapped his chest "—she'll be with you." Kane grunted and doubled up.

"I'm calling the hospital."

"Don't!" he said through gritted teeth. "I've been through worse. Go. Now. I'll meet you there as soon as I can."

Julie hesitated, not wanting to leave him now that she'd finally found someone who knew she wasn't crazy, but if what he said was true, then Theresa didn't have much time.

She placed several of the scattered pills into Kane's hand, poured him a glass of water, and rushed out of the morgue.

By the time Julie reached the park, it was empty except for an old man walking an Irish terrier. The orange glow of sunset still lit the city in a ruddy glow. The streetlights snapped on, ineffective for the moment.

Julie sat on the same bench Kane had and stared at the eclectic antique store across the street. The fountain, which she could see clearly in the window, was dormant. She had been positive when she'd sat down that she would find Theresa; but she was nowhere to be found, and Julie's initial confidence was turning into feelings of failure and a growing belief that this had all been another delusion, that Theresa wasn't real, that Kane wasn't real, and all she was doing was sinking herself deeper into a world of her own making.

Julie clawed her fingernails down her arm to snap herself out of it. She tried to slip into the same mind-set as the day before, but as the western sky dimmed and night marched over the city, nothing happened. Nothing at all.

How had she done it last night? How had she seen the Others as she was approaching Kane with the revolver?

And then Julie wondered. Maybe *she* hadn't done anything. Maybe *Theresa* had found her. Maybe Julie had simply attracted her attention in some way, and Theresa had done the rest.

But how?

How?

Adelaide.

Of course. She had been fixated on Adelaide.

She did so again. She thought of the details that were Adelaide: the baby powder smell of her hair after a bath, the awkward but adorable way in which she ran, the way she used to clap after learning a new word, and the way her blue eyes would light up when she smiled.

The way Julie's heart would break whenever Laidey cried.

The hairs on Julie's arms and neck stood on end. The feeling of a million divergences in reality returned. She'd been so focused on Adelaide that she hadn't realized the fountain was alive. Theresa was standing in it, naked, surrounded by dozens of them—thin, shadowy forms full of sharp smiles and hungry expressions.

Hungry, but not for Theresa. Not anymore. Now they wanted Julie—she could feel it—and she knew, somehow, that when she turned, when she looked at the fountain directly, they would all still be there, waiting for her.

They seemed to be proposing a trade. Theresa for Julie. They'd had Laidey for a long time now, and they wanted more. They wanted her mother.

Julie stood and turned.

Theresa didn't look up as Julie approached. One of the creatures put its foul hand on Theresa's shoulder and let the claws sink in. Blood trickled from one of the claws, then two, then three. Theresa cowered from the pain, but quickly stood straight, perhaps having already learned the whims of her masters.

"Let her go," Julie said simply as she stopped at the fountain's edge. She resisted the urge to reach for Theresa.

Several forms broke away from the mass and surrounded Julie. They ate at Julie's consciousness, sucked at it like foul piglets suckling at their mother's teats.

"Theresa, look at me."

She did not. She seemed to be drawn inward. The beast behind her, their ostensible leader, bent down and opened its maw wide. It clamped its jaw around the crown of Theresa's head. Sucking sounds emanated from its mouth as Theresa cowered in pain and fear.

Draw her toward our world, Kane had said, *our reality.* But Julie had no idea how to do that. None. And she couldn't stand here and watch this happen.

There was only one thing she could do.

"Let her go!" she shouted. "You can have me, all right? Just take me!"

The beast stopped sucking and unhinged its jaws from around Theresa's head. Blood began running down her face in dozens of rivulets.

"You can have me," Julie said, more calmly now.

This felt right. It felt good, to save one child, even if it wasn't her own.

The larger shadow smiled, terribly pleased. The others moved in, savoring the moment.

And then, perhaps drawn by Julie's sacrifice, Theresa raised her head. She seemed to recognize Julie.

And then she smiled.

It felt as though Theresa were pouring all of herself into that one magnificent gesture, as though she were giving herself to Julie.

And Julie accepted her. Gladly.

It was the last thing she remembered.

A cool wind blew against Julie's face, bringing the scent of freshly fallen rain along with it. She could feel Theresa,

warm and safe and whole, as clearly as she could feel her
own heartbeat.

Julie opened her eyes. Flashing red lights were illuminating the boughs of the tree above her, flattening everything in a ghostly sort of bas relief. She was lying on a
gurney, and when she tried to lift herself up, she realized
her wrists and ankles were restrained. An ambulance was
nearby, as well as a black-and-white squad car. Nicole was
talking with a policeman and two paramedics while dab-
bing her eyes with a Kleenex. The policeman pointed with
his pen to the stone fountain, and when Nicole answered, he
began writing in his notepad.

"Nicky?" Julie tried to keep the desperation out of her
voice, but knew she had failed.

Nicole turned. She spoke with the policeman and then
broke away. "You're back," Nicole said in a listless voice
once she'd reached Julie's side.

"Nicky, you can't do this. Not now. Not today."

"I'm sorry." A tear inched down her cheek and then
dropped before she could dab it with her Kleenex. "It
should have been yesterday."

Even now, only minutes since she woke, the warmth of
Theresa was noticeably cooler. Would she die when it
cooled completely or would she just return to them? Julie
could afford neither.

"Nicole, you have to listen to me. You have to make
them let me go."

Nicole shook her head. "They're going to take you to the
hospital, and tomorrow Dr. Thierry's going to check you
back in."

"I can come to the hospital tomorrow. Even a few *hours*
from now."

Julie had never seen her sister look so desperate. "Julie,
you had a *gun*. They say it's the same type that was used to
shoot that artist Kane Reynolds."

Theresa was cooling. This couldn't be happening, not

when she'd managed to save one from them. "I had nothing to do with that," Julie lied. "Nicole, *please*."

Nicole looked up and stepped back, a frightened look on her face.

Julie turned her head just in time to catch a black Eldorado crashing into the front of the ambulance. It pitched the larger vehicle sharply to one side, but then, with the high-pitched sound of steel scraping steel, the Eldorado slipped off the ambulance, hopped the curb, and sped toward the fountain. The cop and paramedics sprinted out of its way, but the car missed them by a wide margin and collided with the fountain. The engine was still revving high, and it churned its way off the fountain and accelerated into a row of parked cars. The Eldorado's rear wheels kicked up two rooster tails of wet grass and dirt as it failed to bulldoze a huge blue Suburban. The policeman and paramedics ran toward it, and Nicole stepped forward, her hand to her mouth.

Julie felt something at her wrist and realized Kane was at her side, undoing the thick leather restraints. It didn't take him long, but it felt like minutes, minutes that would allow Nicole or the cop to see her. But the cop was shouting for the driver to kill the engine, his gun trained on the driver's seat, his flashlight illuminating the interior; Nicole and the paramedics were transfixed by this long black car that had come out of nowhere.

Kane helped Julie to her feet, and moments later they were heading through the dark streets.

"I don't get it," Julie said. "Who was driving the car?"

"A brick," Kane said as he limped out into the street and hailed a cab.

The next few minutes blurred, Julie terrified to speak in front of the cabbie, and in no time they had reached the morgue. A sheen of sweat covered Kane's bald head and face, and he was limping badly as he led her into the vault room. He pulled Theresa's drawer open, and Julie stared at the beautiful girl whose life had been stolen, a life Julie now contained within her.

"What do I do now?"

"Just wait," Kane said as he mopped his brow.

It didn't take long. Julie coughed, hard, several times. She felt something coming up, as if she were vomiting. She held her hand over her mouth and caught it just as it slipped between her lips. An object like an elongated egg rested in Julie's palm. It was translucent white with an iridescent quality like mother-of-pearl. She could feel Theresa waiting within it, thankful and tender and scared.

Julie, knowing in her bones what she had to do, placed the egg against Theresa's lips and pressed. Theresa's mouth opened, welcoming her soul back to her body.

Moments passed, Julie painfully aware of her own breath. And then Theresa's eyelids fluttered.

And opened.

Julie began to cry.

She hugged Theresa tight and rocked her back and forth as Theresa began crying as well. "It's going to be all right."

The sound of sirens came through the broken window, faint but growing in intensity.

"You have to get going," Kane said.

"Where?" Julie asked, willing to do whatever it took.

"Take her to the St. Agnes orphanage. Sister Relda will know what to do."

"Will you meet me?"

The sirens grew stronger as they walked out the front door. Kane locked it behind him. "Not right away. I need to let the cops take me in." Julie was about to speak, but he smiled and continued. "Don't worry. My lawyer kicks some serious ass."

Julie knew she should take Theresa and run, but the realization of Kane's efforts over the years threatened to overwhelm her. "How long have you been doing this?"

Kane took a deep breath and gave her a half smile. "Since I was rescued from the other side."

A simple answer, but one filled with implications. "There are *more* of you?"

"A few . . . Not enough." Kane guided her to the edge of the street and pointed to a darkened alley.

"Will you help me to find my daughter?"

Kane nodded. "It won't be easy, she's been there for a while, but yeah. I'll help."

Julie stepped in and hugged him as a huge weight was lifted from her. She would no longer be alone. She would no longer have to live helplessly.

The sirens grew suddenly stronger. Kane broke away and pointed again to the alley. "Hurry up."

She smiled and led Theresa away. Just before she entered the alley, two squad cars squealed onto Main. Kane sat down on the curb and waited, pointedly ignoring Julie and Theresa.

Julie moved quickly, not wanting the police to get a look at them, and in minutes they were blocks and worlds away.

When they were getting close to the orphanage, they stopped at a crosswalk, waiting for a truck to drive by, but a red light caused it to stop right in front of them. It was a Breyer's delivery truck with mirrored sides.

Julie stared at her wavy reflection and Theresa's, her pride bittersweet that it wasn't Adelaide she was guiding to safety. But she had nothing to be ashamed of. Far from it. She had found a new purpose in life. With or without Kane, she already knew she was going to do this again, and again, and again.

"Don't worry, baby girl. Mama's coming."

And then the truck pulled away, taking her reflection with it.

GOD PAYS

Paul Genesse

October 17, 2012

Nina's throat burned as if she'd swallowed glass and chased it down with battery acid. She went into a coughing fit, and pain exploded inside her gut. Nina grabbed her belly, trying to keep her intestines from spilling out. A crescent-shaped incision ran from side to side. Her fingertips dragged along what felt like staples curled into her skin. She forced her eyes open and realized she was in a dark hospital room with a monitor flashing numbers at her bedside. Tubes snaked from her arms, and something that smelled like old plastic hissed into her nose.

They cut me open, she thought, then tried to sit up. A wave of nausea knocked her back down. The door opened, and a thirtysomething-year-old man with short sandy brown hair walked in carrying a coffee cup.

"Nina, you're awake!"

His voice and upper-class British accent were so familiar. He reached for her, spilling coffee on himself as he knelt at her bedside.

"*Elliot.*" Her voice crackled with relief from seeing the man she loved so much. The strength in his hand comforted her, and Nina tried to shake the fogginess from her mind. "What happened?"

"You had surgery." He put a straw in her mouth, and she sucked down some cold water from a bedside pitcher, soothing her raw throat. "Remember?"

Nina blinked, not remembering at all. She fought the urge to cough again and took a slow, deep breath.

"They took out the tumors, and your uterus is fine." Elliot smiled, showing his slightly crooked teeth.

Memories of her fiancé, Elliot, flooded back. They had met in Mexico City at a Mayan Studies conference two years ago when she'd given a presentation on the linguistic evolution of the modern dialect of Yucateca Maya. They'd been together ever since. He was the first person she told after the doctor said she had abdominal cancer—hell of a thirty-sixth birthday present. "They got it all?" she asked, her brain working again—although at the speed of a hungover grad student.

Elliot squeezed her hand and nodded. "The pathology report will be back in a few days, but the doctor said he thought they caught it in time. Everything will be fine."

Nina let out a relieved sigh. She wanted at least one child and knew Elliot hoped for two. Grandmother Márquez would be so happy. Still a chance for babies. Too bad Elliot wasn't Spanish. Her family in Barcelona would never get over it. At least he wasn't French.

The cough took her by surprise, and the pain erupted in her abdomen once again.

"I'll get the nurse, darling." Elliot vaulted toward the door and slipped out of the room.

She hacked up some mucous into a tissue, expecting it to be filled with broken glass. The phlegm must have been caught where the breathing tube had been. She suddenly felt light-headed and very weak. Something warm and wet was on her inner thighs. Her hand touched her incision. It felt dry, not bleeding. She reached further down. It was coming from between her legs. *Damn, I've pissed the bed.*

She pulled her hand out. The coppery smell wafted into her nose, and bright red blood stained her fingers. She pulled the covers back and gasped at the bloody mess spreading out from her groin.

"Nina!" Elliot shouted as he flung open the door. "Nurse! She's bleeding!"

Everything will be fine. Right, Nina thought as nurses swarmed around her bedside. She lost consciousness as the expanding pool of her own blood spread to the middle of her back.

A month after the surgeon cut out her damaged uterus to stop the hemorrhaging, Nina found herself alone in her house. She hadn't seen much of Elliot since she'd come home. He claimed all the traveling to meet with clients was to make up for the time he had spent at the hospital. Nina knew it was bullshit. He was a consultant with a trust fund to fall back on. They both knew he didn't need to work. The truth was he didn't want to be with her and she knew why.

When he returned a few days later she blurted out at dinner, "We could adopt." Nina had been trying to find a way to say it with tact, but after hours and hours, it was the best she could do. Elliot's cold response and quick exit from the house sent her to drinking, hard, something she hadn't done since NYU. The truth was, *she* didn't even want to adopt, so Nina could hardly blame him for his response.

She skipped her chemo appointment the next day and got on a plane. She had to escape, and Belize had always been her favorite place to do fieldwork. Nina was going to spend what time she had left at the ruined Mayan city of Lamanai. She rented a house, joined an excavation, and spent a month trying to forget Elliot and her old life.

Still, the memory of what had happened in the hospital made her shudder. Nina couldn't forget the smell of her own blood. She sucked air through her nose, using the pungent scent of the moist jungle around her to erase the coppery blood smell.

The frown-shaped scar across her abdomen throbbed a little to remind her of current reality. Nina put her hand on it, sensing the emptiness where her uterus had been. Better if she'd died then, rather than face dying in a long, drawn out way. The cancer had spread to her lymph nodes and was proliferating all over her body. *But there's always a bright side*, the sardonic voice in her head reminded her. At least she was alive the day the world was supposed to end.

December 21, 2012, the winter Solstice had been predicted by the Mayan calendar to be doomsday for the past 5,125 years. It had become somewhat of a joke in the Mesoamerican Studies department at Vanderbilt University before she'd left to have her surgery at the university hospital. They had even started a countdown to the apocalypse on a calendar in the staff lounge, but the events of the past weeks made her wonder. The increase in earthquake activity, volcanic eruptions and the electromagnetic fluctuation in the earth's core were happening at an alarming rate. Magnetic impulses from the sun and deep space were bombarding the planet and had wreaked havoc on the satellites, power grids, and cell phones for the past month. Seismologists were practically screaming about the probable eruptions of at least two super volcanoes, Yellowstone and the island once called Krakatoa.

Even worse were the global leaders calmly reassuring the public that nothing was out of the ordinary when everyone knew otherwise. She stopped watching TV after she'd seen the third geeky astronomer on a talk show explaining why the sun, the earth and the black hole at the center of the Milky Way galaxy were now lining up for their once every 25,800-year concordance. The massive black hole in the heart of the galaxy might be the cause of the increased magnetic activity, and its full force would hit Earth . . . tonight. It's nothing to be afraid of, they all said.

How the ancient Maya knew this rare cosmic event was going to happen and predicted its occurrence thousands of years ago was another matter entirely. It was a question Nina had been contemplating ever since her master's thesis on Mayan epigraphic conventions related to astronomical predictions. The glyphs told some interesting stories about the world already having been destroyed and reborn four times. This Fifth World was due for a reboot. Considering all the violence and suffering, Nina decided that starting over was a really good idea.

She shook her head and missed Elliot for a moment as she walked into the ruins alone. At least she wasn't Christmas shopping at some mall with mind-numbing music playing in the background, or sitting on stockpiles of food and water in a remote shelter with survivalists. What was the point of worrying about the apocalypse? Dawn had come hours ago—in several time zones—and the planet had not ceased to exist. It was just like the whole Y2K scare in 2000 when so-called experts predicted global catastrophe because computers supposedly couldn't figure out what date to display though Google could reference all 431,000,000 mentions of sex on the Internet in 0.06 seconds. *Please,* she thought, *Come up with something real to worry about, like global warming, famine in Africa.*

Or cancer . . .

Pretending she was already a ghost who couldn't perceive the living, Nina did not acknowledge the crowd of tourists and the throng of local villagers gathered in the grand plaza of Lamanai. They had come for sunset and the upcoming end of days. She felt so removed from them, even the friendly archaeologists who had let her join the dig. A group of them stood at the back of the crowd. Nina kept her head down and tried to avoid them.

"Profesora Carreño, ¿qué tal?" An archaeologist from la Universidad Autónoma de México named Miguel Alvarez stepped out of the crowd. She ignored him. *"Bix a bel?"* He switched to Yucateca Maya, literally asking her: How is your road?

His accent was atrocious, and she immediately regretted ever teaching him the phrase. Nina strode away, acting as if she didn't hear him. Alvarez and the others always invited her to have a beer with them after the workday. She always declined and went back to the little house for a lonely dinner.

She had pushed everyone else away, including Elliot and her entire family on both sides of the Atlantic. Why let in complete strangers? This was her diagnosis, and she would deal with it in any way she damn well liked. None of them needed to know what was wrong. She would live out her days in Lamanai doing what she loved—studying the ancient glyphs on crumbling buildings and sitting on the beach watching the Caribbean roll over the white sand. Her body would be shipped back to Spain when she was dead. All the arrangements had been made, and the money from selling her house in the States would pay for it all when the time came.

Time, damn it! The long shadows cast by the ruins snaked across the ground, a warning of the imminent sunset. Nina had never gotten used to how fast the light faded in the tropics. She walked quickly into the less spectacular part of the city, far away from the crowds. She tried to find a place to watch the sunset before it was gone completely. Each one seemed so precious now.

Nina stopped in front of the same short pyramid she had been drawn to ever since she had come to Lamanai as an undergrad. The structure, known as the pyramid of Ix Chel, the goddess of the moon and fertility, had always beckoned her.

Vines and small plants grew on it like parasites, trying to claim it for the jungle once again. Bas-relief faces of a goddess with a headdress of snakes stared out from the ends of the stone balustrades. Not a single speck of colorful paint remained from when it had been constructed over a thousand years ago. The cementlike stones were light gray with white and black patches staining their surfaces. The steps rose at a steep incline to a flat platform where the ancient fertility ceremonies had been held. Maidens had been sacrificed to the goddess there.

Nina always resisted the urge to climb up during the many times she'd stood at the pyramid's base over the past thirteen years. A sense of dread always crept into her heart whenever she stared at it. She couldn't explain why she was afraid. She just was.

Stop being a scared little girl, Nina thought. *Today is the day.* She held her abdominal scar as she climbed the steps, feeling the burn in her legs and finding it funny that the woman without a uterus was going to the top of a pyramid dedicated to the fertility goddess on the day of the apocalypse. Her wry grin faded, and with each step as less and less oxygen reached her brain. Her mind wandered, and she felt dizzy halfway to the top. After a brief rest she crawled on her hands and knees to the highest platform. Panting, she hung her head, then pushed her black hair out of her face.

Exhausted and wishing she'd eaten dinner, Nina dragged herself onto the ancient altar. The rectangular stone had been worn down by centuries of rain. She turned over, and the clouds obscuring the horizon made the sunset less than spectacular. Nina found herself staring at the dark green mass of jungle that covered the abandoned city. It still boggled her mind to think of the thousands of people who had fled Lamanai over eight hundred years ago. No definitive trace of them had ever been found, though everyone knew that drought, famine, and wars had all been factors in their demise. She wondered where the people had gone. Some thought north to Chichén Itzá. Adding to the mystery were the other Mayan people from the Yucatán who had taken over Lamanai. It was well documented that they too wondered what had become of the inhabitants of the amazing city.

Nina finally caught her breath and tried to get off the altar. The stone had started to make her uneasy—like when she'd been in a haunted castle as a girl. She stood quickly, and dizziness took hold. A cold prickly fog filled her skull. Her head spun as if she were going to pass out, and the light on the horizon started to fade. Nina fell back onto the altar and lay down. She stared into the blackness swirling above her. Her body felt as if it were floating as the sun disappeared over the horizon.

The longest night of the year had begun.

When she finally opened her eyes, twinkling stars loomed in the heavens. Smoke drifted into her nostrils, and she bolted upright. Half a dozen short-statured men carrying torches stood in a circle around her. They wore ritual headdresses with long green quetzal bird feathers. They had decorated their brown skin with tattoos, and all had painted their shoulders with red ochre.

Nina's heart leaped, and she wondered how the locals had kept alive the religion of the Maya. Were they about to perform some secret ceremony? Her trespass would not be welcome, and the fact that she was on a sacrificial altar scared her speechless.

Heart pounding in her chest, Nina faced them. She noticed their pierced noses and the scarification across their chests. Even the locals with Mayan ancestry didn't do such things anymore. Perhaps the upcoming end of their ancestor's calendar had changed all of that. It was the day to embrace the old ways. A new fear shot through her body, and she jumped off the stone, which seemed stained black with blood in the darkness.

Six of the men came forward with stern faces so unlike the friendly ones of the locals who worked on the dig.

"¿Cómo está?" Nina's voice wavered, though she imitated the local dialect of Spanish perfectly. They didn't respond, so she tried Yucateca Maya, *"Bix a bel?"*

The men glanced at each other, then parted down the center, opening a path toward the steps.

Nina meekly headed for the stairs, thinking about using the Yucateca Maya phrase for thank you, *Dios bo'otik,* which literally meant God pays. Considering her location, mentioning a deity seemed like a bad idea. She kept her mouth shut and hustled toward the steps.

As she prepared to take her first step down, a sea of

torches carried by thousands of people at the base of the pyramid registered in her mind. She froze in place, too stunned to think.

The men seized her arms. They held her in place so the crowd could gape at her. Nina glanced back at the altar and noticed a man in his fifties holding an obsidian knife.

A strong rumble shook the pyramid and plaza below. Her foot slipped, and Nina fell forward. Strong hands grabbed her by the arms before she tumbled down the steps like the headless body of a sacrificial victim. She fell onto her back, her fall cushioned by the two men who had grabbed her. They held her until the tremor stopped and the collective gasps from the mass of people below started to quiet.

Nina made eye contact with the knife-wielding man. She tried to think of all the reasons she should not die on the altar. The most compelling reason of all was on her flesh. Nina pulled up her shirt. "No children," she said in Yucateca Maya as she showed them her scar.

The man pointed at her abdomen. "Ix Chel."

The others stared at her half-moon shaped scar. She had never thought of it before, but it was indeed a symbol of the moon goddess Ix Chel.

The older man sheathed his knife, then motioned for the others to help her down the pyramid.

She had to thank him for sparing her life. *"Dios bo'otik." God pays.*

He nodded to her respectfully and lowered the black knife.

The men helped her stand. They steadied Nina even as vertigo made her reel backward. A man on each side led her down the steps. They had tattoos that symbolized the Mayan god Kukulkan—though they were slightly different from the ones she had studied. They were more complex, intricate, evolved.

The men kept silent, using their strength to keep her from falling. Nina's legs didn't want to work, and she couldn't shake off the daze afflicting her. It was as though she'd woken up in the middle of a sleep cycle and couldn't make her brain function. She tried to concentrate. This was insane. Who were these people?

Despite vertigo threatening her every step, Nina kept stealing glances at the men around her. Had they stolen the jade jewelry from graves or robbed a museum? She might have to call Esteban at the Antiquities Ministry and report them.

The oldest man who walked behind her shouted down to the plaza in what sounded like an archaic dialect of Yucateca Maya. He yelled something about "Ix Chel" and "the Fifth World."

Daring to glance down at the now murmuring crowd, she couldn't believe that there were so many people gathered. They seemed to be staring at her, and as far as she could tell, they were all wearing Mayan costumes.

Her feet touched the stone plaza, and she stared out at the throng of men and women. Many had painted their necks and faces with ochre and yellow paint. Large wooden earrings dangled from stretched earlobes. Carved bones pierced cheeks, noses, eyebrows, and chests. She looked into their expectant faces and realized none of them were mestizo. They were short and reminded her of the genetically separated tribes deep in the Amazon who had little contact with the outside world.

A group of women with intricate large-beaded necklaces gathered around her. The oldest of the women, a crone with deep wrinkles, lifted Nina's shirt to expose the crescent shape across her belly.

All of the women gasped at the sight. The crowd surged forward to catch a glimpse as the old woman tried to remove Nina's shirt. The buttons befuddled her and the crone drew a small obsidian knife to cut them. Nina undressed herself and kept on her white athletic bra, hoping her action would satisfy the mob.

Thunder rumbled in the distance as the old woman took Nina's hand and gently guided her forward. The crowd parted, though everyone gawked, trying to catch a glimpse of her. She had no choice but to go where they directed. The women herded her toward the main plaza where the largest pyramid of Lamanai had stood for centuries.

Blazing torches revealed that the familiar buildings were not there. A row of three large pyramids painted dark red rose up where a market plaza should have been. The palace complex opposite was much larger than Nina remembered. And when had everything been painted red? The stone should have been dull gray with years of stain. Mind reeling, Nina stared up at a massive pyramid lit with scores of torches. It was far larger than the biggest pyramid in Lamanai and reminded her of the great pyramid of Chichén Itzá.

She must be dreaming. In case she wasn't, Nina allowed herself to consider the possibility that she was not in Lamanai. Had she passed out on the pyramid of Ix Chel and then been carried to some unknown city by a secret Maya cult? It was impossible that the archaeological community had never heard of a place such as this.

Staring upward, she noticed the stars were all wrong. The constellations she had memorized as a teenager and written about as a Ph.D. candidate were absent. They had been replaced by a whole new array of heavenly bodies. Even the moon had odd-shaped dark patches and lines so different from Luna.

The strange moon, the massive pyramid, the people, and the stars told Nina that this was impossible. This was not the Yucatán, and if the stars were part of the Milky Way, she wasn't seeing them from Earth.

The ground shook again, and a rumble filled the plaza. The cobblestones began to undulate, rising like the scales of a serpent. Nina fell to the ground along with the mass of people. Women screamed, children wailed, and stone structures crashed down in the distance. Fear replaced Nina's daze.

An interminably long time later, when the earth stopped

heaving, a trio of men with ornate headdresses helped Nina to her feet. They hustled her toward the yellow painted steps of the great pyramid following a cadre of others. A woman met Nina at the base of the high pyramid and painted her surgical scar red with a bold finger stroke.

Unanswered questions and a rising terror overwhelmed Nina's mind. Another woman rubbed blue paint into a circle around the scar. This was not happening. Blue was the color of sacrifices.

Adrenaline surged through Nina's veins. She resisted as the men urged her up the steps. She turned to flee, and the men seized her limbs. They hoisted up all one hundred and two pounds of her. The men marched up the steep steps carrying her with a grim resignation. Nina's primal instincts told her to fight like a demon. She could thrash, try to bite and kick until she was spent. She could call them every swear word she had ever learned, and as a linguist she knew a lot. But at that moment, Nina forgot all the foul insults. If this was going to be her end, it was going to be with dignity. What did it matter? The cancer would win eventually.

The men breathed hard as they reached the top. She smelled sea air and knew they must be on the coast—just as Lamanai was. They set her on her feet in front of an older man with what appeared to be a long toothpick pierced through his nose. He stood in the doorway of the square chamber covered with a vaulted roof. He wore a headdress with a snarling jaguar ready to pounce.

He spoke slowly, and Nina began to understand the inflections and grammar of his dialect of Yucateca Maya. She guessed he said, "Your road has ended here with us, daughter of Ix Chel." He pointed to the sky. "The Cosmic Mother has come to the center of the dark rift. The thirteenth Baktun cycle is complete. I, Muan-Balam, the Keeper of Days, know that this Fourth World will be destroyed. Tonight."

Her linguist's mind processed the words, their roots and possible meanings. *Muan-Balam. Bird-Jaguar, an obvious title,* she thought, then wondered aloud what had happened to the Fifth World—Earth. "Fourth World?" Nina asked.

"Do you not know where Ix Chel has sent you?" Muan-Balam asked. "Do you not know what will be asked of you?"

Nina suppressed a shudder, still not believing, then found her voice. "Tell me of this Fourth World." Nina mimicked his dialect as best she could, trying to keep her scholarly mind from considering what was happening.

"Dress the daughter of Ix Chel so she may come into the Temple of the Fathers." Muan-Balam motioned to the other priests. A man came behind her and slipped a sheath dress of white and black material over her head. The dress had an oval-shaped area that exposed her painted belly. A robe with long quetzal feathers and jade beads was put on her shoulders. On her head he placed a carved wooden headdress of coiled snakes, another symbol of Ix Chel. Her wrists were adorned with jade bracelets, and around her neck was placed an exquisite necklace with a pendent carved in the shape of the crescent moon.

Muan-Balam motioned for her to follow, and along with an entourage of men dressed as Mayan priests they entered the ceremonial chamber. Bright torches and braziers lit the entire room. Nina smelled sweet and earthy incense that reminded her of copal resin.

A stone altar lay in the middle. It was set into the floor—sized perfectly to accommodate a man or woman lying on his or her back. It was curved like a bow so the sacrificial victim's ribs would be spread apart, making the job of extracting the heart a little easier.

Nina's eyes lingered on the altar. Muan-Balam spread his arms in front of the back wall filled with rows of painted glyphs. They ran beside each other in symmetrical squares. Cracks ran through some of the plaster epigraphs, and a few seemed about to crash to the floor if the ground quaked again.

"Daughter of Ix Chel. I will tell you of two worlds." Muan-Balam pointed to the glyphs and began to speak. She began deciphering the epigraphs before he uttered a word. She had studied images like these for half her life—but never had she seen them in perfect condition.

Muan-Balam told the tale in a somber voice. "The fathers of Lam'an'ain were attacked by fierce warriors from the south. The Blood-Takers."

Nina recognized the name Lam'an'ain as the ancient Maya word for modern Lamanai. Her ears took in every sound, her mind translating as he spoke.

"The gods had cursed the southern cities, and they needed the blood of captives and slaves to honor the gods to bring back the rains. The thirsty cities looked for salvation, and Lam'an'ain had the wisdom of the righteous people. The fathers of Lam'an'ain came from the Fourth World. They were the keepers of the magic. Many who fled the drought and war came to the city of the fathers. The corn was eaten. Famine came, and all the people knew suffering."

Muan-Balam moved to the next row of glyphs. "The armies of the Blood-Takers arrived outside the starving city. The fathers of Lam'an'ain knew their people would die in the battle to come or from hunger. The Fifth World was in chaos, and the bloodthirsty gods had won. The last king of Lam'an'ain, Hun-Ahau, knew of one way to save the people. Hun-Ahau used the magic of the fathers. He gave his blood to Hunab-Ku, the father of all the gods, and became the Father Bridge back to the Fourth World from where his line had come. The people of Lam'an'ain were sent back to the Fourth World, leaving Lam'an'ain in the Fifth World, where the Blood-Takers would have an empty city."

Nina rocked back, the weight of the robe and headdress unbalancing her.

"Do you know what I say?" Muan-Balam asked.

"Yes."

Muan-Balam touched his tattooed chest. "My ancestors came back to the Fourth World from whence they had come. They knew this world would end when the thirteenth

Baktun ended. The fathers chose to take the old road back to this world and live for a time, rather than die on the altars of the Blood-Takers in the Fifth World."

A faint rumble had been building as he spoke, and now the pyramid shook. Nina heard the people outside clamoring about. A cracked section of glyphs fell to the floor and broke into several pieces.

Muan-Balam faced her. "Daughter of Ix Chel. You must choose."

"Choose what?" Nina took off her headdress.

"You are the only one here whose blood is of the Fifth World. If you give it freely, you will become the Mother Bridge back to the Fifth World for the people outside. You will save them."

I can never be a mother, she thought, holding her belly where her bleeding uterus had been cut from her body.

"If you do not take this road . . . all of us will die. None will go to the afterworld of the gods. No more of our people will be born. The line will end."

Nina felt woozy and considered the possibility that she had been given some hallucinogenic drug. Muan-Balam must be a cult leader who had crafted a clever deception, then deluded native people into following the old ways. She was done playing his sick game. Nina threw the headdress against the altar. "I will not be the Mother Bridge."

"Please. You must give yourself freely."

"No." Nina let her feathered robe fall to the floor.

"Then all of our roads will end tonight." Muan-Balam walked somberly toward the steps of the pyramid—probably to address the crowd.

Nina glanced again at the altar and followed the men out of the room. Another rumble shook the pyramid, and she stumbled, clutching the doorway as the crowd below screamed and more structures crashed down. She ended up on her knees as a block of stone smashed down behind her. Nina crawled away from the doorway toward the edge of the pyramid. Thousands of people had climbed onto the tall structure, filling each level of steps with their huddled masses. Many more were still trying to climb it, but there were so many still in the plaza below. Near the top platform, the wealthy folk, with all of their fine clothing and jewelry clung to each other. Little children with terrified eyes held onto their mothers and cried. A girl with wide eyes stared at Nina. Large tears ran down the child's cheeks.

A massive boom like thunder exploded over the city. Ears ringing, Nina gripped the stone as they pyramid shook. She felt the same panic as the people around her. Maybe this wasn't just an earthquake? Was it really the end of the world?

Muan-Balam tried to stand and address the people. Another massive tremor hit the pyramid, and he fell backward. The grand palace toppled down in a great crash, and the collective screaming of thousands of people filled the air. The crowd surged up the steps, packing them tighter. The weaker people were pushed aside and fell to the lower levels to land atop those huddled there.

Club-wielding warriors fought the masses back as they tried to scale the steps and get to the top. Blood and tears fell to the stone. Muan-Balam stared at Nina and he shouted, "The end will come in a great flood."

She was instantly chilled to the core. That was what ancient Mayan manuscripts said. The Dresden Codex in particular was very clear. It would be a flood. The smell of the sea intensified. A wall of darkness came from what had to be the coastline. Blackness enveloped the trees.

A curtain of dark water entered the plaza. A hundred feet tall, it engulfed the people. The gigantic tsunami hit the pyramid, covering the lower three fourths. Nina watched in horror as the water came higher, frothing white with debris and bodies. *This was the end.*

Nina rolled onto her back, facing away from the destruction. Muan-Balam had crawled toward her. "Daughter of Ix Chel, how is your road?"

She wanted to tell him it was just a tsunami caused by the massive earthquakes, but it was much more.

"The flood will not stop," he said, "until all of the people are drowned. We few who were closest to the gods may live for a time in the flooded world that Hunab-Ku has abandoned."

Nina glanced back. An even taller wave rushed toward the pyramid. More people would perish, though at the top of the pyramid she might survive, waiting to join the others in death.

"They will all die unless you offer yourself to the gods," Muan-Balam implored her.

"How can my death save your people?!" Nina shouted.

"You are the daughter of Ix Chel, born in the Fifth World. You are a speaker of the sacred language."

Nina suddenly knew the reason she had dedicated her life to keeping the Mayan language and therefore the ancient people alive. It was why she had suffered through the post-graduate education that kept her from having children. It was all for this moment. "I offer myself to the gods."

Muan-Balam extended his hand.

Nina took it. They stumbled into the ceremonial chamber. The braziers had been knocked over, and broken stones lay strewn on the floor. Muan-Balam helped her lie on the altar, her blue-painted belly facing the ceiling. The pyramid shook as waves battered against the stone. Muan-Balam raised a long obsidian knife. The roar of the water filled Nina's ears. The blade cut through her scar. The excruciating pain made her fingers dig into the stone. Blood leaked out, and Muan-Balam reached into the gaping wound.

Nina smelled the sea and felt the wind on her face. Her back ached, and she felt cold stone under her. Turning over, she realized she was lying on the altar of the pyramid of Ix Chel. Her hand went to her belly. Her scar was there. No fresh incision. No blue paint. She got to her feet and went to the edge. Moonlight revealed the dark shapes of modern

Lamanai. The trees of the jungle stood tall. She couldn't see any evidence of the tsunami or earthquakes.

The bouncing beam of a flashlight caught her attention in the plaza below. Someone stopped and shined the light up toward her. A voice cut through the darkness. *"Hola, ¿qué tal?"* a man asked.

"Hola." Nina tried to see who he was.

"¡Profesora Carreño!" He sounded shocked.

"Si, soy Profesora Carreño."

"¡Al fin te encuentro! Un momento." He shouted into a hand-held radio, then started climbing up the short pyramid.

It was Miguel Alvarez. The archaeologist helped her climb down the steps using his flashlight. "We've been looking for you for three days. Where have you been?"

Nina glanced at her watch in disbelief. It read December 21, 11:34 PM. "What day is it?"

"December 25."

"What happened here on the Winter Solstice?" Nina asked.

"Nada." Alvarez grinned

"No earthquakes, tsunamis?" She thought, *No gatherings of thousands of native people in Mayan costumes?*

"Nada. The Mayans were wrong." Alvarez smiled bigger. "Except someone came looking for you."

"Who?"

A group of jogging men with flashlights came into the plaza. Two local boys led an out-of-breath white man to where Nina and Alvarez were standing.

"Elliot?" Nina couldn't believe it. He hadn't shaved in days, and dark circles hung under his eyes.

"Nina." He wrapped his arms around her. She hugged him tight.

Nina kissed him, put her hands on his stubbly cheeks. "I'm so sorry." She didn't know what to say. What had just happened? Nightmares didn't last three days, and her watch said maybe three hours had passed. It didn't matter now, only Elliot did. "You came to find me?"

"I couldn't let you be alone for Christmas." He kissed her again, then got down on one knee. He held up a diamond ring that sparkled in the moonlight. "Nina, will you marry me?"

She stood in shock, instantly forgetting every word of every language she had ever learned. He started to look nervous. She suddenly remembered how to nod her head and did so. His wide grin helped her remember a few English words. "Yes. I'll marry you." They hugged, and Nina felt the tears she had held in for so long streaming down her face.

Three months later Nina and Elliot sat in her oncologist's waiting room.

"Antonina María Carreño Trimble?" The nurse asked.

"Yes." Nina stood up, holding hands with Elliot much too tightly.

"The doctor will see you now."

They followed the nurse into doctor Weatherford's personal office, for once not an exam room. A wide cherry-wood desk kept the patient and doctor at a respectful distance. Nina found herself sitting in the plush leather chair where the bad news was always delivered. At least this time her husband was with her. It was her third visit to the hospital in three days. They'd done the scans more than once, drawn a gallon of blood, and still no one said anything.

The pain and bloating in her abdomen had come back. Just like the last time, when the tumors had started poking into her bowels. She thought, *I'm not going to let them cut me open again. And no chemo or radiation. Just put me on a morphine drip and let me go.*

Doctor Weatherby came in slowly and sat down. He looked at her, his bushy gray eyebrows bunched together. "Nina, all the tests have been done twice. The chiefs of several departments have looked at all the results. There is no question as to your condition."

Nina felt like she was going to faint. "Just tell me."

"You're pregnant." Doctor Weatherby sat back in his chair.

"I'm *what?*" Nina nearly collapsed and Elliot developed a sudden case of malaria.

"Pregnant." Doctor Weatherby seemed as stunned as Elliot.

"But . . . I don't have a uterus."

"I used to think that as well." Doctor Weatherby stared at her chart. "I was the one who removed it."

I am the Mother Bridge, Nina thought, then recalled Muan-Balam cutting her open. She said, "Dios bo'otik."

"Darling, what does that mean?" Elliot asked.

"God pays." Nina touched her belly and felt the life stirring within.

JACK OF THE HIGH HILLS

Brenda Cooper

(Make sure there's real magic in the High Hills.)

*Jack figures in most stories told about the High Hills:
He's short, stocky, and blond with blue eyes and wide
shoulders. He has a way with wood and metal and feelings.
In some stories, he stands by the waterfall door and greets
those who come and go. Some say he makes sure no one
crosses who shouldn't, but if you ask him, he'll tell you
that's not his job at all. But if you look closely, he may have
two fingers crossed behind his back.*

*If the world has beat on you in spite of your good heart,
Jack might lend a hand. Particularly if you're young and
even more if you're a girl, and yet his care for you will be
innocent (he won't touch you in the wrong places, or sweet-
talk you into a line of coke or going home with him). But
even though it seems as if he's been here as long as the
Sawdust Festival has been on the Laguna Canyon Road, he
didn't see it until the year the festival turned seven and he
turned fifteen.*

Jack stared down the dirt road in front of Ginger, Old
Alfred's swaybacked roan. It was his turn to watch. The
old man slept beside him, bundled in a red and gray wrap

that the widow Smitty had made him while Alfred and Jack fixed her barn doors and stacked in hay for her. It was good to be on the road again; Old Alfred and the widow had made him a third wheel. The last four places they'd stopped hadn't featured anyone young enough to be able-bodied, and now that he was almost grown, he really wanted to see other people his age. Girls, if possible. But even boys would be nice—anyone to talk to, about any subject except repairing things.

The sun crept over the hills, painting the ocean on Jack's right luminescent blue-green and making Old Alfred bury his head deeper on his left. The road was far enough up-bluff from the sea that it was mostly dirt and completely empty. But as they approached a eucalyptus grove near where a thin fall stream trickled through brown grass toward the sea, a sob floated across the clear air. A girl's cry, more a catch in the throat than a scream. Another female voice answered it, too softly for Jack to make out the words.

A flash of bright red moved between the thin boles of the trees and emerged into the bright sunshine. A slender blonde girl in a red dress that was too short for common sense and hugged the tops of her thighs. Behind her, a taller figure, also blonde, dressed in a long flowing blue skirt and a white shirt. They crossed the road and raced toward the beach, like bright spring butterflies blessing the dull browns of the Coast Highway. It was hard to tell if the taller woman was chasing or following, and maybe that was a fine distinction anyway. Regardless, they were too far away for him to make out their features. The cool fingers of a destiny shiver ran up his back.

They hadn't seen him.

Jack licked his lips and glanced at Old Alfred. His benefactor would say it didn't concern him. It wouldn't do to make Alfred mad; there were other boys that wanted his job.

He looked back at the women.

They were worth getting in trouble for. Jack pulled

Ginger to a stop and shook Alfred's shoulder, thrusting the reins into his hands before he was really awake enough to do more than clutch them by reflex. "I'll be back soon," Jack whispered, and he jumped off the running board, hitting the ground so hard his feet stung. If he looked back, Alfred's eyes might demand an answer or two, so he didn't. He ran at an angle to the road, watching the two strangers— for they must be strangers—as closely as he could. He didn't want to spook them.

He needn't have worried. Lost in their own argument, they didn't look behind them at all.

Their voices carried snips to him. Red dress, "I don't care. He loves me."

Softer, more reasonable. "He's giving you . . ." Some of the words whipped away, ". . . dependent."

Repeated, ". . . don't care."

A long string of words, some he didn't understand, some he did. *Shelter,* and *call,* and *anybody.*

The taller one was lecturing the one in the red dress. She looked young to be so like Alfred. He was close enough to see that red dress girl was younger than he was and the other one older, but only by a few years. After he crested the last little hill of grass before the beach, he slowed to a walk so as not to scare them.

Maybe he did, and maybe he didn't. Scare them, that is. It was hard to tell. He could see the older one really well now; she was striding up to him with her fists in balls. "Who the hell are you?"

He opened his mouth and then closed it again and took a step back since she was still coming at him. "I'm Jack."

"Jack who?"

"Just Jack." She was nose to nose with him, her eyes a brilliant green and her cheeks touched red by the sun. "Pleased to meet you." He offered a smile meant to be a truce flag.

She stood her ground, her feet planted in the calf-high brown grass, her gaze almost a gale force. He stopped stepping backward. "I fix things." He jerked his head toward the wagon. "Old Alfred's apprentice. What do you need? I mean, I followed you down here in case you needed anything." He took in her strange clothes again. "Where are you from?"

The words seemed to pop out. "Laguna Beach." Then she clamped her mouth into a tight line.

Laguna Beach? He'd never heard of it. He could smell her now, something sweeter than he'd ever smelled, flowery.

She shook her head at him. "We don't need anything." She called to the other girl. "Caroline! Come on!"

"Don't leave!"

"And don't follow us, either!"

Well, that was a challenge if he'd ever heard one. He glanced at the wagon. Best not. Best go back. But . . .

The older girl was ahead, Caroline following her now, heading for the eucalyptus grove. Just like girls: Let a boy come around, and they did the opposite of what they were doing in the first place. What was he? Poison?

The wagon hadn't moved. He'd have to pass it. And so what if he let them get a head start? He knew the hills. It wasn't in him to run right past Alfred, but he stopped on Alfred's side of the wagon. His benefactor watched him calmly, even though he must have seen the girls. In fact, it kinda looked as though he was *trying* to be calm. His face was relaxed, but his fist clenched tight on the reins. "I think they're in trouble," Jack said. "I want to follow them. It's time to stop for breakfast anyway. What if we stop by the trees? I'll feed Ginger and you can eat while I find the girls."

Alfred's smile was a hard line across his thin face. "Looks to me like you already found 'em and then they left."

"Well, I couldn't just go with them. I had to see you."

Alfred patted the bench next to him. "They're already gone."

And they were. There was no sign of them by the eucalyptus trees any more. But he knew there was a path beyond that, folded up in the hills and going inland a half hour or so. A smattering of houses huddled near an oak grove up the path. They'd gone there a few years ago. Alfred had left Jack watching the horse and wagon while he went into the houses to get and spread news. He looked up at Alfred. "What about my plan? We stop and you eat?"

While he waited for an answer, Jack watched Alfred's face carefully. The little muscles by his ears were tight and hard, and the creases in his forehead had deepened. But even though he looked scared, his voice came out calm. "I can stop in and visit Gisele, and you can look for the girls."

"Thanks!" Jack went around and hopped up, hardly believing he'd gotten the chance so easy. He took the reins back and clucked at Ginger.

"You won't find them," Alfred said.

Sure he would. "Why not?"

Alfred didn't answer.

Ginger broke into a slow trot, her head so high that for a moment she almost looked like a yearling instead of the old beast she was. Surely a good sign.

Alfred just shook his head and slumped down again, half asleep, while the wagon rocked up the path between the hills. When they got to the circle of oaks, Jack rushed to tie Ginger to one of the thick low-hanging branches with room to graze, and then he dug up an apple and day-old bread from the Widow Smitty, shoving it into his pockets before getting a share for Alfred. When he handed a slice of the bread up, Alfred ignored it and grabbed Jack's hand. His face had lost its tense look, and he just seemed sad. "Take care, boy. You'll need other eyes to find those two." He broke his gaze away and took the bread, just holding it.

There was magic in the High Hills. In fact, all along the coast. Nothing Jack could *do,* maybe since at least a few stories said he wasn't born here. But even if he couldn't do the magic, Alfred had taught him to *see* the magic. He just had to look soft and sideways until it firmed up. Gisele's little carved animals that came alive. Rocks that had fairies under them. Trees with a purpose. Sometimes spells hung around people's necks or stuck in their pockets or the toes of their shoes.

Was Alfred saying the girls were magic? They didn't seem like magic.

Alfred's voice wafted down from above him. "Go on with you."

Jack went. The path was too thin for a wagon now. He passed a white house with clear and hard magicked windows, and then he was walking along a stream. From time to time he made out the girls' smooth tracks. A handmade stone bridge crossed the water, and then the path wound up a hill with no more than a few token trees, getting high enough for the midmorning salt breeze off the ocean to faintly scent the air. He tried softening his gaze to see what else the tracks had to say, but there wasn't any special glow or color or anything. The tracks were the same no matter how he looked at them. The girls' were the most recent.

He nearly bumped his nose on a flat wall of rock that defined one side of the hill, like a garden terrace. The reddish-brown wall was the same color as the dry grass. The tracks ended right there, directly in front of the rock. They were muddled a bit, so the girls had stopped, but there was only one set of their tracks in each direction.

Maybe the rock was an illusion. Except it didn't look that way, and when he touched it, it was hard and rough under his fingertips.

The path stopped here, but there was room to walk a way. So he walked up and down, looking for a way up the rock. He called out, "Caroline!"

No answer.

He looked sideways and soft at the rock and the world around it, all over again. It did, maybe, seem a little brighter right where the path stopped.

He leaned into it.

Nothing. It took his weight. With his ear right by the

rock, he heard water. The sound made him blink. It wasn't
the stream; that hadn't been so loud when he walked right
by it. He closed his eyes, listening, using only his ears and
shutting out everything else. The way Alfred had taught him
to see was to believe he would, so he heard the water so
crystal clear he knew it was there.

He stumbled forward, water sluicing over his neck and
head.

His feet were soaked, his ears assaulted with the thick-
ness of water falling onto a pond at his feet and the babble
of voices, girls and women and kids and . . . He opened his
eyes, still standing directly under the water. A haze of colors washed in front of him as sun turned the drops sticking
to his lashes to prisms. He took a step forward, and the
color resolved to people. Not the two girls. Or maybe. How
was he supposed to tell? There were more people than he'd
ever seen in one place before.

He'd just walked through a stone wall!

He wanted to lean back, make sure he could, but what if
this was his one chance to follow Caroline and the beautiful angry girl? There was no doubt their bright clothes and
accents were from here. He reached a single finger back
through the water, testing. No stone. Just space.

So he could get back.

He stepped over a low stone wall to get out of the pond
and onto a wooden boardwalk. He sniffed. Sawdust. Heaven
for a handyman like him! Fire and sweaty people and eucalyptus grease and butter and something salty. Under it all,
the same salt tang from the ocean.

Nothing for it but to go look for the girls. And to find out
where he was and if this was Laguna Beach. People made
way for him, and only then did it dawn on him that no one
seemed to have noticed him walk right through a stone and
a fall of water. Dang.

After the boardwalk ended, paths lined with sawdust led
in all sorts of uneven ways, so he picked one at random and
walked down it. A wooden structure on his right held

shelves of pottery. To his left, a small dark-haired woman sold leather shorts with beads on them. And just past her, a man with silver and blue jewelry in cases with magicked windows. So this place was magical, too. Maybe more than home.

He looked for anyone he knew.

Best to look for red. There was a red baby's dress. Bright red flowers on a man's shirt (where did they get such pretty things?). The red bodice of a dress on an old woman. He kept going, moving a little faster than the crowd. A red shirt on a tall, thin boy. A woman with red pockets on her jeans.

There! A red dress. He raced toward it. The girl had dark hair and leaned against a young man's arm, looking up at him with doe eyes.

"Hey!"

He turned. She was right behind him. Not in red, not Caroline. The other one, with her fists all round again. "I told you not to follow us."

"Are you always this mad?"

She gaped at him, her mouth open and no sound coming out, her fists still clenched. Then a tear slipped down her cheek.

"I don't mean you any harm," he said. "I'm just curious."

She looked away from him. "I'm sorry. I've been on the other side five times now, and I never saw anybody. I took Caroline because I wanted her someplace I could talk to her, and she's always mobbed. I thought you were the beginning of it over there."

The beginning of what? "I'm Jack," he said.

"You told me that." She was really very pretty, her eyes wide set and her hair the color of cornsilk, although not as fine. Sturdy and strong.

"I'd like to know who you are," he said.

"Oh." She was quiet. "I'm Caroline's friend." She looked down. "Or I was. Marla."

There it was. Her name. "Thanks. Pleased to meet you."

She eyed his clothes again. "You're from over there. On the other side of the waterfall."

It was a statement. "And you're from here. And Caroline is in trouble of some kind?"

She was walking now, but looking back, so he started walking beside her. He had to walk pretty close to hear what she was saying. Her voice was all silky anger. "Just the same trouble she's been in since she turned twelve and started singing on TV. Men follow her, and they give her coke and pot and try to get her to date them, and she gets all fluttery sometimes. Right now, she's fluttery over a silver-smith." He must have looked as confused as he felt because she shook her head. "I bet you don't have TV. I'm saying she's famous. Everybody knows her, or they think they do. But nobody sees her as a person. They just want her. It's not fair."

"So you were trying to talk her out of this silversmith?"

"Yeah. And the handyman. And the guy with the frog pots." She grimaced. " I thought if I showed her . . . what do you call it over there? Is it Laguna Beach, too?"

"It's the High Hills."

"Oh. Well, I found it a few weeks ago. I thought if I showed it to her, she'd stop and listen to me."

"And then I interrupted. I just . . . wanted to meet you." He looked around. "There aren't very many people over there. There's some, and a few young people like us, but since I'm always going around with Alfred, I don't see them very much. Know some names." They stood at a crossroad of sawdust paths and Jack took the one he thought led fur-ther from the waterfall. "But you saw some people. I know you passed the houses by the oaks and all."

"I always sneak by them." Marla was pretty when she laughed.

"So where's Caroline now?"

Marla shook her head, and he swore he caught the glim-mer of another tear just before she swiped the back of her hand across her cheek. "She didn't like me telling her what to do. She acts like she thinks she's better than me, but I know her. I know she's just scared."

"Do you want me to help you find her?"

"Why? Do you think she's cute?"

Jack shook his head. Then he realized that was wrong, too. "Are you trying to protect her from me, or you trying to protect me from her?"

She smiled at that. "I'm sorry. I lost two boyfriends to her, but she didn't mean it."

That wasn't exactly an answer. "How come there's so many people here?"

"It's an art festival. Like a five-week-long party. Everybody from town comes, but people come from all over the States, too." She pointed at a man with a something silver around his neck on a strap. "That guy with the camera is a tourist. See how his skin is so white?"

He still understood half of what she said, the rest of her words shadow-puppets in front of a fire. It made him want to stay forever and ask her a thousand questions. "I should go back. Alfred'll be waiting for me."

She stopped and looked at him, and then she held her hand out and took his. "Not yet. Let's go listen to Caroline. So you'll understand."

He let her lead him, looking around as they went, fascinated with the color and the smells and the huge variety of people. More than a few of them waved at Marla. She tugged Jack through a crowd ten people or more deep, and fully surrounding a circular lawn. Caroline stood hushed-up still in the middle of the grass, still wearing the red dress, and behind her two girls and a guy with long hair sat and played guitar. Caroline opened her mouth, and sang. Her voice was a songbird's, trilling and high, except loud like a red-tailed hawk. While she sang, she moved so her belly moved all by itself, then her arms, then all of her, and his eyes had to follow her moving and his feet wanted to move with her. The whole time he felt like the mass of people now behind them was going to break over the flimsy wooden barrier between the golden sawdust path and the green lawn, between the crowd and Caroline.

But they didn't.

After she finished the song, a great clapping rose up, and she looked over at Jack and Marla and pursed her lips and narrowed her eyes. Then she looked away, without really acknowledging Marla at all. He felt Marla slump a little beside him, as if Caroline's disdain had taken an inch off her height.

Caroline never looked back at them. She kept the crowd's attention, and for the next song, Caroline and the audience sang the chorus together, and Caroline clapped her hands and led them. Marla joined in, her voice so soft it nearly got lost on the wind. The audience seemed to feed on Caroline, or maybe demand that she feed them. Even children gazed at her wide eyed and bounced to her beat. Men seemed particularly starved, although when Jack felt Marla's hand in his, he was happy with that. He leaned down and whispered in her ear. "I'm going. Care to come with me?"

She followed him back through the crowd, which had swelled even more, and they finally popped out into fresh air and afternoon sunshine. "See how they love her?"

"Yes." In fact, all he'd seen for singers was wandering pub bards who earned drinks for tips and, once, a family that sang at a wedding. "It must wear her out." He was getting worn out. He wanted to stay, but even more, he wanted a breath of home. "Can you take me back to the door?"

Marla nodded. "Will you come back tonight? Caroline's mom thinks she's staying over at a friend's, so she can stay here with me."

"You're spending the night at the festival?"

"I live here in the summer."

She looked a little defiant again. It made him lower his voice a little, and take her hand back into his. "You don't have a family?"

"Sure I do. I just don't live with them anymore."

She didn't look like she wanted to be pushed, but he did want to see her again. "If I can get back."

"Sure you can. You got here, right? You just have to be back before they turn the fountain off. So after dark your time."

He could hear the waterfall now, so they were getting close. "I mean if Alfred lets me come back. I'll try."

She stood as tall as he was, so she only had to lean in a little to plant a brief kiss on his forehead. "I've got to go . . . I need to go see how Merle and Susan are doing and then catch Caroline before she finishes singing. Make sure she doesn't go do something stupid."

Her walk was full of purpose and speed, and he smiled at the idea of her going off to care about other folks. Maybe she'd care about him one day. Except that could be like being loved by a lightning storm.

The waterfall accepted him and spit him back out, dry, into the High Hills. It was glorious to bathe in his own smells and hear two crows scolding each other. The sun hung so close to directly overhead his shadow pooled at his feet. Hadn't it just been midafternoon? Not that the length of his shadow was his worst confusion. He hurried to down the path to find Alfred sending small gray lizards scurrying away from sun-warmed stones.

Alfred sat in the back of the wagon, leaning against a bale of timothy hay the Widow Smitty had given him for Ginger. He had one foot up on the side of the wagon, and the other splayed out, the picture of patience. He arched an eyebrow as Jack came running up to him, short of breath. "Well, what did you find?"

And so Jack told him about everything except the kiss. Alfred clearly feigned surprised when Jack told him about the waterfall door, and he winked when Jack talked about Caroline's voice.

When Jack finished, he asked, "Have you ever been to Laguna Beach?"

Alfred looked sad. "Only some people seem to be able to go through the doors."

"Doors?"

"There's more'n the one you found." He picked up a little magicked glass box he kept paper and pens in. "See, this stuff comes from there. A little trade happens, though not much. The doors don't seem to let more'n a single person can carry through."

So glass maybe wasn't magicked but just brought over? "You told me I might not have been born in the High Hills." He stood up straight and looked back the way he'd come. "Am I from Laguna Beach?"

Alfred shook his head. "Probably not. The church-woman I got you from came from way up the coast. But she said you were probably born on that side of the world."

"I want to go back tonight."

Alfred looked sad again. "Some people get stuck over there and never come back. Happened to Gisele's sister, so she never goes and never lets her son go, either."

He could still feel Marla's hand and hear Caroline's voice. "I need to go."

"All right, then."

Jack jumped up beside the old man and settled in, watching the dry oak leaves clack together in the sea breeze and thinking about gateways and Marla while he heard Caroline's high, sweet voice in his head.

When the last gloaming of the day finally came, Jack shrugged into his fringed leather coat and walked up the path. He sat with his back against the rock, watching the dark folds in the hills get blacker and bigger until all the hills were shadows and the stars tiny fires above his head. This time, the stone let him go through as if he or it were mist.

It looked like Gisele's tales of fairyland. Ropes of light had been strung around and between all the booths, and little lights twinkled like stars beside all the paths. The crowd had shrunk together in age; there were no children and few old people. But plenty of teenagers like him and Marla. After he stepped on the path, his feet and even his leather coat wet (he should have thought about that!), he stopped and leaned against a wooden railing and looked around for Marla. Or Caroline. The least she could have done was be close by; he'd never find them in the crowd in the dark.

He watched the people go by, making a list in his head of all the things he wanted to ask about; metal belts and red leather boots and music with no players. After he'd stood there about an hour, he gave up and walked off, listening for Caroline's song or Marla's intense whisper.

He found the lawn, ringed only a few people deep. An older woman in a long white dress plucked at strings on a harp, her music slow and wistful. Her audience drifted in and out like small shore waves. Nothing like Caroline's spell. He kept going after that and was far away from the waterfall when a loud voice from the air proclaimed, "The Sawdust Festival will close in fifteen minutes. Please head toward the exits at this time, and enjoy the rest of your evening."

Jack hesitated. He'd seen no sign of Marla or Caroline. Artists had started packing up jewelry. A few were making last-minute deals, the purchasers looking over their shoulders as if telling time to just stop for five minutes.

Had he been dumped?

He started walking the wrong way, like walking inland up tidal flats, trying to retrace his steps quickly. By the time he crossed the open area below the waterfall door where people sat and ate at little tables, the space was empty expect for a vendor or two still cleaning a booth. Overhead lights started to flick off, one by one. He raced up the steps and onto the wooden boardwalk, but before he got there, the waterfall stopped. He splashed across the almost-still pond, and thrust his hand at the rock. It took skin from his knuckles. He stepped close enough to it for his chest and belly to lean against the rock, and imagined the High Hills right on the other side.

He didn't fall through the stone, or hear the High Hills on the other side.

Lights kept winking off until only the biggest lights at the intersections of the paths and a few faint lights in booths remained. A handful of sullen stars shone in the gray-black night.

Jack crawled up the waterfall rock and sat as still as he could in a dark shadow, listening. Artists chattered softly to each other as they walked toward the street exits. Stranger sounds came from the direction of the exits; humming noises and the occasional sharp honk or squeal. Loud music that passed him by the in the distance, as if someone ran and played it. He'd heard it before as background to the rest of the festival chaos, but now it sounded more ominous.

He should have gone back through the door as soon as he realized Marla wasn't around.

As night deepened, he searched for signs of home. An owl hooted from somewhere in the brush-covered hills above the festival. A hawk cried for its dinner. The darting dark shadows of field mice flit through the dimly lit food court below the waterfall rock.

Sitting here wasn't doing him any good. Apparently the door wasn't going to work for him until the water flowed again. Or maybe it wasn't going to work for him at all.

That was no thought to have.

He slid over and then down the face of the rock, avoiding the pond so his feet had a prayer's chance of drying. There wasn't enough light to see into many of the booths, but at least most of the paths were clear. He started walking.

Up one path, he crossed over a red wooden bridge that went over a stream. At a corner, he leaned away from looming figures, and then looked closer and laughed. They were bears, all rough-hewn wood decorated with seashell and paint eyes and smiles. Each one held out a hand in friendship. Another booth had smooth wooden mushrooms for stools, and under each stool a wooden dwarf sat with a pipe or a book or a fishing pole, as real as Gisele's carvings be-

fore she breathed life into them. He could just see the joy
on her face if she saw them. He was used to created things
and magic, but there was more—uniqueness—here than
he'd ever seen in any one place. He started whistling softly
as walked the paths, searching every shadow.

A desperate whisper made him jump. "Jack! Be quiet!"

"Marla?"

She emerged from behind the wooden wall of a jewelry
booth, her fingers to her lips. She whispered in his ear.
"Thank god you're here. You can help me look."

"For what?" Although, surely, it was for Caroline.

"After I walked you back, she was gone. And she was
going to stay over with me tonight. Caroline wouldn't have
left on her own. Or if she did, she would have come back."

He wasn't entirely sure of that, but he held his tongue.
"You think she's still here?"

"She doesn't drive or have a car, so where would she go?"

"Car?"

Even in the dim light, her frustration with him was clear.
"Cart with an engine. Never mind, she's here. I know it.
And I know she's in trouble. She wouldn't lie to me."

"Okay. Where have you looked?"

Her shoulders fell. "Everywhere."

"I've been walking a while and I haven't seen anybody."

"Not even Guy, the handyman? Tall man with dark hair,
looks like a raven?"

"Nobody."

"He usually patrols. I've been avoiding his place so he
can't kick me out." She took his hand and started walking,
her voice resolute. "I guess I can't avoid it any more. It's the
last place to look."

He followed, his frustration with her for abandoning him
evaporating at the worry in her voice.

Marla stopped in front of a big gray-painted wooden
door with a latch on it and a sign that said, "Need Help?
Contact the Admissions Desk and ask for Guy." She leaned

in close to Jack, her breath fast like a rabbit's after a scare. But she knocked on the door anyway.

No one answered.

"It's always locked," she whispered as she tugged on the door.

It swung wide open to reveal a big room with wooden walls and a wooden ceiling, handmade from what looked like scrap wood. Tools hung on the walls, some familiar, some strange. One whole wall was lined with workbenches.

Alfred would be fascinated. Jack was trying to count the huge variety of hand saws and had got to ten when Marla tugged him toward a door he hadn't gotten around to noticing yet. "This is where he lives," she whispered. "Besides me, he's the only one who lives here all summer. And he doesn't know I do, although I think he suspects. He was following me and Caroline a few days ago. He creeps me out." She pushed the door open and then gave a little cry and raced forward.

By the time he got to the door, Marla's cry had turned to sobs. She knelt on the floor beside Caroline, one hand on Caroline's chest. He raced to Caroline's other side. Bruises bloomed across her delicate cheekbones and one eye was swollen shut. Her bottom lip had split, and a thin trickle of blood had dried on her chin. She'd taken the beating at least a few hours ago, and didn't look like she'd moved since. But even in the dim light, she looked a little more alive than dead. "Is she breathing?"

Marla looked both furious and completely lost. She nodded, shifting to sit at Caroline's head. "But I don't think she's okay. Can you find water?"

They were on the floor in a narrow bedroom, with three wooden walls and one natural rock wall that sloped away a bit. The bedclothes were mussed and one pillow was on the floor. Nothing looked like the door to a bathroom or a sink. "I'll find some."

He went back into the big outer room, where he found a sink that trickled clear water into a slick green cup beside it. He hurried to Marla's side, handing her the water. Marla dipped her fingers in and brushed them over Caroline's face, washing the blood from her chin. The still girl didn't even flinch. Marla looked up at him. "She's breathing. She just won't wake up." Marla bit her lip and looked questioningly at Jack, then shook her head, and thrust the water glass into his hand. "Stay with her while I call for help?" And then she was gone out the door.

He dribbled some of the water over Caroline's face, her bruises an affront now. Everyone had seemed to want her, but who would do this? Hurting people never got you what you needed. He swallowed hard, angry now, and took Caroline's hand. What kind of world was this? The High Hills weren't perfect; he'd gotten black eyes from bigger boys more than once. But it was all in fun, and they'd all sat down and had dinner afterward and laughed. Caroline couldn't ever want to see whoever did this to her again. Maybe he should never have come here.

Boots scraped across the door frame and he looked up to find two young men in bright yellow and another one in blue inside the doorway. The tallest of the two in yellow waved him aside and then they were moving clearly expert fingers over Caroline's arms and legs. He stood up and stepped out of the way, near Marla and the man in blue. She was saying, "Do you think he did it?"

The man nodded. "Guy had a rap sheet that included beating his wife. We've been watching him, but he hasn't been any trouble." His eyes were on Caroline's bruised face. "If it was him, I'll catch him." He turned to look directly at Marla. "I'm sorry. I hate it when we can't keep the bad guys away from pretty girls."

Marla swallowed hard. "I know you try, Clete."

Clete gave Jack a searching look, and then his eyes passed back down. "You two better go. You weren't really witnesses anyway. The call came in from someone who didn't stay. I'll find you and tell you where she is in the morning."

Marla raised up on tiptoe and kissed Clete exactly the way she'd kissed Jack before he left, then she took Jack's hand and led him down a dark path and around the corner before she stopped. "They'll take care of her. Clete knows about me, so he doesn't want me caught up in anything official."

"What does he know about you?"

She grinned. "That I look after all the other runaways. Some of 'em call me 'Mom Marla,' although I'm not like that, not really. I get enough money to eat by helping out at the women's shelter."

Is that what she thought he was? A runaway? "Was Caroline a runaway?"

Marla shook her head. "No. Maybe if she had been I coulda helped her more. She lives with her mom, but her mom's no good." A tear slipped down her face. "It makes me so mad."

He might have never met anyone so good, even if she was a tiny bit bossy. But the tear told him it wasn't easy for her. In fact, maybe she was in more trouble than Caroline, but she just couldn't see it. "So who helps you?"

She wiped her face and blinked up at him. "People like Clete and other folk."

"Can I help you?" The words had escaped his mouth before he thought of them at all, but they sounded right.

She stared at someplace past his shoulder, her face a mask.

"I won't hurt you. I just want to help."

"I'm not looking for a boyfriend," she said quickly. "Just help. You can't work for the women's shelter, though." She was so silent he heard her breath and another owl and, far away, the waves. Then her face brightened. "I bet there's a handyman job available for the rest of the festival. I know someone to ask in the morning. And I'll be taking care of Caroline for the next few days, so I'll surely need help then."

He grinned. She did need someone to take of her. She

was so skinny it would be good if someone reminded her to eat from time to time. Surely Alfred would let him stay and help for at least a few days. Maybe he could bring him through a few of the tools and show him, so they could make copies for the High Hills. "I'll go see Alfred in the morning, and convince him to let me stay for a few days. I bet he won't mind." And maybe it didn't even matter if he did mind. That was a good thought to have, even though he loved Alfred. Maybe it was time for him to take another boy. Or soon, anyway.

He was rewarded with another brush of her lips on his forehead. "Come on, I need to go find Lisa and Julia—they're down on Main Beach."

"Don't you ever sleep?"

She grinned. "Every morning, when all the bad people are sleeping, too."

"I'll go with you if you'll stop and eat something first."

She took his hand and led him toward the back of the festival. "When the gates are closed we go this way."

Whether or not he got her to eat anything, this would be a grand adventure.

THE SILVER PATH

Fiona Patton

The man heard singing, the words whispering through his mind in a singsong cadence that seemed both familiar and unfamiliar, but having heard such snatches of doggerel passing through the veils of time before, he ignored it, turning his attention instead to the edifice before him.

The Tower of London was an imposing fortress in the spring of 1554; difficult to enter and even more difficult to exit. The man had spent a great deal of money to gain his entrance and even more to assure his exit, but it had been worth it. The events of this day needed careful guidance if they were to become the forerunners of a golden age and not a tragic notation in the annals of history.

Standing behind the wrought-iron gate that separated the small, formal garden from the rest of the inner ward, he could just make out a young woman seated beneath a flowering almond tree. She had her father's hair and imperious manner and her mother's poise and beauty. To his specially trained eyes, destiny swirled about her like a mist off the sea, and for a moment he simply gazed upon her. However it was not she whom he'd come to see today but the boy crouched, crying, behind a low yew hedge some distance from her. Bringing his mind back to business, the man drew closer, studying the child carefully.

The boy was no more than four years old. Physically unremarkable, his light brown hair was neatly trimmed about his face, and his clothes, made from plain and serviceable cloth, were well patched but not threadbare. He was thin rather than emaciated and grubby, as any boy his age might be, but he carried no marks of poverty or abuse upon his body. A ball made from a pig's bladder lay forgotten to his right while a handful of blooming violets and daisies, already wilting, lay scattered to his left.

The man spoke.

"John Cross."

The boy jerked his head up, his tear-swollen eyes widening in alarm, but when he saw that the man stood on the other side of the locked gate, he rose uncertainly.

The man gestured him forward. "You're wondering how I know your name," he said without preamble.

The boy nodded warily.

"I know a great many things, John. I know the past and the future as well as I know the present. I know you're the son of Tower Warden William Cross and that you were born on Palm Sunday. I know your mother believed that you were destined to be a great healer, but when her midwife pressed a silver threepence into your hand to ensure it, it burned you instead, and you carry the mark to this day."

The boy dropped his gaze to stare at the tiny scar puckering the palm of his hand with a frown.

"Your father believed it was an ill omen," the man continued, "foretelling that silver would pass through your hands like water, but they were both wrong. Silver won't pas through your hands, John; you will pass through silver. A child born on Palm Sunday may find many treasures hidden, for he can walk the silver path if he has someone to guide him. I will guide you."

The boy frowned again.

"You don't need to understand me," the man assured him. "You will one day." He turned to stare across the garden once again.

"She's very beautiful, isn't she, John?" he said, gesturing towards the woman.

The boy nodded.

"She was brought here on your very birthday, yes? And for the past seven days you have given her comfort, bringing her flowers and playing such games as might lighten her stay within these walls."

The boy's face twisted with renewed unhappiness. "Da says I can't go to her no more," he said miserably. "But I weren't doin' no harm. She were sad, an' I made her smile. I gived her flowers an' I played football for her. She liked it," he finished in a low voice. "Da coulda let me stay."

The man gave him a stern look. "Your father was doing his duty by you," he said, allowing a hint of steel to enter his voice. "These are perilous times, and he just wants to keep you safe. The lady will be great one day, but she has many enemies who would not hesitate to crush a child who strayed across their path."

He crouched down so that he and the boy were eye to eye. "So if that child were to remain by her side," he added, "he would have to seek the aid of a powerful ally of his own."

The boy's expression grew hopeful, and the man nodded. "Yes, John, together, you and I might just be enough to stand by her against her enemies. Shall we try?"

The boy nodded, then his lips began to tremble. "But . . ."

"But?"

The boy hung his head. "Da said I mustn't talk to her no more or I'll be whipped."

"You won't have to talk to her. All you have to do for now is to watch over her for me in secret. When it's time for you to act, I'll come for you, and together we'll take a stand that may go down in history. Can you be patient until then?"

The boy nodded his head vigorously, and the man beamed at him.

"Very good; it's a bargain then." He put his hand through

the gate railings, and the boy took it. The tiny scar burned between them for an instant, and then the man was sitting back on his heels. "What's that you're playing with?" he asked in a conversational tone, content to discuss trivialities now that their business had been concluded.

The boy glanced behind him. "'Sa football," he answered.

"Do you like to play with it?"

The boy nodded his head as vigorously as before. "It's Da's," he explained. "He won it playin' street football in London when he were young." The boy's eyes widened with excitement as he recounted the story. "He says it seemed like the whole town came out to play, an' they played all through the streets for four whole days." He held up four dirty fingers to demonstrate. "An' Jack the butcher an' his brother Ham tried to take the ball from Da. They tried to punch him inna nose." He aimed a blow at his face. "But Da dodged and ran and won and got to keep the ball an' a silver threepence as prize."

"The very same silver threepence given to you when you were born, no doubt," the man added. When the boy answered in the affirmative, he nodded to himself. "That connection would have crafted the first clasp on his silver path," he mused. "And that explains the ball's role."

"When I'm grown up, I'm gonna be as good as Da," the boy declared. "I'm gonna win the ball an' win the prize an' punch Tom, the butcher's son, inna nose."

"I'm sure you will. Give it your all when you play, John. It may be more important than you think. It may become yet another clasp on your silver path." Glancing at the sky, the man stood. "I must away now."

The boy squinted up at him. "When will you come back?"

"Not for some years. So many, in fact, that you may not remember me when we meet again."

"I'll remember you," the boy declared stoutly.

The man smiled. "I'll be there when next you meet with

our lady. On that day I will hand you something to give to her. In the meantime, you must watch over her for me in the utmost secrecy. None can know of our bargain, for her sake and for ours."

The boy glanced behind him. "Can she know?" he asked. "Can I tell her?"

The man's eyes gleamed for an instant. "You may, but go quickly before you're discovered. Tell her that you can no longer bring her flowers but that you and I will protect her always."

The boy ran away happily. A moment later he approached the woman, glancing about to make sure that no one was watching them. She bent to hear what he had to say, smiled gently at him, and then raised her head. The red of her hair shone like fire in the sunlight as she met the man's eye. For a moment the force of her personality wrapped about him, her cool gaze assessing him for any hint of threat or betrayal, and then she inclined her head in regal permission before rising to disappear inside the Lieutenant's Lodgings behind her.

As the boy came running back to retrieve his ball, Queen Mary's astronomer, Doctor John Dee, stood a moment making his own assessment of the Lady Elizabeth, then took his leave of the Tower of London. There was still much work to be done if the silver path was to be made ready by the time she and young John Cross required his services again.

"Do you remember me, boy?"

Eight-year-old John Cross reluctantly pulled his attention from the coronation procession. He and his father had been standing in Little Conduit in Cheapside for over three hours hoping to catch a glimpse of Her Majesty Queen Elizabeth, but all he could see beyond the crowds was the top of her gold-covered litter. The man who'd spoken to him was dressed as a player, one of many enacting a dozen pageants along the route for Her Royal amusement, but John recognized him at once. He nodded.

"And do you remember my parting words to you?"

John nodded again.

"Then here." Pressing a small Bible into his hand, John Dee nudged him forward. "She has seen it and she is waiting to receive it. Time to strengthen the silver path."

John glanced worriedly at his father, who just jerked his head at him. "Do as yer told, Jackie," he said brusquely, pulling the ever-present football from his arms. Then he smiled. "Go on, lad; go meet the queen."

He moved forward in a daze. The crowds seemed to melt away from him as he followed the crimson-clad guardsman sent to escort him to Her Majesty. As he stepped through the multitude of brightly garbed courtiers that made up Her Royal entourage, a murmur went through them, but he had eyes only for the woman he'd played football for, the woman he'd pledged to watch over four years ago. She accepted the Bible from his hands, brushing the place on his palm where the tiny scar still burned him, and her smile seemed to outshine the sun. Then the crowds engulfed him once again, and the procession continued on its way to Westminster without him.

The screaming of a hundred competitors made him run that much harder, dodging the flying fists of the butcher's son intent on snatching the ball from his arms.

John Cross was fourteen. It was the second time he'd joined in the Shrove Tuesday mob football game throughout the narrow streets of London. Last year he'd lasted a single hour before a shipwright the size of a house had knocked him down and broken his arm. He'd never even seen the ball. This year he'd been more cunning. He'd kept to the shadows until he'd seen the ball carrier hurtling past, then one well-placed kick and the ball was his. And so was the mob. He ran.

Generations of kings had tried to outlaw the game, but it was rumored that Her Majesty was in sympathy with the mob, that she received regular reports on the various games throughout the city, and so he ran that she might hear that he had reached the goal and won the game. For her.

A fist flying out from the shadows ended his dream for another year.

When the darkness receded, two men stood over him, and he quailed back until he recognized the younger of the two.

The man gazed down at him with a concerned smile. "Are you all right, John?" he asked.

The boy nodded angrily, rising to his feet. He glanced about, but the mob was gone, following the new ball carrier down another winding street. The silence made him want to gnash his teeth in frustration.

"Then compose yourself," Dee ordered. "There's someone I want you to meet. This is Richard Mulcaster, headmaster of the independent school Merchant Taylor's in the parish of St. Lawrence, Pountney."

John tugged at his forelock uncertainly, and the second, older man gave him a stern look from under a pair of bushy eyebrows.

"You play the game commendably well, boy," he noted. "However, mob rule football has very little to commend itself."

John closed his teeth on an unthinking response, and Dee chuckled.

"Richard's a powerful proponent of the game, John," he said. "It's played and played well at Merchant Taylor's but with proper rules, sides, and standings, and proper training masters. It's a game of skill, not a game of violence. Do you think you might excel at such a game?"

John squinted up at him. "I could, sir, but . . ."

"But?"

"But how? I'm apprenticed as a Tower warden, and proper football's not played at the Tower."

Dee shrugged. "A minor detail. If your father and the headmaster here agreed, you could go to Merchant Taylor's this very term. You'd learn Latin and Greek and mathematics, even theater and music. And play the game as it should be played." He took a step forward. "It's important, John," he said urgently. "It's another clasp on the silver path, another step closer to the day when we must stand against Her Majesty's enemies."

John scowled up at him. "But when will that be?" he complained. "It's been eight years already."

"In point of fact, it begins this very day, once we conclude our business here. So, could you make a scholar for Her Majesty's sake, John?"

The boy nodded solemnly. "For Her Majesty's sake, I could make a priest, sir."

"Well we won't ask that of you." Dee turned. "What do you think, Richard?"

Mulcaster favored the boy with a penetrating stare. "Do you know your catechism, John?"

"Yes, sir."

"And can you read and write?"

"Yes, sir."

"In Latin?"

The boy frowned, and Dee rolled his eyes. "Don't be cruel, Richard," he admonished. "You know he can't, and you yourself said that you honored Latin but loved English. Come, be kind, you know the boy will do."

The older man smiled slightly. "Yes, I suppose he will. Very well, Dee, if his father agrees, I'll take him on. However . . ." He turned back to the boy. "Remember, John, the bursting of shins and the breaking of legs is unworthy of the game and those who play it. It will not be tolerated at my school." He turned. "I'll see you at supper, Dee."

"Thank you, Richard."

Once they were alone, Dee turned to back John. "So, what ever happened to that threepence we spoke of?" he asked in a conversational tone.

John fished a small cloth bag hanging by a piece of twine from under his shirt. "Da said you talked to him at the coronation procession, that you said he should trust me to keep it safe."

"And I see that you have. Very good. Come, we have much to do."

He turned at once, making his way through the narrow streets at a swift pace. John followed at a half walk, half trot, and eventually they came out onto a wider avenue, a row of fine, tall houses on one side and a belt of green, treed gardens, protected by gated, wrought-iron fencing on the other. Dee entered the central house, gesturing the boy in behind him. As he moved about the shuttered front room, lighting various candles, John glanced around with undisguised curiosity.

The room was large, paneled and beamed in dark timber, with yellowed plaster walls and a black, iron hearth giving it a warm, safe feeling. The only furniture was a huge iron-bound trunk and a wooden table set on a square of shimmering red cloth. As he drew closer, he saw that each table leg stood on a thick, wax tablet inscribed with unfamiliar letters. A single piece of flat stone, its surface polished to a mirrorlike finish, lay in the center of the tabletop.

"Are these your lodgings, sir?" he ventured.

Dee gave him a strange look. "No, John, they're simply rooms I let for business purposes."

Crossing to the table, he indicated the piece of stone. "Do you know what this is?" he asked.

The boy shook his head.

"It's a scrying mirror. Every moment in time is a world unto itself, John, as perfectly formed as a line of pearls strung together by the silver clasps of symmetry and connection. With this mirror I may gaze upon them: past, present, and future. Look and you may see them too."

John bent over the stone obediently, studying his own faint reflection in the candlelight, thin and scattered with freckles and a few pimples and smeared with dirt; but when the image changed, he shouted in alarm. A beautiful young woman with pale, white skin and golden-red hair was stepping onto a land of dark, mystic lakes and mist-covered hills. He glanced up in confusion.

"You saw a young woman, yes?" Dee asked. "A queen, both regal and beautiful?"

"Yes, but not . . ." John's voice dropped. "Not our queen."

"No, not our queen. The Scottish queen. She returned to her own lands near three years ago, and since that day the world has become a dangerously unstable place, steeped in conspiracy. The queen, our queen, would have her make a marriage that would strengthen both their realms." He bent over the stone with a frown. "But I can't see it, John," he said. "The future's pearl is hidden in a miasma of intrigue and betrayal." He straightened. "My stone isn't powerful enough to lift it clear, and that's where you come in. You must find this pearl."

"But how?"

"By walking the silver path; the silver clasps that binds one pearl of time to another. Fourteen years of symmetry and connections have made it solid. It's ready, and so are you."

"I shall explain further," he added as the boy gave him a confused look. Reaching into his pocket, he drew out a small, silver ring, setting it on the table beside the scrying mirror.

"This was my mother's. And before that, her grandmother's. Her grandfather was a silversmith in service to the house of York, and he fashioned it for her from a solid silver buckle given to him by another Elizabeth who would one day become our queen's own grandmother. Connections, John, and symmetry, in dates and names and events, all combining to build the clasps that make up the silver path."

"And that's another connection?" John asked, indicating the ring with a frown, struggling to understand. "Silver ring, silver path?"

"Very good, yes. Silver, John, the child of the moon, born from the union of earth and sky, it contains an inherent power far beyond that of any one physical form. It is not within the pearls, it is without, binding them together; past, present, and future in an unbroken line." He held up the ring. "It was a buckle, now it's a ring. What form it may have taken in the past and what form it might assume in the future is immaterial; it was, and is, and always will be silver in its most basic and elemental nature.

"Like your threepence. What was it before it was stamped with King Henry's visage, and what will it be when your own use for it has passed?"

"What, sir?"

"What indeed? You can only know that if you follow its path from one pearl to another." Dee leaned forward. "And that's what you must do, John; you must follow your three-pence where it leads you until you find its new form, and you must bring it to me."

The boy blinked. "Bring it?"

"Of course. Remember what I told you eight years ago. A child born on Palm Sunday may find many treasures hidden. Silver is not within, it is without, it is the clasp, not the pearl, it is hidden, but it may be found by walking the silver path."

"But how do I walk it?" John pressed. "I'm not without, I'm within."

"You will walk it through the symmetry and connections of your own life and experience that will draw you from one clasp to another." Reaching into the trunk, Dee drew out an old pig's bladder ball and set it beside the ring and the scrying mirror.

John stared at it and then began to laugh.

"That's not . . ."

"It is."

"But how did it come to be here?" John stared at the trunk as if it were bewitched. "My father made me pack it away when I began my apprenticeship."

"I wrote to him, requesting it," Dee asked in a dismissive tone. "I am a man of powerful influence John," he added sternly when the boy's expression did not change. "Your father was only too happy to oblige me.

"Now, as to its purpose," he continued. "The ball is connected to your threepence, and it is connected to the queen. With it, you will be able to navigate the silver path to find the former in order to do your duty by the latter. Do you understand?" He held out the ball.

Accepting his old plaything, John tucked it reverently into its familiar place under the crook of one arm, then nodded.

"Then let us begin."

Singing.

There were no chairs in the room, so John sat on the floor with his back against the iron-bound trunk, the silver threepence in one hand and the ball in the other. Dee moved about the room, lighting more candles and snuffing out others until the room was lit to his satisfaction, then caught the boy in an intense stare.

"You must be both wary and steadfast," he warned. "The future will likely be quite different from anything you may have experienced before, more wonderful or more terrible than you can possibly imagine, so you must hold fast to your goal. Keep your duty to the queen and your passion for the game foremost in your mind and you will return safely. Are you ready?"

John nodded.

"Good." Dee straightened. "Now, it is customary to focus the power of a working through a word or phrase that holds some meaning for it, strengthening it through symmetry and connection. Can you think of such a word or phrase?"

John thought for a moment, then nodded. Squeezing the threepence in his hand, he closed his eyes, speaking the words he'd first heard at the coronation procession.

"The rose is red, the leaves are green, God save Elizabeth our noble Queen."

• • •

The words seemed to fall into the room as if he'd uttered them in a vast, echoing chamber. For a moment it felt as if nothing had happened, and then suddenly there was terrible rending in his mind and body as if some great animal were trying to tear him to pieces. He opened his mouth to scream, and then he was on his knees, retching and shuddering in pain. When the spasms passed, he opened his eyes, staring about himself in shock.

The room was gone. Instead, he was curled up on the floor of an empty choir stall, his stomach twisting in nausea and his head pounding. A strange snatch of song whispered through his mind, a song about storms and light and silver, and then there was nothing but a deep, sanctified hush that wrapped about him like a shawl. His vision cleared, and he found himself gazing up at an ornate misericord running along the underside of the hinged seat before him. The shelving projection had been lovingly carved to depict two figures facing each other, and he laughed suddenly as the dim light revealed them both to be in the act of kicking a round ball that hovered in the air between them.

"Symmetry and connection," he whispered. "Duty to the queen and passion for the game. It really worked."

He peered over the edge of the choir stall. A great, stone cathedral rose up before him, and he swallowed suddenly; but as the scar on his palm began to burn, he felt it pulling him in the direction of the vast, shadowy nave, and, with an excited grin, he vaulted over the choir's wooden door, eager to discover what his threepence had become.

"A poor box! I robbed a poor box!"

The return trip had been just as instantaneous. When the music in his head faded and he finished retching, John glared at Dee as the man rummaged about in the trunk, choosing and discarding several small bowls until he found one painted black on both the inside and the outside. Carefully filling it with water, he placed the silver shilling John had brought back with him in the bottom of the bowl.

"Yes, yes, yes," he replied absently. "From Gloucester Cathedral if I understand your description aright. And dated 1664 as well. Remarkable symmetry."

"Remarkable?" John gawked at him. "I just robbed a church! Not only am I a thief, I'm an apostate!"

"Nonsense. Besides, I believe you're using the term wrongly." Crossing to the window, Dee opened one shutter a crack, allowing a fine shaft of moonlight to fall into the room. He turned the bowl until it caught the light, then glanced up with an impatient expression. "I explained this to you before, John. The silver in this coin is no different from the silver in your threepence. It is, in fact, the very same silver transmuted through time and use to a new form. How can you steal your own silver?"

"But . . ."

"If it makes you happy, you may melt it down into something more recognizable for 1564 and return it to the poor box in Gloucester Cathedral once we're finished here. Now if you don't mind . . ." He bent over the bowl. "Or had you forgotten the reason you went to rob a church in the first place? Answers, John, answers to very important questions."

He bent over the bowl once more, leaving John to stare down at his threepence suspiciously.

An hour later, John held the threepence in one hand and the shilling in the other, staring from one to the other in confusion. "I understand how this can be two different forms in two different times, but how can it be two different forms in one time?" he asked.

Dee emptied the bowl out the window, then placed it back inside the trunk before giving him an absent shrug in reply.

"That is one of the great mysteries inherent in the metal

itself," he said. "Even the most powerful alchemists of antiquity never knew the answer."

John frowned down at the shilling. "The queen's face isn't on it," he noted.

"Hm, what? Well, of course it isn't," Dee snapped. "Her Majesty was born in the year of Our Lord 1533. Did you in all honesty believe that she would live to be one hundred and twenty-one years old?"

John winced. "I hadn't thought of that, " he answered in a subdued voice.

Dee's expression softened. "No, I don't suppose you did, boy." he said gently. Plucking the shilling from his fingers, Dee placed it in the trunk beside the bowl, then began to snuff out the various candles. "Still, be of good cheer," he added as the room began to fall into darkness. "With our aid she may yet live and reign to a venerable age unheard of in the annals of royalty, yes?"

John nodded. "So, did you find your answers, sir?" he asked.

Dee frowned. "I did, and it was as I suspected: intrigue and conspiracy and the worst of decisions made." He shook his head. "But what to advise the queen? What indeed?"

"The queen?"

"Yes. I have an audience with Her Majesty on the morrow."

John grew very still. "Can I come?" he asked quietly, struggling to hide the emotions that made his heart beat painfully in his chest.

Dee studied him intently. "Yes," he said after what seemed like an eternity. "But you must not speak or give any indication that you were part of tonight's workings. Alchemy and astrology, while unofficially sanctioned by the royal family, is not sanctioned by the church. I would hate to find you imprisoned or worse. Do you understand?"

John nodded.

"Good." Dee placed the ball into the trunk as well and closed the lid, snapping a heavy iron lock into place before he straightened. "Now, off you go; see if you can rejoin the game. I will send someone to fetch you by noontime tomorrow. And remember, tell no one about the events of this evening."

He shooed John out the door, then stood a moment, staring at the top of the white tower, just visible in the distance before locking the door and heading off in the opposite direction.

And John heard singing.

"No, Dicky, you must concede that there can be no use of hands whatsoever, or there's no skill to be had."

John froze in time to keep his head from banging against the underside of what appeared to be a large drawing room table. As the strange music whispered through his mind again, he wrapped his arms about his stomach, gritting his teeth against the nausea that threatened to make him vomit. Around him, a dozen pairs of legs in exotic shoes and what appeared to be long, narrow breeches of some fine cloth stretched out under the table around him.

Seven years had passed since he'd first walked the silver path. His time at Merchant Taylor's had been spent on the football pitch, learning the intricacies of a more disciplined style of play, and in the classroom struggling to keep up with schoolmates far more learned than himself. When his studies had been complete, John Dee had exerted his influence once again to send him to the vaulted halls of Cambridge University, and John Cross had left the world of tower wardens and mob football games behind forever.

His patron had summoned him to that shadowy room half a dozen times in those seven years, and, with his battered old toy in one hand and his threepence in the other, he had visited halls and churches and homes. He had stood in a crowd of tradesmen and sailors, watching a football game played well into the night on the green grass of Smithfield's, and hidden in a closet in Ashbourne in Derbyshire while two wine merchants had come to blows over whether a hood was as good as a ball. And in each place, the burning of his palm had drawn him to a spoon or a key or a ring. Once he'd even found himself on the sun-drenched cobblestones of a Florentine square on the feast day of St. John beside a priest wearing a finely crafted silver crucifix on his belt and listening as the man harangued the opposing team in language that no English cleric would ever have uttered in public.

And each time it was the same. He had only to touch the item to find himself back in John Dee's room, his stomach twisting, his mind echoing with the same familiar snatch of music, and the silver clutched tightly in his fist.

Dee would place it in his blackened bowl, and it would give up its tiny allotment of vision. He had seen revolts and conspiracies, explosions and murders and banishments. Each time he would hasten to the queen with his findings, and each time, with his doubts dismissed by Dee and his efforts rewarded by a short and silent audience before Her Majesty, John would return to the world of studies and football.

This time had been much the same except for the urgency of the summons. He had been pulled from his bed in the middle of the night, arriving to find the candles already lit and the bowl waiting. Dressed in mud-spattered traveling clothes, Dee's face had been pale and gaunt, but when John had asked him what was wrong, he'd simply snapped at him to "get on with it," shoving the ball unceremoniously into his hands.

With the now familiar snatch of singing still whispering loudly in his ears, John crouched beneath the table, feeling the burning in his palm which told him the silver he required was directly above his head. But he didn't dare move as another, more nasal and much less reasonable sounding voice now spoke up from his left.

"I must concede nothing of the kind, Arthur. We always

employed a toss for goals at Eton, and I don't see why that has to change now."

Another voice belonging to a stockier pair of legs to his left now spoke up. "Oh, leave it both of you; we've been arguing this point for over an hour. We are all agreed, yes, that there shall be no tripping or hacking and no wearing of projecting nails on the soles or heels of the boots?"

A chorus of agreements followed this remark. "Very well," the stocky legs' owner continued. "Then let's adjourn for some supper before I grow faint from hunger and return to the matter of hands once the matter of bellies is addressed."

"You always were a delicate one, Charles," the first voice said, but, nonetheless, he lead the scraping back of various chairs. The legs receded to the muted sound of hard-heeled shoes hitting heavy carpet, and when all was silent, John slowly crept out from under the table, stretching his own stiffened legs.

He found himself in one of Cambridge's private studies, one he had been in himself on several occasions. It looked much the same, and he paused a moment to glance about the room, noting both the familiar and unfamiliar surroundings. The sound of shouting drew his attention to the tall, lead-paned windows along one wall, and it was with no surprise that when he crossed the room to glance down at a well-manicured lawn, he saw a dozen people kicking a ball back and forth with admirable skill.

He watched until the tolling of the University bell brought him back to the task at hand, then turned back to the room with some reluctance. Discarded pens and paper lay scattered about the table, and at the place where Dicky's legs had sat, the lid to a rather full inkpot lay forgotten. John carefully replaced it to keep the ink from drying out, glancing down at a piece of parchment on which a well-rounded hand had written the words: "The Cambridge Rules for Football, 1848." Unable to resist, he reached for it, and his hand brushed against a small silver box. As he felt the familiar nausea in the pit of his stomach that told him he had once again found his silver threepence, the door opened and two young man of about his own age stepped into the room.

They stared at each other for a long moment, then John had the box in his hand. The last sound he heard was Arthur's voice exclaiming, "I say, Dicky, that fellow's stealing your snuffbox."

His return found Dee in a much more relaxed frame of mind. Holding the snuff box up to the light, he chuckled with pleasure. "Eighteen forty-eight, you say? Another date of symmetry and connection. Excellent."

Leaning against the wall, John ignored both nausea and signing, crossing his arms to regard the snuffbox with a reproachful expression.

"How so?" he demanded.

"I took my master's degree at Cambridge in 1548. You see, John, how everything is connected?"

"I see that, as always, I'm a thief," John groused in reply.

Dee shook his head in impatience. "You really must come to grips with this," he said as he reached for the bowl. "Silver has had value for mankind for centuries past, and it will continue to have value for centuries to come. In each age men have laid claim to it, but it is the metal of the moon and cannot be owned by mere mortals. Hmm." Turning the snuff box back and forth, he grimaced. "I need a bigger bowl.

"There are vile conspiracies afoot that must be stamped out at once, John," he said as he rummaged about in the trunk again. "Never forget that's why you walk the silver path. You are not a thief, you are a defender of the realm and a champion of the queen, however secret.

"Ah, here we are." He poured the water from the first bowl into a somewhat larger one and dropped the snuffbox unceremoniously into it. "Now," he said as he bent over it, "let us see what we may see."

• • •

"No, this won't do."

"What do you mean it won't do?"

"I mean the future is as murky and uncertain as it was on that first night all those years ago but the present is infinitely more dangerous. This won't be enough to lift the future clear of it. I must have more silver."

It was 1568. John was thirty-six, Dee forty-nine. The older man's beard was streaked with more gray than brown now, and John's own was beginning to climb up either side of his forehead. After his time at Cambridge, he had obtained a position as a teacher and training master at Merchant Taylor's under his old headmaster, Richard Mulcaster. He had not seen much of Dee in the previous fifteen years. The alchemist had spent most of his time traveling on the Continent and off on one expedition or another, searching, with the queen's backing, for the Northwest Passage and other ways to counter the growing threat of the Spanish navy.

Relations with Scotland and France had been stretched near to the breaking point, with increased fighting breaking out between Protestant and Catholic factions in England and in Europe with every passing year. John had not been at all surprised to receive Dee's summons that spring. The powerful were calling for the death of Mary Queen of Scots and Her Majesty, Queen Elizabeth, had summoned her royal astronomer to give counsel, and so John had been summoned to find that counsel for him.

The silver watch he'd had taken from a wealthy merchant while the man had been watching a production of Master Shakespeare's *King Lear* a hundred years after it had had been written had been the largest item his three-pence had transmuted into yet. With his stomach still twisted in pain and the words, "a base football player," still ringing in his ears, he stared at Dee in astonishment.

"You want me to find more silver?"

"Yes, yes." Dee waved one dismissive hand at him as he lifted a large crucible from the trunk. "Times are dire, John, terrible, terrible decisions are to be made, as I've told you, and they must be made with as much knowledge as possible. You must walk the silver path again. You must."

And he heard singing.

"No, no! It's still not enough!"
Dee raged about the room as a large silver bracelet joined the watch in the crucible.

The old familiar snatch of song pounding in his head in time with the overloud beating of his heart, and fighting down the cramps that threatened to spill the contents of his stomach onto the floor, John gazed up at him blearily, but he willingly caught hold of the ancient football once again.
"The rose is red, the leaves are green . . ."

"Almost, John, almost. Please, you must try again. The clock is a masterpiece, a work of genius, but it's still not enough. You must try again for Her Majesty's sake. John? John, can you hear me?"
"The rose is red . . ."

Singing, always singing; the same song, as if from a thousand throats growing ever louder and ever closer with every journey.

" 'Ere mate, you all right?"
John shook the man's hand off his shoulder, nodding mutely as the twisting of his stomach and the pain in his head threatened to make him faint as the music slowly receded.
"You been to a fancy dress ball or something?"
"Something," he managed.
"Well, you'd best shake it off, the match is about to start."
"Match?"

"Aston Villa? For the FA cup? Blimey what have you been drinking?"

Somehow he managed to stagger to his feet, and, aided by the man and three of his friends, he made it to the stadium where half the town of Birmingham was already gathered in noisy anticipation. His benefactors paid for his ticket and helped him into the stands, passing several bottles of beer back and forth while he watched, mesmerized, as the local side played the game he loved with such wonderous skill and enthusiasm that he would never forget it for the rest of his life.

Later, when the celebrations finally wound down and the last of the revelers had staggered off to their own beds, he stood in front of a darkened shop window, staring lifelessly at the object of their adoration. The shopkeeper had left the shutters down so that the entire city might see the dawn sun light up the beautiful, silver cup, but even now, the faint moonlight across its rounded flanks gave it a fey, ethereal glow. His threepence had made a new home for itself somewhere in this radiant symbol of the sport he'd loved for so long—somewhere in the lovingly crafted base, the finely wrought handles, so delicate and yet so sturdy, or the tiny figure of the footballer standing so proudly at the very top. But Dee would melt the entire thing down in his crucible to find the future that would give him his answers for the present.

For the past.

For the space of a single heartbeat, John considered the wild notion of turning around, walking away, and never setting foot on the streets of London in the sixteenth century ever again.

"The rose is red, the leaves are green . . ."

His expression bleak, he picked up a broken piece of brickwork and hefted it in his hand as the scar burned a sear

of pain from his palm up through his eyes and into his
brain.

"God save Elizabeth, our noble queen," he whispered.

And the singing rose up in his mind once more.

"You've done well, John, now rest; you must rest now."
Back in the room, Dee held the FA cup above the crucible, marveling at the workmanship. "Yes," he breathed.
"This is magnificent, and so much silver. It will be enough,
yes, now it will be enough."

John said nothing. Forcing himself to his feet, he pushed
the door open and half fell into the street beyond, willing to
face anything rather than watch the beautiful trophy vanish
into the fire.

The evening sky was clear and cool, the spring breeze
bringing him the scents of almond blossoms and violets. He
wandered aimlessly, feeling both deeply sad and incredibly
weary until he fetched up before the old Water Gate at the
Tower of London. The warden peered at him, then with a
silent nod, opened the gate and ushered him inside.

"Halt! Who goes there?"
"The keys."
"Whose keys?"
"Queen Elizabeth's keys."
"Advance, Queen Elizabeth's keys. All's well."

John stood in the doorway of the warden's lodgings, listening to the ancient challenge. His father stood beside him,
leaning heavily on a thick, oaken stick and silently smoking
his pipe. Finally the older man glanced over at him.

'I'm glad you're not abroad this night, Jackie," he said.
"There's an ill wind blowin'."

John nodded his agreement. Together they went inside,
closing the door behind them as the last words of the Chief
Warder came to them over the wind.

"God preserve Queen Elizabeth."

Between them the two men whispered, "Amen," with the rest of the guard and escort.

Nearly a full year later, Mary Queen of Scots was executed on a cold winter's day. What Dee had advised Her Majesty was a secret known only to the two of them; for the first time in twenty-three years, John Cross had not gone with him.

"What can you possibly want?"

John stood on the threshold to Dee's room where the old man had summoned him, arms crossed as Dee opened the door. It was March 24, 1603, forty-nine years to the day from when a four-year-old boy had brought flowers to the Lady Elizabeth in the Tower and played football for her to lighten her stay within its imposing walls. Behind him, they could both heard the herald's cry, "The queen is dead; long live the king."

Dee shook his head wearily. "Few ever receive what they truly want, John," he said. "Please, come in. The wind is cold and I am an old man."

John entered suspiciously, casting a withering gaze at the cracked old football in its place in the center of the table. Dee lit one or two candles, then set the taper to one side.

"Fewer still can know the time of their own end, and maybe one alone might have the power to overcome it. I will die in five years' time. My fate is sealed, and I am resigned to it. But you, John, if you remain in this place and in this time, you will not live to see the springtime come again. That is when the silver in your threepence will move on to another steward in 1604."

"Symmetry again?"

"And connection." Dee leaned against the table for a moment, breathing hard, then straightened his shoulders. "But there is a way, John, that you might yet cheat death. With my help."

John shook his head. "I'm tired, Dee," he said. "As tired as you. Perhaps I'm as resigned to my fate as well, now that Her Majesty is gone."

Dee chuckled dryly. "Don't be too swift to accept death," he admonished. "Not until you hear me out. With consummate skill, I have separated your threepence from every silver object you obtained over the years, and I have minted it into a very special coin. It will lead you onto the silver path for one final destination. How long you might live there I cannot say, but at least you'll have a chance."

He set a large silver coin on the table, and with some trepidation, John reached out for it. It gleamed in the candlelight as he read the words, "Elizabeth. II. Dei. Gratia. Regina. 1953." He looked up in wonder. "Can it be possible?" he breathed.

Dee nodded. "I told you long ago, every moment in time is a world unto itself, as perfectly formed as a line of pearls strung together by the silver clasps of symmetry and connection. Another Elizabeth has ascended the throne. Will you go and do your duty by her now, for however long you have left?"

John nodded slowly, the great weight that he had felt at the Queen's death suddenly lifting.

"Then you will need this, I think."

Dee handed him the ball, and John tucked it automatically into the crook of his arm. "Speak the words John, and don't look back."

Pulling the threepence from the tattered, old bag around his neck, John pressed it against the newly minted coin, feeling the scar begin to burn.

"The rose is red, the leaves are green. God save Elizabeth, *my* noble queen."

And stepped forward into a shining silver light.

The room filled with the smell of almond trees and violets in bloom. Dee heard a great noise, and for a split second he saw a vast stadium of people dressed in Her Majesty's own crimson colors. As John disappeared into their midst, Doctor John Dee heard the crowd singing the very same music he himself had heard so many years ago.

And then they and John Cross were gone.

HEAR NO EVIL

Alexander B. Potter

"I think something is wrong with my ears."

I glance at Evan, slumped in the passenger seat, staring out the window at sheep. "Your ears? Do they hurt?"

"No, but I can't hear as well. I can't hear my voices anymore."

"Your voice? You can't hear yourself talk? I don't understand." I say that frequently since I took up with Evan, but he doesn't seem to mind.

"No, I can hear me." He looks away from the passing scenery. I cut my eyes over at him again. His uncomprehending, troubled expression tugs at my chest. "I can't hear *my voices*. The ones in my head."

My eyebrows rise, despite my best efforts. "Some people would say that's a good thing."

He tilts his head forward until he peers over his new glasses at me. "I'm *not* some people, Victor."

I grin. "That's for sure. Sorry, honey." I can't say I'm surprised to hear he has voices in his head. Once I got past his ability to heal with his hands—on faith, he'd say—everything else paled by comparison. This is a new one, though, and does strike a note of worry. "I didn't know you had voices."

"No? Sorry. Didn't realize I'd never mentioned it."

"That's okay." There's a lot Evan doesn't think to mention. I've come to understand it isn't intentional, or at least not personal. He's cautious about how much he shares about his differences, even with me. "Tell me now."

"They'd usually be commenting on the sheep."

The sheep. Okay. "The voices like sheep?"

"The entities like sheep," he corrects, scanning out the window. "At least some do. They're not all partial to sheep."

"Understandable," I offer. "Can't expect *everyone* to like sheep. They may look cute from a distance, but they stink and they're none too bright."

"Exactly." His satisfied smile eases the pang in my chest. My ability to 'speak Evan' keeps improving.

"No sheep appreciation today?"

"No. And that's odd."

"Maybe the . . . ones," I can't *quite* bring myself to say entities, "that like sheep aren't around today? Are they all present all the time?" Scary thought.

"No, they aren't. That's a good thought, except I'm not hearing them at other times, too. Remember the kittens?"

Do I ever. He convinced me to help him volunteer for the Windham County Humane Society. We did the kitten room last week. Kittens are not only messier than cats, they're also friskier, and they find more places to hide. And come three or more to a cage. Adorable, but chaos. Evan's much better with chaos than I am. "They like kittens, too?"

"Yep. And not a peep. Also, no comments on people I pass on the street. No debates. No whispering at the movies."

I wondered how Evan never mentioned this. Sounds like a crowd in there, and an opinionated one at that. "Do they bother you?"

"Some do, but those don't stick around." The sudden, feral edge to his grin surprises me. "The bothersome ones get the hint quick that they can't get a foothold on me."

"Ah." That makes . . . sense. Evan sense.

"No singing either."

"They sing?" Of course. If they talk, why not sing. "What do they sing?"

"James Bond theme songs, mostly."

"Is *that* why you're always humming *Tomorrow Never Dies* and *View to a Kill?*"

He nods. "You know how easy it is to get a song stuck in your mind. Try having it sung inside your head. They love those heavy beats and over-torqued vocals. Sometimes I wish they'd never heard Brandon's Bond Themes CD."

"So," I aim for casual, "do any of them . . . these voices . . . is it anything like Brandon?" I hesitate to bring up Evan's old lover, three years dead but entirely too present. At least, he was too present until a little over six months ago. But since Evan mentioned him, I figure what the hell. I haven't told Evan that Brandon's ghost stopped coming around. At first I didn't notice. When I did . . . Evan and I don't talk much about Brandon. It's weird enough the ghost only visits me when Evan isn't present. I don't like emphasizing that I get to interact with Brandon—even dead— when he doesn't.

"No, not like Brandon. Well, yes . . . but not. They're *like* ghosts, but they're *not* ghosts. Brandon was—"

"Special. I know."

Evan gives me that look over his glasses again. "Victor. You're much saner than Brandon was."

I have to smile. "Thanks. Sometimes I wonder if that works against me, rather than for me."

He reaches over and squeezes my knee. "No. It doesn't. Brandon was difficult."

That's one word for him. Still, the reassurance does my head—and heart—good. The road ahead is lined with cars parked on the shoulder. I slow down, pulling in behind the last car, and shut off the ignition. "Given your distinct lack of Christianity, do you ever feel a little . . . off, coming to these Dummerston church functions?" The strawberry supper suggestion had surprised me, since I know church sponsorship conflicts with Evan's worldview.

He laughs, shaking his head. "This church has the sweetest people. It doesn't bother me."

Grinning, I open my door and get out. "So, the voices. They're not ghosts, but—"

"We can talk about it later. You know . . . people." He waves his hand at the people walking toward the Grange as he joins me.

I shrug, grabbing his hand in mine. "I don't mind. Let 'em listen and see how boring their own lives are."

He shakes his head, the shy smile reaching back into my chest and poking me hard. "People look at you funny if you talk about voices."

I squeeze his hand. "Whatever makes you comfortable." Hating the world just a little bit more, I follow him into the church supper.

When Cat comes by my office the following Monday, I cut my phone call short, waving her over.

"Hey, thanks for coming." I jump up and pull a chair closer for her. She's so different from Evan it's almost comical—tiny, so petite where he's taller and rangy; long dark hair, styled straight today, against his sunny blond mess that I constantly have to remind him to even comb; dark brown eyes to his blue; perfectly put together opposite his complete lack of style. She hugs me, then sits. The hug destroys the deceptive image of fragility her fine bones and small frame convey. It's like embracing flexible steel. Her voice underlines the message for anyone who misses it.

"What can I do for you? You sounded urgent."

The notable similarity is in the huge eyes Evan shares with all his sisters. The colors vary, but all have that arresting gaze. I've always wondered if there were any less visible parallels. Time to find out exactly how deep the similarities run. I lean against my desk. "Has Evan always heard voices?"

Her shoulders square minutely, her posture tightening.

Her face shutters. "Voices?" The warmth leaves her neutral tone.

"Relax. I'm not looking to have him committed or sent off for 'observation.' I just want to know if he's always had this . . . aspect of his gift. He hasn't mentioned it to me before, and I'd like to know how far back it goes. I figured you, of anyone, would know." The tense body language belies her unaffected front. The Trevalyen sisters are so damn overprotective. Good thing, overall; it's probably how Evan reached his twenties with most of his innocence and good nature intact.

"The healing came first, but I'm under the impression the voices have been around almost from the beginning. Our mother . . . well, it fired her anxieties."

I'd wondered. Mama Trevalyen is extremely protective, too. Daddy Trevalyen also, for that matter. The more the school counselors inquired about Evan, the more her protective instinct ran toward, "How about we get very quiet and make sure no one finds out you're a lot smarter than anyone thinks, and *please* don't mention you believe you heal people with your hands." Since it meant Evan could stop seeing doctors and sitting through counseling sessions he didn't understand, he agreed readily. He also got plenty of hard-learned, early lessons from his peers about what was, and wasn't, okay to talk about.

Despite my reassurances to Cat, hearing that the voices aren't new relieves me. Much as I love Evan and believe in his sanity, sometimes it's hard for a simple Vermont country guy like me to pry my mind *that* far open. Meeting the ghost of Brandon did a lot to blow my mental doors open, if not right off their hinges, but I still worry that being as different as he is might eventually affect Evan's stability.

"Has he always talked about the voices as 'entities'?"

"No." Cat smiles, memories obviously surfacing. "He didn't *always* have a wild vocabulary. Or, well, he probably did, knowing him, he just didn't use it. When he was little he called them 'people,' and sometimes 'clomp beasts.' "

"Clomp beasts?"

"When we were growing up, he used to drop to the floor and wrap himself around my lower leg and just hang on, going to dead weight. Shouting 'clomp beast!' " Her face gets serious. "When he started having so much trouble explaining that he saw people, he started using 'clomp beast.' If we pressed him on what he meant by 'people,' he got . . . weirded out. Told us they weren't people."

Considering her description of clomp beast, I wasn't sure the analogy made me comfortable. "So these things attach themselves to him? Cling? Won't let go?"

My worry must have shown. She relaxes further and shakes her head. *My* protective instincts regarding Evan always reassure his family. "No, because remember, Evan always knew how to let go. He would if I really needed him to. Clomp beast is an affectionate term, not a scary one."

I know I'm about to make her uncomfortable again. I toss out the hard one, trying for that casual tone that keeps Evan talking. "Do *you* hear voices? Does anyone else in the family?"

I can almost hear the whiplash of tension that rockets through her, bringing her ramrod straight in the chair. Electricity ought to be crackling off her hair. Her eyes narrow. "No. We're not like Evan. He must have told you that."

Actually, he hasn't. I've asked him a few times if anyone shares his gifts, and he usually laughs it off with, "I don't think they see them as gifts." Any further pressing meets with gentle evasion. "The reason I ask is because he says he can't hear them now. He thinks something is wrong with his ears. I've dissuaded him from that, but he's fixated on the idea that something's wrong with *him*. I'm not so sure. I thought if anyone else in the family experiences anything similar, I'd ask if they've noticed changes."

Surprise runs over her face like water before she cloaks the expression. She sits back in her chair, expression thoughtful. "You need to understand. We're not like Evan." She stares at me with those piercing eyes until I nod. "But I can make a few inquiries. I'll call you tomorrow." She comes to an obvious decision. "Some of us do have experiences." Her mouth clicks closed, and she adds abruptly, "Not like Evan."

"Got it. Thank you. Anything you can share might help me figure out what's up with Evan's voices. It's disturbing him." I lift both hands and shrug, as if that explains all.

She nods. For her, it does.

The phone is already ringing as I walk through the office door the next morning. I run to my desk and pick up with a breathless, "Hello."

Cat's voice comes crisp over the line. "It's not just Evan."

"Meaning you can all hear voices, or none of you are hearing voices now?"

"Cute, Victor. I wasn't lying. None of us hear. Not like Evan. Some of us don't experience anything. But some . . . have dreams."

"Dreams?" I have dreams, and I'm not metaphysical in the leas—

"Very *accurate* dreams. Startlingly accurate. Before things happen, or as things are happening somewhere else, that we couldn't know about."

"Oh! You have *dreams*." Morning person, I'm not. "Prescient dreams."

"If you want to call it that." She sounds cagey. "And one of us sees colors."

"In the dreams?" I notice she's not identifying any of the sisters with gifts by name.

"No. Around people. Some people."

"Auras?"

"No," she snaps. "Just *colors*. They shift with the person's mood."

So do auras, I think, but I bite my tongue.

"Also, some of us have . . . *indications* of ghosts."

"What the hell is an 'indication of ghosts'? Is that like finding indications you have mice?"

Her tone remains serious. "Somewhat. We don't interact with them, they don't interact with us. We've just had indications they've been present. Things that can't be explained any other way. And our mother—" she hesitates. "Knows things. Odd things."

I sigh. "I get that you don't like talking about this. I appreciate that you're doing it at all. But . . . 'knows odd things'? You're going to have to do better than that. Until I met Evan, I'd never seen anything like this."

She mutters something I don't quite catch, then continues. "My mother has premonitions. About murders. When someone's been murdered, particularly women, she gets clear images of . . . what happened. Sometimes in dreams, sometimes daytime flashes. It's extremely unpleasant. What she sees always ends up being what actually happened. She won't talk about it. She's done everything she can to stop it."

A chill walks down my spine. "Has it stopped?"

"For the most part. She distracts herself. It used to happen when she thought about a murder too much, after reading the newspapers. So she doesn't think about murders too much anymore. Doesn't even read the articles."

"Wow." I'd distract myself, too.

"Anyway, my point is it's not just Evan. Everything's stopped."

"Everything?"

"None of us have had any of *those* dreams for over two weeks. Closer to a month. The one who sees colors isn't seeing them. No ghost indications for a good month. Mom hasn't had any flashes, although she's been suppressing for a while now."

"Ordinarily, you'd have a dream or something in the space of a couple weeks?"

"I didn't say *I* had dreams." She pauses, calming her voice. "But yes, it's rare for all of us to go without experiencing anything at all for this long. We don't chat about this, but when I brought it up, everyone knew. At first they didn't notice. You spend most of your life ignoring something, you don't immediately realize when it's gone. But everyone I talked to realized that something . . . was absent."

"Thank you. This is really helpful."

"Is it?" She sounds doubtful.

"Not in getting an answer, per se, but in getting a bigger picture. Confirming it's not . . . Evan's ears."

I hear the smile in her voice. "Trust him to think it's his ears."

"He's a straightforward kind of guy. He can't hear voices, must be his ears."

"Reasonable logic," she laughs. "Glad I could help. Let me know if you need anything else from the family. Keep me posted."

"Of course." I hang up and settle into my chair, staring at my dark computer. Oddly, Evan's approach of "simplest explanation first" often works. The catch is what Evan thinks of as simple and obvious doesn't always jibe with what everyone else thinks. I try to put on my "Evan hat," which I always picture as one of those warm fuzzy sheepskin hats with earflaps—cute, dorky, gets the job done, and quintessential Vermont. The tourism department may disagree with me, but I've always thought of Evan as embodying the essence of our state—quirky.

So, the Trevalyen family members are all missing their "experiences." Unlikely anything is wrong with all of them at the same time, ruling out organic causes for Evan. Meaning something wrong on the other end, with the entities? Although how that works, when Evan is the only one who actually hears entities—

Evan hat. Think simple. Don't overcomplicate.

Just because the others don't see, hear or talk to entities, it doesn't necessarily mean entities aren't involved. The entities aren't ghosts, but who says the sisters' "indications of ghosts" aren't indications of entities? Dreams, premonitions, visions . . . couldn't those all be inspired by entities?

Maybe the entities can't communicate as bluntly with the rest of the family. Maybe they can only whisper to them through images, through the subconscious.

Seeing colors around people. I don't know what the hell that is. Sounds like auras to me, no matter what Cat or whoever sees them says. I always found auras absurd before dating Evan. Now, why not? How auras connect with these entities, I can't figure. Seeing auras sounds like a sight-gift rooted in the seer. Unless the entities give off the glow that people think of as auras. That means the entities are on other people, though, not with the Trevalyens. I also don't think that theory fits with the definition of auras, not that the definition is necessarily accurate. But maybe these entities that hang out with Evan *do* also surround other people, and they *are* what the sister sees. And now those entities are missing, too.

Or maybe I have no clue how any of this works. I resist the urge to bang my head on my desk. The only thing I know for *sure* about "entities" is they *don't* talk to me.

Unless you count Brandon's ghost. He talks to me.

Of course, he's disappeared, too.

Evan looks up from the Scrabble board spread out on the living room floor when I get home. "Hi! I'm using Scrabble."

"I see that. How was your day?"

"Quiet. Yours?"

"Busy." I kick off my sandals and fold myself down on the living room rug next to him. After leaning over to get my kiss hello, I glance at the board. Words cover it, built on each other as if he's playing an opponent—more words than are numerically possible until I see he's using two sets of the letter tiles. "Whatcha doing?"

"Trying to see words in the words."

I puzzle at that, then concede defeat. "One more time?"

"Seeing if the words say anything to me. Sometimes I get messages that way."

Interesting. "How does it work?"

"I just play with the letters, make words. Sometimes as I'm putting letters down I make words I wasn't even planning to make."

"Cool. Anything coming through?"

He gives me that dazzling smile that makes every nonsensical conversation we've ever had so worth it. "Have I told you lately how much of a relief you are to me? How wonderful it is to be around you?"

My cheeks flush. My casual acceptance of his odd pronouncements, of his inability to think linearly and communicate like other people, means the world to him. He hasn't had many people in his life who make the effort to listen and follow what he says, and work as hard at understanding as he works at explaining. Brandon was a bastard, but that one thing he always did right while he was alive—listen and try to understand. "You're sweet."

"But no, nothing in the letters."

I look at the tiles. Something tugs at my brain. I tilt my head, squinting. An ice cube slides over my spine. "Evan, did you set this up with any patterns in mind?"

"No, I just make random words, waiting for inspiration. Why?"

I point to the board and trace my finger from word to word. Unconnected, with gaps as large as two spaces between the individual letters, the word "help" appears backwards four separate times.

Feeling like six kinds of a fool, I unscrew the peanut butter jar, calling, "Brandon! I need to talk." I burn sage, light a candle, sit down cross-legged, meditate on the flame and him. I feel even more stupid, but summonings and séances always happen by candlelight, and Evan puts a lot of stock in sage. I ignore the niggling feeling that Brandon is laughing his ass off at me and focus on getting a crystal-clear image of him. He's extremely attractive, as the dead go, so it's not difficult. I close my eyes, remembering him exactly, down to the clothes he was manifesting.

Open my eyes.

Nothing.

I've never summoned. I don't know what I'm doing. Brandon always just . . . hung around. Appeared wherever and whenever he wanted. That's why Evan thought of contacting him. Brandon ignores "rules," if any rules exist for the afterlife and ghostly visitations. He does things other ghosts aren't, or shouldn't be, able to do. Personally, I theorize that has a lot to do with Evan and the amount of time they spent together before and after Brandon's death.

But Evan went out to dinner with a couple of his nieces because of Brandon's history of not appearing if Evan is home. Except this is Evan's territory, not mine. Nothing metaphysical ever happened to me before Evan. Nothing metaphysical happens to me now.

Suddenly my mind clicks over. *Evan*. I get ready to feel like an idiot again and raise my voice. "If you can hear me, and you're just staying invisible to be a pain in the ass, Evan's having trouble. *He* needs you to talk to me." I concentrate on Evan instead, focusing on the troubled expression on his face lately, the sick feeling I get when I can't help.

Five . . . seven . . . minutes slowly tick by. Nothing.

I push to my feet. Brandon's a contrary bastard, but it's possible he's affected by whatever this is, too. It's hot, and I'm tired, frustrated, disappointed. I've been stretching my brain's boundaries a little too much the past couple days. I strip off my shirt and head for the shower. Ten minutes later I step out from under the water and stare at my fogged bathroom mirror. Writing stands out, where someone drew with a finger through the steam, the words dripping.

Kill. Die. Buy local.

I can say with certainty it's not Evan's sense of humor, but I know whose it is. "About time," I call out, wrapping a towel around my waist. I walk into the living room and see my peanut butter floating in midair. I talk in that general direction. "Where you been?"

Slowly coalescing mist hangs in the air. A disembodied voice intones, "Obey the mirror."

I snort. "Please. I date Evan. I already buy local and never eat strawberries out of season. And you know Evan doesn't even let me kill the spiders."

"Yeah, that used to drive me nuts." He falls into his normal voice as he materializes all the way, with the same lopsided grin I remember—the one that flashes a little too much canine and gives him a dangerous air rather than a happy one. "You did such a traditional summoning," he waves the peanut butter at the sage and candle. "I thought you deserved a traditional haunting."

"Buy local?"

"Traditional Vermont, then."

"Right. Thanks for showing up. Have any trouble?"

"Trouble?"

"Getting here? Hearing me?"

He gives me another familiar look, one of his favorites—the one that says, What's your damage? "No trouble."

"Nothing got in the way of your manifestation?"

"What are you asking? I might be able to answer better if you stop being so damn obscure. I felt a need to visit you. So I thought about being here. That's all it takes. I concentrate and I'm . . . here, instead of there."

"And where is 'there'?"

"Wherever I go when I'm not here." He walks to the chair in the corner, climbs up on the seat, perches on the back of it. His body submerges partially into the chair, the upholstery showing through his legs. It's disconcerting, so I try not to look.

"And where is *that*?"

He shrugs. "Your guess is as good as mine. Not *here*. At peace."

I ponder that. He looks calmer than I've ever seen him. Despite his constant laconic attitude, even in death he usually carries tension around him like extra clothing, a dissatisfaction that radiates. Today, I just sense calm.

"How is it you wander back and forth whenever you want?"

He smirks. "Apparently I've got a deal with the devil."

"Right."

"You don't believe me?"

"I don't believe in the devil," I correct dryly. "I'm sure you would never be dishonest."

"If you're in the mood to have your worldview radically shifted, I could arrange an introduction."

The problem with Brandon—okay, *one* of the problems with Brandon—is that it's incredibly difficult to tell when he's kidding. "Thanks, I'm all set."

His expression screams "wuss." All he says is, "So what's wrong?"

"Evan's having difficulties."

"Last time I looked in, he seemed great."

"How often do you look in?"

"Time is a hard concept for me these days. What's the season?"

"Almost July."

"Oh. It's been a while."

"I haven't seen you since winter," I confirm. "Evan," I pause, still having trouble saying it. Though if anyone understands, it's Brandon. "—isn't hearing voices."

"At all?"

"Nothing. For two weeks. His sisters aren't experiencing any of their . . . experiences either."

"The sisters are special too? Holy fuck! I always wondered about that!"

"They never told you?"

"They never liked me."

"They liked you fine. They got pissed at you for offing yourself and leaving Evan to pick up the pieces."

He winces. "Yeah, I suppose so. Moving right along."

I repeat Cat's summary. He listens with avid interest, but when I finish, he shakes his head.

"I don't know. Nothing's different for me. I don't do any other . . ." he waves a hand, "woo-woo stuff. I don't have ghost buddies. I'm either here with you, or . . . there." He shrugs and jumps down off the chair, tossing the peanut butter to me. "But tell you what. I'll go have a chat with Lucifer and let you know what he says. 'Kay?" He flashes me his sincere charming grin, the one with no sarcastic edge, reminding me there was once someone that Evan fell in love with in this man. "Nice seeing you, Vic." He blows me a kiss and he's gone.

Evan and I lounge on the sofa watching a TV show about cakes when Brandon pops into view in front of us. I let out a startled yelp and spill my popcorn. Evan's mouth falls open.

Brandon looks remarkably solid tonight, none of the wavering, artistic-foggy look. He nods to both of us, his eyes catching on Evan. "Got some news."

I straighten, keeping one hand on Evan's thigh.

"Lucifer says something's keeping everything in his dimensional reality from interacting with this one."

"Dimensional what?" I say at the same moment Evan says, *"Lucifer?"*

"Yeah. We . . . talk," he answers Evan.

Evan's face falls, stricken. "But—no, that can't be— You're *not*—"

"Oh! No, I'm not in *any* kind of hell. Not anymore. Lucifer's . . . interesting. He's not what you'd think. You'd like him." He grins. "Can't you guess? Humanity's always gotten him wrong. We don't understand much of anything about his dimensional reality, but I think you get more than most. You two would get on great."

Evan ponders for a moment. "Okay," he says simply, face clearing. "I'll take your word for it."

"Dimensional reality?" I prod.

"Right. This is the human plane of existence, that one is . . . his. Well, theirs. Evan's entities are there. He didn't feel comfortable with me hanging out long. He was antsy. Never seen him like that. He kept saying, in this *meaningful* way, that I needed to go settle where I was most comfortable, fast, and not be caught wandering. But he wouldn't say by what. He looked stunned that I'd been able to talk to you and that I could materialize in his dimensional reality. Which is weird, because I've done it before." He shrugs, confused. "This is not a guy who's easy to surprise."

"Why did he want you gone?"

"If I didn't know better, I'd say he was nervous." Brandon shoves a hand back through his shaggy black hair. "He kept looking around, like he was watching for something, and then he'd go unfocused for a minute, which he does when other stuff is going on for him. He told me nothing was moving back and forth, and if I didn't want to get stuck one side or the other, I should get somewhere comfortable and stay."

"That was it? We already knew that. Guessed anyway."

"No, I wouldn't leave until he explained some stuff."

I have to laugh. Leave it to Brandon to out-stubborn the devil.

He nods at Evan. "Your voices—"

"The entities," Evan supplies.

"Yeah. They're not ghosts."

"I know."

"Of course you do." A half smile lifts the corner of his mouth. "They exist with him on this other plane. Two dimensions," he holds out his hands, palms down, one about two inches above the other, "that exist really close to each other. So close," he brings the top hand down to the bottom hand and intertwines his fingers, "they practically take up the same space. Except not exactly the same space—like a step to the left through an invisible wall. When you're there, you can *almost* reach out and touch everything that's here. It's like his dimensional reality exists on another frequency,

one that's too high for humans. Like dog whistles." His eyes
glitter suddenly. "And get this . . . there's more than one additional dimension."

My brain skips, fighting the information. I struggle to
get it back on track.

"But this is the closest. They can *interact* with this dimensional reality, but they can't *act on* it. They get
through, observe, walk around, move occasional objects.
They don't have much sway, and even less so with the av-
erage human, but they try. Interacting isn't the same as
communicating. They can't do that in the direct sense, unless," he points at Evan, "someone opens up and invites
them in. Then they can talk, appear, very directly. That's
unusual. Mostly they communicate with humans in really
subtle ways, because we're not too bright, to their way of
thinking, and just don't pay any attention." He pauses, eyes
narrowing at Evan. "I'm not telling you anything you don't
already know, am I?"

Evan looks embarrassed. "It's what I figured."

He grins, shaking his head. "Well, you're right, as
usual."

"Why can't they communicate even with me now?"

"And why are they spelling out 'help' on my Scrabble
board, *backward?*" I add. "And why can you get through?"

"They're spelling 'help' however they can because they
need it, but they're much more limited in what they can do
right now. All they can do is nudge, which is probably why
it was backward, and why you can't hear them, Ev. Near as
I can tell, I'm getting through because I didn't know anything was wrong. See, ghosts are separate from either dimension and can wander both. Most ghosts who cling to the
human dimension are unquiet, uncomfortable. I've been
comfortable lately."

"At peace," I murmur. He meets my eyes, smiles, and
nods.

"Ghosts at peace don't usually travel. I've always been

able to move out of . . . wherever I go. The devil isn't even sure why but he has a theory that—"

"—it has something to do with Evan," I chorus with him, and we both grin. Evan looks at us suspiciously.

"The ghosts that hang around the human dimension have all gone to ground. Spirits are good at sensing disturbances, feeling when energy is being disrupted. The restless dead know something is up and are keeping their heads down. I didn't have a clue." He pauses. "It's also possible, Ev, that your sisters' 'ghost-visits' are actually entity-visits. They say they have evidence that 'ghosts' have been present. It's entirely likely, given the way the entities *love* you, they like hanging around the rest of your family, too. Either way, entities or ghosts, activity overall is just . . . dampened."

"But because you didn't know that, you can move?" Evan sounds confused.

"And because I don't care about what I'm *supposed* to do, and I'm willing to ignore a lot of discomfort."

"So it's getting harder even for you?"

He nods and holds out his solid-looking hand. "No in-between stages. I'm either manifested here completely, or I'm not. Somebody walked in here who isn't sensitive, they'd probably see me. It would take someone in deep denial to miss me right now."

Evan nods. "You're very tangible. But does he . . . the devil . . . know what's blocking interaction?"

"He says it's us." Brandon winces. "More accurately, *you*. Humans. I don't count anymore although he said the ghosts had a part in it, too. He didn't elaborate. He was very eager to get me *out* of his dimensional reality completely, to the point he finally pushed me out." Between one word and the next a shudder convulses Brandon's frame, and I can see directly through him. He solidifies with an obvious effort. "Okay, that's different. I think I need to go be at peace now." His entire form flickers. He gets a determined look on what I can see of his face. The flickering stops, but he remains transparent. He directs all his attention at Evan and speaks with obvious effort, his voice hollow-sounding. "Great seeing you, Evan. Things are good, really." He blinks out of sight.

We sit staring at empty space, then look at each other. I don't like the speculative look coming over Evan's face.

"The entities need help, and they're asking me. Victor, doesn't it make sense that if they can come here, I could go there?"

"No," I say automatically. "Absolutely not."

"But I like them. I want to go help. They need me."

"They're asking you because you're the only one who can hear or is even trying to! Just because you *can* get the 911 call, doesn't mean you're the one to respond to the emergency!"

"But Victor . . . who else is there?"

I'm such a sucker.

"We should wear black. We're infiltrating."

I don't argue. What the hell. Brandon said Lucifer was worried about something. Whatever it is, I'd love to avoid catching its notice. Maybe black will help. If I can even get through. I don't doubt Evan will. He figures if he makes it, he can bring me with him. I'm not convinced. *I'm* not gifted, or special. I'm keeping calm by concentrating on his confidence.

I have to smile, though, when he's standing in the middle of the living room, dressed all in black with a black bandanna over his hair, pressing outward with his hands. He looks like a mime who forgot his makeup. My amusement fades when his hands start vibrating.

He stops, arms dropping. "I can't push through."

"You say your healing is like opening up. Brandon talked about the entities needing invitations. Maybe it's less push, more give?"

He brightens. "You're good at this, Victor."

No, I'm not, and I'm afraid he's about to find that out in

spades. "You want to help. The healing comes when you *want* to heal."

"So don't push. Concentrate on *wanting* to help and—" His eyes close, hands reaching out in front of him. Fingers disappear, then the palms and up to his wrists. Eyes still closed, he grins. "It's working!" His arms disappear up to the elbows. He pushes outward to either side. I hear a sound like wet silk tearing, and he's bathed in a soft peach glow, as if light spills through an opening in front of him. He opens his eyes and stares, obviously seeing more than the apartment wall.

"Get ready, Victor." He presses out further, and the glow gets stronger. His arms are vibrating again. He steps forward. One leg disappears.

I leap, grabbing the back of his shirt. "Wait!"

"Shhh. We're infiltrating!" he whispers.

"Just don't disappear." I look over his shoulder, and I can't see the far wall, but I don't think I see what he sees. The peach glow seeps around a solid mass of swirling gray clouds in our living room. That sight cannot be making Evan's face so beatific. All I see is what looks like a vertical thunder storm. As the thought appears, small blue flashes dart through the clouds. "Evan? That doesn't want me coming through."

"Open your eyes, Victor. Then you'll see."

Easy for him to say! He was born with his eyes "open." I've never been able to see. Right now I *don't* need his grammatically correct Yoda pronouncements. He moves his other foot forward, and he's disappearing into the clouds. They flow around him, an inch from his skin, as though he's walking under a waterfall. My hand on his shirt is going with him, but the clouds close behind. An electric zap hits my arm, making my hand spasm. Only force of will keeps my fingers clenched on fabric. "Evan!" I panic.

He calls back, "Take your advice, sweetheart. Do you *want* to come with me? Focus on the want."

I realize I *don't* want to go with him. I don't want him to go. I just want to keep him safe. More zaps singe my arm. My fingers don't want to grip. One more step and he'll be gone. This is going to shut me out. I pour everything into *wanting* to keep him safe. And dive forward.

Lightning crackles from all sides, scorching clothing, burning skin. I want to help Evan. I feel the jolts straight through to my heart. *I feel bad about these entities and all, but I want to help Evan, and he's going there.*

I stumble out of the cloud, heartbeat erratic, hot sensations of multiple burns pulsing through me. I stare. We're in our living room, just . . . not. Everything looks vaguely peachy and fuzzy, like it's all encased in orange Jell-O. Evan stands in front of me, shining with an eye-blistering white glow.

"You made it!" He reaches out, fingers whispering over my burns. Coolness follows his touch. "Ow. Your disbelief hurt. Or, your *belief* that you couldn't follow. It was strong." I don't like the dreamy, cult-leader way he's talking. Then he adds, "Your hair is standing straight up." That's my Evan.

"Alternate dimension, right? Something about me may as well be straight."

He laughs, putting his hand on my chest. The pain and scorched feeling fades. My heartbeat stabilizes. Seizing muscles relax so quickly I stumble. I catch myself against him. "Turn down your wattage, honey. I think you're more powerful here."

"Really? That could help."

I certainly hope so, because we're going to need it. I have no idea what we're supposed to do. So far we've gone from one version of our apartment to another. Evan snags my hand and drags me to the door.

"We should go."

"Where?"

"Outside. There's no one in here."

"Is there usually?"

"Sure." He leads me out the front door. "I hear voices everywhere."

I want to ask more, but in the moment I'm too overwhelmed. Outside is different. The strange sense of orange gelatin between me and everything else remains, but oddly it doesn't make everything *look* orange. Out here the peachy glow is somehow under everything, adding radiance but leaving colors clear and intense. Some things—living things—glow, the soft emanation adding to their vibrancy. The flowers in the neighbor's small garden give off bursts of red and yellow in shades I've never experienced. The trees are so green I find myself getting lost in the leaves.

I startle out of leaf-contemplation when Evan calls out in delight, and hurries across the parking lot. So much for stealthy infiltration. I follow, catching sight of his goal a moment later. Something that looks like pure light caught in a moving, shifting glass vessel is moving toward him. Vaguely humanoid, when it reaches him, it envelopes him in what can only be a hug. I'm reminded of the glassblowers at the Simon Pearce gallery up in Quechee, when the fire is caught in the heart of the glass and it's red hot, just at the point it will drip. Evan speaks rapidly, pausing as if hearing answers, but I can only hear him.

"—been worried. I haven't been able to hear. Victor says it's not my ears, but Brandon says Lucifer told him it's us humans. I want to help so I came here. I could try. I don't know—"

The entity lifts its . . . head, I guess, and now sound reaches my ears, like a faraway song I almost recognize, haunting and maddening. Instantaneously, others appear. Not all are humanoid, some little more than a blob of glassy glow. The number increases faster than I can count as they swarm Evan. Panic rises in my chest. The entities shrink in tandem from my direction.

Evan whirls, lifting a hand to me. "No, Victor, don't. Don't be scared."

I tear my eyes away from the pulsing mass of amorphous

entities, and another flash of terror hits. Evan's eyes are twin suns, giving off the same fiery yellow shine as the entities, the clear blue irises and black of the pupils burned away. I'm losing him to them, to that difference I've worked so hard to understand. He's bleeding away . . . he speaks their music, he's more them than us. He always has been. I always knew I'd lose to this, to the difference, to the Other . . . everything I can't touch and don't understand.

His face grows anguished. The trilling at the edge of my hearing hits a sharp, painful peak. "Please, d-don't be fri-ightened. Fear p-pushes them away. It h-hurts."

The stutter that only appears when Evan is really over-tired or incredibly distressed jars me out of my instinctive reaction. I don't want to cause him pain, but I don't want to lose him. "Don't leave me too far behind. I don't know how to follow."

"I'm not g-going anywhere without you. If you can't follow, I won't go." His simple Evan-logic beckons as much as his reaching hand.

Breathing shallowly, I push back against the panic. They're pressing as close as possible, but they aren't smothering him, and he isn't any the worse for wear. He's still standing solid and human, not disintegrating into a glowing glob. He's moving through them as if they're water, hands stroking, touching each. Where his fingers trail, deep blooms of red feather cut through the yellow light, creating waves of breathtaking, swirling oranges. He may have qualities like them, but he's *not* one of them. They swarm him because he's different from them, too. He touches them the way he touches humans. Healing touch.

Breathing becomes easier. My feet take me to his out-stretched hand. "I don't want to hold you back either."

His fingers curl around mine. "I need you to hold onto my feet, Victor. Someone has to, or I really will float away. Brandon couldn't. He could see truth, but he was too unstable. My family can't, they won't look at the truth even when it's rearranging their furniture while they sleep. You can. You're solid, stable, but you see, too."

"But I don't, Evan. I can't understand a word they're saying. I almost didn't make it through. I practically gave myself a heart atta—"

"You got here. You reach for it, through the fear. It's okay if it's not natural as breathing. You try. You keep trying. You force new ideas into that practical mind of yours. You stretch. You're *open*. And you can hear. Listen. It's like seeing."

I stare at him, not knowing how to explain that sometimes I just don't comprehend.

"How did you see to get here?"

"I followed you," I answer immediately. He nods. Can it be that easy? Just . . . follow his lead? I move closer to him and throw everything into the *want*, my desire to help him do what he needs to do, so I can protect him. Keep him grounded. *I'm sorry you guys are in trouble, but I need to know what's up so I can keep him safe.* He *needs* me.

For the first time, I believe it. He really does. Something tight and knotted inside me relaxes. The keening notes in my head surge.

::—stand why he can't hear us? You'd think something would rub off on—::

::—see him with the kittens? He can't—::

::—humans are fundamentally lazy! Can't be bothered to extend their senses—::

"We are not!" I snap in a tone worthy of Cat. The rushing crescendo of voices stops. "Some of us don't know what senses to extend! Or how—" I break off. Holy fuck. I can hear them. And understand them.

They're all looking at me. Instead of glassy vessels of light, definition starts to appear—facial expressions, though not always where you'd expect a face to be. "Faces," I manage, hearing the squeaky note in my own voice but unable to control it.

Evan leans close to my ear. "We're translating what we see and hear in symbolic ways that make sense to us."

"I'm not really seeing faces?"

"You're seeing faces. You're just reinterpreting what the entities look like through a form your brain comprehends."

"Oh." I see surprise, joy, satisfaction, doubt. "Yeah, I'm hearing you," I direct at the doubting one. He . . . he? . . . nods and smiles.

::Well done. Sorry about that comment, but humans do appear lazy to us. That's what has us in this predicament.::

"Human laziness?"

::Laziness. Human apathy, anger, fear. The usual culprits. Your kind are prone to the lower, heavy emotions. Unfortunately, there are also those of our kind prone to them.::

"Remember when I told you about the ones that can't get a grip on me?" Evan leans his chin on my shoulder. "Those. The ones that used to chase Brandon and cling to him, that drew him all the way down. Little dark clouds. Sometimes big dark clouds."

::They're getting through the barrier fine,:: another voice chimes. Literally. The voice reminds me of wind chimes. ::Your world, your region in particular, is so fearful, so angry, unhappy. Deep, deep sadness and discontent. A crisis of dark emotion. You're all pushing us away, making the barrier less permeable. We can't help if you don't let us through.::

"And you want to help?" I don't mean to sound suspicious, but if I'm supposed to be the grounded one here, I want to do my job.

::Yes.:: The voice sounds like it's smiling. ::We want to help. It's what we do.::

Another entity snorts. It's the only word for the noise it makes. ::What we do is meddle. Strengthening the barrier is keeping us from having any *fun* and giving it all over to the ones who play in the heaviness, who love to see the joy sucked out of everything. All emotion has power. We have a taste for contentment, but dark emotion produces just as much juice. More, the way your lot is pumping it out. All you humans wander around in deafness or slide into feeding *them*. Occasionally one of you opens up and hears. The central conceit of human beings—you meditate and wait for us to come to *you*. All we can do is make suggestions. You *could* come visit us on occasion.::

Evan makes a startled sound. "You *want* us to come here?"

::Why not? We should always come to you? Most humans we get are experimenting with astral projection and accidentally end up here. They run the other way when we make contact. If you lot tried a little more we wouldn't be in this mess.::

Evan's grip on my hand tightens. "Before, you could get into our world through those open enough to invite you in. Now—"

I catch the wave at the same moment. "Now even an invitation isn't enough. We need to actively come to you, open the barrier from our side."

::Exactly,:: comes a breathy voice by my ear, making me jump. ::Your dimension is just . . . draped with this thick, disgusting miasma. We can't get through, but if you come to us, we still have access. Influence.:: It laughs—I think—making a sound like jingle bells. ::We do like our influence.::

Evan nods, excited. "If I come visit and give you access by opening the barrier from our side, will that work?"

"It'll help, but it won't solve the problem." My brain is making sense of it now. "The miasma they're talking about isn't an external thing to us, to humanity. Humanity feeds it as fast as you could poke holes in it. Faster, if it's reached a point of preventing contact from this dimension to ours. We all feed it. We created it ourselves. We all need to work to dispel it."

::Exactly so.:: Wind Chime Voice faces me. ::Our opposites here exacerbated the problem, but the fact remains, evil exists. In all dimensions. Primal evil that is larger than any one, yet resides in all of you, just as primal good. When humans give in to fear, apathy, distress on a large enough scale, the emotional plague takes on a life of its own and spreads.::

I interrupt. "Primal evil. That's . . . not Lucifer, right?"

::Lucifer?:: The jingle bell laugh next to my ear is joined by a dozen other incarnations of amusement, from leaves rustling to waves lapping and birds chirping. ::You humans and your hang ups about Lucifer.::

Wind Chime takes over again. ::No. Lucifer is . . . misunderstood. He is a threat to evil's preeminence. It feeds on the self-inflicted misery of both the living and the dead. Lucifer does in fact preside over hell, but not as your literature would have it—not one single place of damned souls, but all the myriad hells the dead create for themselves. He works to release the dead from the hells of their own making. In doing so, he cuts evil's supply line from the dead, as we work to cut it from the living.::

"Which you can't do anymore. And now Lucifer's work is compromised too, because I'm guessing he can't access the dead as easily, or cut through their own misery to free them to peace."

::Appropriate conclusions. And so primal evil is strengthened, and those who battle it, stymied.::

"We all choose what we feed," I murmur, suddenly put in mind of uncounted reminders from daily life—in jokes, therapy sessions, stories, quotes from famous thinkers—that each of us is responsible for our emotions, that they're the only thing we truly control. Every day, we each make countless choices—how we respond to each other, to circumstance, to the world and its vicissitudes. And the dead . . . the dead choose their hells.

All the entities focus on me again, with intense watchfulness. "What?" I look around, unsure.

::You've chosen well, Evan,:: says Breathless, still right at my ear, the jingle bell laugh sounding.

Evan grins, his arm around my shoulder. "Brandon found him for me. But I figured out what I was supposed to do with him." I wonder what I missed, until Evan squeezes me. "You're right again, sweetheart. That's all they mean."

::We try to promote the message of personal choice to humanity in as many ways as possible,:: a new voice adds from the crowd. ::You humans lose the focus of it so easily.::

"So that's how we help. Help people choose." I nod. I can hold onto Evan's feet while he does that. Keep him from getting too outrageous in his efforts, make sure he doesn't get committed. "Help people choose to feed the higher emotions. Remind them they control the choice on a daily basis."

::And come visit,:: reminds the snorting entity.

"Will do," Evan confirms. He glances at me, and I nod. Moving out of the circle of entities, he reaches out and parts the dimensional barrier with ease. He glances over his shoulder as he takes my hand. "Bye." The chorus of good-byes rings in my ears as we step through onto our parking lot. I pass easily, with no electrical storms. The air sucks closed behind us with a soft pop.

The area is deserted, so I don't think anyone notices us stepping out of thin air. Evan looks more . . . solid, some-how, than I've ever seen him. I wonder if I look more ethe-real. I squeeze his hand. "Think we're up to the job?"

He leans into me as we cross the pavement to the lawn. "Now I know how to poke holes from our side, that part's golden. The rest . . . not simple, but we can work at it. Together."

"No superheroes or climactic battles with this one. Just a daily slog, over and over, in an uphill battle. Nobody to pop in and save the world." *Not even you.*

Not even me. The knowledge reflects in his eyes. "I al-ways told Brandon that might have worked at some point in history, but not now."

"Born at the wrong time?"

He shakes his head, smiling, as we go inside. "I always

thought he might have been," he says gently, touching my cheek. "But not me." He leans up and kisses me. "I'm good with here and now, where you are." He winks and heads for the bedroom.

I watch him walk away, then step to the refrigerator for a drink. The note stuck to the peanut butter, which we now keep in the fridge because it's organic and separates, looks like it's written in red lipstick. Lipstick? I tear it off with a groan.

"Hey, Vic, talked to Lucifer again. I'm on the job, too! Partner!"

Followed by a little red heart, and a flourishing "B."

Below that, a much smaller postscript is written in pen. "I never was any good at staying on the ground. Hold onto those feet of his."

No worries, Brandon. I will.

ABOUT THE AUTHORS

Brad Beaulieu has been writing fiction for some time. His tastes (both reading and writing) lean toward the fantasy end of the spectrum, but he's been known to dabble in science fiction from time to time. His first sale of any kind was to the *Deep Magic* online zine in the summer of 2004. His first professional sale was the story "Flotsam," which won second place in the Writers of the Future 20 contest and debuted in August of 2005. He works as a software security consultant and lives in Racine, Wisconsin, with his wife, daughter, and two cats. He enjoys cooking spicy dishes, playing tennis, and hiding out on the weekends with his family. His Web site can be found at www.quillings.com.

Donald J. Bingle has had a wide variety of short fiction published, primarily in DAW themed anthologies but also in tie-in anthologies for the Dragonlance and Transformers universes and in popular role-playing gaming materials. Recently, he has had stories published in *Fellowship Fantastic, Front Lines, Pandora's Closet, If I Were an Evil Overlord,* and *Time Twisters.* His first novel, *Forced Conversion,* is set in the near future, when anyone can have heaven, any heaven they want, but some people don't want to go. His most recent novel, *Greensword,* is a darkly comedic thriller about a group of environmentalists who decide to end global warming . . . immediately. Now they're about to save the world; they just don't want to get caught doing it. Contact Don at orphyte@aol.com and purchase his novels through www.orphyte.com/donald bingle.

Lillian Stewart Carl's work often features paranormal/fantasy themes and always features plots based on mythology, history, and archaeology. The latest of her fifteen novels are *The Burning Glass*, third in the Jean Fairbairn/Alasdair Cameron mystery series, and the romantic fantasy *Blackness Tower,* which divulges the origins of the character of Magnus Anderson. She explored Glastonbury in the epic fantasy novel *Lucifer's Crown*. Of her mystery, fantasy, and science fiction short stories, eleven are available in a collection titled *Along the Rim of Time* and thirteen are collected in T*he Muse and Other Stories of History*, *Mystery, and Myth*. Lillian Stewart Carl's Web site can be found at http://www.lillianstewartcarl.com.

Brenda Cooper has published fiction in *Nature*, *Analog*, *Oceans of the Mind, Strange Horizons*, in the anthologies *Sun in Glory; Maiden, Matron, Crone; Time After Time;* and more. Brenda's collaborative fiction with Larry Niven has appeared in *Analog* and *Asimov's*. She and Larry have a collaborative novel, *Building Harlequin's Moon*, available now in bookstores. Her solo novel, *The Silver Ship and the Sea*, was released in 2007. Brenda lives in Bellevue, Washington, with her partner Toni, Toni's daughter Katie, a border collie, and a golden retriever. By day, she is the city of Kirkland's CIO, and at night and in early morning hours, she's a futurist and writer. So she's trying to both save and entertain the world, with sometimes comical results as the two activities collide and, sometimes, blend. Neither, of course, is entirely possible.

Paul Genesse told his mother he was going to be a writer when he was four years old and has been creating fantasy stories ever since. He loved his English classes in college, but he pursued his other passion by earning a bachelor's degree in nursing science in 1996. He is a registered nurse on a cardiac unit in Salt Lake City, Utah, where he works the night shift keeping the forces of darkness away from his patients. Paul lives with his incredibly supportive wife, Tammy, and their collection of frogs. He spends endless hours in his basement writing fantasy novels, short stories, crafting maps of fantastical realms, and occasionally copy editing manuscripts for a small press publisher. His first novel, *The Golden Cord: Book One of the Iron Dragon Trilogy*, was published in 2008, but his current project is *Medusa's Daughter*, a fantasy set in ancient Greece. He encourages you to contact him online at www.paul genesse.com.

Over the past twenty-five years, **Nina Kiriki Hoffman** has sold novels, juvenile and media tie-in books, short story collections, and more than two hundred short stories. Her works have been finalists for the Nebula, World Fantasy, Mythopoeic, Sturgeon, and Endeavour awards. Her first novel, *The Thread that Binds the Bones*, won a Stoker Award. Recent works include the young adult novel *Spirits that Walk in Shadow*, her short science fiction novel *Catalyst*, and the fantasy novel *Fall of Light*. Nina works at a bookstore, does production work for *The Magazine of Fantasy & Science Fiction*, and teaches short story writing through her local community college. She also works with teen writers. She lives in Eugene, Oregon, with several cats, a mannequin, and many strange toys.

Jody Lynn Nye lists her main career activity as "spoiling cats." She lives northwest of Chicago with two of the above and her husband, author and packager Bill Fawcett. She has written over thirty books, including *The Ship Who Won* with Anne McCaffrey; a humorous anthology about mothers, *Don't Forget Your Spacesuit, Dear!;* and over ninety short stories.

Fiona Patton was born in Calgary, Alberta, Canada, and, grew up in the United States. In 1975 she returned to Canada and now lives on seventy-five acres of scrubland in rural Ontario with her partner Tanya Huff, six and a half cats, and a tiny little Chihuahua that thinks he's a Great Dane. She has written six fantasy novels for DAW Books, the latest being *The Golden Tower*. She has also written more than two dozen short stories, most of them for DAW anthologies edited by Tekno Books.

Chris Pierson was born in Canada, and now lives in Boston, Massachusetts, with his wife, Rebekah. He works as a writer and designer of online games, including *Lord of the Rings Online* and is the author of eight novels set in the Dragonlance world, including the Kingpriest Trilogy and the Taladas Trilogy. His short fiction has recently appeared in the anthologies *Time Twisters, Pandora's Closet,* and *Fellowship Fantastic*.

Alexander B. Potter resides in the wilds of Vermont, editing and writing both fiction and nonfiction. His short stories have appeared in a wide variety of anthologies, including a number from DAW Books. He edited *Assassin Fantastic*, the award-winning *Sirius: The Dog Star*, and co-edited *Women of War* with Tanya Huff, all for DAW Books. He can be visited at www.alexanderpotter.com, his home on the Web.

A member of an endangered species, a native Oregonian who lives in Oregon, **Irene Radford** and her husband make their home in Welches, Oregon, where deer, bear, coyote, hawks, owls, and woodpeckers feed regularly on their back deck. As a service brat, she lived in a number of cities throughout the country until returning to Oregon in time to graduate from Tigard High School. She earned a B.A. in history from Lewis and Clark College, where she met her husband. In her spare time, Irene enjoys lacemaking and is a long time member of an international guild.

Born in Wisconsin in 1967, **Steven Schend** fell into the world of fantasy quite quickly, growing up on L. Frank Baum's Oz books, Edgar Rice Burroughs' Tarzan and Barsoom novels, and Ray Harryhausen movies. It was only a matter of time before comic books and other fantasy and science fiction corrupted his brain permanently . . . but in a good way. For the past seventeen years, Steven worked full-time or freelance as an editor, developer, designer, writer, or assistant manager for TSR, Inc., Wizards of the Coast, Bastion Press, Green Ronin, and the Sebranek Group. Steven has written scores of magazine articles and role-playing game products, though he hopes to match that track record with his current stint as a fiction author and free-lance novelist. Steven's called various places in Wisconsin and Washington home over the years; he now hangs his hat in Grand Rapids, Michigan, where he teaches writing at a local college and works feverishly on novels and stories of his own.

Anton Strout was born in the Berkshire Hills, mere miles from the homes of writing heavyweights Nathaniel Hawthorne and Herman Melville, and currently lives in historic Jackson Heights, New York (where nothing paranormal ever really happens, he assures you). He is the cocreator of the faux folk musical *Sneezin' Jeff & Blue Raccoon: The Loose Gravel Tour* (winner of the Best Storytelling Award at the First Annual New York International Fringe Festival). In his scant spare time, he is an always writer, a sometimes actor, sometimes musician, occasional RPGer, and the world's most casual and controller-smashing video gamer. He currently works in the exciting world of publishing—and yes, it is as glamorous as it sounds. His first novel *Dead to Me* is in stores and is the first in an ongoing fantasy series.

Sherwood Smith

Inda

INDA

0-7564-0422-2

New in Paperback!

THE FOX

0-7564-0483-3

Now Available in Hardcover

THE KING'S SHIELD

0-7564-0500-7

To Order Call: 1-800-788-6262

www.dawboks.com

The Novels of
Tad Williams

To Order Call: 1-800-788-6262
www.dawbooks.com

Patrick Rothfuss
THE NAME OF THE WIND
The Kingkiller Chronicle: Day One

"It is a rare and great pleasure to come on some-body writing not only with the kind of accuracy of language that seems to me absolutely essential to fantasy-making, but with real music in the words as well.... Oh, joy!"   —Ursula K. Le Guin

"Amazon.com's Best of the Year...So Far Pick for 2007: Full of music, magic, love, and loss, Patrick Rothfuss's vivid and engaging debut fantasy knocked our socks off."   —Amazon.com

"One of the best stories told in any medium in a decade. Shelve it beside *The Lord of the Rings* ...and look forward to the day when it's mentioned in the same breath, perhaps as first among equals."   —The Onion

"[Rothfuss is] the great new fantasy writer we've been waiting for, and this is an astonishing book."   —Orson Scott Card

0-7564-0474-1

To Order Call: 1-800-788-6262
www.dawbooks.com

Kristen Britain

The **GREEN RIDER** series

"Wonderfully captivating...a truly
enjoyable read." —Terry Goodkind

"A fresh, well-organized fantasy debut,
with a spirited heroine and a reliable
supporting cast."—*Kirkus*

"The author's skill at world building and her feel
for dramatic storytelling make this first-rate
fantasy a good choice." —*Library Journal*

"Britain keeps the excitement high from beginning to end, balancing epic magical battles with
the humor and camaraderie of Karigan and her
fellow Riders." —*Publishers Weekly*

GREEN RIDER   0-88677-858-1
FIRST RIDER'S CALL   0-7564-0209-3
and now available in hardcover:
THE HIGH KING'S TOMB 0-7564-0209-3

To Order Call: 1-800-788-6262
www.dawbooks.com

DAW 7